Memories of the Dance
by

Keith Neely

"Paramedics routinely experience a slice of life that few others ever observe. They work with life in crisis, and see the very best and worst of individual and community behavior. Keith Neely is in a unique position to show us life from this angle, a perspective that will give most readers fresh insights about America and Americans. Keith's work with national EMS issues has established his credibility as an academic and health care professional. His new book confirms that we should add successful novelist to his list of credentials. Like his first book, I found this novel to be captivating, beginning to end."

Jeffrey Michael, EdD
Chief, EMS Division
National Highway
Traffic Safety Administration

"Keith Neely tells the EMS story like no one else. His fiction comes directly from the real world of inner-city care at both its best and worst."

Kate Dernocoeur
Paramedic
EMS Author

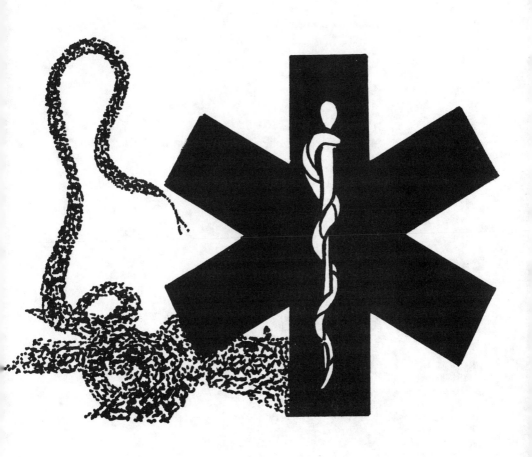

Memories of the Dance

An EMS Novel
by

Keith Neely

VISTA PUBLISHING, INC.

Copyright © 1999 by Keith Neely

Edited by Pat Clutter, RN, MEd, CEN

Cover Design by Thomas Taylor of Thomcatt Graphics

Vista Publishing, Inc.
422 Morris Avenue, Suite One
Long Branch, NJ 07740
(732) 229-6500
www.vistapubl.com

This publication is designed for the reading pleasure of the general public. All characters, places and situations are fictional and are in no way intended to depict actual people, places or situations.

Printed and bound in the United States of America

First Edition

ISBN: 1-880254-59-X

Library of Congress Catalog Card Number: 98-61857

USA Price $18.95
Canada Price $24.95

Dedication

For all of you who still carry the memories.

And for all of you who help to soften them.

Meet The Author

Keith Neely is the author of **Street Dancer,** his first novel about Denver paramedics. He is an Assistant Professor of Emergency Medicine at Oregon Health Sciences University and he contributes frequently to academic and professional emergency medical journals. He lives in Portland, Oregon with his wife and family.

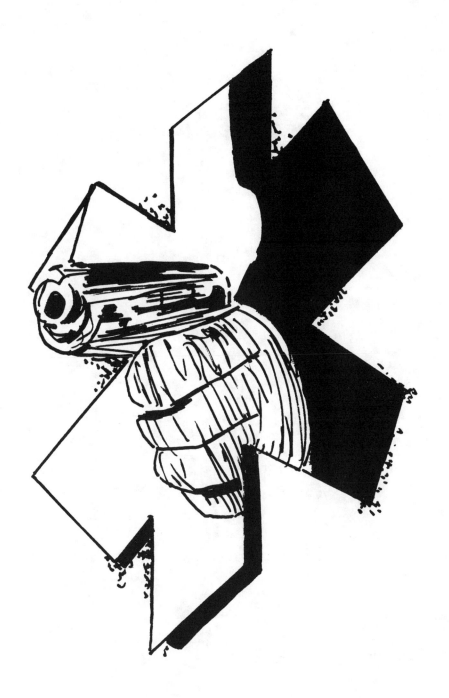

Chapter 1

Banjo bent his wrist over the ambulance steering wheel and drummed his fingers impatiently on the dash board. Clayton, his rookie partner, rested his hands quietly in his lap. The wide bay door yawned open before them and led into the gray basement of the Denver jail. When the door was high enough to allow the ambulance emergency lights to clear, Banjo idled the car forward until the hood nearly touched another iron mesh gate straight ahead. That door remained closed while the one behind them creaked back down and banged the concrete floor. Then the gate in front raised. It carried a sign that warned, "**Check Weapons at Cage**." Banjo looked at his partner. "Better get out your throw down so you can check it at the cage."

Clayton knotted his dark brow. "My what?" His voice was deep and full.

"Throw down. You know. When you shoot someone who doesn't have a gun you throw down yours to make it look like his."

Clayton still looked lost.

"Never mind. Police joke." The gate stopped. Banjo drove forward and parked against a loading dock. When they got out Banjo, hands buried in his pockets, left his partner behind. Clayton carried the medical kits and made no effort to catch up.

Clayton irritated Banjo--worried and irritated him. When Banjo returned from Vietnam Clayton was still in elementary school. When Banjo became a Denver paramedic sixteen years ago, Clayton was still too young to drive. When the field instructors passed the rookie through the field training program they commented on his wry humor, sudden temper, and an odd predilection toward mystical philosophies. They also predicted he would soon be the best paramedic in the city. Banjo objected to this. He was the best and he wasn't going to let some rookie who couldn't grasp a police joke take his place.

But Banjo, according to his habit of close observation, had to admit Clayton had a gift. Patients responded to Clayton the way an animal sometimes settles quietly to music. He had the knack of anticipation, so important to all paramedics, and could see where circumstances would lead. But Clayton's abilities were exceptional beyond that. He seemed to possess a second sight. He knew of things to come. Clayton, sensing something, told Banjo earlier today to be careful. This galled Banjo immensely, priding himself on his own intuition, and prompted Banjo to be a little more lax than he otherwise might be. He wasn't going to be cautioned by a new employee.

Still, seeing his partner's unusual skills, Banjo worried that he would one day be set aside by the rest of the paramedic division when it shifted their respect to Clayton. So he kept Clayton at a distance, preferring to ignore that which he found unpleasant. Clayton seemed satisfied to be by himself and stare off to some far horizon.

The cage was a booth of thick reinforced glass and steel overlooking the basement jail entrance. There was a policeman inside. Banjo nodded and said, "Hey."

The voice of the office caged inside was small and distant. "How are you this fine Spring day?" The officer flipped a switch and a loud click echoed inside the yellow metal door in front of them. "Come on in. You guys up for a little life savin' this afternoon?"

Banjo asked, "Whatcha got? They told us to get on over here but didn't say for what." Banjo pulled open the heavy door and let it swing shut behind him. Clayton had to grab at it with both hands before it locked him out.

"Some guy we busted in a raid last night conked out."

"He breathing?"

"Don't know. The guys upstairs sounded kind of excited though. Called back two, three times wonderin' where you were." The officer stepped from his cage and punched an intercom button next to the elevator door. "Ambulance! Basement up!" Banjo noticed his empty holster. They waited.

Light from the dropping elevator car slid down the crack between the two doors which presently spread open. Another officer ran the controls. His hair was as gray as the concrete basement floor. He squirmed uncomfortably on his padded stool, favoring his left hip.

"Where to?" he asked when the paramedics stepped in.

Banjo looked at Clayton who shrugged his eyebrows. Banjo asked the policeman. "Don't you know? We were just sent to the jail on an overdose."

"Hell, I only drive this thing. They gave me this job when I had my hip replaced. I don't really know where I'm going. Hold on a minute." He reopened the door and called toward the cage. "Malcolm. Malcolm! Which floor?" The glassed in officer twisted his mouth then picked up a telephone. After a moment he held up five fingers.

The elevator jolted when it started. Banjo said to Clayton, "I'll bet you think this is real exciting. Some guy maybe not breathing up there needing us." Before Clayton answered, Banjo told the officer, "New guy. Gets excited a lot."

Clayton gave them no response and this also raised Banjo's ire. Banjo had heard Clayton was a full blooded Sioux Indian. He had the look of one-- tall like a wooden Indian, dark, smooth skin, black hair, and nose like a rock outcropping. Banjo supposed an Indian might have access to the spiritual side, allowing Clayton to see bigger things; to shrug off Banjo's little leveling taunts. Clayton seemed to meditate and this also led Banjo to speculate along these lines. It made him shiver. If Banjo couldn't touch it, see it, or bring it under his control he would rather not deal with it.

Yet Clayton's silent music touched him. Within Clayton's stillness Banjo heard the noise of his own soul. Within his partner's inwardly held power, Banjo saw his own feeble attempts to bend the world to his wishes. Clayton contained the peace of a quiet forest. Banjo crashed around like a badly driven car. Banjo wanted to touch Clayton. So he said, "I'll tell you, Clayton. After about the zillionth overdose it's just another day at the office."

The policeman studied Clayton. "He don't seem to need much calming down." He added, noting Clayton's necklace

3

from which hung a claw as thick and long as a finger, "That's quite a piece, son. It's almost big enough to check at the cage."

Banjo said, "You can tell. This rookie's churning inside."

Clayton rested his eyes on them both then let them drift away. One side of his mouth tightened and drew back, the most response Banjo could get from his distant partner. It would be easier, Banjo thought, to perturb a tree.

The elevator jerked to a stop and the doors spread open. The officer pointed to several policemen. "Must be down there where all those people are. Suppose?" Then he said, "Wait a minute. If that's the prisoner I'm thinkin' of, he's a real bad one. Even all doped up last night he banged up two, three of our men. You be careful."

The warning startled Banjo, being the second one that day. A little chill shot up his spine. A moment of fear clenched his stomach. When faced with danger, he always wondered if he would do the right thing. If he had to, would he offer himself up and save another before himself? Faced with death, would he still do his job?

One vile instance in Vietnam could have answered that but the moment passed before he could muster up the right impulses. His scares on the streets amounted to surprising moments of terror that his partners had dealt with, or passed before requiring anything from him. He had never been forced to concluded that he was about to die then do what he was expected to do. He did not know if he was that brave. So his stomach churned and his palms slickened whenever that moment seemed imminent.

They stepped out of the elevator. Stiff little wire cages protected bare light bulbs screwed into the concrete ceiling. Rows of doors, each heavy with a post card sized window at eye level, extended down either side of the white corridor. "He's in here," gestured a policeman. "He stopped talking to us about an hour ago."

Clayton stopped. "Wait a minute. Why did they wait so long to call us?"

Banjo ignored the suspicion in Clayton's question. "Probably thought he was sleeping off a drunk. Which, in fact, he probably is."

4

Banjo took in the details of the cell. He had to notice everything. If he could see it he could prepare for it and account for it in his plans. He avoided surprises for surprise destroyed control. He inspected and sniffed and listened for all the details. Banjo conceded that this was a great difference between himself and Clayton. Clayton's power eased outward from him and spread like silence through an attentive audience. Banjo had to cast about feverishly with his influences and stay on his toes.

The prisoner wore a black silk shirt which bagged on him. Most of the buttons were missing. His shiny, cuffed, and sharply creased trousers were torn and bloody at the knees. He wore no belt or shoes or socks. Yellowing toenails curled over the ends of each long, bony toe and dirt filled the creases in between. He lay balled up on the plastic bench bolted to the wall. Vomit covered the floor and made it slippery and dangerous. Banjo gritted his teeth and swallowed hard to prevent the smell from causing his stomach to revolt. "Where'd you find him," he asked.

"We rounded him up on a crack house raid early this morning," said an officer.

Banjo took a long step to avoid the slippery vomit. He moved the gaunt man's head to see his face. "Clayton, he's not breathing. Give me the suction and get a tube ready." Banjo slipped the suction catheter into his mouth. Toothless gaps interrupted the line of caked teeth. Banjo took small breaths to keep from gagging. The suction tube made loud, sucking noises in the man's mouth. Gravy thick fluid carrying shreds of meat rushed into the catheter. "Get a line and give him some Narcan," he told Clayton. Banjo slipped a curved plastic airway into the man's mouth and used a bag and face mask device to breathe for him.

He watched his partner feeling patiently for veins. Clayton walked his gloved fingers gently along the skinny arms searching the road maps of dark needle tracks for a vein.

Banjo worried. "Anytime you're ready. He'd sure like to breathe again."

Clayton closed his eyes and, as though caressing a sculpture, felt a small area of skin close to the man's elbow.

His hand moved slowly then froze and his fingers palpated carefully. He twisted the man's arm and his eyes fixed on a certain spot. Clayton sank the needle beneath the skin where Banjo saw no evidence of a vein. Blood flashed into the syringe. Clayton tenderly advanced the slim plastic catheter. He fitted IV tubing into the needle hub and watched the fluid to see that it ran well. As it flowed he injected a small syringe of medicine. Soon the man stirred and his chest expanded without Banjo's assistance.

"Nice shot," Banjo complimented, glad he did not have to start the IV.

Clayton told him, "He's going to fight when he wakes up. Better get a good hold of him."

Banjo waved him off. "I can talk him down."

Soon the man's legs stirred. He gagged and reached for the plastic airway filling his mouth. Banjo slipped it out for him and said, "How ya doin', partner?"

He woke up and made eye contact with Banjo. Panic swarmed in the prisoner's eyes. He bolted to his feet. Banjo stepped back, gripped by sudden fear. Face to face, Banjo saw the panicked eyes narrow meanly and fill with rage.

"It's all right, partner. We're paramedics," Banjo said hurriedly, vainly. The prisoner balled his fist. Muscles in his shoulder gathered. "We're just here to ..." Banjo wondered if this would hurt. His head exploded in pain and snapped back. He slammed against the opposite wall. He slumped to the floor and saw Clayton dive across his line of vision, plunging straight at the man. Blurred blue uniforms piled on top of Clayton and the prisoner. Men swore and grunted. Shoes scraped on the slick concrete trying to gain purchase. There was a cry of pain that was choked off.

When the shock of his own pain cleared, Banjo tried to stand. He pushed off the floor but his hands slipped on the cold vomit. He scooted to dry concrete. Banjo regained his feet and positioned himself to fight but the tangle of uniformed bodies had already quieted and begun to relax.

They got up slowly, watching the prisoner for renewed aggressiveness. The man's wrists were cuffed behind his back. The IV Clayton had delicately started was torn out. It did not bleed from the site. Clayton stood, blood dripping from his nose, but he paid no attention to it. He fingered his neck and Banjo noticed that the necklace had been torn away. Clayton stepped back quickly to see more of the cell floor and found the necklace under the bench. He clutched it in his fist and buried it in his pocket.

A plain clothes officer was the last to stand and when he did so he shook vomit from his heavily muscled arms. Banjo saw the characteristic bulge of a weapon under his Denver Broncos warm-up jacket. He wondered how the other got it past the policeman in the basement. A lightening strike scar slashed across one cheek and his floral shirt stretched taut across his thick chest, pulling at its buttons. "Such a little man," he mumbled running a finger down each arm to scrap off the last of the slime.

Banjo recognized him. His name was Zagata and he was hated by other policemen for reasons Banjo vaguely understood had to do with drugs and gambling. Zagata made a point of knowing all the paramedics. Banjo mistrusted him intensely and avoided him whenever possible.

Zagata turned to the other officers. "Where's Rocky? Where's that partner of mine? Someone in that pile sounded like they got hurt."

Banjo heard a muffled voice. "I'm right here, Larry." An officer squatted against the cell wall. He held a bloody hand over his nose. "The guy kicked me a good one," he said with a nasally twang. "I think he broke it."

Zagata wiped his hands on his pants then kneeled next to him. He gently pulled his partner's hand from his face to examine his nose. "Well," Zagata said in a soothing way as a father might say to his son, "at least you'll be all right in a little while. Let's have the paramedics take a look at you."

Banjo noticed Clayton staring strangely at the prisoner. Then he dropped to his knees and his fingers darted to the prisoner's neck. "Banjo, he has no pulse. He's arrested."

"Damn right he's arrested," answered Zagata. Loathing swept the caring from his face. His scar squirmed like a snake. He looked seriously at Banjo as if to ask him to set this new paramedic straight. When he recognized Banjo his face opened to a glad smile. He boomed as though calling across a bar, "Banjo! My favorite paramedic. How the hell are ya?"

Banjo, still puzzled by Clayton's actions, automatically returned the pleasantry. "Hey, Zagata." Banjo now felt the cold vomit through his clothes. His head hurt. He touched his forehead with the back of his wrist looking for blood. "Clayton, what are you doing?"

"I can't find a pulse. Someone get these cuffs off."

"He's under arrest, son," Zagata told him in a fatherly way.

Banjo suddenly comprehended Clayton's actions. He dropped to his knees. "Get them off, Zagata. We have to go to work on him."

Zagata fumbled in his pocket. "Lot of fuss for someone selling drugs and killing our kids, don't you think, Banjo; for such a little man." The friendliness was gone from his voice and his scar shifted about again.

Clayton turn toward the policeman. His face darkened with such rage that for a moment Clayton's anger made Banjo as nervous as Zagata's unpredictability did. A little uncertain, Banjo said, "Lighten up you guys. Let's just do our job."

*****

At Denver General Hospital Banjo watched the efforts to resuscitate the prisoner long enough to conclude they were hopeless. He took his time writing his report then chatted awhile with a nurse. He did not want to return to the ambulance until his partner had cleaned the vomit off the floor and stretcher. Banjo went to his locker in the dayroom for a fresh uniform shirt. After washing up he felt clean once more and returned to the ambulance. Clayton sat on the bench staring at the fresh sheet on the stretcher. Banjo said, "Well, so you were right."

"That was stupid and you know it!" Clayton fixed his dark eyes hard onto Banjo's watery blue eyes.

Banjo indignantly drew himself up straight. "You take some risks out here." This drew no response. Clayton looked elsewhere. Banjo at least demanded attention if not respect. "Listen! You did exactly what you should have done. Don't ask for a medal."

Clayton told him flatly, "Partners don't do stupid things. You could have gotten hurt. I could have gotten hurt. You may be the senior partner here but I'm not just a potted plant. I knew what that prisoner would do. You should have figured it out, too."

Banjo looked at Clayton's deep eyes. Clayton's anger was subsiding but his strength remained. He was grateful for Clayton's immediate response. It was just that sort of instantaneous action that fate had not yet required of him. Banjo noted small drops of blood still collecting at Clayton's prominent nose. He said, "You took a pretty good shot there. Better go clean up. I'll take care of whatever's left here."

Clayton asked, "Do you know that cop? Zagata?"

"I see him around once in awhile."

"He killed that guy."

"What guy?"

Clayton shot an extended finger toward the emergency department. "That guy! For the love of God, who else do you think I mean. I was on the bottom of the pile and I saw it. That cop did more than throw a simple head lock on him. He twisted or squeezed or crushed something. I don't know. But that man cried out and I heard his dying gasp. When I looked into that cop's face I saw something. He killed him."

Banjo narrowed his eyes and challenged Clayton's fierceness. "Just exactly what did you see?" Clayton did not answer. "Did Zagata choke him or hit him? What did you see?"

Clayton's jaw muscles loosened. He looked away. "I didn't see, but I saw."

"Don't talk mystical to me. What did you see?"

He slapped the bench with his open palm. "I saw! Not here." He pointed to his eyes. "But here." He tapped his chest. "I know he did something."

Banjo spoke slowly as though explaining an important complexity. "Things happen fast out here. This guy died. He

9

probably took a ton of drugs. You didn't see anything. You're new around here. You don't get that kind of intuition after a few months on the street. You spend ten, twelve years down here, then we can talk about intuition."

Clayton's suspicions were plausible, but it went against reason to let a new paramedic accuse a policeman of murder on a hunch, especially a supernatural one. Banjo knew they could report the suspicious circumstances but that would only serve to stir up rumors and incite the police. Banjo did not want to disturb the understood promises that accompanied that protective relationship between the street cops and paramedics. As the senior paramedic Banjo had to weigh these things. If Clayton had actually seen something, if others had witnessed it, that would be one thing. But a suspicion? Even the cops had rights. A prompt police response could not be taken for granted. Banjo could not allow Clayton to report this. The decision was made, but he wasn't proud of it.

Greatly agitated, Banjo turned to leave the ambulance. He swung back and stuck a finger in Clayton's face. "I'll tell you something else. Zagata's mean. Even cops hate him. Understand that? If you aren't sure and you tell anyone about this, there'll be such a firestorm around here. God knows what Zagata would do. So drop it. Don't get cross wise with Zagata. Maybe if another cop reports this first, then you could say something."

Clayton held Banjo's eyes a moment, then focused off. Banjo left the ambulance.

Banjo's energy failed him quickly, as it did lately after bad calls. His concentration started to wane. Banjo touched his forehead. He felt the tender knot where he had been struck. He decided a beer would be in order after this shift.

*****

In his weary state, the twisted designs etched in The Parlour's frosted glass door made no sense to Banjo. They circled and entwined like snakes in a ball. If he followed one he lost it. These mysterious convolutions, forming no particular pattern, allowed his imagination to create any pattern he chose.

He sought relief here many times following his shifts as a Denver paramedic, and each time Banjo came to The Parlour for a beer he saw different pictures in the opaque etchings. After caring for a man stabbed in the belly he saw intestines. Other times he saw open gashes full of wiggly blood vessels, tendons, and muscle. Once in the glass markings he saw a dying, defiant Viet Cong soldier who, after staring furious hatred straight into him, disappeared beneath the muddy surface of a river. He never knew what would snag in his memory and spring ferociously alive again.

This time he saw an impossible snarl. "Like my head," he said to the complex designs. He pulled on the cool brass door handle.

Inside the dark bar he pointed at the bartender. "Jackson! I'll have one."

"With or without?"

"With. And heavy."

The Parlour that spring afternoon contained only saxophone music and a single slim column of cigarette smoke rising into a curl above a man sitting alone at the bar. Banjo went to his particular corner booth with high back bench seats. He tossed his backpack down and he sat there, safe and private, the fake brick wall comfortably at his back. This isolation calmed him, as a secret place is calming; but beneath this comfort lay his vast loneliness. The special and courageous voice required for one to seek closeness had, within Banjo, gone mute.

Positioned as he was, Banjo could see who entered before they saw him. Anyone coming in had to wait in the dim orange light for their eyes to adjust. This light pleased him and he wished he could scoop it up and take its sweet sadness home. It made The Parlour a perfect refuge for his private thoughts. A beveled mirror hung next to him and cleaved his reflection into precise, disassembled diamonds and kept his pieces from connecting. He liked to play with his fractured likeness.

11

Jackson brought a glass of beer and a double shot of Jim Beam. Banjo raised one finger to hold the bartender and put the shot glass to his lips and jerked his head back. Gritting his teeth and sucking air Banjo handed back the glass. "One more just like it," he gasped.

He felt himself loosen up. Waiting, he drummed two fingers to the saxophone music and watched soundless activity on a television set hung from the wall. A fresh Jim Beam was placed before him. Banjo sipped, then cooled his throat with a swallow of beer. Now a comfortable numbness moved into his fingers. Before his fingers grew too clumsy he removed two safety pins from his breast pocket and pinned a square bar napkin over the shoulder patches which identified him as a paramedic. He sighed deeply now and, for a moment, foggy contentment smoothed over the sharp edges of the ambulance calls he had run during his just completed shift.

The Parlour was an old friend. Sixteen years ago, some forgotten partner had brought him here still stinging from his first shift. The stinging softened with the hard liquor and loud talk among the paramedics around the table. It was a tradition even then to safety pin anonymity over their shoulder patches. So it was honor, not caution, that Banjo observed this afternoon as he did the same.

Banjo unzipped his backpack. He removed a book sized journal with a worn corduroy cloth cover and thumbed through the entries. There were nine long detailed entries. Each was written in Banjo's rapid scrawl that even he had trouble reading. Each was written on exactly the same date each year. He carefully turned a some pages and read a few lines. The image of an old partner came to him. This partner also was an old friend who had come here with him, so many years ago. Banjo drew a deep breath and sighed out. An old Denver Paramedic shoulder patch marked where the sloppy writing ended and the clean pages began. He picked it up and placed it in the palm of one hand and touched it gently, as he might flower petals, with the fingers of his other hand. He considered it sadly for many moments then placed it between the journal's cover and first page. Banjo slipped a ballpoint pen from his breast pocket and clicked out the writing point. He glanced once more suspiciously around the bar to assure himself that nobody invaded this intimate privacy with a rude gaze. He wrote.

> *Well, John, how are you doing? Another year's gone by since I talked to you.*

He looked up and checked around once again. The man and his column of smoke had disappeared.

> *Ten years ago tonight, old partner. Eleven thirty-six on that warm spring night when life was new and love was in the fuckin' air, to be exact. But who's keeping track? Reagan was President. He got shot right around then. God, I still can't believe what a hero they made of him. Just for being in the wrong place at the wrong time.*
> *I still can't get that night out of my head. Did you ever think about something after it happened and wonder about all the little things that led up to you being there? I was thinking about calling in sick that shift. You might still be around if I had. I was hungry just before that call. We could've gone out of service for dinner. And if I had driven a little faster we could've beaten that fire engine and parked where he did instead of out in traffic. Then you wouldn't've taken your ride on the hood of that car.*

Banjo sipped his whisky, bit his lip, and blinked his eyes clear.

> *I think about things like that. I wonder if you hurt badly or if the lights just went out. The car was going sixty, seventy miles an hour. What was that like? I know I hurt. Hell, I was useless. I couldn't even find you. But that can't*

13

be changed.

Not much has happened around the paramedic division this year. Chief is still Chief; talks in circles to his pipe smoke and paints his pictures. Periodically he touches down in reality to see what's going on. Lately, he's been touching down on me. He's after me for my drinking.

He's got me seeing this therapist now. We sit in his little office and talk. But he was in Vietnam himself so he's okay. We still have Half Deck. He's still the same little, piss-ant supervisor; twisting us around with his stupid work schedules. Dan's doing really well. He's one of the field instructors now, though he and the rest are turning out a different breed than you did. These new kids lack something. They don't have the same appreciation for tradition and dedication that you required. But the Chief likes them. You'd still be proud of Dan. He's a far cry from the clumsy rookie you almost fired. The division needs people like him. And me. I can talk to him a little.

What else is going on around the old homestead? I've got a new woman. Lauren is her name. Southern girl. We've been seeing each other off and on for the past couple, three months. When we talk I'm absolutely dying to tell her things; like how much I feel about her, how I hurt sometimes after a bad shift, what it was like for me growing up. She's really sweet but, I don't know, when I try to tell her certain things or touch her she kind of backs away. Says she needs to go slow.

But you know me, I get a woman I think likes me and I get in a hurry to stake a claim on her so I know she'll never leave. I have to know that because, you know, I couldn't tell her personal things otherwise. She might go out

and tell the next guy. So I get in such a hurry
for her to touch that cold spot in me, I screw it
up. I chase 'em and when I get them to turn
and look at me I decide there's something wrong
with them; something that makes them less
than I want. My mind goes blank. I've got
nothing to say. It's so stupid. I'm forty-two
years old and I'm still chasing the perfect
woman. I never really know what she's
thinking.

Banjo put down his pen and thrust the empty glass over
his head. "Nurse!" After a few moments he felt it taken away
and a fresh glass was placed before him.

He wiped his eyes on his shirt sleeve and looked again to
see if anyone noticed. He picked up the pen.

I've been getting these memories that won't go
away, John. I mean memories. Capital M. It
seems like I've always had them. But lately;
last year or so, boy. Sometimes they make me
forget where I am. Ever had those? You never
talked much about that sort of thing, did you?
Sometimes I'll see the face of a boy I had years
ago who drowned. Or some old things from
Vietnam will come back. Or I'll see those
burned up kids you and I pulled out of that
garbage dumpster.

Banjo breathed harder and bumped his fist against his
mouth. His stomach began to twist. He gulped some fresh beer
and bolted his shot of whisky and held that glass in the air.

They're hurting my job. I miss work. Afraid of
what I'll see. I get a little loaded. You know.
Sometimes I just can't put the uniform on.
Can't set foot outside. I get these awful things
in my head so I try to close everything out and
bottle things up. And when you do that you

*become a jerk. Like me. And you get loaded
alot. Like I do. You become a jerk. And a
drunk.*

*I don't feel anything for patients. If someone's
not shot or stabbed then it's just another
bullshit ambulance call. I used to have fun out
there, John. Now the Chief wonders if I'm still
fit to work the streets. That's what's been
happening. Some year.*

"Excuse me?"

Banjo twisted sharply toward the voice and covered up the page with his arm.

"Are you alright, Banjo?" The bartender stood at Banjo's booth.

"I'm fine. Why?"

Jackson waited as though assessing Banjo's sobriety.

"I'm fine. Go away."

"Okay. Let me know if you need anything."

Banjo watched him retreat. He quieted himself and moved on to other news.

*I got this new guy a month ago fresh out of field
training. I think he's an Indian or something.
Of all things. He wears a bear claw the size of
your thumb around his neck. The Chief hires
the strangest people. Dan kicked him loose too
soon and I have to baby sit him. It's like his
mind is only one third on the job and two-thirds
in the trees somewhere.*

*We had a hell of a call the other day, this new
guy and I. Clayton's his name. Got a stabbing
out of the 7-11 up on Federal. We get there and
this guy has a knife sticking out of his chest and
you can actually see it bobbing with each heart
beat. And he's talking to us like nothing's
wrong. I mean, like 'Nice day if it don't rain'.
Couldn't believe it. We were real careful with
him, you can bet. Got him in and Denver*

16

*General opened him up and sure enough, there
was the blade right in the heart muscle. The
guy turned out fine. What a great save that
was. Clayton took it like it was no big deal.
That was Friday. Then this afternoon. Clayton
thinks a cop killed some drug dealer we were all
fighting with. He didn't actually see anything,
mind you. I'm saying south and he's headed
east.*

Banjo emptied his beer and held the empty glass aloft.

When Jackson reached the booth he asked, "Are you sure?"

"Yeah. Why?"

"Banjo, you've had three doubles."

"Who's counting?"

"I am."

"Fine. One more beer and one more shooter. Then I'm going." Banjo sipped from the full shot glass and blackness settled over him. His head became more than his neck and shoulders could bear and he felt himself collapse inward, as though all the air had rushed from him. He whispered, "*Shit*", as a storm hit his soul and winds tattered his pleasing numbness. He dropped his pen and used both trembling hands to hold his head together. Images cycloned behind his closed eyes. A steel blue shotgun barrel spit fire. His chest spasmed against the blast. A small girl struggled against flames climbing her hair and curling her ribbons black. He saw dark eyes accusing him.

The memories twisted, disappeared and reappeared, dived and re-emerged like the etched knots in The Parlour's frosted door. His stomach churned and he swallowed hard so he would not throw up. Fire climbed pig tails. Fire jumped for his chest. Banjo dug his fingers into his eyes. He breathed harder and the room suddenly became too hot to bear. Cigarette smoke stung his eyes. His head swirled. He heard screams. They were loud and piercing and filled his brain. He hit his head with his fists. He chewed blood from his lips.

Something gripped his shoulder. He searched the middle distance above him for what had hold of him. He heard a man's voice. "Banjo."

"What?"

"Banjo, are you all right?"

"What?"

"Let's get you home."

"What!" A familiar face emerged from the other side. "Dan, what are you doing here?"

"The bartender called the paramedic division and told us you might need some help."

"Who?"

"Come on. Let's get you outside."

Banjo felt a hand under his arm. He stood, then stumbled back into the booth for his journal which he focused intently upon and placed gently into his backpack. Dan pulled him up once more and Banjo allowed himself to be guided outside. He hesitated a moment. He saw the mysterious frosted lines in the door window and said, "Oh, that's where I was."

"What happened, partner?"

Banjo cooled in the evening air and gathered his strength. His stomach settled and the breeze dried his palms. Dan's face was clear now. "I had too much to drink on an empty stomach I guess. I'm all right."

"I've seen you drunk. It's more than that."

"I'll call Lauren."

"She's still on an ambulance."

"I'll wait." Banjo ached to see her.

Dan took his arm again. "Let me take you back to the Debbie J. I'm parked right over here." Banjo pulled away but followed, his head hung down like a sad dog.

*****

Banjo fumbled numbly at the lock with his keys then handed Dan his key ring. Steel bars secured the windows of his apartment and wide, untended Juniper trees blocked the sun.

Dan opened the door. A heavy recliner, alone on one side of the room, faced a wall of treasured stereo equipment. These days music seemed to be his only reliable company. A bowl containing some soggy corn flakes from this morning sat on a metal dinette table. Sugar was spilled on it and a lone fly buzzed lazily over the area. The air in his apartment smelled old and stale and locked up. The telephone, its cord bridging from the wall, sat next to the cereal. Banjo dropped heavily into his recliner, leaving Dan to find his way to one of the straight back kitchen chairs on either side of the dirty table.

Dan asked, "Are you going to fix yourself some dinner?"

Banjo shrugged. He was hungry but lacked the energy to do anything about it.

"What do you have? I'll fix you something."

"Might be some hamburger."

Dan went to the kitchen. Banjo heard the cabinet doors bang one after the other then the refrigerator door open and shut. Banjo liked the clatter. It was the noise of someone taking care of him. The sounds warmed him and gave him the rare feeling of coziness that, gratefully, he did not have to ask for. He followed the sounds to the kitchen. Dan was cracking eggs into a skillet.

"Hamburger's frozen," Dan said. "I left it out to thaw. Eat it in a day or so before it spoils."

"Yes, dear."

Dan said to the sizzling eggs, "Feeling better?"

"I get bad memories sometimes, you know."

Dan jerked his head in a tiny nod. "Sure."

Banjo knew that vague response. It announced boundaries Dan did not want crossed. John Greystone also could create acres of protective distance with just such a gesture.

When Dan was a young paramedic he had hurried to become just like the granite walled John Greystone who revealed nothing and displayed only harsh strength as the head field instructor. In time Dan, too, began this solidifying transformation. He arrested this change after Greystone died.

But there were moments when the apertures to Dan's and Banjo's deeply hidden soft spots would align to each other. This occurred sometimes when they were weary or frightened or when the things they saw on the streets took them too far from what they knew to be right and decent. Then they could turn to each other and touch each other and it would be like a cool hand to a feverish brow.

But this was not one of those moments. Banjo pulled back, waiting for a better time. "Just some memories. That's all."

"Your name comes up in supervisor meetings. You're skating on pretty thin ice. Everyone knows you're missing work. Bars call the division to come rescue you." Dan paused before asking, "How's counseling?"

Banjo sighed. "You and how many others know I'm seeing a gooney bird?"

"Just those who need to know."

"It's fine. I mean... it's okay. The guy just asks questions. I talk." He shrugged.

"Is he helping?" Dan stirred the eggs. Then he chopped some green onions and sliced ham that was dark and hard. He scraped these from the cutting board into his cupped hand and scattered them among the eggs.

Banjo bumped his mouth with his fist. "I appreciate your concern, Dan. Really. I do. But I'm fine."

Dan slid the eggs and ham onto a plate and poured Banjo some milk. "You want me to stay awhile?" Dan asked over his shoulder, going after his coat.

Here it was again; the opening, the offer of help. But Dan had been distant when Banjo broached the rawness of his memories. He could not risk his great secrets to a living man unless the circumstances were exact. Banjo shook his head. "I'm all right."

"Give me a call later if you want to talk. You look like you're withering up inside."

Banjo snapped a salute and Dan left. Heaviness set in as soon as the front door closed. Banjo lifted the telephone receiver. He jabbed the automatic dial button. Two rings were followed by the quiet whir of an answering machine about to speak.

He hated this game. She never answered her phone. She would wait for the message then decide if she wanted to talk. He wondered who she was with. Anger flashed through him. "Stupid broad."

"Well," began the recording. Her voice ... He loved the soft, draggy Georgia song in her voice. It was smooth like silk sheets, sweet like fragrant breezes. "If you think I'm this easy to track down you had just better guess again. I might be out saving lives or I might be out spending what little they pay me, or then again..." great sigh, "...I might sitting right here at home, talkin' to my toaster, waiting for you to call." Laughter. "Leave your name and number after the little beep and I'll get back to you... maybe."

"Stupid recording." Her machine beeped. "Hi. This is Banjo." He gave his voice a flat, disapproving tone, hoping that was all he would have to say. After a disappointing pause he added, "Thought I'd call and say hello. Give me a ring when you get home."

Without lifting his feet or straightening his shoulders Banjo went to the kitchen for a beer before returning to his sparse supper table. The vinyl chair cushion sighed under him when he sat. He sipped his beer, propped his head tiredly against his fist and said to Greystone, "I've been needing someone to talk to, John; really talk to. It's hard to find anyone these days who understands how hard the streets can be. But you do."

He took a deep breath and it shuddered on its way out. "I'm still a good man, old partner. I'm a good man. Do you believe me? You've been here where I am. You've seen guys get like me. You believe me, don't you? Nobody knows me anymore. Maybe Dan a little, but not really. Not in the way I need. I'm a good man, John. I need someone to tell me that. Don't I at least deserve that?"

Banjo listened to the silence grow. His dark apartment was emptier still after Dan's soothing kitchen noises and Lauren's distancing answering machine. He wished Dan had known his thoughts and stayed.

He heard voices in the parking lot just beyond his door. A car door slammed and the engine started. The car backed away taking its sound with it. He heard the light step of a child running up the cement stairs outside and along the balcony above his front window. A TV was on in another apartment. He heard clanking overhead and knew his neighbor was lifting weights. But those noises were a universe away. He was here, disconnected and alone. His wilting soul begged for things he was afraid to ask for. Banjo hung his head over his dirty supper plate. Tears fell into the unwanted bits of scrambled egg.

Chapter 2

Morning sun cut the shadow on Banjo's bed. It was early and he rose and opened all the curtains wide to drive last night's blackness from his apartment. He went to his patio and bared his chest to the sun. In the warming brightness his headache receded. Lavender clematis climbed the close by fence that defined his small backyard and patio. Banjo kneeled to pluck new green shoots of weeds from the clean flower bed. He smoothed off the dark earth again and wiggled his fingertips together to flick the dirt away, then rose and returned to the kitchen.

Inside he poured orange juice. He considered adding vodka but thought not; his mood was light, so instead he inserted **Voices of Spring** into his CD player. A tile mosaic of a man playing a piano hung above his sound equipment. Banjo liked how oddly shaped, pretty little pieces could be arranged into a beautiful picture. On good days, as this one seemed to be shaping into, he believed his odd pieces also could be coalesced into a finely shaped whole.

Banjo filled with energy. His mind turned fresh and clever and he toyed with a plan.

He intended to get another partner. Banjo's dedication to the division was pure. He carried the division's stories and transferred its traditions to the young. His being had taken on a paramedic's identity as though the blue and white uniform colors had dyed his soul.

But Clayton was not cut from the same cloth. Despite his extraordinary skills, Clayton did not iron his shirt or trim his hair or tend to the other details of pride. His passion was the wilderness. He spoke intensely of the mountains and loved the cold shock of mornings when he camped during winter. He spoke of the paramedic division as a utility item, when he spoke of it at all.

In the years since Greystone's death a different kind of paramedic had been recruited. More of them, like Clayton who had a degree in anthropology, had attended college. Banjo, who had no schooling apart from high school and paramedic training, found this discomforting. They tended to be interested in things foreign to him. One partner had been strictly vegetarian and would not eat the free donuts Banjo could get them because they had been deep fried in animal fat. Other partners read. One read Steinbeck, Hemingway, anything he could get his hands on as long as it was, as he would say, *fine literature*. Others had studied pre-medicine or pre-law or pre-any number of other things as they sat beside him in the ambulance. And soon enough, they moved on.

Very few remained truly dedicated to the paramedic division, or showed respect for the older, street wise, if less well educated paramedics and their traditions. Paramedics used to spend time with paramedics. He remembered the parking lot parties held long ago on Friday nights in the lot just across the street from Denver General Hospital. They would bring beer and invite the cops. They would be proud and glad to be together.

Other times whole groups of them would fill The Parlour. Now, he alone visited to call up his old partner and remember long gone paramedics wearing white shirts with napkins pinned over their shoulder patches. Banjo had tried to tell Clayton the old stories. Predictably, he wasn't interested, but Banjo persisted, reasoning some seed of pride might take root and blossom.

But his years of experience and story telling got him only loneliness among these new kids who came and went, heading elsewhere, going right on by him, hardly noticing.

The Chief was responsible for this. He hired people who were as different from one another as ornaments on a Christmas tree. With John Greystone gone, there was no one to sift through the young. The place no longer bore his old partner's stern stamp. It resembled another of the Chief's rambling collections, like the paintings and photographs covering his office walls, and Banjo feared soon there would be no more room for him.

Clayton represented all of that. He was respectful enough of Banjo but it resembled the coerced respect parents demand from children toward the dottering elderly, not that which is freely given to a mentor. Banjo really wanted another partner, preferably Dan or Lauren. So Banjo wondered how he might engineer the change. Perhaps he could convince Half Deck to change his mind.

The bright waltz, his clean flower bed, and warm sun elevated Banjo's mood and contributed sweetness to the scheme he molded. He smiled. It was Friday. The streets would be wild tonight. And he would begin to work on Half Deck.

*****

Before starting his shift, Banjo entered the supervisor's office without knocking and sat on the corner of an empty desk. Half Deck worked at his computer. He still wore his bullet proof vest though he had not worked on an ambulance in years.

"Ron," Banjo said.

"In a minute." A toothpick rode Half Deck's nervous tongue back and forth across his mouth. A porcelain Elvis Presley, its face and body frozen in contortion, stood on his monitor. An Elvis photograph was neatly thumb tacked to the bulletin board. Pinned next to that was a scratched off lottery ticket.

Banjo wound up a toy ambulance and watched it clatter erratically across the desk top. When it stopped, he set it to running again and watched it drive over the edge of the desk. He hoped he could do the same to Half Deck.

Over the years, Banjo had watched Half Deck move paramedics' initials from one neat square to another on his computer spread sheet. Everyone had partner and shift preferences and the Chief, wanting happy people, would insist Half Deck accommodate as many schedule requests as possible.

The toothpick Half Deck gritted in his teeth jumped crazily every quarter when he struggled with combinations that kept the right people happy and his targets miserable. He had a genius for small boxes on a computer screen, so his schedules were a masterful mix of politics and revenge. Once done he would unveil them smugly one day before they were to begin and answer protests with an indifferent wave of his hand. He never changed a schedule after posting.

Banjo dismissed Half Deck's authority. He removed himself from the anxieties surrounding schedule changes, relying instead on his seniority and generally good standing with the Chief to assure him a shift and partner he preferred. These things had failed him when the last schedule was posted. He felt hurt and wondered if he had slipped from favor. Banjo began maneuvering for a change in the schedule already carved in stone.

Banjo interrupted again, "I wanted to thank you for giving me Clayton."

Half Deck stopped typing and turned up his radio. He snatched the telephone and dialed. He waited. Then he hit the receiver to disconnect the call and pushed the redial button. After a moment he repeated the sequence. Banjo counted four tries. Finally Half Deck asked into the receiver, "Am I the eleventh caller?" His body stiffened. "Yes!" He listened. "Uhh, let me think. That would be Pat Boone in **State Fair**." Half Deck held his face in anticipated delight. "Oh joy! Thank you."

He hung up and turned smugly to Banjo. "The radio station just gave me two tickets to the Ferrante and Teicher concert." His toothpick stuck jauntily in the air. When Banjo did not respond, Half Deck said around the toothpick gripped in his teeth, "What exactly did you want?"

"Wanted to tell you I appreciate having Clayton with me."

"I updid my database and it gave us a fine schedule, didn't it?"

"Ron," Banjo laughed. "You can either up-date or re-do. But you can't up-did anything. That isn't a word."

Half Deck lowered the toothpick's trajectory until it pointed sharply at Banjo. "I'll cook up my language any way I want."

"Whatever," Banjo grumbled, returning to his intentions. "Clayton saved my ass yesterday." He stepped off the desk and bent to retrieve the toy ambulance. He casually wound it up again waiting for Half Deck's curiosity to drive him to inquiry.

"Well! Talk to me. What happened?"

"Some dirtball junkie in the jail drop kicked me in the head. Clayton was on him before I hit the floor."

"Took a shot in the head, huh. Must be why you weren't hurt. Did the police take him down?"

Banjo pushed the truth. "Clayton threw him around a little before Zagata got ahold of him."

His toothpick jumped. "Zagata! Knowing Zagata he did more'n get ahold of him."

Even as his stomach squirmed, Banjo waved off Half Deck's suspicion. He was anxious to keep the attention off Zagata and away from the little belly jerks of guilt he had been experiencing when his thoughts turned to events at the jail. "Those stories have been around for years. He's all right."

"All right! He's got drug money all over him. You watch yourself. I always say that about Zagata. Isn't that right? Don't I say that? He'll smile in your face and slice you open. You keep your rookie away from him. I like that boy. He won't say much but he isn't afraid to take a guy down. Not like some of the puffs we got down here these days."

Banjo played his first card. "I heard Dan and some others talking about the new schedule."

"It's a done deal," Half Deck warned. With one finger he brushed down a twisty mustache hair that tickled his nose.

"Just so you know. I heard Dan and a couple other field instructors saying Clayton should be on nights with weaker people; especially ones who couldn't hold their own in a spot." Though Banjo had never heard such a conversation, he knew Dan's thoughts ran generally in that direction. "Remember how Dan got hurt on a night shift, hit by that bullet up at the Delphi Hotel while he shielded a patient from gunfire?"

"Dan was a fine one for getting himself into picklements when he was younger," Half Deck said. "But you were his partner. Didn't do him any good having a senior man with him that night."

Banjo quickly defended himself. "I was downstairs getting equipment. But I was the first one back in when shots were fired. A less experienced guy might have bolted and who knows what would have happened. The least would have been a black eye for the division." Banjo huffed out a laugh. "I can see the headlines now: *"PARAMEDIC RUNS. PATIENT DIES."*"

Half Deck shook his head. His toothpick drooped in his lips. "Well, the schedule's done. If Dan or the others want changes, they'll have to get them to me in writing a month before the next one's due out."

"Good. I'd hoped you'd say that. I want the guy with me. So don't go trying to impress Dan and the Chief by changing things like you could read their minds." Banjo could just detect Half Deck's left eye squint as an idea struck him. Banjo raised his hand in farewell. "Well, I have to get back out there. Just so you know."

Half Deck nodded and spun back to his computer.

Banjo went to his ambulance and the dispatcher assigned them to cover a district from Colfax Avenue.

*****

Banjo loved waiting for calls on Colfax. Up here life tumbled fast and head long. Beauty and stink, laughter and gunshots, sharp color and hard concrete existed so closely that a person could easily step from one to the next just by turning a corner, stepping into a shadow, or opening a door. Up here Banjo felt that thrill kicking around low in his belly that told him something astonishing was about to happen. Anticipation shimmered off the hot pavement. It pounded in the music blasting from monster, twin speakered radios carried on shoulders. It rumbled from the heavy engined, gaudy colored pimp cars cruising past. And it rippled in the muscled chests posturing for the sleek, curving legs that beckoned on Colfax.

He remembered high school. He once strutted about and drank beer and hungered for such smooth, brown legs as these to be clutching his. He thought a time or two he had found them. They walked away, though. His wife's legs certainly had. And after her came Eden, the only woman he believed he ever loved. She walked away, too. What about Lauren? Now there were legs.

He wanted Lauren from the first time she walked ahead of him and he looked at them climbing all the way up to her perfect, palm fitting ass. Those legs remained just a little too far ahead of him, though. In time, he assured himself. In time. He let the rustling in his pants play out.

"Clayton," Banjo said, feeling the need to tell a story. "See that big old gal dressed in traffic light red?" Banjo pointed to a woman bent over garbage cans next to apartments on their left. "That's the Countess. She's been up here forever. Used to go down to Broadway Piano and play the Steinways. They'd let her for awhile. We'll get her every once in awhile when she forgets to take her seizure medicine. She's a little crazy but generally takes care of herself. Dresses like she just got nuked by radiation, though. Her clothes just about glow. I like her." Clayton, his eyes closed, grunted his half interest.

A garbage truck rumbled past. An orange and blue Bronco's banner flew from its radio antenna. Banjo burst out laughing and pointed. "Look! Look! Look! Those are the cops. Must be their new undercover rig. See the magnetic sign on the door? *'Denver Garbage Removal: If It Stinks, We Haul It.'* I love it. Next time we see it we'll have to go talk to them."

They sat for an hour. The radio remained silent. "Pretty slow for a Friday," Clayton observed.

Banjo was bored. "I remember sitting right here once with Dan. It was slow just like this and I told him we we're going to get something good. After a couple hours of growing moss we got sent up to district one. We had just gotten there when some whacko blew into a gay bar right over there and opened up with a nine millimeter. Had four guys killed. We'd've heard the shots."

"I get those feelings, too."

"Uncommon for a new guy," Banjo reminded him, feeling his irritation grow.

"I've always been intuitive," Clayton explained. "My great grandfather was a Sioux medicine man. I think I get it from him."

"Uh-huh. Well, you may be out of field training but you're a rookie for a year, remember. You do what your partner says and don't be doing things on the fly just because you think you know things others don't." Clayton said nothing.

Banjo insisted, "Besides, I knew that prisoner would be squirrely."

"I was just making an observation," Clayton said. "I didn't mean anything by it. Indians are very intuitive. We know all about stupid white man tricks."

Banjo thought. "But that prisoner was black."

Clayton smiled and his eyes twinkled. He dabbed at his triangular nose, reminding Banjo of the blood that had dripped from it.

Banjo realized Clayton's little joke spoke of him. He felt his ire rising but let it go. "Well," he mumbled as a dismissal. "Maybe you do."

They listened to the dispatcher quickly assign four ambulances to different calls. Afterwards, the dispatcher moved them into Denver General to cover the city from there.

As he parked the ambulance in the division lot, Banjo saw Lauren striding toward the paramedic day room. He hopped out of the ambulance and followed. She saw him coming and waited. When he reached her, Lauren hooked an arm through his. "Banjo!" She seemed to be delighted, which Banjo took as encouragement."

He loved her smooth, drawly voice and smiled like a tickled baby.

"They ran me around with two or three late calls last night so I didn't get your telephone message until after midnight." She jammed a fist onto her hip and jutted her jaw. "Like those dispatchers couldn't find another ambulance out there somewhere." She lowered her voice and took his hand. "Are you okay? You sounded terrible on the phone."

"I had the heebie-jeebies. I'm fine now, though."

She furrowed her brow and drew closer to him to rest her head against his shoulder. "I'm so sorry. Do you want to get together and talk soon?"

Banjo laid his head upon her hair and smelled her perfume. He jumped inside. "That would be nice. What's a good time?"

She removed a small notebook from her breast pocket. Banjo noticed writing in every square of her calendar. "Well, I'm working overtime tomorrow on my first day off so that's gone. I'm throwing a birthday party for Doug Chambers. Do you know Dougy? He's one of those emergency medicine residents. He and I go skiing sometimes when the mood strikes. Let's see. Well, darn. The next day? No. How does next Saturday sound? My goodness, I am a busy child, aren't I? Call me tomorrow. We'll figure this out."

Nothing ever occupied Banjo's days off. "Great. Whenever is fine with me."

She turned to leave and said over her shoulder. "Don't forget. Call me. We'll jabber about where we're gonna go."

Chapter 3

The next morning Banjo stood sideways at the mirror puffing out his chest and drawing in his stomach. He had just called Lauren and gotten her, not her machine. He smiled and felt light on his feet. Their date, their wonderful, long evening alone together was scheduled, after more page turning in Lauren's pocket calendar, for next Tuesday. Probably. She had to check one more thing. He slipped on a tee-shirt and let his anticipation play. He knew just how the evening would go.

Dinner would be quiet and nice; rich with time and right for speaking deeply about himself. He would bring up the memories. Surely, seeing his torture, she would draw close again and say quiet words. Maybe he would find a piano and play a little for her. He paused in his thoughts. The piano had been a long time ago. Perhaps Lauren would be the one to unlock his dormant music.

Banjo imagined them at her apartment, on her cozy sofa, amid the vivid colors in her living room. They would first lay together and kiss, lightly, lingering, barely touching, then deep; not the little pecks on the cheek and hugs, as the sum of their affection had thus far amounted to. Then he would rise and take Lauren by the hand to her bed. Their breathing would catch in their chests. When their bare bodies touched and the coldness deep in the middle of him had warmed, he would sigh a deep, releasing sigh.

Banjo moved from his bedroom mirror and lifted a bullet proof vest from his dresser drawer. He held it before him as though assessing its fit. He had not worn this in some time, but the attack at the jail had been as quick as a snake strike and he found himself needing this security.

He liked how the vest made his chest look bigger. Lauren once mentioned how good she thought policemen looked with their uniform shirts tight around their second chance vests. He dropped the stiff, firm A-frame over his head and felt it cover his chest and abdomen. Banjo fastened the Velcro straps at his sides and adjusted the vest for tightness. He worried a little about taking a knife in the side where the front and back halves touched but did not protect.

Banjo turned from the mirror to polish his black work boots to his old Marine Corps spit shine. Unusually hungry, Banjo opened the refrigerator. He found milk, beer, and salsa. He poured the milk onto stale corn flakes and spread a thick layer of sugar over the top. At the table he pushed his thumb against a curl of laminate that was coming unstuck from his table top. He gave himself permission to replace the table with something long and elegant when Lauren came into his life. He thoughtfully stirred the sugar into his cereal.

After breakfast Banjo pulled on his boots and lifted his coat from the back of his vinyl rocker. On his way to work he switched on the radio and banged the dashboard in his old Toyota pickup. A love song scratched intermittently. He had stopped listening to them when Eden left years ago. Banjo turned it up to hear over the rattles and bangs that came from all directions in his truck.

He expected he and Lauren would go through some hard times. Perhaps he would be stabbed in the side. From his hospital bed he would look up and see the agony in her face. He would hold her as she dampened his cheek with her tears.

*****

At work Banjo thumbed through the thick accumulation of paper jamming his division mailbox. He discarded nothing, taking something out only to look at it and put it back; this to deliberately frustrate the memo writing supervisors who could find no room in Banjo's tightly filled box. Banjo saw nothing new and was about to let his mind float back to Lauren when he heard bedroom slippers slapping at heels and smelled woody pipe smoke. A little sense of alarm went through him. He knew the Chief was near and Banjo's quick street cleverness did not serve him in the presence of the Chief's powerful radar.

The Chief was tuned to the personalities of his paramedics. He knew their subtleties. He could read their faces, their sagging shoulders, the bounce in their step. Understanding this, the Chief, in his loose, distracted manner, could nudge and suggest in quiet ways to create the context of change. He governed with a long tether and quick eye until his soft touch detected disorder. He rooted out dissonance with a fast jerk and sharp words, and when the division returned to equilibrium he would once again lighten his grip on the reins.

The Chief's persistent pressure had moved Banjo to see a therapist. Banjo felt other invisible forces to curb his drinking, too. He did not believe Jackson, the bartender, had called the division. He suspected the Chief had sent Dan to keep an eye on him. Banjo knew he was being focused upon and reasoned that the rambling narrative he was about to receive this morning would ratchet the pressure up another notch.

Banjo's growing respect for the Chief corresponded with the Chief's growing attention. So if he felt naked when addressed by the Chief he also felt cared for. For the time being anyway, he knew he would be treated kindly.

But, Banjo worried, the Chief could be unpredictably forceful; throwing off his strategic cleverness and useless last name formality to be sternly blunt. When determined, the Chief could not be resisted, and Banjo, feeling thus captured and out of control, would recall his own father's rages and hate the Chief until these moments passed.

"Ah. Mr. Stanley. Good afternoon."

"Hey, Chief," Banjo replied absently, still fingering through his mailbox.

"A moment on the verandah, please? We'll sip gin and watch the heron come and go."

The odd remark was well within Banjo's range of experience with his boss who often wandered a bit before warming to his point. He checked his watch. "My shift starts in a few minutes."

The Chief nodded and extended an arm toward his office. Banjo walked ahead, listening to the slip-slap behind him.

A graying beard covered the Chief's brown, sun weathered face. The face carried sadness, like that of a long grieved death or failure. His shoulders slouched tiredly and his long arms dangled as though poorly attached. But his grip was sure when he took Banjo's shoulder once in the office and guided him to the intended chair. There was cleverness in his eyes.

A saber hung on the wall behind the Chief's desk; the sort a Civil War officer might have swung over his head to rally troops for battle. He painted pictures and took photographs. Only thin strips of wall remained exposed between each photo and oil painting. From earlier visits to this office gallery he knew the Chief created a small oil painting of his family every few years. The Chief was married to a doctor and they lived in the mountain foothills in the house he built. The children were taller in each picture.

He photographed the telling details of beauty on his land west of Denver. He turned a crooked fence running up a hill into a gracefully curving line. He caught mist snagged within a small stand of aspen.

And amid the collection that seemed hung with no organization or categorization in mind, Banjo noted the watercolors of important events in the division's history. He saw the one of an apartment house in flames with one lone white shirted paramedic standing in front. That was the Golden View Apartment fire and Dan was the paramedic.

The Chief closed his door softly and sat behind his desk. He seemed a little preoccupied, a little melancholy. "How long have you been with us now, Mr. Stanley?"

"I don't know. Sixteen years or so." He saw another watercolor of the Delphi Hotel where he and Dan had been caught in a gun fire. "You're pretty good with a camera and a brush, Chief."

The Chief shifted his attention toward his paintings. "The time of the downtown hotel fires."

Banjo wrinkled his forehead in question.

The Chief clarified. "You joined us about the time of a series of fatal downtown arson fires. I mark time not by calendars but by associated circumstances and events. Without anchors, time for me scatters like startled birds launching from a tree."

Banjo liked that analogy.

"I started here," the Chief continued, "after college when we still drove smooth riding, red-and-white Pontiac ambulances and transported bodies to the morgue. I was appointed Chief just as I laid the foundation for my house and have been Chief through the raising of two sons; not long enough to be a father but far too long, I think, to be Chief."

The Chief kicked off his slippers and thudded his heels atop the desk cluttered with papers and files. His socks, brown and threadbare, clashed with his navy blue uniform pants. "Such a legacy in those moments of time captured there," he said, pointing with the stem of his white clay pipe at the paintings. "Do you know what that legacy is? My friend, do you know the one and only thing we have a right to expect from this business ..." He drew a breath through his pipe. "... of pretending we can put peoples' dreams back together?"

Banjo, focusing on a watercolor of Greystone, heard only a fragment. He turned back to the Chief and made a little questioning sound in his throat.

"Change is the only thing we can expect. Everything changes. To survive, we must also. I think every new paramedic comes to us with a certain, slowly expended capacity for change. When that is used up ..." He shrugged.

Banjo struggled to put these comments into a context. "Something wrong, Chief? You seem kind of down."

He brushed away Banjo's concern with a wave of his hand. "I must keep this division in a state of change or it will grow stale and rot. The soil must continually be tilled."

Banjo watched the Chief's eyes drift toward the watercolor of Greystone.

"We started here on the same day. His passing was a great and heavy sadness. Jonathan and I were school mates, you know. Very close school mates."

Banjo turned back to the Chief whose eyes remained on Greystone. "No kidding?"

"He joined the Navy out of high school and I went to college with an eye to becoming a teacher or a minister. He and I changed little from those early days. He wanted to bring the military ways to this division and I suppose I see this place as my parish or classroom. The conflicts we had before he died." He puffed smoke again and looked at something in the bluish cloud beyond Banjo's vision. "I am the godfather to his children. Mildred and I still see them when Patty comes to Georgetown." He turned to face Banjo. "Did you know Jonathan's former wife, Patty? Lovely woman. Something went out of me when he died."

The Chief cleared his throat as he did when swinging into his subject. "I am recreating a new head field instructor. Thomas, our last one, was not successful. He prematurely judged too many new paramedics ready for the streets. The young people here need a more rigorous gold standard. The cadre of field instructors need stronger leadership."

Banjo grew attentive. He wanted that job. He would return Greystone's discipline to the division and keep his memory alive. The current field instructors, including Dan, did not instill the important values.

The Chief smiled at a distant memory. "I remember when Daniel Cravens started down here. The economy was good then. Denver was flush with money. The city gave us money to build our dispatch center then and purchase a new fleet of ambulances. I remember when he sat right there in that chair." He pointed to where Banjo sat. "Such a boy's face he had. Now it's a man's face, hard in some ways. I offered the position to him this morning. He accepted. I feel very good about that."

Banjo's instant of delight crumbled into disappointment.

"Mr. Cravens will be a good center for our young to revolve around until they are ready to find their own orbits."

Banjo shifted his feet under himself and prepared to stand. "Is there something we needed to talk about, Chief?"

The Chief smiled toward his smoke cloud. "Yes."

Banjo returned to his slouch.

"You've had a long and successful street career. You're fortunate. You've avoided the physical injuries, but like so many of us, you have sustained such grievous psychological ones. I appreciate your ability to think in different directions. Like me, your mind runs happily perpendicular to the rest of the world. We need that in our supervisory ranks, you know." The Chief paused.

Banjo's thoughts froze. "Chief," he warned, "I am not supervisor material."

"Exactly. You still have sparkle in your eyes. You have that wonderful, playful pragmatism, that responsible optimism. You would turn some of our supervisors on their ears." He chuckled and Banjo knew the Chief thought of Half Deck.

The Chief placed his pipe in the ashtray. He touched his fingertips together then carefully laid his long hands palm to palm. "Banjo, I will be frank."

Banjo knew the arrow had been aimed and released. His stomach began to grind on itself.

"You have serious problems. We both know that. I want you off the street and I want you to apply for the supervisor's position that has just opened. I want you to think about how this can prolong your career here. I want you to think about how you can contribute in different ways. You will still be in uniform. You will work a car from time to time, as other demands permit. You will be the senior management representative on the night shift. But you can no longer be a street paramedic."

Banjo sprang to his feet and heat filled his face. "No way, Chief. No way I'm going to be a supervisor. No way you're getting me off the street."

The Chief cleared his throat and crossed his arms and Banjo knew this discussion was over. "Is there anything you would like to bring up with me, Mr. Stanley?"

Banjo crossed his arms. "Yeah. Put strong paramedics on nights with weaker ones. Clayton would be a good one to use. I think you ought to try it."

"Yes, Mr. Lameroux is exceptional. Have you discussed this with our scheduling supervisor, Mr. Humphries?"

"I mentioned it."

"We have discussed this in previous supervisor meetings," The Chief answered vaguely. "Perhaps it's time to revisit the idea."

"Yes. Why don't you."

*****

Clayton asked, "Are you going to do it?" He and Banjo waited in their assigned district and listened to the dispatcher send other ambulances on calls. Bored with the long stretches of silence Clayton could maintain, Banjo had told him about his conversation with the Chief.

Banjo answered, "Too much paper work and bullshit, and the Chief, which is the same as bullshit." Then he reconsidered, as he had a number of times that day since receiving the Chief's proclamation. There was something intriguing about being in charge at night. He might be Lauren's supervisor. With the extra money he could afford nice things for his apartment. His new rank could put him on a more equal footing with the physician Lauren had been mentioning a little too frequently. "I don't know. I might go ahead and apply just to see what it's like." But saying that caused heartache.

"The Chief probably wants you in there to liven up the place."

"That's what he said." Banjo liked his partner's clever insight. He saw Clayton again flying head first at someone who hit him so fast he could not move to avoid it. He warmed to his new partner.

Something caught Banjo's eye. A man in loose red and orange clothing entered the 7-11 they sat next to. Banjo pointed. "Look at that guy."

"A Rajneesh," Clayton observed.

"A what?"

"A phony spiritual leader from India took over a town up in Oregon years ago. That's one of his followers. They all

39

dressed in red like that. Their head man had something like 90 Rolls Royces, an altogether unique economic situation for someone seeking meaning. He was quite the item."

"You like that stuff?" Banjo asked, wondering about Clayton's spells of silence.

"What stuff? Rolls Royces? Sure."

"You know. Meditating, chanting stuff."

Clayton nodded.

Banjo waited for more. Then he asked, "What happens when you do it?"

"I'm with myself mostly, and it's quiet."

"Don't you need incense and weird music?"

"No."

"Oh." Banjo caught Clayton watching him. Clayton shifted his attention out the windshield. Banjo pushed a little more. "What do you do when you're with yourself?"

Clayton drummed his fingers once on the arm rest. "Listen."

"To what?"

"Myself."

"Do you talk to yourself more than you talk to your partner?"

"Sometimes."

"Shee-it. I'm getting out."

"Banjo," Clayton answered, stopping Banjo's exit. "It's private, what I do. I'll tell you about it sometime if you're more than just casually curious."

"Another time." Banjo hopped from the cab and slammed the door. He jerked open the market's glass door. He bought chocolate milk and Fritos and grumbled inwardly about the thousands of dollars he must have nickel and dimed away in convenience stores waiting, bored out of his mind, for ambulance calls. After he and Lauren were really together and he was making more money, Banjo mused, they would fix each other nice gourmet sack lunches. At the cash register he heard the siren yelp. He hurried to the ambulance and climbed in. "What do we have?"

"Someone sick at the chicken place down on Arizona."

"A sick case," Banjo complained. "Don't we have another car down there?"

"They were sent to cover a fire."

"Well, why don't they run a car over from Station Eleven." But Banjo resigned himself to the call. "Crap. Everyone else gets good calls. We get crap."

Banjo steered using the webbing between his left thumb and index finger. His elbow rested casually on the window frame. The ambulance flowed smoothly around cars like water past rocks and Banjo tilted his open carton of chocolate milk to compensate for the ambulance sway. He rested the carton between his thighs when he ate the Fritos.

The fat restaurant manager met them at the door when they arrived. Banjo ate here often and knew the manager. He smelled chicken frying and corn on the cob and the melting butter that was poured over it. He was hungry again.

"Hey, Dick," Banjo said

The manager nodded and gestured helplessly toward a woman sitting at a table. She cradled her head in her arms which rested on the table. Banjo approached and got a whiff of her. She smelled like chicken soup to his sensitive nose and his new appetite was shot. He looked her over. Her hands were in full view and nothing rested near which she could snatch and strike with. Black crescents of dirt lodged under her fingernails. Her shoes were several sizes too large and her socks were rumpled at her crossed ankles. Banjo figured she couldn't be too sick. Nobody ever died with their legs crossed. She breathed normally and her color was pink and healthy.

Banjo stood at the table. "What's going on, hon?"

She did not respond. Banjo turned to the manager. "You know her name, Dick?"

"Pamela, I think."

"Pamela."

She mumbled into the crook of her arm. "What."

"What's going on?"

"I've been weak for week."

"Weak for a week?" Banjo repeated, amused.

"You heard me."

"What are you doing in here?"

"I came in to eat. What else?"

Banjo decided he didn't like her back talk. "Sit up, Pamela. I can't understand you." He leaned in and pulled on her shoulder. She sat upright. "Did you eat anything?"

"No. My belly hurts."

"How long's that been going on?"

"I've had pancreatitis and cirrhosis of the liver and that's been going on for a long time."

"But what's going on right now that you had this man call an ambulance?"

"I didn't ask."

"Then why did he call?"

"I don't know."

Banjo turned to Dick who said, "She comes in, sits down just like you see her there, and doesn't say anything when I ask. Pretty soon I heard her crying so I called you guys."

Banjo squeezed the back of his neck and thought. He turned back to Pamela. "What do you want us to do for you?"

"I want to go to the hospital"

"Why?"

"Because my stomach hurts!"

"You said that's been going on a long time. What do you want the hospital to do for you now?"

"I don't know. Make me feel better."

Banjo raised his eyes searching for patience. He turned to Clayton and gestured for ideas from his partner. Clayton shrugged his own puzzlement back to Banjo. This irked Banjo. He figured someone who could predict the future could help him a little with a surly woman. Banjo took a deep breath and slid in next to her. He took her blood pressure and examined her. "Can you walk?"

"No."

"Why not. You walked in here."

"I'm drunk."

"Come on, Pamela." Banjo pulled her by the arm and she slid to the edge of her seat. She stood under his continued pull then folded to the floor. "Get up, Pamela. We don't have time to mess around. We'll take you in but you have to help us. Now stand up." He pulled. She stood. She curled to the floor again. Banjo turned to Clayton and ordered, "Get the damn stretcher."

The back of the ambulance grew thick with her chicken soup smell. As he wrote his report Banjo felt something warm and wet on his pant leg. Urine ran off the mattress, soaking him where his leg touched the stretcher, then dribbled to the floor. He jerked away as though burned and lifted his feet to avoid the urine spreading across the floor.

"Pamela, why didn't you tell me you had to pee. Goddamn. We have things to do that in." She remained curled up on her side facing away. He slid open the windows to release her suffocating smells.

At Denver General Banjo rolled her off his gurney onto a hospital stretcher. Outside he shoved the gurney to Clayton and told him to clean it up.

His skin crawled where she had dampened him. Banjo took surgical scrubs from the emergency department and went into the bathroom. He removed his damp pants and threw them to the floor and scrubbed his leg red. He thought about the clean, sweet smelling house he and Lauren would have.

It would be full of light and flowers; the kitchen open and airy with copper pots and pans hanging from a wooden frame over the stove. Plants would fill a window box that looked upon the smooth, green lawn. Navajo tapestry the color of sunsets would quiet their rooms of adobe and wood. On Sunday mornings sunlight would stream over them as they sipped coffee and read the paper in bed. He would know just which section of the paper she would want first ...

Banjo stepped on his urine soaked uniform pants. His fantasy vanished. "Jesus," he muttered, pulling off the damp socks. "My head's in never-never land while my feet are soaking up piss."

Clayton sat in the dayroom reading a magazine when Banjo jerked open the bathroom door. "If I was a supervisor," he told his partner, "I wouldn't have to put up with this shit anymore."

Chapter 4

Ernie Webster crossed his legs and cupped his hands together in his lap. "What would you like to talk about today, Banjo?"

Ernie wore a burgundy sports jacket over a sky colored shirt. A bow tie of pastel colors accented his shirt. A yellow rose arched delicately from a narrow vase on a small table to Banjo's left. Banjo could just detect its sweet fragrance on the leading edge of each breath. Tissues also sat on that table. A waste basket underneath waited for them after they had been moistened and wadded. Banjo, noting the colors and delicate smells surrounding Ernie, considered his therapist a little too interested in womanly things. Still, like himself, Ernie had known the jungle terror of Vietnam so Banjo allowed him into the edge of his confidence. Banjo screwed up his mouth in thought. Ernie waited quietly.

The therapist could wait like a statue. They must teach that in therapy school, Banjo thought. The guy could probably sit the whole hour all composed and comfortable just waiting for him to say something. That made Banjo nervous. Unusual calm meant undisclosed power.

Banjo used that trick on the street. When someone tried to intimidate him he would become tranquil and the aggressor would fall silent as fire dies when oxygen is choked off. So Ernie had him a little off balance. Banjo drummed his knuckles against the arm of his chair. He wiggled his toes inside his Hush Puppies.

"I have a date tomorrow," Banjo answered.

"Oh, really. With Lauren?"

"Yup. She finally slowed down long enough."

"From what you've told me, she sounds like someone with lots of irons in the fire."

"Well, I guess I'd like to be one of them."

Ernie chuckled and smiled. Banjo liked the way his eyes twinkled. Maybe Ernie was someone who enjoyed chasing women after all. Banjo decided to give him another tiny glimpse of his world. "I took a shot in the head the other day. A guy dropped me before I knew what happened."

"How does a street wise paramedic let that happen?"

Wishing to avoid such questions, he arched his eyebrows and responded with a puzzled look.

"Cleverness and intuition are your strong suits. I wonder why you didn't see that coming."

"It's like the war," Banjo said, carefully changing the subject. "Next thing you know, you're dead."

Ernie's face slackened and his eyes shifted into the middle distance where Banjo often searched. "I know."

Then Ernie ceased being a therapist. He became a man dogged by his own memories and Banjo could talk to him. "What's interesting is that I knew he would be jumpy." Banjo averted his eyes as he did when revealing his secrets to a living man. "He overdosed and we woke him up with some medicine. I know those kind are dangerous and I knew he would do that. But I stood there anyway."

Ernie nodded.

Banjo bumped his fist against his mouth. His stomach hurt. "I guess I was careless."

Through Ernie's office window Banjo could see a fire station. Sirens and red lights swam behind his eyes. Banjo closed them. Weariness settled into his shoulders and he felt himself collapsing inward, as though all the air had rushed out of him. He felt thin and wrinkled and likely to be blown away. Ernie, a great distance away now, vanished before the memory of Greystone's death.

The accident report had chronicled that night's events in stilted police language. Banjo still could recreate from memory the police report's two critical and neatly typed paragraphs. The first summarized his partner's last moment of life; the last, Greystone's first moment of dying:

Paramedic Greystone of the Denver General Hospital Paramedic Division radioed ambulance arrival at this location at eleven thirty-six p.m. on this date. Mr. Stanley, driving the ambulance, found no suitable area at the side of the freeway to park and elected to park the ambulance on the freeway fast lane shoulder. This location was adjacent to the damaged cars. Fog was very heavy.

Mr. Stanley exited the ambulance onto the freeway shoulder. Mr. Greystone exited onto the fast lane. A forty-four year old male subject driving a 1968 Ford Fairlane sedan northbound on I-25 breached the flare line at a high rate of speed. Subject struck Mr. Greystone in the right thigh area with the front bumper. Mr. Greystone rolled onto the hood striking his head on the windshield and was carried a distance of approximately seventy-five yards. Subject then swerved the car throwing the victim into brush between the north and southbound lanes of the freeway. Subject fled and a subsequent police pursuit led to his arrest. A heavy odor of alcohol was noted in subject automobile and on the subject.

Banjo's recollection bore none of the report's chronological coldness. He saw the highway again. Red and blue and white and orange emergency lights danced madly in the dark and threw piercing beams at crazy angles through the gathering fog. A crumpled vehicle, too damaged to recognize, rested in the brush between lanes. Banjo got out. Greystone got out. Thump. It must have been a car door, he remembered thinking.

Someone yelled, "Oh, God, no!"

That made no sense to Banjo. Things seemed fairly well settled here. People were under control.

"Your partner!" cried someone else.

Banjo noticed the fading zoom of a fast car heading away and was alarmed, thinking that the police had closed the freeway. He then looked across the ambulance for Greystone and saw police officers running for their cruisers. The shock of understanding hit him and he thought he would fall to the ground.

The sounds ran through his mind.

Thump. "Oh, God, no!"
Thump. "Oh, God, no!"
Thump. "Oh, God, no!"

"What's going on, Banjo?"

Banjo turned his unfocused gaze toward Ernie. "What?"

"You were gone for a minute. I was wondering where you were."

"Oh, I saw the fire station and remembered some things."

"Anything you want to talk about?"

Banjo shook his head no. Adjusting the direction of conversation again, he said, "It was like I wanted to get popped. I started wearing my second chance vest again. If somebody could get me with a foot ..." Banjo let Ernie draw the obvious conclusion.

"Is that the only reason, because you got hit in the head once?"

Banjo laughed and resettled himself in his chair. "Maybe I should wear the vest on my head."

"Well, it seems that wearing a heavy vest on hot days is a little much. Don't you think?"

Ernie was beginning to sound like a therapist again, asking questions that made Banjo fidget. "What I do is dangerous," he answered a little too loudly. "People out there want to hurt us. Dan got shot. Greystone got killed. I took one between the eyes. I just want to be smart."

"Would a vest have helped in any of those circumstances?"

"So? You tell me how to protect myself."

Ernie avoided the taunt. "I don't know why you're wearing a vest, though I have an idea why you got hit. Interested?"

Banjo waved a consenting gesture at Ernie.

"I think you let it happen." Ernie waited.

Banjo showed no emotion.

"You bring up Greystone and the war frequently. I think you feel some guilt about both things." Ernie waited again.

Banjo did not move.

"You and I were warriors. We were taught that there is glory in offering ourselves up for a cause. It occurs to me that your cause may be atonement."

Banjo jerked his head back with disbelief. "You think I want to punish myself, like I have a death wish, or something?"

"It's just an idea." Ernie waited again.

"Hell of an idea," he laughed. But deeper currents moved him more often these days, and in these he caught a glimpse of truth. He shut his eyes against the cauldron of ill-defined emotions churning inside him.

Ernie chuckled. Banjo liked that. Ernie's laugh made the fears building in him seem less significant. He gave Ernie another peek inside.

"I don't know where they come from, but sometimes I get these flashbacks. I'll see things that happened when I first started with the division. They swell up and fill my whole head. I mean I've always remembered these things. But this past year ... They're not memories, they're storms. I forget where I am. I can't see anything."

"What kinds of things do you see?"

Banjo's fist went back to his mouth. "The night when John died. I see that."

"What do you feel when you see that?"

"Same old thing. I killed him."

"No you didn't. A car killed him."

"It wouldn't've if I'd parked somewhere else."

"Where else was there to park the ambulance?"

He chuckled bitterly. "There must have been someplace better. I just parked the car. The inside lane was clogged so I parked where I did because it was close to where patients would be. I didn't really look for a better place. My usual sloppy way. I do what it takes to get by. That time it killed my partner."

"A car killed your partner, Banjo. Don't you think Greystone had some responsibility there? Don't you think he should have looked before getting out onto a freeway? You would have looked."

"I suppose." Banjo rested his heavy head on his trembling fingertips. "Sometimes I see myself getting shot."

"Did that actually happen."

"No. A guy held a shotgun on Greystone and me one time. We were on a stairway and all of a sudden he appeared on the landing in front of us. He pulled the weapon. The barrel almost touched John's nose. There was no place to go. I found myself imagining what it was going to feel like and whether I would let it kill me outright so it wouldn't hurt, or try to protect myself somehow."

"What happened?"

"Greystone started talking to him like there was nothing wrong. Said, 'How you doin', partner? We're paramedics. I understand someone upstairs is hurt.' No fear. No anger. Just, 'How ya doin', partner?' We stood there a few seconds, him lookin' at us down the side-by-side barrels, us looking up into big black holes. Then he put the gun down. Sometimes I see steel blue barrels flashing at my chest."

Ernie shook his head in disbelief. "Greystone had guts."

"I have no idea what I would have done." Tears gathered in his eyes. "He got us out of that one. You know what? Strange as it sounds, I've been through Vietnam and years on the street and I never got a scratch."

"I'd say you're damn lucky."

"I lost friends in both places, but I got away clean. I was always just out of harm's way. On the other side of the ambulance or just down the hall, like I was when Dan got hit. That's not right, somehow. Nothing's supposed to last on the street."

"There's nothing wrong with surviving."

"But it's plenty wrong not being there when your partner needs you."

A quiet electronic beep interrupted Banjo's thoughts. "We have to stop for now," Ernie told him quietly. Banjo gathered in his emotions and put them back in their proper place. Feeling awkward in the transition, he patted down all his pockets searching for his check book.

"If you forgot again," Ernie told him, "you can pay me next time."

"Thanks." He stood. With the spell of intimacy broken Banjo began to feel silly for revealing so much of himself.

Ernie looked at his calendar. "Would you like to make another appointment now or call me later?"

"How does next Thursday look? I'm off Thursdays."

"Thursday's good." He made a note of it then wrote the day and time on a business card and handed it to Banjo.

"Take care of yourself, Banjo."

Banjo opened the door into the waiting area hoping nobody would see him come from his session. A woman sat in the waiting room, legs crossed, foot bobbing nervously as she flipped magazine pages. Her glance darted impatiently from Banjo to the therapist. Ernie told Banjo again to take care of himself, and, seeing her, gestured and said, "Come in, Annie. I'll be right with you."

A queer twinge of jealousy struck Banjo. For a fleeting moment he believed himself so special he should have Ernie's attention all to himself. In the next moment he felt himself on a mental health assembly line: one in a string of broken hearts passing under the therapist's nose.

Banjo headed home. He felt not quite put back together nor touching the ground; as though his spirit had left his body and had not gotten entirely tucked back in. He had to concentrate, feeling that, if he did not, he would float off somewhere.

*****

Banjo hit the automatic dial again. Two rings. "Well. If you think I'm this easy to track down ..." Banjo dropped the hand holding the receiver to his side. When he heard her machine beep he raised it again.

"This is Banjo. It's Monday night. I've been calling since Saturday. Do we still have a date tomorrow, or what? Call me." He slammed the receiver down. "Goddamnit! We're supposed to have a date and she's out with that doctor!"

Banjo kicked the table, sending it scooting loudly across the linoleum floor. The telephone crashed to the floor. He went to the refrigerator. Banjo swept aside the hamburger gone rank that Dan had left to thaw and looked for something else to eat. He found nothing so he took two beers. He popped one open and drank it down without taking a breath. He opened the next and sipped.

He went to his bedroom. In the bottom dresser drawer, beneath his second chance vest he found his baggy of finely ground dry leaves and cigarette paper. Banjo tapped a neat line of marijuana onto the paper, licked the long edge and gently rolled it between his thumb and index finger. He lit it with an old Zippo lighter he bought in Vietnam. He took the cigarette and beer back to the out of place table. He alternately gulped and inhaled. His anger at Lauren swelled.

He wanted to kill her. He ached to see her. She was trifling with him. He knew it. She was off somewhere with that doctor not thinking about him unable to sleep for the excitement of seeing her. He'd like to put her on that stairway with that shotgun staring down at her. She would say something stupid like what's on her answering machine, and boom. Only Banjo, in front trying to protect her, would get it, not her. That vision flooded before him. He saw the barrel, the long glinting barrel, explode orange. He shuddered and the muscles in his chest contracted. His breathing picked up, his stomach folded, and he began to sweat. Again, the barrel flashed. He reached for his beer. The barrel flashed. Banjo sucked hard on the cigarette then cooled his throat with the beer. The barrel flashed. Lauren ran away screaming, leaving Banjo bleeding and silently dying. Then, Banjo knew, she would realize how stupid she had been. Then she would see Banjo for the good man he really was. Then she would cry wretched tears to have him back. There she would be. That would teach her. Dingy broad. He would love to get her on that stairway.

Banjo drank a third beer and checked his watch. Feeling numb, his raw feelings protected at last, he went back to the bedroom. He lifted his vest above his head and dropped it over his chest and abdomen. Next he put on his uniform shirt and adjusted it over the vest. His boots had lost last week's shine but Banjo did not care today. He pulled them on and went to the bathroom to brush his teeth twice before leaving for work.

Chapter 5

Three beers and a joint just before work was Banjo's limit. He could function just fine with a little beer and marijuana in him; perhaps even a little better, he reasoned, relaxed as he was. Mastery on the street demanded a clear, relaxed mind and an exquisite intuition. And, as the chemicals blunted his blinding pain, he believed also that they heightened his awareness. Banjo took command of his ambulance feeling elevated and powerful and equal to Clayton.

The calls were easy. Their first was a cardiac arrest. Banjo and Clayton found her on the bathroom floor next to the toilet, from which she slid during a bowel movement. Brown feces smeared the white seat and the clean bathroom stunk. Her eyes remained open and her corneas were dried out and wrinkled. A pool of jelled blood spread from under her head like a deep purple aura. They knew she was dead but her husband begged them to try so they did.

Later a teenage girl ate a hand full of sleeping pills because friends spread a rumor that she was pregnant, not just fat. Banjo put her on the stretcher, checked her blood pressure, and held her hand on the way to the hospital.

Most recently, they saw an old woman who wanted them to get her husband out of the house. He called her a bitch and a cunt and threw beer cans at her. He told them to go to hell, he knew his rights.

Banjo said bullshit and called the police. The old man threw beer cans at them so the police arrested him.

Easy, Banjo thought, full of power and into the rhythm of the shift. His calls were at such intervals that he could relax between them and say hello to the nurses he liked. He dropped by his apartment to look after his clematis which, in the unusual spring time heat, were a little droopy. He listened to

Mozart as he watered, pulled a few tiny weed shoots, and gently fingered the soft dirt beds. Later, he and Clayton even had time to eat their slices of pizza.

Feeling just fine, Banjo could appreciate Clayton's solid competence, though his dirty shoes galled him. Clayton had not challenged him today. The shift was smooth. Clayton integrated his routines into Banjo's style. He anticipated well and was prepared for the next step in patient care. Banjo began to trust him. Reaching this point, Banjo was even curious about his partner's mystical religion. In fact Banjo felt a little nudge of guilt for recently slipping a word and a wink to Dan who had in turn suggested to Half Deck that he might impress the Chief if he moved Clayton to a night shift.

After they finished their pizza Clayton parked the ambulance in the shade of an elm tree next to a golf course. Clayton closed his eyes. Sweat dripped fast inside Banjo's vest and the shade gave him cool relief. He watched a golfer swing lazily at his ball then lug his clubs through the heat after it.

Quickly bored, Banjo turned up the police radio. He liked to listen to the police when he had nothing else to do, hoping to overhear them dispatched to a shooting or an auto accident, which in turn could lead to something interesting for him to do. He heard an officer answer his dispatcher with, "Roger."

Banjo reacted sharply to draw Clayton into conversation. "Roger! Nobody says Roger anymore."

Clayton moved to see Banjo.

Banjo looked at him. "Did you hear that?"

Another officer called for an ambulance to the Corona Hotel to check a fifty-five Adam. Clayton wrinkled his forehead in question.

"Fifty-five Adam," Banjo answered, "might be a sensitive incident code, like for a rape or bomb threat or something." He was eager. "That's close by and we'll get that anyway so let's just head on over there." Soon, when the ambulance dispatcher ordered them to the Corona Hotel to check a death, Banjo stated the obvious. "I guess a fifty-five Adam is a DOA."

Clayton double parked the ambulance next to the police cruiser. An officer slumped against his car and covered his face with one hand. Banjo approached and greeted him tentatively,

"Hey. Whatcha got?" He tried to peek between the policeman's fingers.

He jerked his head upward to indicate someplace in the hotel. "It's a baby girl. She was found dead. Room four twelve."

Banjo felt the memories stir as they entered the hotel. They stood in the lobby and called the elevator which stopped at most floors on its way down. They could hear the polite ding and the rustle of foot steps entering and exiting the car on the floor just above. Then the elevator slid into hearing, dinged, and opened. A heavy woman with sparse hair stepped out. "Oh, dear," she said, recognizing paramedics. "Who are you here for?"

"We were called to check on someone," Banjo answered flatly.

"Is it Mrs. Irving, six-oh-two? She's been so ill lately."

He said, "No, ma'am."

"Well, I'm sure you boys will take good care of whoever it is. You do such fine work, you paramedics." She touched Banjo's arm.

Banjo closed his eyes as the doors slid shut. "They have no idea, Clayton. People getting on and off this thing don't have a clue there's a dead baby up there. I wish I could go back to the time before I had to see such things face to face."

Blackened pigtails, carefully tied with red ribbons, shifted gently in the gathering winds of his memory. His hands trembled. He swallowed again and pushed down against his stomach. He sought out Clayton's large, comforting presence next to him.

He felt Clayton's hand at his arm. "Would you like me to go first?"

The door opened. Banjo sniffed the air out of habit. The hall was quiet. He checked room numbers in both directions. He took a deep breath. "No, I'm okay. Just stay close."

Banjo hoped a police officer was in the room. Bad calls were easier if he was not the first to see. He needed to know how bad the baby looked before he saw.

An officer writing in his notebook stood outside the room and looked at Banjo and Clayton but said nothing. "Where we going?" Banjo asked him.

"Kitchen's to the left," he said, reading what he had written. "Try not to disturb anything. Investigators are coming."

"The kitchen," Banjo said, confused. "The baby's in the kitchen?"

"Check the counter." He avoided looking at the paramedics.

"She's on the counter? Did someone beat her up and leave here there? How's she look?"

He looked up and his face was drawn. "I personally haven't looked."

An empty crib stood at an odd angle from the wall, as though someone had kicked it in that general direction. Urine and feces stained the newspaper that served as a mattress. Strangely, Banjo wanted to run his fingers along the crib rail to touch this evidence of recent life but did not, remembering the policeman's warning. Even dead, the infant created a presence. He expected baby noises. He looked for toys. Banjo checked again for Clayton.

An awareness of life just ended hung in the quietness. This little something, which Banjo believed was the spirit waiting momentarily in some nearby, nearly detectable dimension before moving on, always gave him a chill. Banjo felt this every time he checked a death.

Clayton grabbed Banjo's shoulder and pulled him back abruptly. "Something's wrong."

Banjo turned to him. Clayton's worried frown startled him. Banjo looked back toward the kitchen for an intruder.

"Something terrible has happened here, Banjo. Something awful."

"Do you see somebody in here?"

He looked about the room. "This is a bad place. Let's just get in and out quick."

They passed through an archway into the kitchen. There was no baby on the counter. A microwave sat next to the stove.

"There's no baby in here. Clayton, go get that cop."

"There is. Look." He pointed at the microwave.

Banjo looked. He took a step and made out a shape that reminded him of a small turkey. Banjo clapped one hand to his mouth and the other to his stomach. "Oh, my God." He turned to his partner. "Clayton. This can't be. Oh, God, this isn't true." Banjo took a step closer. The baby's curled up outline became clearer through the blackened glass door. He stared. He knew if he opened the door a small part of him would die. He resented the police for not warning him. Banjo checked once more for his partner. He stepped to the counter, closed his eyes, and pushed the door latch. He heard the door pop open and felt as if he were about to be executed.

A warm, cooked meat smell washed over him. He remembered Thanksgiving dinners. He opened his eyes. Her hands were at her mouth and balled into tight fists. Dry wrinkle lines extended from her eyes squinted shut and she grimaced toothlessly at Banjo. Her skin looked as though it would crack and fall away if he touched her. He wondered if he should check for a pulse. He did. She felt warm and dried up. Banjo rocked her back and forth and she moved as a unit. He turned to Clayton but did not know what to say.

Then Banjo looked back. He made the baby into a fascinating abstraction. He stared at the tiny details: the unnatural wrinkle lines creasing the skin on the back, the uncharacteristic redness and tight fists. He tried to stick his finger into one and could not. The thought of pulling her out horrified him. He remembered how easily drumsticks were pulled off well done turkeys.

Clayton said, "She's dead, Banjo. Let her go."

Banjo separated himself from the moment's reality. He built a circumstance in which such a killing could happen. A monster not long ago had been in this apartment, lifted the baby from that filthy bed, and carried her without gentleness to where he now stood. It opened the microwave and crammed her in. Then it closed the door, selected a time, and turned it on. It would have heard the fan running.

He thought of Lauren. He must talk to her. He needed her soft words. A thought struck him. At this moment he envied supervisors. Right now they were looking at paperwork on their desks. Half Deck was probably straining over whose initials to put in which tiny box. Clean papers and neat little boxes appealed to him greatly at this moment.

Suddenly he was back and imagining how the baby girl died: small hands curling into tight fists as she screamed silent screams behind the small glass door; skin drawing taut and wrinkling. Then, as though a plug were pulled, his energy drained away and darkness fell over him. Banjo took an off-balance step backwards into Clayton. Something in his stomach convulsed. He flung himself forward and a foul taste filled his mouth.

Strong hands took his shoulders, led him somewhere, and sat him down. He felt something cool and wet placed in his hands which he put to his mouth. He heard his name quietly called. "Banjo, are you all right?"

He looked toward the voice. "What?"

"Are you okay?"

Banjo ran a hand across his face to wipe away sweat. He cleared his throat and checked the front of his shirt. "Sure. Why?"

Clayton quietly told him, "You threw up in the sink. Are you all right?"

When light returned to Banjo's eyes he found himself in the living room in a chair. He blessed whoever brought him here for not leaving him in sight of the microwave. Clayton kneeled next to him. The policeman who had remained outside jotting in his book now stood near.

Banjo sucked cool water from the wash cloth. "I had a touch of the flu last night. I guess the smell got to me."

Another voice boomed. "I thought I heard one of my boys on the radio coming over here." Banjo startled and quickly turned to the voice. Zagata rested an elbow on the baby's crib and grinned at Banjo. "Smells like you had a touch of the party bug last night, too."

Zagata's face was cheery and the scar lay as a pale line across his cheek. He smiled and chuckled. Banjo hated him and wanted to spit remaining bits of vomit into Zagata's face. But fearing the cop, Banjo remained distant.

Clayton patted Banjo's back. "It got to me, too, partner." Banjo noticed how obviously Clayton ignored Zagata.

The first officer said, "We have a police chaplain who's real good at helping with these things. You want me to call him?"

"No."

Zagata answered like a coach. "Ol' Banjo don't need that shit. He's a real paramedic. He's seen worse than that in Nam. Haven't you, Banjo?"

The policeman ignored Zagata. "He can be here in ten minutes. Happens to all of us one time or another."

"No. I'm fine. Really."

Clayton said, "I think it's a good idea. We can stay out of service for awhile."

"I said, I'll be fine."

"I know I won't sleep tonight," said the policeman.

"Well, hell," Zagata swore impatiently. "No sense just arguing. I'll call him in. Look at you guys," he grumbled, reaching inside his Bronco's warm-up jacket for his portable radio. "A goddamn bunch of men in uniform who can't even decide what to do."

Clayton exploded to his feet. "Fuck off, Zagata! Get back in your goddamn car and get out of here."

The smile fell off his face leaving surprise behind. Then the face hardened and the scar began to move. Clayton and Zagata stared coldly at each other across the stunned silence.

The first officer stepped between them. "Aren't you out of your district, Zagata?"

"I go where my friends go," he said with his eyes still fixed on Clayton. "Make sure they stay out of trouble; mind their P's and Q's."

Banjo stood. He took deep breaths and smelled his vomit and alcohol in the kitchen sink. He wiped his mouth again with the wash cloth then tossed it to the chair. "Come on, Clayton. What I need to do is brush my teeth and get some air. Let's get back to Denver General. Our shift is about over anyway."

As they left Clayton stepped close to Zagata and, holding his gaze steady, cuffed him lightly on the arm. Banjo saw Zagata jerk and tense but he did not retaliate.

They drove back to the hospital. Banjo worried that Zagata, smelling alcohol, would report him. He worried that he would never forget that smell, the dried out crow's feet wrinkles at her eyes, her tiny, tight fists. He worried that if he ever had a baby it would die, too.

Nearing Denver General Clayton spoke. "I meditate, you know. I focus on my breathing and repeat a sound over and over in my mind. When I do that everything quiets down and I don't feel the shock of this job so much."

Banjo listened but did not let on.

"Sometimes when something really bad happens I go out into the mountains. There I remember I'm connected to something much greater than myself and much more important than what happens day to day. I can put things into perspective. I'm going there after work tonight. Would you like to come?"

"How do you put a cooked kid in perspective?"

Clayton shook his head. "I can't. But I know her spirit is at peace and will live a better life next time around, perhaps as a strong and free eagle."

Banjo's chest jerked as he neared crying and he covered his eyes. He pictured a frail young soul lifted out of the room as he had stood there sensing it and placed into a strong-eyed eagle sailing grandly on mountain winds. He bit his lip to hold back his tears.

*****

Banjo dropped the keys on the driver's seat and left the ambulance for the oncoming crew. He considered walking over to The Parlour to soften the ache hardening inside him but Clayton interrupted those thoughts. "Let me show you something," he said. "It'll just take a minute."

Banjo wanted to decline but Clayton's had defended Banjo against Zagata. In Banjo's system of honor Clayton deserved his respect. He preferred to drink beer alone but he would go with his partner.

They passed through the emergency department and into the lobby. Clayton led Banjo to the elevators and pushed the upward pointing arrow. Banjo remembered the little dings he heard as they waited in the lobby of the hotel. "Where are we going?"

"Up to the helipad. I like to go up there sometimes."

"You like to watch helicopters land?"

"Just wait."

The elevator arrived and they rode it to the top floor of the hospital. Exiting, they walked along a short hallway to a locked door. Near it was a wall telephone. Clayton picked it up and said, "Paramedics on the pad for a tour." Banjo heard a click inside the door and Clayton pushed it open.

A gentle wind stirred. The mountains were clear. Noise from the streets far below was muted by the distance. Banjo's mood was revived by the cool breeze and he untucked his shirt and loosened the straps on his second chance vest. He lifted his arms away from his sides to let the cool air circulate around him. Clayton walked across the rooftop pad to the side facing the mountain and sat. He dangled his feet off the edge of the pad. He unbuttoned his. "Sit down, Banjo. Take a load off."

Banjo sat, hanging his feet into nothingness. The wind soughed as it moved amid the hospital structure.

Clayton took several deep breaths and closed his eyes. Banjo worried that his partner would drift into meditation and forget about him. "I have to be lifted above what happens to me," Clayton told Banjo. "I have to get above it, even if it means sitting up here on the pad."

Banjo looked out to the Rockies. They were sharp and hard in their clarity. He wondered if an eagle soared up there on the wind. He nodded at Clayton's necklace. "What's that?"

Clayton fingered it. "My grandfather gave this to me when he gave me my Sioux name. It's a bear claw and it brings good luck, good fortune, good health; all good things generally."

"You have another name besides Clayton Lameroux?"

"I have a couple. I was named Two Clouds when I was born. When I was thirteen my grandfather gave me this bear claw and named me Talking Fox. He died right after that. I've worn the necklace ever since."

Out of his depth but curious anyway, Banjo asked, "So ... like, were you born on a reservation, or something?"

Clayton was respectful. "No. I was born right here in Denver and stayed put."

"Do you go to an Indian church? You're awfully religious."

Clayton laughed at this. "Indian church. Our land was our church. The sky was our church. The rivers were our church. Usually the oppressive culture burns churches. But look." He gestured outward. "We had streets and 7-11's built over top of ours. That's why I have to leave the city to feel connected to my beliefs."

Banjo cocked his head in greater curiosity. "So, what exactly do you believe?"

Clayton was thoughtful. "Well, we believe that we grow by seeking understanding in the four great ways: wisdom, illumination, introspection, and innocence. Those represent the four points of the medicine wheel." He drew a circle in the air with a finger and touched the four chief compass points. "The medicine wheel symbolizes our mythology and guides us. To grow we have to give up our old ways of seeing and seek the lessons of the great ways. In particular, our first important lesson is understanding that all perceptions are true to the perceiver. And we believe that every person is a living power that has always existed somewhere in time and space. I think we all existed before and will again. That little baby did, and will again.

"When I seek one of the four ways, I go where it is quiet and I can feel the spirit of things." Clayton lifted his chin toward the mountains. "I feel that out there. Out there I am connected to all things. I feel the harmony of all things. I know that the blood of my grandfathers flows in the rivers, and the air they breathed fills the wind, and that the bones of my ancestors are buried beneath my feet. When I am in that place, I feel timeless and changeless even though I am a seeker of change. I sense my place in the universe and I am embraced by something."

Banjo looked at Clayton without speaking. His partner stated it all without hesitation or embarrassment. Banjo could not have articulated his love of music as well. Still, he craved for an answer. "How does all that help what happened today?"

Clayton's eyes lowered from the mountains. "Doesn't, I suppose. I just try to stay strong."

This disappointed Banjo. The two did not speak for awhile. Presently something else interested him. He asked Clayton, "Why did you bump Zagata back there?"

"I was counting coup. It's a sign of great courage to touch your enemy during battle. Counting coup is a source of power."

Banjo was shocked. "Are you planning to do battle with him?"

Clayton thought again. "He's an evil man. I think he's someone we'll both have to face."

Banjo waved both hands in front of him. "Wait, wait, wait. Wait just a minute. You're not doing battle with anybody. He's a crazy cop. That's all. You leave him alone. He'll leave you alone."

"He knows that I know what he did and I'm sure he's figured out that I've told you."

Banjo angrily slapped the helipad deck. "Good Lord, what makes you so sure about things you can't see?"

"I sense things. I don't know; sort unsettled feelings, I guess you could say." Clayton touched his bear claw. "My great grandfather was a medicine man and frequently had visions. He was very powerful and greatly honored by his people. Sometimes I think I have some of his power. This bear claw originally belonged to him."

"If you keep raising hell with Zagata maybe I should get one of those for myself."

"It works better as a gift. If I could give you something to help you, I would. That's why I wanted you to come up here. You need to get above the streets; away from what is bad. Maybe that will help a little bit."

Banjo felt a sudden touch of affection. "You know, I hope you haven't taken it to personally, me treating you like a rookie. It's always been the way we do things."

Clayton nodded. "Traditions are important to you. They're important to me, too. But you need to know our traditions are different. I'm not one to drink beer and pin napkins to my shoulders."

This hurt Banjo's feelings but he did not show it.

*****

Banjo prepared himself for bed that night with marijuana and beer. But thoughts of the baby nevertheless found their way in. Blackness gathered and his shoulders accumulated weight.

The telephone rang just when he had determined to watch television until late rather than try to sleep. Supervisors looking for overtime were the only ones who called this late. He would not have answered the phone except to break the escalating swirl of images. He sat at the table and lifted the receiver. "Talk to me. I'm listening."

"Hello, my dear. Do you hate me clear out to the edge of time?"

Happy shock lifted him. "Lauren! I've been trying to call."

"I know. I can be such a hard dog to keep on the porch. I went back to Atlanta for my sister's wedding. What a clambake that was. We had relatives from all over and I had Uncle this and Auntie that, people I don't know from Jerusalem, telling me what a wonderful sight I was. They pinched my cheeks and declared, 'Oh, aren't you such a lovely grown up girl now.'"

Banjo fell into her mesmerizing Georgian drawl and his dark feelings tattered and fell away. He smiled as he listened.

"Say, have you ever seen a wedding cake with a donut on top? My sister ... Samantha's her name. She met this man in a donut shop over french crullers or some such. She's a stitch, that sister of mine. Just the bees knees, as mama says. You'll have to meet her sometime; my sister that is. Say, you still up for a little nonsense tomorrow?"

"Sure. If you are."

"Oh, heavens, I wouldn't think of standing you up. How about dinner. There's this wonderful little spot over on Pennsylvania Avenue. They call it the Plum Tree Cafe. Don't you just love that name. They have those little outdoor tables."

"That's just up the street from me."

"Oh, aren't we clever and convenient about this."

Banjo took this to mean they could easily return to his apartment after dinner. His heart raced. He would have to clean up and get some good wine.

She didn't elaborate. "Well, sugar, it's late. I should let you get your beauty rest. Goodness knows I need mine. I'll make reservations for six-thirty. You be on time. I'm not one who likes to be kept waiting around by herself."

Banjo chose to believe this was another seductive hint. "I'll be there." His springy resiliency returned. He would go to bed now and when he woke up he would have just a few more hours to kill before he saw her.

Then he saddened. A few hours after that their date would end. He wanted to clutch her to his chest. The sweet things never lasted long.

*****

Banjo walked to the restaurant. A block short he stopped dead. That smell. That warm, meaty smell. It floated from the restaurant and swirled warmly about his head. His stomach moved and he began to sweat. Banjo closed his eyes to steady himself.

Banjo continued when the evening breeze shifted the dinner aromas away. The tables were covered with linen. Women in colorful dresses sat with men in jackets and ties. They looked so comfortable at their intimate tables. They smiled and laughed easily. He wished he had been somewhere else when the police called an ambulance to check a DOA at the Corona Hotel. He lived a million miles from these people.

He found Lauren. Her dress, an explosion of summer flowers, clung to her and flowed along the lines of her body. He followed the perfect outline of her thigh and watched her breasts, as loose and free as her dark hair, rise and fall gently with each breath. His own breathing quickened with the sweet stirring below his stomach.

She looked up. A smile, a truly happy-to-see-you smile, brightened her face. Banjo laughed. Lauren cocked her head teasingly. "Hello, m'dear."

"Hey," he answered, grinning like a teenager.

She reached for his hand. Banjo held her fingers gently as he sat, and for several moments longer after sitting. She spoke first. "I apologize for not telling you I would be out of town." Her voice flowed sweetly like golden honey.

Banjo shrugged one shoulder. "That's okay. It worked out." He wanted to crush her in his arms, crawl inside her, sleep at her side forever.

She leaned across the table to speak so others would not hear. "Who had that poor little baby? Why, it was all over the news. Police think a bizarre cult or some such was responsible."

"That was mine." The morning paper also had taken Banjo back to the Corona Hotel. His fist went to his mouth and bumped.

Lauren's smooth forehead furrowed. Banjo saw the baby's wrinkled back. Lauren stared at him then closed her eyes. "Lord," she said. "Please protect me from ever seeing such a thing. Life's too short to be hurt that way."

A waiter appeared with a towel folded neatly over his arm. Lauren spoke up, smiling so sweetly, "We've been chit-chatting. Can you give us just a minute, please?" She watched him walk away. "Well, doesn't he have the prettiest little swing in his bottom."

Her face swung hungrily back to his. "Tell me what it looked like. Was it all burned up and charred?" She caught herself. Her face softened with sympathy and she reached again for Banjo's hand. "Oh Banjo, I'm sorry. That must have been so awful for you. I can get carried away with the gruesomeness sometimes. I know that. I am so sorry."

But the shock had already struck. The question had invaded. Like a gawking bystander, she wanted ugly details. The woman he imagined would never be so unbecoming. Lauren's beauty slipped. Her perfection failed. He answered vaguely. "She looked like a dead kid."

"God love his children. I hope the precious thing didn't suffer long."

Banjo saw the baby's toothless grimace, her tiny clenched fists. "Hard to tell."

"How long do you suppose it ... was it a little boy or girl?"

"Girl."

She touched her fingertips to her cheek. "Oh, poor thing. Banjo, I'm so clumsy with pain. Can I do something to help? I know you must be hurting. You've seen so much." She looked at him for a moment then asked, "How long was she in there?"

"The inside was still warm when I opened it. Not very long."

"My dear God, it had just happened. How did you survive that? Could Clayton help you?"

Banjo nodded.

"Thank goodness for that. Clayton seems so gifted in that way --helping others with feelings and that. What kind of place was it?"

Banjo thought. Though he always noted details, he could recall nothing of the room. "I don't know. I must have been fixed on the microwave."

The waiter returned and stood a polite distance off. Banjo pulled his fingers away from her hand. The waiter took their requests without writing them down. Lauren ordered Cornish game hen. Banjo asked for a pasta salad, the one thing on the menu with the fewest associations with a microwave.

Lauren turned back to him. She was eager. "What did she really look like?"

"I don't know. Looked like someone tried to fix a turkey in a microwave."

She touched her fingers to her mouth. "I'm so awkward with these personal trouble things. But I'll listen. Will that help?"

Banjo changed the subject and they spoke of small things until dinner arrived.

With exaggerated dignity the waiter brought their meals. He dipped at the waist to place their food before them. Banjo and Lauren watched in silence. Then she said, "I hear the pasta salad is wonderful. I would have ordered that but I'm hungry enough to eat a stump." She tore off a leg.

Banjo lurched back. He left the table and hurried up the block hoping to reach odorless air before vomiting. He stopped when he could no longer smell the restaurant and leaned against a car. He turned back to see how far he had come.

Lauren and other patrons stared in silence. From his distance he mouthed, "I'm sorry," but stayed put. She stood and came to him.

He jammed his fists deep into his pockets. She crossed her arms. "Do you mind telling me why you bolted from our table?"

She stood right there but she was worlds away. "I'm sorry."

"Banjo, I can't go back there now. I'd be mortified."

"I'm sorry. Really I am."

"Is it that baby?"

He nodded.

"Did something remind you?"

He nodded again. "I can't go back there."

She let her arms unfold and openness returned to her face. She touched his arm. "Wait here, sweetie."

She returned to the restaurant, said something to the waiter, then dropped a bill on their table and came back. She took his arm. "I'll fix us something back at my place."

Banjo liked her apartment. She had already created the brightness and light he hoped to create with her someday. Yellow and white daffodils extended from a clear crystal vase sitting on the window sill. Lace covered the windows so that sunlight bathed the oak floors in quiet, old fashioned shadow patterns. Exotic orange and lavender floral designs covered her sofa. Similar pillows spilled to the floor. A kaleidoscopic quilt made from odd squares of cloth draped over a rocker. Watercolors, posters, children's finger paintings, books, magazines, all of strong and crashing colors, filled up the empty spaces so that Lauren's eclectic clutter spread color about her home like a great splatter painting.

But the vivid chaos left Banjo disoriented. He could not bring order to her place. There was no focus such as his stereo equipment and facing chair represented. She had no nest anywhere, no most comfortable spot, no place littered with newspapers, a coffee mug, and the debris of loving use. Her colors flowed from one room to the next without reason or thought, like Lauren herself; moving from here to there, always moving past, moving on, moving elsewhere.

She made a tuna fish sandwich which she served with green lettuce and a bright wedge of orange.

Lauren settled herself in a chair across from him. "So, tell me what happened."

Banjo stared at his plate. He wanted to explain but he could not organize his thoughts. "I don't know."

"Was the baby just more than you could absorb all at once?"

Banjo recalled her intrusive questions about the baby. She had seemed to crave for details then prayed not to see the real thing. 'Lord,' she had said. 'Protect me from ever seeing such a thing.' Banjo certainly hadn't wanted to see that either. But he went into the kitchen, popped oven the microwave, and let that cooked meat smell come over him. He made the sacrifice. She was not willing to cross the same bridge. He could not respect that. She wore the uniform but her commitment flowed as superficially as her unfocused decorations. They were pretty but that was all.

Banjo gave the best answer he could put together. "It's hard to keep an appetite after that."

"I can't imagine!" She leaned across and lightly stroked his cheek.

He kissed her fingers and stared into the middle distance. He disengaged his brain and allowed only his rhythmic breathing into his awareness. That relaxed him some. He heard his name. He wanted to ignore it as he would an early morning alarm clock but he answered, "What?"

Lauren looked puzzled and inadequate. She held out her hands in a gesture of helplessness. "Do you want to talk?"

"I'm sorry."

"You don't have to be." She dallied with her sandwich and looked away.

He took that to mean his presence no longer interested her. "Lauren ..." He wondered how the evening had led to his need to be rid of her. "This kid got cooked. The restaurant smelled just like her. I couldn't sit there anymore."

She nodded. Her face was sad.

He closed his eyes and his head grew heavy. "I guess I'd better get going."

"Banjo, I do wish I was better at this sort of thing. You look like you have the weight of all your ancestors sitting on those tired shoulders."

He looked at her pretty, worried face. "This isn't how I imagined the evening going." She started to speak but Banjo shook his head. "I'll be okay in a couple days after my head clears up.

"Are you sure?"

"Yeah, I expect." He stood. On his way out Banjo noticed her answering machine, the black box that kept her callers at bay. And the box told a truth about her. All means of access to her were blocked.

Chapter 6

Banjo used a pencil and poor handwriting to complete his application for supervisor. He turned it in at the last moment. Two other paramedics applied also. One had previously been a supervisor, resigned to return to the streets and, finding no pleasure there either, decided unhappily that a supervisor's office was preferable to an ambulance. The other, Eric, was a body builder when off duty. He dressed neatly and wore jewelry and expensive black loafers as though expecting never to get dirty. Seeing the three candidates, paramedics shook Banjo's hand and wished him luck. Banjo felt obligated to apply. He envied the paramedics who did not face these choices.

But he liked being in charge. He would be the night supervisor. The division would be his when he came to work. Nobody would look over his shoulder and Half Deck would no longer control his life at schedule change every three months. Perhaps this would compensate for losing Lauren.

A Beethoven piano concerto played on the CD that June morning. Banjo directed the music with one hand. During a quiet passage his thoughts shifted automatically to Lauren. He had imagined this music in their house. Sadly, he discarded the notion. She wasn't the woman he figured her to be. He sighed and his thoughts comfortably dissolved again into the piano chords. Then he remembered his plans for the evening.

He was having dinner with Half Deck and his parents that night. Half Deck said he wanted to urge Banjo into the supervisory ranks, but Banjo figured this was at the prompting of the Chief, not the worthless supervisor. Banjo dreaded the idea but later devised a way to make the occasion interesting. He had convinced Dan to come along and looked forward to the evening.

*****

Banjo rode with Dan and admired his friends substantial Saab automobile. He envied the smells of new fabric and leather. Soft-rock music surrounded them like a halo. The music bored him though, like Dan sometimes could.

Banjo remembered when Dan was an enthusiastic kid who loved everything about being a paramedic. Dan brought his saucer eyes into the dayroom on his first day, took one look around, and asked for the bathroom. He argued his ideals with Greystone who by then had been very tired for a long time. He elbowed his way outrageously into Eden's life and pushed Banjo aside. Banjo had put up a brief fight. He had taken Eden to a bus bench on Colfax Avenue, offered her champagne, and asked her to marry him; to keep her away from Dan. He would have done it, too. But she had to have her Danny-boy. Banjo eventually forgave Dan but he, Banjo, never really got over Eden.

Dan had other amusing impulses. His honesty when he drank frightened people and Banjo liked to party with him just to hear what he would say. He once told a doctor he was a stupid, over priced technician. Another time he nearly picked a fight with a biker. Banjo had forgotten what that was about. People watched carefully how much Dan drank in those days.

After Greystone died, Dan changed from a happy, clumsy boy into this careful, respected, but monotonous man driving his Saab. Banjo missed Dan's playfulness as much as he missed his dead partner. He wondered if the granite hard Greystone started out like Dan, if Jonathan Greystone was ever Johnny.

Dan turned a corner and shifted gears. The power pushed Banjo into his seat. He thought of his rattly Toyota pick-up and wondered where all his money went. He wondered just how much Dan was worth, having inherited his huge Victorian house from his odd landlady. Maybe Dan was so settled because he did not need this job and stayed only because he liked the place and could tell the Chief whatever he pleased.

Banjo burned to ask Dan about his money. But Banjo, who rarely saw a paycheck that could last the month, found this wealth disconcerting and mysterious so asking him bluntly was out of the question. They would first have to get drunk, which Dan rarely did these days.

Banjo decided to bring Dan out of his stuffy shell tonight and sneak up on the subject. Dan was many things Banjo wasn't, he knew, but he wasn't nearly as clever. He harrumphed his throat clear. "Whoever first called him Half Deck sure got that right."

Dan looked disgusted. "You sure you want to do this?"

Banjo smiled, full of satisfaction and mischief. "I want to see how he lives. This is a guy older than the both of us. He still lives with mom and dad, worships Elvis, and wears long sideburns and leisure suits. Now aren't you just a little curious about him?"

"Not that curious."

"He's been a supervisor since before anybody can remember but nobody ever sees him outside work. When he asked me over, he told me to bring a guest. I couldn't resist, you lucky dog."

Dan narrowed his eyes. "Why me?"

Banjo laughed, delighted. "Because I love getting serious guys like you into trouble. You've worked with me long enough to know that."

"That's what I thought."

Banjo considered his comments then made a connection. "Speaking of serious guys, I've really gotten to like Clayton. He's quiet and spooky sometimes but I like him. He's steady. Like you. I think I'd like to keep him. You don't suppose Half Deck took all that stuff about moving Clayton to nights seriously, do you?"

Dan did not engage himself in Banjo's high mood. "I guess we'll find out next schedule change."

"Just like Greystone," Banjo complained. "You never play anymore."

Half Deck lived in brick house painted white. The black shingled roof shined in the summer twilight as though it had been shellacked. The lawn was closely cropped and well disciplined. A slab of red, tightly fitted stone ran straight from the sidewalk to the concrete front porch. Small heather clumps, like puffs on a poodle's tail, lined the walk. Two plastic, perfectly erect pink flamingos bordered the walk at the porch step. Banjo tweeked the beak of one, tilting the bird sharply. Dan gave Banjo a look and straightened the bird. He jabbed the doorbell. Three tones, loud as church bells, sounded.

Half Deck called from a distance, "Mother, they're here! Get the door!" They heard hurried steps. The door opened. A globe of white hair, perfect and full like a dandelion seed head, bloomed around her face. She wore an apron over a dress that dropped straight to mid-calf.

"Good evening, Mrs. Humphries. I'm Banjo and this is Dan. We work with your son down at the hospital."

"Oh, yes, yes. How nice to meet you." She tugged at the screen door latch which stuck. She flapped her hands at it. "Calvin, this darn lock!" She took the latch in both hands and rattled the door. The latch popped and the screen sprung open. They jumped aside. She patted her hair back into perfection.

Banjo smelled roast beef. He saw the baby. He pulled her arm and it tore from her shoulder. Banjo took deep breaths and forced his mind back to the present.

Mrs. Humphries extended her hand. "I'm Missus Humphries." Banjo shook the wet palm. She pulled it back self consciously. "But you already know that. Ronnie's just in the kitchen finishing dessert. It's chocolate macadamia nut cake. He's quite proud of it. Ronnie! Come say hello to your friends!"

"Mother, get them a beer and set them down. I'll be out when I can."

She clasped her hands at breast level. "He can be so fussy when he's cooking. Make yourself at home." She gestured to the sofa encased in clear plastic. "Would you like a drink?"

Banjo answered, "Whatever you have is fine."

"Just make yourself comfortable. I'll be right out." She winked. "I'll shake Ronnie loose from that cake of his, too."

Dan said, "Tell him to take his time."

Banjo's eyes twinkled at Dan. "We begin to get the picture."

They heard a loud slap in the kitchen. A new voice, high and shrill, commanded, "Damn you, get away from that beef!" Two cats streaked from the kitchen and disappeared down a hall. A skinny man stood in the kitchen doorway jerking his fury filled face about. He wore no shirt and a few white curls of hair poked from his pink chest. He seized the strangers with his eyes. "I'm Ronnie's old man. It pays to keep your rolled up newspapers around when you have beasts. Helps when the wife and kid get out of line, too. Isn't that right." That wasn't a question but an affirmation. He nodded with certainty and set out after the cats.

Dan and Banjo sat on the davenport. Plastic rustled under him. "This is like a play with real strange characters," Dan said. "Except these are actual people. I mean, actual people."

There was another loud slap then hissing. Low slung cats flashed into the living room, toward the davenport and slithered underneath.

"Calvin!" Half Deck shouted from the kitchen. "Leave those stupid things alone. You're going to make them psychiatric or something."

The bony man huffed to save face and sat in an overstuffed chair. "Damn beasts are everywhere, getting into food, trash. Why, every time you flush the toilet they come rushing in. Have to see the turds circling, I guess. Never seen anything like it." He unrolled his newspaper and snapped it flat. He held it in front of his face. Behind him Banjo noticed a photograph on the wall. It was importantly secured to the plaster with screws. Half Deck's father, wearing an old Denver Police Department uniform, stood rigidly at attention next to another officer who held himself less erect and whose hat sat cockeyed on his head. Banjo recognized this carelessly dressed officer. His name was Harry Bancroft; Captain Bancroft. He had been held responsible for drugs stolen from the evidence locker and was directed to retire. He did so in 1980, then killed himself in 1981. Banjo found it interesting that Half Deck's peculiar father was once a police officer.

"Well now, gents." Half Deck approached. He wore a blue leisure suit over a white shirt unbuttoned to the middle of his

75

white chest, skinny and boney without his second chance vest. He carried three cans of beer. When he reached the sofa he popped two open. He gave one to Banjo and kept another. He tossed the third unopened can to Dan. "This is an occasion, Banjo." He raised his can to Banjo. Dan opened his beer and drank, ignoring the toast. "You are about to join the elite supervisorial ranks; the leadership that makes this division the best damned paramedic division in the whole USA." He drank deeply.

Banjo tossed down a quick gulp, fascinated by the narrow sideburns extending below Half Deck's ears. His hair tapered down closely to the back of his white neck. He smelled of barbershop hair tonic.

Dan, with his fingers laced behind his head, stared into space. Half Deck now recognized him. "Didn't mean to ignore you, Daniel. But I want to make Banjo feel important. We supers aren't the most appreciated bunch so we take care of each other. Isn't that right? So I'll just focus in on him in the beginning so he'll know what I'm saying. See?"

"Uh-huh."

Banjo smiled. "Dan's always a little uncomfortable in new situations." He smiled at Dan and kicked his foot.

"No reason to be uncomfortable around here. We're just folks. Isn't that right, Calvin?" The little man nodded without looking from his paper. Half Deck joined them on the davenport, situating Dan in the middle, and swung his knee onto the cushion. "You know, Banjo," he said past Dan, "we have the best job in the world. I mean it. Think about it. Denver General is a good city hospital and being a paramedic there is a good city job."

"You won't get rich," interrupted his father from behind the newspaper, "but you'll get your retirement. Isn't that right, Ronnie? Didn't I tell you that?" He nodded sharply at them again to certify his conviction.

"Calvin's right. And we get to work around those pretty nurses. A guy likes to sneak a peak down their scrub tops. Isn't that right, Banjo? I've seen you."

"Which one do you like, Ron," Banjo asked slyly.

"I like Sherry. Sherry's a nice one. I mean a **nice** one."

"I know what you mean. I know what you mean, too, about this being a good job. We work with real fine people. Dan here's become my best friend. I was with him the night he got shot at the Delphi Hotel. He hung in there with me when I went half crazy after John died."

Half Deck's face took on a far away look. "We lost a good one there."

Banjo feared this conversation would come to close too his aggressive memories so he nudged the talk elsewhere. "Dan here tells me you're an Elvis fan."

Dan's mouth popped opened.

"You like Elvis, Daniel? Would've thought you were too young to appreciate Mr. Presley. You really have to be at least into your forties like Banjo and I to appreciate the era. When I turned twenty-one Irma and Calvin took me to Graceland. I'll never forget that birthday. Let me get my scrap book."

Dan finished off his beer. "Actually, I could use another one of these."

"All right, sir." When he stood and went to the kitchen, the cats peeked from beneath the davenport and padded silently across the floor.

"Muffles. Raindrop," warned Half Deck's father, watching. "Don't you even think it." Eyeing him, the cats broke into a trot. "Goddamn beasts!" He pushed out of the chair and rerolled his paper. The cats hit the shiny kitchen floor and skidded sideways. The old man, bobbing his head about, chased after with his threatening paper club.

Dan turned sharply to Banjo. "Did you two team up to make this a miserable evening for me? You guys talk about me like I'm not even here."

"I like seeing how people live. I like getting into their world."

"Well, you're getting into mine. This whole family is getting into my world. Gives me the creeps."

"Half Deck makes a big deal about being the senior supervisor. He thinks it's his place to bring new supervisors into the fold. He's harmless."

"How on earth did he ever get to be a supervisor?"

Banjo loved the fun. "Threw away the mold when they made that one, didn't they? Back then all you needed was seniority. He's got that. Swears he won't leave until he wins the lottery. The Chief has him under control, though. Keeps him away from everything but the schedule."

Mrs. Humphries carried a platter of roast beef. "Boys," she called in a sing-song way. "Dinner." The old man, now wearing a navy blue Denver Police Department tee-shirt, marched behind with his rolled newspaper.

Half Deck pulled the chair from one end of the table. "Banjo, you get the place of honor." He pulled out another next to Banjo's. "Irma."

"Thank you, sweetheart." She patted her perfect globe of hair, smoothed her apron, and carefully sat.

He pointed to the chair opposite his mother. "Calvin, you sit there and carve the meat." Dan found his way to the remaining chair.

His father cut the roast and dark juice filled the serving platter. The cats circled the table. The old man held a drippy slab of meat motionless on the carving fork and watched until the cats settled themselves near a heat vent.

Banjo got the first piece. He watched bloody juice run from underneath it and cut a small bite. Half Deck cut a chunk from his piece and chewed. He stopped. He took the bite out of his mouth and returned it slowly to his plate. "Irma, it's not done enough. Take it back and cook it some more." She stood without a word and took her son's plate, not bothering to ask if others wanted less bloody meat.

"She's such a goose sometimes. Can't even fix a roast."

The old man extended his fork. "You watch that talk about your mother. That woman's been feeding you and wiping your butt since the day you were born. Isn't that right?"

Half Deck twisted his neck as if to see out the front window.

"Isn't that right!"

Half Deck strained toward the window. He said, "I believe the Finesilvers just came home. The Finesilvers," he told Dan and Banjo, "were in Houston visiting their son who is an astronaut."

The old man turned to the cats. "You beasts better stay put if you don't want to be launched by your tails into orbit." He nodded at them.

They ate while Half Deck waited in silence. Soon the microwave beeped. Banjo's breathing quickened and he was afraid to see what would come out. Mrs. Humphries reappeared with her son's plate. He put the rejected bite back into his mouth and tested. "Perfect. It's perfect."

"Don't talk before your food's chewed up," ordered his father sopping up red juice with a slice of white bread. "If you don't chew your food up first, who will?"

Banjo coughed to mask his laugh.

Banjo tasted the red wine offered from a screw top bottle. It was sweet as syrup and he could drink it only if he held his breath. Dan made a face and shuddered when he tasted his. Banjo found this bothersome. His plans to invade Dan's personal history depended upon Dan's alcohol loosened tongue. Half Deck and his father drank their glasses empty and refilled them. Banjo forced his down and encouraged Dan to drink but didn't imagine either of them abiding more than a couple. But Dan did drink the first and was working steadily on his second. Banjo watched, very satisfied. After dinner Mrs. Humphries stood, wobbled, patted her apron and hair, and began to clear the dishes. "You boys go have your wine in the other room while I get dessert dished up."

Half Deck and his father drank more as they waited for cake. Dan also had two more glasses. Banjo stopped on his second, but determined if he didn't feel drunk he could at least pretend and thus perhaps draw Dan out. Dan's head moved about loosely and Banjo knew he was becoming nicely inebriated.

"Cards?" Half Deck asked when the cake was gone.

Dan protested, "Shit, no!" Half Deck's surprised face fell slack.

Banjo burst into surprised laughter. "You have to understand Dan and his liquor. When he drinks he gets a little too honest. That's why he's cut back. Pour him another and let's see what's on his mind."

"Nope, Banjo. No more. That stuff's rot gut. Besides, I gotta drive."

"We'll call an ambulance." Banjo held out the wine bottle to Half Deck and his father.

"None for me," said the old man. "Gives me the wine shits. I'm going to bed."

Banjo poured more for himself, Half Deck, and moved to Dan's glass. Dan objected, Banjo ignored him, and Dan downed the contents. A trickle of red wine trailed from the corner of his mouth. Half Deck gulped his glass. Banjo sipped from his and decided to assess the level of candor in the room. He looked at Half Deck. "I need to ask you something?"

"Ask away."

"You know," he said in a slurry way as though truly intoxicated, "I wouldn't be saying this except that I know I could trust you. We may work together pretty soon."

"We **will** work together," Half Deck corrected, leaning heavily into Banjo. "You have to maintain your mental positivity about this."

"Something I have to know." Banjo considered his words. Dan looked about to go to sleep. "Do you know they call you Half Deck? I need to know why they call you that. Half Deck. That's like saying your elevator doesn't go all the way to the top; like you're a taco short of being a full combo meal; like all your lights aren't on. Know what I'm saying? I mean, if we're going to work together I'd like to know that about you."

Half Deck's chin dropped slowly until it touched his chest and he looked like a beaten man. "Yes," he said to his lap. "I know. That is the sort of cross any supervisor must bear."

Dan laughed quietly to himself.

"That's been my ball and chain for sometime."

"Why?" Banjo asked with exaggerated concern.

"Who knows? Why do they call you Shrink Bait?"

Dan exploded into laughter and doubled over, knocking their wine glasses to the floor. He picked his up and filled it again.

"Shrink Bait! Call me what? Shrink bait?"

"Well, you do see one, don't you?"

"Hell, no!"

"Oh, Banjo," Dan countered. "You do too. Everyone knows why the Chief wants to make you supervisor. He figures you're less dangerous in an office than on the street."

Half Deck nodded. "The Looner does know his people, Banjo. I agree with Dan. The Looner wants to bring a period of calm to your life. In fact, he asked me to invite you over."

"I don't need any goddamn calm!"

Dan, laughing too hard to hold himself upright, fell into Banjo.

Banjo shoved him away then tugged Dan's arm. "Let's go."

"I can't drive, Banjo. I'm too wobbly. Besides, nobody means any harm calling you Shrink Bait."

"Is that what you, my best friend, call me behind my back? Let's go. We're getting out of here."

"Maybe Half Deck can drive us."

"Half Deck isn't driving us anywhere. Dan, get UP! I'm leaving. I'll walk if I have to."

"Banjo," Dan laughed. "I can't drive."

Banjo gulped for air. Noise like a jet liner roaring filled his head. He dropped Dan's arm and rushed for the door. The screen door stuck and he rattled it savagely until it sprung open. The air outside cooled him. Dan followed him out. Banjo pointed a finger. "You stay away from me. Anybody who calls me that is no friend of mine."

Dan walked crookedly across the short brown grass to Banjo and dropped to his haunches. "Oh, lighten up. You can play mind games with others but nobody can mess with you." Dan imitated the old man's nod. "Isn't that right?"

"Did you tell?"

Dan slowly raised his face to Banjo's. "Tell what?"

"You know. Did you tell anyone?"

"About your counseling? You really upset about that?"

"Did you tell?!"

"No. It's not a big deal. Besides, you're not the only one talking to someone about the crap we see everyday."

"Who else? You?"

Dan groaned quietly then lay back on the grass. "Half Deck stayed in the house. I told him to call us a cab. I think I'm gonna be sick." He closed his eyes.

Banjo sat cross legged on the bristly grass next to Dan. "Are you seeing one?"

"You can't even say the word. You're not crazy, Banjo."

"Are you?"

"No." Then Dan teased, "You mean crazy or seeing a shrink?"

"Go to hell."

Dan sat up, draped an arm around Banjo's shoulders, and tipped against him. "Oh, relax about this. You'd only be crazy if this stuff didn't get to you. You're normal, more or less."

He shrugged Dan away and changed the subject. "Are you rich? I mean, how much did your landlady give you?"

"She gave me her house."

"That's a monster house. It must be worth at least a couple hundred thousand."

"Maybe three and a half, four."

"Why?"

"Why what?"

Banjo ignored the question in response to his question. "Do you really need this job?"

"Yes and no."

"Shee-it. You're as spooky as Clayton. Can't you just answer a damn question?"

Dan lay back and closed his eyes again. "I think I'm gonna be sick."

"Shit," Banjo whispered to the grass.

Without opening his eyes, Dan answered, "Violet was eccentric. I was lucky. I don't know why she gave me her house. But when she took all her money and went traveling, she gave it me. That was that. Maybe she felt sorry for me because my wife had just moved out. Maybe she loved me like a son. I don't know. I don't try to figure why or if I did something to deserve it. It just happened. No reason. Why?"

Banjo lay back and looked at the night sky, starless for the blanket of smog closed over the city. It was a waste to look at the sky, he knew, needing not filth but sharp, clean needle points of light for his darkening mood. He thought of Clayton and the mountains. He looked at his drunk friend. "Just wondering was all. I like to hear about guys that get lucky. Makes me think it's possible for me. I like to think I can finally meet the right woman or fall into a fortune or something. Like there's something out there for me."

Banjo suddenly needed to express an insight. He sat up. "When I think of the streets I feel ..." He shuddered, hearing himself discuss rarely touched feelings. "The streets are fun and I'm comfortable there; sometimes I'm more at home there than anywhere. Being good there is who I am." He trailed off again, trying to reach in and reveal what struggled to be seen. "Work doesn't mean what it used to. It can't explain everything in my world. There's no color out there for me anymore. There's no plan or organization. I think of work and I see that." He pointed to the sky. "I see something dark and gritty and not very healthy. I want to look up and see the north star. I want a north star inside me. That's what I want. But that's so far away.

"Remember that baby girl cooked in the microwave? I've been trying to write her off saying that's that. What's done is done. Like Greystone would have said. But I can't." Banjo's fist went to his mouth, bumping. "Clayton thinks her soul was lifted out of her and put into another life, maybe an eagle's. I like that. I need another way to look at things, partner. I'm lost." Dan did not answer. Banjo looked over and saw him staring into the smog. "Whatcha thinking, partner? Don't leave me now."

Dan shrugged one shoulder. "I remember one time wishing I was like Greystone--always in control. I envied that. I wanted to be just like him." He took a deep breath and held it. He raised to an elbow and turned away as if to vomit. He did not and lay back down. He sighed and continued. "Pretty soon, what do you know--I became John Greystone and there went my north star. Then there went my marriage. And I went to hell. I turned out screwed up, bound tight, and oh shit, when is that goddamn cab gonna get here?"

"Did you find what you were looking for?"

"Jesus, Banjo. Do we have to talk about this now? I'm suffering here."

"So am I, Dan," Banjo answered quietly.

Dan lay still and closed his eyes once more. He took deep breaths. He belched. He patted Banjo on the pack. "I know, partner. I know. Did I find *it*," he said, restating Banjo's question. "I don't think we ever find *it*. Sometimes I think ..." Dan faltered again. "Sometimes I don't know what I think. Finding is listening to a little voice and doing what it says. Finding is discovering important things about yourself. If I found anything important, I found that the right place to look is inside me."

They were quiet. Banjo looked at Dan. His eyes were closed and his breathing was deep and even. He thought Dan might have gone to sleep. Banjo turned back to the thick night sky. He said, "You remind me of John. You still have some of his hard edges and little gestures that tell people to stay away."

Several moments passed. Banjo decided Dan had gone to sleep.

"I miss my ocean," Dan said. "I miss hearing breakers. I once lived along the Oregon coast near headlands. I remember Dad telling people that Maxwell Point stuck into the ocean like a thick fisted arm. Oceanside was right down next to the headlands at the end of a windy road. We would take that road to get home from where ever we were. It twisted through the fir and manzanita that made the road seem like a magical green tunnel. We'd go around a certain bend and down a hill and suddenly there was Maxwell Point and Three Arch Rocks and there was home, quiet and protected next to those huge headlands where houses were perched like birds." Banjo closed his eyes to listen.

"We had an old house with a creek next to it. A weathered foot bridge crossed it and my mother used to worry I would fall off. I had to cross that bridge and walk down the hill to get into town. The ocean was right there, and I grew up to its sound. The surf was always drumming, gulls screeching, wind whistling through trees ..." Dan sighed. "I'd go to the bakery every Saturday morning for pastry. That and the eggs mom fixed was our family breakfast on Saturday mornings.

You could get a dozen different donuts for seventy-four cents."
Dan stopped and thought. "That was home. Everything made
sense there. If I could do it, my friend, I would bottle that up
and give it to you right now so you could feel the way I used to."

Banjo looked at him and smiled. It was a relaxed and easy
smile that came from his distant spot. Dan's face held a
searching look, a longing look, a sad and mournful look.

The taxi arrived. Banjo stood and reached down. Dan
took his hand. They got into the cab and Dan let his head fall
against Banjo. Banjo gave the taxi driver Dan's address.

*****

The following morning a stranger checked equipment in
the back of Banjo's ambulance. Banjo demanded, "What are
you doing here?"

"This is my new shift," he said. "I just finished field
training."

The sudden loss of Clayton was piercing. He gathered his
indignation, puffed out his vested chest, and marched into the
supervisor's office. Half Deck sat hunched before his computer;
the telephone receiver was nestled between his shoulder and
cheek. Seeing Banjo, Half Deck narrowed his eyes with
suspicion and calculation. Last night Half Deck's old man
watched the cats this same way. Half Deck raised one finger,
telling Banjo to wait. He scratched a lottery ticket. He
punched the telephone redial button, listened, punched again,
listened, and finally hung up. Half Deck turned, crossed his
arms, and waited.

"Where's Clayton?"

"On nights. The division needs strong people on nights
with weaker staff. We want someone like Clayton who can take
down a dweeb now and again and keep his partner's tit out of
the ringer." He nodded his father's certainty. "Isn't that
right?"

Banjo snatched the wind up toy sitting on another desk and flung it to the floor. It cracked in half and the gears started to run. The fractured toy spun in circles on the floor as Banjo exploded from the office.

Chapter 7

Banjo propped himself up on the ambulance stretcher. Through the back doors flung wide to allow in the fresh evening breeze which had come at last, he watched the city below turn sunset red after passing through the white hot summer sky day. Brown grit ringed his collar which was clean that morning. His armpits were sweaty and slick. He lay motionless with one leg on the stretcher and the other on the floor where it had landed when he had collapsed. He tingled with weariness. He ached deep inside his joints. Moving took more energy than he had.

Watching the city change colors was enough for him right now. At these moments he took time to see subtle changes. Shadows advanced eastward from the densely packed skyscrapers, themselves reflecting the sunset flaming over the Rockies. The opposite horizon took on a deepening blue. Closer, as his eyes darted randomly, stubble grass, ugly and ignored during the day, shifted gracefully. Banjo moved to relieve his stiff back.

Colors. Banjo took time to see the colors below where he and Dan rested in a parking lot overlooking the city. The slowly changing sunset light created a crayon box of colors. Gleaming downtown towers reflected the western sky, at first strong and blue, then moving into fire colors, and finally subsiding into purple glows. Earth colored brick buildings grew rich in the approaching twilight. The shadows, in that time of light and dark, placed the colors in sharp relief. Banjo smiled. Only this living picture framed by the open ambulance doors concerned him now and this was enough and it filled him with peace.

Dan stirred in the front. Banjo smiled again. He got lucky with the summer schedule. Half Deck must have forgiven him to put him with his old partner. And a city hiring freeze stopped all promotions. With Dan, this past month, their shifts were like the old days together, before Greystone died, when Banjo's life was simpler. They knew each other well enough to read minds. Calls were effortless. Neither had to ask, the other knew. When they entered a room both sensed immediately if the patient was critical, sending each into well practiced, mutually supportive routines. Banjo would start the IV and talk to the patient. Dan would attach the heart monitor and tell Banjo what it read. A certain look from Dan alerted Banjo to watch out for something. A little joke from Dan told Banjo that things were too tense and he needed to calm people down. Banjo signaled the same thing by slowing down the normally clipped cadence of his speech. In a tight situation, if one said, "Let me think", the other needed to step in quickly and offer advice. And both knew the other would protect his back. Calls were smooth and quiet. They could insert themselves into chaos and step out again easily. Just like the old days.

Banjo talked more to Dan since his self revealing conversation on Half Deck's lawn. They talked about their marriages. Banjo rarely admitted anything about his except that his home bound wife simply stormed out one day; the same day he and Greystone pronounced dead two kids caught in a garbage dumpster fire. The children had crawled in and set the fire. Neither could get out. Banjo climbed in to lift the charred bodies to Greystone. One wore pigtails left curiously intact by the flames. They moved gently in the breeze. When Banjo got home his wife complained about the neighbor's dog leaving feces in the yard. Banjo told her to shovel it herself. After that, divorce.

But there was more he had put away. In painful twists of his stomach he conceded to Dan that he married her because he was afraid of being alone. She was the first woman after Vietnam who liked him. Once married he never believed it would last. He did not understand why, though he often believed anything important was temporary. He was afraid to have children for the same reason. Like those kids in the dumpster, they could go outside one day and never return. So he never completed connections. They would be broken anyway. Ernie Webster kept telling him that this didn't have to happen, which was easy for him to say.

Dan talked, too, sometimes. He missed the predictability of the marriage, but not how Karen made him feel less than whole for wanting to be a paramedic. Banjo reminded Dan that Eden also may have had something to do with their divorce. Dan nodded and said yes. And Dan also had felt stuffed into a box which defined the person Karen wanted him to be. Then Dan burst free from the box and the marriage collapsed. Now Dan dated but not enthusiastically. Banjo admired Dan. He seemed content to live alone, not desperate for a woman.

Banjo shifted again to relieve the pain in his back. He groaned against his tightening muscles and tried to count his calls from the past eight hours. Ten calls? Twelve? They all ran together. Busy shifts took more out of him these days. A shooting or cardiac arrest left him tingling with fatigue. He remembered when those calls were a wild carnival ride. Now, if there wasn't that same thrill, at least there was satisfaction knowing nobody could handle calls better than he. Control. Smooth, clean control. He loved it.

Banjo's mind fell to Zagata. He had been showing up more on his calls. Zagata's presence was like a growing stain that could not be washed out.

His mind roamed back through the calls. What had happened within these past eight hours, Banjo tried to recall. In just eight hours ... His forgetfulness struck him. Oh yes. A construction worker died in an elevator shaft. The elevator below started up. He said to someone outside the shaft that it wasn't going to stop. Dangling from rigging attached to the top of the shaft, he hurried to get out. He struggled and became more entangled as he watched his death winch noisily up the shaft. He told a fellow worker, "I blew it. This time I really blew it." He reminded Banjo of a cartoon character run over by a steam roller.

They had the usual two or three seizures and overdoses. Those were so frustrating. None, in their irrationality, wanted to go to the hospital. They all were agitated and difficult and would just as often jerk out of Banjo's grip and run off as go in.

Banjo remembered a DOA in there somewhere. But he wasn't sure if that was today or yesterday. She had been dead for days before neighbors called the police. She lay in bed so hugely bloated and purple Banjo was afraid she would pop if he touched her. He smeared Vicks Vap-O-Rub under his nose to block out the smell. Later one of their regulars called. Said she hadn't had a bowel movement in a month. Drunk and laying around in her nightgown, she complained that her husband refused to give her an enema. Dan and Banjo made her walk to the ambulance and sit on the squad bench on the way in.

That afternoon they hurried to one of the downtown towers now brightly lit. In the women's restroom on the 27th floor a beautiful woman dressed in a business suit lay crying on the floor. Her stomach hurt and it was rigid as a board. She got dizzy if she sat up and her face was the color of the white tile. Banjo stroked her hair and told her that he suspected a ruptured ectopic pregnancy. She denied any chance of pregnancy then cried with heartbreaking sobs. And just before coming up here the dispatcher sent them to a man down in Cheesman Park. Dan and Banjo looked at each other and knew. They walked to the figure comfortable curled up on his side, woke him, and told him a place to go where the public would not see him.

There were some other calls, maybe a big one buried in there somewhere. He couldn't remember. But everyone of them left an ache. He loosened further and his hand slid off his chest to the mattress.

The downtown buildings sparkled as evening advanced. Their white lighted windows, illuminated in checker board fashion, shimmered through the heat still rising from the pavement. All the sky was deeply blue, slipping to black, and the breeze felt very good. Banjo's eyes fell shut. He dreamed. He found himself in a beautiful and very familiar home. Light and green plants filled the rooms. He heard music. Dishes clinked in the kitchen and the warm sweet feeling of love snuggled him. He went to the kitchen looking for Lauren. He found Dan. Banjo startled awake. He wondered if they had a call. The radio remained quiet. Dan slouched behind the steering wheel and said nothing. Banjo took one more look at the twinkling buildings and lay his head back onto the stretcher. With the peaceful twilight colors receding into darkness Banjo, let his mind drift where it comfortably would. Lauren came to mind.

She bent over him. "Banjo!" Her long hair enclosed his face in a warm curtain. She was crying but Banjo did not understand why, so comfortably protected was he. An awareness came to him. His days on the street were over and he was going away, though he did not know where. He had given everything. He had done enough. Now he could be proud. But why did Lauren cry? He saw her lift a hand from his chest. It glistened red with blood. "Banjo!" she called after him from further away.

"Banjo," Dan called from the front seat. "Wake up. We have a call."

Banjo jolted awake in the dark. He tingled uncomfortably from the forced awakening. He mumbled, "What?"

Dan leaned from his front seat to see into the patient compartment. "We have a shooting over in the projects. Some guy opened up with a shotgun. Supposed to be two down and some hostages."

Banjo's heart raced. He saw a shotgun flash. His chest muscles tightened. He scrambled to the front as Dan sped away from the fairyland sparkle of downtown lights. The electronic siren yelped to life. Sleep still muddled his head. He couldn't think. "Where we going?" he asked Dan.

"Sun Valley projects. We're right on top of this. Police won't be there yet." Dan punched the accelerator. The engine screamed and the power pushed Banjo into his seat.

"How many are down?"

"Two. Supposed to be hostages." Dan spun the steering wheel and the ambulance cut sharply around a corner. Banjo struck the door. He felt the ambulance drift sideways. Dan hit the gas pedal again, snapping the ambulance straight. Several blocks away Dan killed the siren and lights and cautiously slowed.

Banjo wanted more time to think. He wasn't ready to see shotgun damage. "Wait for police before getting too close," he cautioned Dan.

Dan pointed. "There they are." Silent and dark like sharks, four police cruisers appeared in front of the address. Dan stopped half a block away. Police officers, weapons drawn, slipped from their cars.

Banjo took Dan's wrist. "Hold back." He hoped all the victims were dead. It would be easy to go in, pronounce the obvious deaths, and leave them where they lay. He did not want to stare down at them on the way to the hospital. He knew those red, meaty wounds; the detached limbs. He had seen the floor of his ambulance slick with congealed sheets of blood. Not tonight. He just wanted to go home tonight.

"Police are waving us in." Dan hopped out. Banjo, on the exposed side of the ambulance, adjusted his vest to make sure his sides were covered. He ran crouching to the back door and crawled the length of the ambulance floor to get the trauma kits. They ran to the sergeant. The apartment remained dark and quiet.

"We're setting up a perimeter," the sergeant told them. "We have a negotiator and the Special Services Unit coming. We understand people are down in there so we may go in real quick."

"Do you want us to go in behind you?" Dan asked.

Banjo's stomach twisted. He looked at his watch. His shift ended in twenty minutes. Not tonight. He should be back at Denver General waiting for his relief.

"I want you guys close. We'll drag them to the door then they're yours."

Banjo watched blue uniformed police officers, nearly invisible in the darkness, scatter like fast shadows to all corners of the building and disappear. Banjo guessed at least ten revolvers and shotguns were now trained on the windows. Soon a team approached the front door. They shouted, *"POLICE! OPEN UP!"* They heard no response. A policeman kicked in the door. Others hurled heavy rocks through the windows and swung their weapons in. Banjo held his breath waiting for gunfire. Moments passed. Then minutes. A light came on in the apartment and weapons along the perimeter appeared. Then an officer with his revolver holstered stood in the doorway. He shrugged. "No one home," he called to the sergeant.

Banjo let out a sigh and slid down the side of the sergeant's car to the pavement and sat holding his knees to his chest.

*****

Banjo sat on Ernie Webster's deeply burgundy sofa the next afternoon. He rested his feet on the coffee table situated close and held his knees to his chest. A wide bouquet of peonies, also burgundy, sat on the table and Banjo could see them between his feet. "I had this dream last night." Banjo shifted his eyes from Ernie. "I think it was a nice one. I'm not sure. I might have been dying. Lauren was there crying and her hand was bloody after it had been on my chest."

"Sounds like a nightmare to me."

"No. I felt nice in it. I felt like someone had given me permission to quit being a paramedic."

Ernie wrinkled his brow. "Do you need permission to quit your job?"

Banjo thought. Ernie wore a Hawaiian shirt, flashy with exotic birds. He waited patiently, his hands folded comfortably in his lap. That effeminate little mannerism irritated Banjo. Banjo answered, "No." Ernie waited some more. Banjo directed his eyes out the window to the fire station to occupy himself until Ernie realized Banjo was playing the same little game.

"Why would you feel good about being told you no longer had to be a paramedic?"

This conversation wearied him. "Beats me. It felt like I was being allowed to go home after a long struggle. Flying back from Vietnam was the same way."

"That is a metaphor often associated with death: going home, returning to a peaceful place, having all burdens lifted."

Banjo felt exactly this way in his dream. He went back to it and recalled new pieces. "I was on stairs. Like the time Greystone and I had."

"When Greystone calmed the gunman?"

Banjo nodded. "I've always wondered what would've happened if I was first up the steps. Greystone was there only because the apartment building was on his side of the ambulance, closer to him than me. I've never been right up to the edge like that. I don't know which way I'd jump. My worst thing was Greystone getting clipped. We couldn't find him at first and when we did I was such a basket case I couldn't help him." Diverting his eyes again, he added, "I felt like I left him when he needed me most."

"He left you, Banjo. Remember? He should have looked before getting out of the ambulance."

"He was in trouble. I wasn't there to help. It's very simple, really."

"Greystone is dead, Banjo. Sooner or later you'll have to let him go. You can't carry his responsibility forever."

Banjo dropped his forehead to his knees as Ernie talked. He held Greystone's hard face in his memory.

"My friend, there comes a time when you have to forgive yourself. You did the very best you could. You can't ask any more."

Banjo stared into the pleasing rich flowers and noticed subtle changes in shading as he followed petals inward toward their dark interiors. He wished he could go there.

Ernie Webster continued. "I had a platoon leader in Vietnam. We both had younger sisters we liked to talk about and we both loved the redwoods in northern California. He vowed that regardless of what it took, he would not let any of us get killed. So he always walked point with an armed hand grenade. Robbie reasoned if he was taken out, he'd get the VC who got him. Patrol after patrol he walked point. For nine months we didn't loose a man. On his last day in country I told him I would take point. We had this big argument about it. But I refused to let him stick his neck out for us on his last patrol. Finally he let me." Ernie paused at the memory. "That was the day the enemy decided if they let three or four of us walk through their ambush before firing they could kill more Americans. Robbie was third back, my usual position. He was the first one killed. Robbie deserved to be in front. I deserved to be dead. I carried that for years.

"Finally I realized he was gone and blaming myself would not bring him back. I needed to go on. So I had a little ceremony for him. I went back to the redwoods and found a spot that was right and told Robbie how I had been feeling and how it was time for me to let go of the blame. That didn't mean I would forget him. I told him neither of us chose to go to war; neither of us chose how the enemy would attack. I did what I did because I loved him and it was the best I could do, though it wasn't enough. Then I planted a rhododendron. Then I cried."

Banjo broke the silence with a heavy, chest heaving sob. "I want Greystone to forgive me," he told the flowers. "I want to get rid of the memories. I want to drive down the street and not see dead kids in garbage cans." He raised his head. "I want to think of a Thanksgiving turkey and not get sick. I want someone to tell me I've done enough," he shouted at Ernie. "I want someone to tell me I can go home now!"

And Ernie Webster replied quietly, "That has to come from you."

*****

Banjo went in for his pay check the following day. The Chief saw him and motioned him into his office. "Let's step down to the river, skip flat stones, and discuss promotion."

"What do you mean, exactly?"

"I mean, of course, I convinced the great City and County of Denver of our need for additional supervisory staff. Our division alone was given permission to promote." The Chief clamped his pipe into his brilliant grin. "And you have been granted an interview."

"Now!"

"Silly boy. The wheels of change don't grind that fast. Come in here," he urged impatiently. A new water color took shape on his easel. In the evolving painting, the Chief and Greystone stood arm in arm. They were younger. Greystone's relaxed smile did not compare to Banjo's memory of his rock hard face. The Chief's younger eyes sparkled with cleverness from the canvas.

"We were a pair," the Chief told him, placing his pipe in the child made ashtray. "Not mischief makers, by any means. We were two over-serious innocents who became close friends. Over the years we came to view this place as home and the contentious paramedics here family. We brought many changes to this division. Greystone created the field instructor program and brought to it his military bearing. He shaped the professional personalities of so many paramedics. He was what a paramedic looked and acted like.

"His death brought a public focus upon our collective identity, showing that we too risk our lives for a greater good. He gave us a new way of viewing ourselves: soberly, perhaps a bit fatalistically, and in a curious sort of way, prouder." He thought for a moment and fiddled with his pipe. "Worthless reasons for a good man to die.

"And for my part," he sighed. "I have led this division for many years now, for good or bad." He shrugged. "Mostly to the good, I hope. Who knows?" He leveled his eyes to Banjo. "The streets would have been more fun.

"More than once I awoke in the morning and announced to my wife that I had wasted my life sitting in this office devising strategies to affect unappreciated change among stubborn paramedics, and losing myself in these pictures of my past when I failed." His lips grew tight and narrow. "I have grown angry at myself and the division for those frustrations. But we all need our cause and this division is mine. If I am to devote my life to something, this is it." He shifted his attention away and Banjo wondered if the Chief struggled to persuade himself of his own words.

"Nothing a paramedic does is meaningless, Mr. Stanley. I nurture the environment in which a paramedic's actions can be expertly carried out. If I don't touch a single patient my influence touches every patient. I won't give my life as Jonathan did, but I will sacrifice other opportunities for this fine place. So my contribution is as great as anyone's here."

The Chief lifted a tin of tobacco from his bottom desk drawer, took a pinch, tamped it into his pipe, and lit it with a wooden match. He puffed until a full, sweet cloud rose around his face. He stared into it as though the ghostly wisps may hold something for him; like solace or a pardon for some harm committed a long time ago that still roosted on his shoulders.

The Chief cleared his throat. "Banjo ..."

Banjo tensed.

"Your days on the street are over. You don't see that but you will. Your interview, by the way, is next Thursday at two p.m. My story, awkward as it was, makes a point. We all want to be heroes. We all want to be respected, revered, looked up to as saviors. While we are often the latter, it goes without notice. I don't want my staff to measure their worth by their risks. I don't want their self respect coming from the admiration of others. I hope they can respect themselves and their work, regardless of their role within the division, for their own intrinsic value."

The office grew hot and confining. Banjo's mind flashed to a narrow stairway where a shotgun quivering inches from his chest held him at bay. Banjo sprang from his chair. "Nobody is going to tell me I have to be a supervisor. There's no way. No way."

"Do you come to work under the influence of any substances, Banjo?"

"What!?"

"Answer my question."

"Are you kidding?"

"Answer my question."

"Absolutely not."

"If you are, you jeopardize this entire division and its public trust."

Banjo's lower lip trembled and pushed out, leaking his sudden remorse.

"My earlier point is this. There are other ways to dedicate your life to this place if that is what you choose. One does not have to be killed or terminated."

Banjo demanded, "Has Ernie been talking to you? If that son of a bitch says anything to anybody I'm out of this place."

"No, I have not spoken with your counselor."

"You've been talking to my partners. *Bastards*! They don't know what they're talking about. Sometimes I drink heavy the night before. Sometimes I have parties where they smoke a little marijuana, but I don't smoke it. I guess my problem is not airing out my clothes good enough or something. I'll talk to those guys."

"I don't have to ask your partners. I can see the changes in your spirit. I hear it in your voice. I see you exhausted at shift's end and know that the joy of this work has left you. I say again, the road you are on is destructive for you and the division. Certainly you are responsible for yourself. But I am responsible for this place and I will not have you, no matter how deep my affection for you, continue with behaviors that are deleterious. You can be a superb supervisor and continue to serve. But you are no longer a superb paramedic. You have two paths, my friend; up or out. I want you here with me."

"I got rights here. Just because I maybe hit a rough spot doesn't mean you can take over my life. I'll call the union. I'll get an attorney. You won't make me do anything I don't want to do."

The Chief searched through his pipe smoke and did not look at Banjo. At last, drawing a breath and returning his pipe to its child made resting place, the Chief said, "I think we understand each other, Banjo. Please think this over carefully."

"You're the one who needs to think. I know my rights." He threw the door open before the Chief could say anything more. The door knob slammed into the wall, starred the plaster, and bounced pictures off their nails.

*****

Swollen with great anger, Banjo yanked open the frosted glass door filled with etchings. He thought the lines were nothing but a jumble of nonsense; a waste of good money; like the Chief and his supervisors.

The Parlour was too dark to see but he knew his way. He saw the bartender's form. "Jackson!" Banjo pointed to his booth in the back corner. "Set me up and don't bother me." Two policemen sat near the front drinking coffee from steaming glass mugs. Banjo recognized the officers but in his highly agitated state, chose to ignore them.

He slugged down the first Jim Beam and sipped his beer waiting for the two additional whiskeys he ordered. Then, with two full glasses of numbing amber before him, he situated himself toward the wall but at an angle to see anyone moving toward him. He sipped and his anger crossed over into fear. His trembling hand troubled the surface of his beer. "Jesus Christ, Greystone ..." He sniffed and took another long gulp that burned a trail down to his aching stomach. "Things are out of control. They're really out of control. You know what? I wish I'd've gotten out on your side of the ambulance. I wish that car had've taken me to a better place. I really do, John. I really, truly do."

Chapter 8

Banjo lifted the empty beer glass above his head. "Nurse!"

Zagata slapped the table and threw his head back to laugh. "Nurse. That's perfect. Just fuckin' perfect. Nurse. I'll have to try that one on the old lady."

Zagata wore a dark blue baseball cap--'Denver Police' was written in white across the front--and leggings, having come directly from his baseball game and interrupted Banjo's reverie. His Bronco's warm-up jacket hung open and Banjo saw his pearl handled service revolver tucked neatly up under his left arm. He wore a Rolex watch. A diamond sparkled in a ring fitted snugly on his thick little finger.

Banjo wondered what Zagata's heavy hands might have done and why he was showing up at incovenient moments. On calls Zagata had a way of watching that made Banjo want to be on his best behavior. Not long ago Clayton told him that Zagata had him under surveillance, too. But in the bar he was everyone's friend, laughing at their jokes and ordering them to put their money away.

Soon Banjo felt the glass lifted from his hand and saw a pleasingly full one placed before him. He vaguely resented drinking beer purchased with Zagata's roll of bill's, which, by the size of it, was mighty suspicious.

Another policeman, so tall his baseball pants did not cover the top of his leggings, hurried for his wallet, as though way over due to buy a round. He smelled of sweat and some part of him always fidgeted, like he had little eternally running motors in his drumming fingers and bobbing feet. He drank only coffee and his eyes chased patrons around the bar.

Two paramedics, who came over after their shift, also dug for their wallets. Both had pinned napkins over their patches. All of them were an unwelcome coincidence. Banjo came here to sit alone and revisit old memories of John Greystone and remember the great calls of his own career that provided evidence of his courage.

"I said," Zagata insisted, "I'll get that." He withdrew the roll of twenties from his pocket and tossed a crisp bill onto the waitress's serving tray. "Keep it, honey."

Smiling, she sat fresh ones all around and refilled the tall policeman's coffee cup. He lit another cigarette from the glowing embers of his last one.

"Banjo," Zagata carried on, "you are one funny man; a truly funny man." He swept his eyes across the others to see that they paid attention. "I watched him haul off a wetback from the train yard once. The kid tried to jump a freight to Pueblo but it bucked him off and threw him under the wheels. Cut his leg off, right there." He drew a finger across his thigh. "Banjo asks him what he thought he was going to do down south and the kid says he was gonna pick fruit. Banjo says..." Zagata stopped the story to laugh. "Banjo says, 'Well, looks like you'll have to find yourself another line of work.'" He slapped the table hard and his laughing turned to loud, phlegmy coughing. "New line of work. That's perfect. Just fuckin' perfect."

Banjo recalled the case with indifference. Zagata's telling of it now embarrassed him.

Roy, one of the two paramedics, changed the subject. "So, Banjo, you going to be the new supervisor?"

Banjo thought a moment and shook his head. "Not if I can help it. Chief seems to have it in his head, though."

Roy had as many years in as Banjo and his slow voice carried an edge of bitterness. He moved his head slightly as he talked so that he never looked any of them square in the face. He especially avoided Zagata's. "What that place needs is someone who knows their way around. Those kids who think they can be supervisors don't know their history; don't see how things need to happen slowly so your morale doesn't go. Like that Eric kid. He's just using us as a stepping stone. He'll be a lawyer one of these days. He don't care about us. And that damn Half Deck, Christ knows that's all he has to play with, wants things his way or no way.

"I was one day late getting my schedule choice to him because the wife couldn't get me hers from work. He wouldn't take it. I had to work three whole months of midnights because I didn't get it to him by the tick of five o'clock. So we need a guy in there, don't you see. And duh..." He searched his beer for the words he wanted. "So..." Roy laughed, trying to end his thought cleanly. He pushed out his lower lip and nodded with certainty. "Lotta guys down here would like to see you take it."

Roy was a reason Banjo did not want to be a supervisor. He did not want to be responsible for Roy's happiness, or that of others.

The other paramedic, Snooper, seemed nearly asleep. Banjo knew differently for he had given her that nickname. Her droopy eyelids gave others the false impression she often dozed. Paramedics and supervisors conversed freely in her presence and Snooper learned more in silence than others did with conversation.

He worked with her last year after her field training. He admired her in his way, as much as he could any woman for anything but her looks. Though she was not beautiful, Banjo liked her face. It was clean and honest like a young boy's, and was framed by straight hanging blond hair. He trusted her because she was blunt with her thoughts and not careful about who heard them and he found himself curiously at ease with her. Her nickname, which she took to with a laugh, was his acceptance gift when she finished her rookie year. During their last shift together she played with new nicknames for him. Afterwards she firmly shook his hand and said it was great being pals.

Snooper told Banjo, "If you don't want to be supervisor, don't be. Nobody can make you."

"Chief has it in his head. He threatened to fire me. Thinks I'll turn into a drug fiend or something if I don't get off the street."

Zagata seized the comment. "Hell. Best way to get promoted around our place is to turn into a drunk. They'll give you bars and put you in an office every time. Captain Sessions' as big a drunk as you can get. I pulled his fat ass over one night for speeding. I could have made him dig deep for that one but I took him home instead. I covered his butt a couple times that way. So now I can do anything I want. Captain won't say shit."

He elbowed the other officer who jumped. Zagata noticed the jolt and chuckled. "Christ, Rocky, I hope I'm not around you when the shooting starts." Then he asked Rocky, "Remember Bancroft? Old Harry Bancroft? There's another drunk I kept out of trouble. Shit, they made him captain and gave him a whole damn district before he up and killed himself. But they say he did that because he was all fucked up in that drug scandal. What a sorry, ass grabbing, finger pointing time that was. Bancroft never could take a little heat. He was such a little man.

"But like I say," Zagata added. "We all need to get along, no matter who we are."

Banjo wondered what the connection was between this remark and drunk captains.

"The Bible says, 'And the lambs shall lie down with the lion...but the lambs won't get much fuckin' sleep.'" Zagata laughed, coughed, and whapped the table. "I'm the lion and you're the fucking little lambs!" He jerked another twenty from his roll and slapped it to the table. "Nurse! Another round here for my good friends."

"Personally," Rocky said, "I think that's exactly what they wanted. Wanted to get rid of Bancroft." The words machine-gunned passed Banjo. Rocky sucked his cigarette to the filter and screwed it into the glass ashtray. He exhaled smoke through his nose. Banjo watched Rocky's eyes darting about Snooper like a hummingbird. "They don't give a shit about you. You try to be a good cop; that's all you can do." He tapped the package of cigarettes in front of him. Then his middle finger flicked the bottom, ejecting a cigarette. He dangled it between his lips and lit it with his shaking hands. "That's all you can do," he repeated. His cigarette jumped with each word.

"Hell, yes." Zagata went on, sprawling his arms, crowding the others. "Far as I'm concerned, if a guy wants to be supervisor, fine. Just keep him out of my way. As soon as you go into the office, you're nothing. You become a little man."

Snooper remained indifferent. "Everybody needs a boss, pretty boy. Even cops who think they have their captain backwards over a barrel." She pulled off his cap and put it on her head. She pointed her chin at him, daring him to take it back.

Zagata's menacing scar shifted. But after a moment he turned his other side to Banjo. "Pushy broad." He laughed it off but it wasn't his buddy-buddy laugh.

Grinning like a teenager at her, Rocky said, "Maybe she likes you, Zagata."

"Maybe she likes you," Snooper repeated, imitated Zagata's way of imitating others. "That's perfect. Just frigging perfect."

Rocky's grin melted away.

Banjo watched Zagata watch Snooper. Zagata inspected her like a snake might a near-by mouse. Zagata's vulgar power fascinated Banjo, but fear held him at bay. He was, disturbingly, eager to remain on Zagata's good side.

Banjo's eyes traveled to Zagata's shiny weapon snuggled warmly against his chest. Banjo's own meager power derived from his white shirt and ambulance. Neither could stop a bullet. He drew his eyes away leaving Snooper to feel Zagata's eyes swarm about her without Banjo's witness.

*****

Banjo hated choices. They meant leaving something behind, closing out options, change. He'd rather be left alone. He envied Roy. Roy was invisible. He came to work, occupied his half of the ambulance for ten hours, then went home. No one would notice if he missed a division meeting or a party. There were no stories about him. No one included him in their plans. He accumulated his years in the division with the unaffected plodding of a tortoise. Banjo wanted to disappear, too.

Lately, though, his mind turned more and more to the notion of command. No one would tell him what to do if he were in charge at night. Even moody dispatchers would not stick him in slow districts and leave him there bored to death. He'd make more money and get to drive the slick supervisor's vehicle. He really liked that. But Zagata was right. Once he became a supervisor, he would be nothing. Like Half Deck, he would wear the uniform but would not be real. His skills would wither. His second sight would leave him.

So he did not know how to respond during his interview coming up in just a few minutes. He waited outside the conference room while the interview panel talked to Eric. Banjo wore corduroy pants and a tweedy sports jacket. He picked nervously at his fingernails.

Soon the door opened. A woman followed Eric out. His muscular body fit perfectly into his fine new suit. He wore expensive loafers that tucked so sweetly into his instep. She said, "Thank you, Mr. Watkins. We'll be notifying the candidates of our decision in a few weeks."

He said with high confidence, "Thank you Mrs. Montoya, but you can call me Eric. And I will most certainly be looking forward to it." He winked at Banjo. Banjo smiled back.

The woman turned to Banjo. "Mr. Stanley?"

"Yes, ma'am?"

"We'll be just a few moments. I'll come get you."

"Thank you."

Shocked, he realized he had put no thought into questions he would likely be asked. Heat rose into his face. Why did he wish to be supervisor? He knew they would ask him that. Why? Nothing came to mind.

"You can come in now, Mr. Stanley." She stood in the door, smiling. "I'm Melinda Montoya, the Career Service representative on the panel." They entered and she showed him a chair. On the far side of a fake mahogany conference table sat the three member interview panel. "This is Dr. Hildebrand. You perhaps recognize him. He is Director of Emergency Services at St. Anthony's." Banjo did recognize him. He did not like this doctor. Hildebrand never listened to paramedics. Banjo nodded without smiling. "And this is Abigail Oxford, the emergency department nurse manager from Porter's Hospital." She was pretty and familiar. "Finally, we have Captain Larry Brewster who is a paramedic with the Colorado Springs Fire Department." Banjo sized him up. He estimated Brewster had half the street experience he had. "Dr. Hildebrand will lead the interview and each panelist will ask pre-established questions, each with one follow-up question. Your responses will be scored and you will be ranked among the other applicants. You will be notified of your position in a few weeks. Your division chief will then hire off that list." She smiled. "Any questions?"

Banjo took a deep breath. "Uh, no."

Hildebrand smiled. "No reason to be nervous. These are straight forward questions not intended to mislead or confuse you. This isn't like you're sitting for your emergency medicine boards after years of training."

Banjo told him in his thoughts, Ask the questions, jerk.

"So tell me, Banjo, after all these years driving ambulance, why do you want to become a supervisor?"

Brewster sighed quietly and shook his head.

Banjo warmed up to him. "Actually," he told Hildebrand, "I've only been the ambulance driver half that time. The other half I was the ambulance passenger. See, we trade off each shift, driving and sitting." Hildebrand's demeanor remained flat. Brewster and the nurse slipped each other smiles. "I guess," Banjo added, "if the Chief really thinks I can do the job maybe I should try." The answer came from the same sarcastic fountain, but upon hearing it Banjo knew it had the ring of truth.

Hildebrand probed. "What do you think?"

"Maybe I'd like to try."

"You're not very persuasive."

"I'm not very certain, to be honest."

Brewster fingered a sheet laying before him. From it he read, "What strengths do you bring to this position?"

Banjo held his shoulders in the shrugged position and thought. "I call bullshit when I see it. I love the place."

"What weaknesses," he continued reading, "would you work on to be the supervisor you would like to be?" Melinda Montoya sat silently to his left taking notes. Her tape recorder was running.

Stupid questions. "I don't know. I don't think much like the other supervisors. That could be a problem. I get kind of independent. I have no patience for meaningless rules. That's not a good thing for a supervisor."

The nurse spoke. "Hi, Banjo. I'm Abby Oxford from Porter's. We've met." He smiled. "What do you mean, you don't think like the other supervisors?"

"Well, like I said, I don't like rules. I do what's necessary to get stuff done. And I just see things differently. When a problem comes up I think that's a chance to make something good happen. Most supervisors just get mad. I get frustrated when people get into ruts and don't ever try to see up over the edge."

Hildebrand asked, "Do you think many years of street experience necessarily makes one a good supervisor?"

"Probably not." Banjo didn't care what Hildebrand thought. "Best street paramedic in the world doesn't know jack about budgets and politics. Probably the more years you got, the harder it is to break into it." He remembered Zagata's judgment of supervisors.

"Is that the case with you?"

Chuckling, Banjo answered, "Probably."

"Let me give you a scenario. You tell us how you would manage it as a supervisor. A field paramedic whom you trust approaches you in confidence and tells you that his partner is using drugs on duty. He relays to you that his partner periodically steps out of the ambulance 'for some air', as he puts it, and then returns smelling of marijuana smoke." Banjo's face froze into a mask. "The paramedic in question is an otherwise good employee, though you yourself have recently noticed he comes to work late and his performance is not as sharp as it was."

Banjo shifted in his chair. He knew he was being conspicuous. Had the Chief said anything to them? Was this another nudge? He looked at the wood grain patterns in the table top and the dark swirls reminded him of the storms that threatened. "That's a tough one," he replied softly. "There's a lot about this job that drives you to just that." He drew his upper lip between his teeth.

Hildebrand filled the silence. "It is a tough one that we in health care face more and more often. How would you approach this?"

Banjo remembered his confrontation with the Chief and his own lies. He recalled the Chief's pained expression as he declared the paramedic division ultimately more important than any single paramedic. "The division is more important than any one guy with a problem," he began. "But I wouldn't throw him away either. I believe we're all closer to becoming that person than we like to think. I would put it to him. I'd say, look, I hear you're getting loaded at work and that can't happen and I'd ask what I could do to help him."

"He denies it."

"I have it from a good source."

"Doesn't know what he's talking about."

"People have smelled marijuana on you."

"I party a little too hard. I have friends who smoke but I don't."

Banjo's stomach twisted painfully. His own lame excuses were thrown at him. What did Hildebrand know? Banjo answered, "That's bullshit."

"Wait a minute! You're calling me a liar."

"You're bullshitting! You're hurting the division." The struggle was within himself; one half calling the other half a liar. One half suffocating, the other demanding he face up to it. Banjo remembered the oldest scene control principle: never get mad. He gathered himself. He said calmly, "People in that circumstance lie. They don't want to see the truth. I would say I don't believe him. I would watch for poor work performance. I would offer any help; counseling, slower shifts, light duty. But in the end, by God..." He drew a deep breath. "I'd fire him if he didn't turn around." Banjo dropped his eyes to the conference table.

The interview continued. The remaining questions were tiresome. Banjo found himself always with two answers; one he left in his head, the other he gave the panel. Brewster wanted to know how he would stay in touch with the street paramedic. He told Brewster, "I'd work a couple shifts a month. That would always be a priority." But he whispered to himself, there isn't a supervisor in the world who stays in touch with his troops. He felt a momentary resentment toward the institution for which he interviewed.

Abby, smiling in such a way that he wondered if she wondered about him, asked Banjo if he had any ideas for change. Banjo smiled and thought, Get rid of Half Deck and make dispatchers trade places with paramedics for awhile. "Give the street people more say in how to run the place."

She wanted to know how.

He struggled to form ideas he never had. Christ, I don't know? "Maybe they ought to elect us." Banjo was stunned, hearing how he had already situated himself among the supervisors. "I don't know. Let them, us, develop vehicle specifications. We work in the cars. Or let us recommend patient treatment protocol changes. Most doctors don't know squat about taking care of people in the field." That shot at Hildebrand felt good. Hildebrand smiled with his mouth but not with his eyes.

Hildebrand said, "I think those are the questions. Is there anything else you would like to add; anything we didn't cover that you would like to share with us?"

Slowly Banjo shook his head.

Hildebrand, giving his spread of papers his attention, mumbled the obligatory, "Thank you."

Banjo stood at the cool dismissal. Abby broke out of her interviewing character. "Banjo," she asked, sounding genuinely curious, "do you really want to be a supervisor?"

"Maybe. If that's where I can do the division the most good."

A macabre fantasy formed in his head. A dark face peered through the window behind the interview panel. Banjo tightened. Blood pounded in his ears. The man spun to face the window and snapped a rifle stock to his scarred cheek and leveled the glinting barrel at Abby. Banjo imagined his dive straight over the table into the crashing gunfire.

His chest spasmed where the hot explosion would hit him. He saw where, between the conference table and window, he would hit the floor carrying the bullet. A woman's anguished cries would penetrate the acrid gun smoke and ringing silence. And finally within his warm cocoon of quiet Banjo would see, from an increasing distance, Lauren's wretched tears, the astonished, admiring looks of the others, and know at last he was truly brave and that he, too, had given all that he had to give.

Chapter 9

Banjo relived his interview. When promotion intrigued him, he anguished over his poor showing. When suddenly desperate to hold onto his field position, he prayed Hildebrand had been sufficiently inflamed. Brewster and Abby liked him, he knew. That was both good and bad. They could sway Hildebrand, arguing Banjo was pragmatic and creative, just what the Chief seemed to want. But Hildebrand could maintain Banjo was neither serious nor committed. Both sides were right.

He waited helplessly as others deliberated his fate. The irony struck him. He fancied himself a master of control yet here he was on a train he could not get off headed where, he did not know.

Memories bolted in and out of his head keeping him wide eyed during the three long nights following his interview. He left his bed to get drunk. He fantasized about speeding cars and blazing weapons, anything that would make him a hero and remove the requirements upon him to choose. But those would never come and being forced to stare into his impenetrable darkness sent him deeper into it.

The police had arrested a suspect in the microwave murder, as the news had characterized this dreadful call. Television coverage took him back to the Corona Hotel and sent the storms swirling again: microwaves, turkeys, hams, dumpsters, pigtails, fire. He struggled each day just to go outside, fearing other triggers, other reminders. He missed a day of work and took a little marijuana before other shifts. His emotions were a puppet on a string. He had no way of knowing when they would be jerked.

Dan helped, despite his shifting emotional distance. Waiting on Colfax Avenue for a call Banjo confessed, "Every time I run a call I'm afraid of what I'll see. Used to be I would go head first anywhere. Now I want my partner to go first. I'll always be right behind. But I just want someone else to see things first."

Dan slouched behind the steering wheel with his right foot jammed against the steering column. A 7-11 coffee cup sat on the console covered with sticky interlocking rings left by Pepsi's set and spilled there earlier. An already read newspaper and food wrappings lay at sharp angles on the floor between the seats. He nodded and Banjo recognized Greystone's terse little gesture. Dan answered, "I can't go into a hotel without remembering the Delphi. I'm always wanting my partners to go up the stairs ahead of me."

Banjo drummed his fingers. He worried about what he wanted to say. "Am I still a good paramedic?"

Dan knotted his eyebrows at him. "What?"

"The Chief told me I could be a good supervisor but I was no longer a good paramedic. I'm good at what I do, aren't I? I wish I knew that. I figure I'm only as good as I was on my last call, but I always find something to criticize. I've been telling myself what the Looner says doesn't mean anything but his comment hit me like a ton of bricks."

Dan answered casually. "Chief was just making a point. He's trying to scare you into taking the supervisor's job."

"Am I good at what I do, Dan. This is my life. Am I good at it?"

Dan remained slouched behind the steering wheel. He looked out the window. "Sure."

Banjo's defenses snapped into place. "What are you guys saying about me in your supervisor meetings?"

"Nothing much."

"Goddamnit Dan, you're giving me Greystone crap. Talk to me!"

Dan shifted in his seat to face him. "I haven't forgotten what you're going through. There just isn't much talk about you anymore. The Chief figures he's given you the opportunity to get straightened out. Now it's up to you."

"What the hell does that mean?"

"You've always been my favorite partner ..."

110

"Don't give me a speech. What's that mean?"

Dan said, "I'm telling you. When I left my field training with Greystone, you were like a fresh breeze. We had fun. You showed me around Denver." He laughed softly. "Remember when you showed me how to tell a female prostitute from a transvestite? You epitomized the streets; all rough and tumble and playful. You could always sense trouble; you always had a way out; an option. I admired that. You could bounce back from anything. When your name comes up at all in supervisor meetings, it's in that connection. You're not bouncing back anymore. We all see that."

Dan turned back to Colfax Avenue. His nervous fingers tapped the steering wheel. "Banjo, think real hard about taking the supervisor's job. I can tell you if you scored even reasonably well the Chief will offer it to you. I know you don't have much respect for him, but I do. He loves this division as much as you do and he is very loyal to the paramedics. He really wants to help you and believes you can serve this place well in administration. So do I. But I tell you honestly, my friend, continuing along your ways is giving the Chief grounds to fire you. And he will."

Banjo also looked out at Colfax. This time he saw no color or fun there, only hot asphalt and shimmering concrete. "I'm only as good as I am on the streets," he said. "The streets are my dance partner and I am their leader. I make things go the way I want. I can be gentle and subtle like a good dance partner or I can be rough if the streets are a bitch. But it goes my way. And I love the dance. I love the dance more than anything. I love it like I love the division; like I loved the Marines. Like I love anything that gives my life meaning and definition. I can't give that up. I sometimes think I'd sooner die out there than let it go."

"You could still run some calls."

"How often does the Chief or any other supervisor run calls. Damn seldom, if ever." He faced Dan directly. "I never told anybody this; not my old shrink Eisenburger, not Ernie. But my old man was an alcoholic. He died while I was still in Vietnam. He used to beat the shit out of me. My mother would run to the bedroom and cry whenever he did. And I kept going back to him. He'd be sober for awhile. Things would be okay. Then he'd go on a binge, come home, and find me. I never felt in control. Christmas would scare me the worst because from year to year I wouldn't know if he'd get drunk at work and not come home, or come home and beat me up, or fall flat into his Christmas dinner. Growing up was like being in a concentration camp. I never had any control over my life. I never knew what the crazy guard was going to do to me. He told me I would never amount to anything.

"I joined the Marines ..." Banjo switched away from that subject. "You know what Ernie thinks?"

Dan moved his head slowly side to side, his face hung slack with astonishment.

"My gooney bird thinks I have a death wish." Suddenly exhausted, Banjo leaned his head against his fist.

"I don't know why I joined the Marines. Maybe to find the family I never had. That was the first time I found men I could trust. You get real close real quick in combat. I had good friends there, but most of them got killed." Banjo shook his head as though chasing away something that buzzed near. He changed the subject.

"I hate the bastard," he said. "I've hated him all my life. Every single day of every single god-awful year I had to prove I was worth the dirt I stepped on. You know what? I envy Greystone. I really do. He died in the line of duty. He gave everything. You could trust him. Remember all the fire trucks and police cars and ambulances at his funeral? And all those men there in uniform standing at attention, crying. I can still see that.

"I saw an old police captain walk up to Greystone's casket. He stood there in full dress looking down at it. Then he gently laid his hand on it." Banjo let a tear slip down his cheek. It darkened a spot on his pants.

Dan nodded, remembering, too. "Captain Bancroft. Greystone saved his live when he got shot."

"He rubbed Greystone's casket and patted it, like a father trying to comfort a son in a lot of pain. Greystone was important to him." Banjo's chest heaved and a sob broke free.

His hand flew to cover his eyes. "Just once I wanted that from my old man. Just once. Just one lousy time."

From inside his black pain he felt Dan's hand on his shoulder. It lay still there for a moment. Then, tenderly, awkwardly it moved back and forth across his shoulders and patted him. Banjo clutched his partner's hand. "Being good on the streets is the only thing that tells me I amount to anything, Dan. I can't leave the streets. It's the only thing I can control."

"You'll be okay, Banjo. You'll be okay."

But Banjo took no comfort from the meaningless mumbling of a man who lived in a world so far from his own. Soon he quieted and took a deep breath. "I'm okay. Thanks." But the confession left him feeling shaken and weak, as though an earthquake had happened inside.

Dan squeezed Banjo's shoulder and patted it again before removing his hand. "Tell you what," Dan told him. "I'll go first into calls if you'll go first up all the stairs."

Banjo chuckled feebly. "Sounds like a deal."

They sat in heavy silence staring out at Colfax Avenue avoiding each other's eyes.

*****

Two weeks later he found the Career Services envelope squeezed into his mailbox. Banjo felt a clutch in his throat, the same grip he experienced when handed orders for Vietnam. That moment, so many years ago, clear, stark, and massive, pivoted him and sent him hurtling unalterably in a new direction which years later landed him right here, at another terrifying departure. He turned the envelope over noticing by its slimness that it contained a single sheet of paper. He held it to the light. It was a form letter. Unceremonious end of a career, he thought. Lauren came to mind and suddenly he wanted to talk to her. He flapped the envelope against his fingers. Then he said, "Screw it," and tore it open.

'Dear Paramedic Operations Supervisor Applicant'. Banjo rolled his eyes at the typical false cordiality. He felt the heavy pounding in his chest. His eyes jumped around searching for the meat of it. He saw a score of 73. Next to the word *'RANKING'*: he saw *'third'*.

"Third! I'm third behind those wimps?" He looked at his notice again and saw similar envelopes in the mailboxes of his young competitors. Banjo let the hand holding his weak results slowly descend. He felt left alone and left out as though he were a child and all the other children had run off to play without him. He said softly to himself, "Shit."

Events progressed quickly. The following day a memo, thumb-tacked to the bulletin board blanketed with old memos, announced that Eric Watkins was the new supervisor.

The Chief called Banjo into his office. Without the typical folderol the Chief simply announced to Banjo that he did not score high enough to justify passing over the others. The Chief apologized. He was friendly but sad and seemed genuinely pained.

Banjo's loneliness grew. He knew then that the Chief had exerted all the subtle pressure he could; had focused all the attention he was going to.

"What happens to me now, Chief?"

"It is up to you, my friend." And that was that.

*****

Banjo ran into Snooper at shift change. She stood like a man, thumbs locked over her heavy leather belt, hips shifted to one side, reading the new memo.

"Hey, Snoop," Banjo said.

"I heard you didn't try hard enough."

"Hired a dandy, didn't they?"

She shrugged. "He's harmless. My guess is he won't last. The Chief probably hired him because he's afraid he'd lose the funding if he didn't stick a body in there." She faced him abruptly, as though challenging. "Who knows, Sunshine. You might get another shot. Sure as stars come out at night I'd rather pick on you than some beauty contestant."

She pulled the new announcement and several other memos off the bulletin board. Walking into Half Deck's empty office she asked Banjo, "Want to have some fun? Sure you do," she declared for him. "You like to mess around." Banjo watched her rummage through Half Deck's desk. She returned carrying scissors and folding the memo. She waved the scissors at Banjo. "But you know better than to fool with me, don'tcha?" Snooper dropped to the sofa and sprawled her legs. "Have a seat. I'll show you what I think of these memos." She patted the sofa next to her. "Wait. Get a bunch of memos," she ordered, "preferably Half Deck's. And don't wrinkle them. It ruins the effect."

Banjo brought a thin stack and sat next to her. She guided the scissors carefully through her sheet then unfolded a doll. Bits of paper fell like snow to her lap. "There. A paper doll. Isn't that the cutest thing?" She taped it to the dispatcher's window. "Let me show you how this is done. Most men aren't too creative." Snooper scooted close to Banjo and snatched a memo from his lap. Her angular elbow and bony hip jabbed him. She read aloud an old note written by Half Deck warning against anyone venturing uninvited into his or other supervisors' offices. "This is toilet paper." She read another concerning uniform allowances. "This is also toilet paper. Let's see how much toilet paper is passed off as meaningful communication. Read your memos."

Banjo scanned his. "Here's one about washing the ambulance at the beginning of each shift."

"That's not toilet paper, that's dreaming. We'll make a star out of that one."

"How about this?" Banjo read, "'To all field staff; from Ronald Humphries, Paramedic Operations Supervisor; subject: collision with police car while on a stabbing.'"

"Who stacked it up with a police car?" Snooper asked.

"I don't remember. This is two years old."

She said, "When I was a volunteer up in Vale I backed an ambulance into a helicopter rotor one time. You never heard such a racket or saw people scatter so fast. Whittled one of the lights right off the roof. Jacked the rotor around pretty good, too."

Banjo chuckled, imagining all the brave emergency people running for cover. He read on. "Recently one of this division's ambulance units responded in a careless and ...'" Banjo stopped and reread. "My God, he spelled reckless with a 'W'."

"Appropriate for the circumstances and the dweeb who wrote it."

Banjo continued reading the memo written in Half Deck's fractured English, "'... and wreckless fashion to a stabbing in a local establishment.'"

"Establishment. I love it. Likely some sleazy bar."

"Where you hang out, probably," Banjo teased.

"Read on, Sunshine."

"'While the crew was inside a police sergeant parked her car immediately behind the ambulance unit. Upon bringing the victim of the stabbing whose neck was slashed out and placing him in the ambulance and preparing to drive to Denver General, the driver threw ...'" Banjo emphasized 'threw'. "'... the ambulance into reverse. The sergeant was in the back of the ambulance at the time. Witnessing the collision with her car which collapted her front end, it is reported that the sergeant uttered a loud scream which in turn further upset the patient who then proceeded to struggle against all efforts to aid him, including biting the sergeant on the hand as she tried to obviate bleeding at the neck with direct pressure. The division tries to maintain good relations with all agencies at all times. This episode damaged that relationship. At all times, do not back up without first seeing what is behind you.'"

"Then run over it," she added. "What an idiot. That's toilet paper for sure. Put it in this pile."

Banjo caught Snooper's spirit. "Let me get some more," he said rising to collect a thick hand full from his mailbox. He sat again close to her. "Where are the supervisors?" he asked, worried they might get caught.

She remained absorbed in her snipping. "Heard one of them talking about a disaster planning meeting downtown."

Snooper fingered through Banjo's memos. "Here. Listen to this. This is from the Chief."

"That's an automatic for the dreaming file."

She read anyway. "'*To my staff:*'" She repeated the greeting, changing it: "To all my children."

Banjo giggled like a boy playing a prank. She giggled as she read. "'*To my staff: The dispatchers have brought a matter to my attention that is concerning.*'" Snooper looked up at Banjo. "He always sounds so stricken when something goes wrong." She continued. "'*Evidently certain cars are reporting their location erroneously, leading the dispatchers and me to believe that cars are out of their assigned districts without notifying dispatchers. The consequence is sending cars believed to be close, but which are not, to emergency calls. The implications to patient care are obvious.*'"

"What pile you putting that one in?" Banjo asked.

"I don't know. What do you think?"

"Let's pin this one back up," he said.

Snooper tossed it into Banjo's lap. They sorted through the rest. They snipped out a few more stars, fashioned another paper doll, and cut out some snowflakes. The stars and snow flakes were dangled from the ceiling and paper dolls covered the dispatch window. The toilet paper was taped to Half Deck's door.

Snooper said, "When he finds out, Half Deck will banish us to nights for sure."

Banjo felt a nice companionship. "I'd like nights again. Get all this supervisor crap behind me and go back to being a regular Denver General vampire."

"Be fun to do that together again," Snooper answered, suddenly shy.

A warning tapped him on the shoulder. If he liked her sassy company too much he might find himself unavailable for Lauren whom he had forgiven and now wished to see again. He considered Snooper. It might be all right if they worked together. Her face was plain and sweet and her sharp bones jabbed at him. She would not threaten his high estimation of Lauren's magnificent legs.

Sure, he said to himself, he could consent to let Half Deck learn who papered his door and thus engineer himself a night shift with Snooper. A night shift might keep him out of the Chief's way for awhile and let all this racket blow over. Banjo could regather his energy there and disappear like Roy. "Sure," he said after a moment's hesitation. "We could maybe pull some shifts together."

Her revealing moment vanished during his pause. She mimicked him cynically. "We could maybe pull some shifts together. If you're lucky, Sunshine. If you're lucky."

Chapter 10

Banjo rose early enough to watch the fresh sunlight fall across his clematis. Lavender blossoms and rich leaves spread vigorously along the close fence. He filled a soup bowl with water, picked a handful of flowers, and arranged them prettily in it. He placed the floating bouquet in front of him as he ate his Rice Crispies.

This was a rare day. The uncertainty that dogged him was gone. His fate no longer rested in someone else's hand. He could move without feeling someone's hand holding onto his belt; breathe without feeling as though someone's finger obstructed his nose. Now, late in the summer, he felt a measure of peace.

Honesty stopped his thoughts. Yes, he admitted, giving the notion its due. He did envy Eric's promotion. But he had avoided an awful decision.

He sat in his huge vinyl rocker situated just so amid his speakers and closed his eyes. Music, powerful and sweet, emerged from the air immediately about his head like a halo. He listened to Mozart and then he listened to music by Aaron Copeland. This music painted music pictures in his mind that captured the tang of something old fashioned and solid like home. And he listened to Strauss' Death and Transfiguration which left him weeping as he imagined the old man, tormented in his death, transformed into beauty and light at the moment he crossed over. He thought of Greystone.

Banjo remained cloaked in his music until he himself was momentarily transfigured. And in that moment he saw beauty that was intrinsic, without connotation; there not because it reminded him of something else pleasing but simply because the beauty existed; perfect, fragile, complete like a full arching rainbow, or love. Joy swelled in his chest. He was lifted so that he no longer felt the chair beneath him. The music became a deep, warm, blue pool covering him comfortably, allowing to float and breathe. For that moment all the world was grace and forgiveness.

The music ended and a tingling silence followed. Banjo held his eyes closed to taste the after-taste of the experience. Chords echoed distantly in his memory and lightness remained in his body. He dared not move. Otherwise the moment would be cut short and his senses awakened abruptly.

Slowly he regained his weight and presence. He noticed his breathing, still and quiet during the music, now resuming its normal depth. He opened his eyes. The electronic equipment facing him sat quietly. A few tiny lights glowed.

Banjo pushed himself upright and went to his bedroom. He removed his pajamas, showered, and dressed himself for work, carefully placing his second chance vest so that the edges touched protectively at his sides.

*****

Waiting on Colfax with Dan, Banjo noticed fascinating things. Out the windshield of the ambulance and a few blocks away rose the gleaming downtown buildings. The world changed dangerously in that short distance from there to here. The temporary people of daytime felt safe and comfortable inside those glassy buildings imposing themselves on the rest of the city. But here, on Colfax, across from the Galaxy Theater showing pornography twenty-four hours a day and in this abandoned parking lot with fading yellow parking stripes and cracking asphalt, the world carried a risk and people walked straight ahead without looking anyone in the eye. A nearby bus bench advertised Paul's Liquor Store down the street. So long ago Banjo brought Eden to this bench, and with a bottle of champagne, proposed to her.

Twin spires topped with crosses reached far into the sky beyond the brick apartment building to his left. Banjo had driven past that huge cathedral a thousand times. Still, though not religious, seeing the many steps leading to those massive church doors left him a little frightened and a little comforted. He admired the protective church in the way he admired the stubborn courage of any hero.

Dark windows in the apartment building across the street hid cautious residents who had a view of this parking lot and of him. Banjo wondered if they watched with dark, impassive eyes while he, only a week ago, tried to save a man whose brains leaked from a bullet hole? Did one of them see that man gunned down and fall right here where green wine bottle shards and cigarette butts accumulated all for a Social Security check?. Did they hear Banjo curse when he cut his hand? Those things and more kept the inhabitants anonymous behind dark windows but brought him to this place full of excitement and anticipation of adventure. Banjo wondered when some inevitable event would take him into that building, behind those windows. That would happen. He knew that would happen.

A garbage dumpster sat next to the apartment building. A gang staked their territory here with their colorful, angular lettering. Banjo liked their colors. Whoever struck with spray cans used imagination. He noticed soot against the building and discoloration on the dumpster suggesting a recent garbage fire. He turned his head quickly to avoid that memory. He squeezed his eyes shut and thought of his music.

"Let's get a cup of coffee," he told Dan.

Dan folded his newspaper and tossed it to the floor between the seats. "Sounds good." He idled the ambulance forward. As he did Banjo could see west along the Colfax corridor to the mountains. The Rockies were ghosted in clouds this morning, their forms only vaguely suggested. Remembering Clayton, Banjo tried to imagine eagles up there somewhere carrying the spirits of small children.

A black man whistling happily waited for the ambulance to cross the sidewalk in front of him. As Dan powered onto Colfax the man nodded respectfully at Banjo. Aloof as a soldier, Banjo nodded back.

Dan drove him east on Colfax toward the 7-11 a few blocks away. Presently their dispatcher ordered them exactly there for someone who was burned. Banjo was pleased that Dan did not interrupt his relaxed state with lights and siren. When a traffic light turned green Dan signaled, waited for a car ahead to complete a left turn, and eased the ambulance into the parking lot as though still after coffee.

Banjo stepped from the ambulance. He removed his long black flashlight from the door pouch, slipped it inside the back of his pants, and adjusted his vest.

He walked in first. The doorbell sounded when he swung the glass door. Dan remained close at hand. Seeing no one, Banjo stopped. He checked the mirror a clerk would use to watch the back of the store. He sniffed the air. There was no smell of gunsmoke. The store seemed in good order. He called, "Paramedics!"

"Back here." The voice was breathy and anxious. "Third aisle in." They found the clerk kneeling on the back of another man. Both were wet.

"Hey," Banjo greeted. "What's happening?"

The clerk stood but kept his foot on the back of the man's head. "I caught the son-of-a-bitch pissing in the cereal. I was holding a fresh cup of coffee at the time so I threw the whole thing on his pecker."

Banjo looked at the skinny, bare-chested man laying in the coffee and urine. "How you doin', partner?"

His face and mouth were distorted under the clerks foot. "How do you think?"

"That really happen like he said?"

"Uh-huh."

"A guy shouldn't be pissing in another guy's cereal, you know."

"Uh-huh."

"You burned pretty good?"

"I don't know. Get this tub of shit off me."

The clerk put more weight on the man's skull. "Listen, buddy. You destroyed about twenty dollars worth of inventory here."

Banjo told the clerk, "Let him up." The clerk stepped away and the other man stood, his legs held apart and his arms away from his body. His red penis poked through the open zipper. He smelled of both fluids.

Banjo looked him over and wanted to chuckle. "Check yourself to see if you have any blisters."

He handled himself carefully and looked. There were none.

Dan told the clerk, "Soak a towel in cold water for him."

"The bastard ruined all that cereal. I'm not getting him anything."

Dan swelled his chest a little and his face hardened. Quietly and with much tight jawed control Dan repeated, "Get a cold, wet towel."

"All the free coffee we give you guys and this is how you treat us." The clerk left and soon returned to the head of the aisle. "Here." He tossed the towel to Dan. Water splattered on him when he caught it. The doorbell sounded and the clerk turned to see. "Good. Finally someone who can do something. I want you to arrest this guy." The clerk told his story.

Banjo heard Zagata's phlegmy laugh. "Coffee on the pecker. That's perfect. Just fuckin' perfect." He turned into their aisle and like a tough movie cop, swaggered to them. Rocky waited at the end of the aisle where he could see the front door. His legs were set to react quickly. One hand rested on his gun which was slung diagonally across his belt buckle. Zagata asked, "This guy really burned, Banjo?"

"A little coffee burn here and there," Banjo answered. "He's okay."

The clerk stood behind the officers. "I caught him pissing in the cereal so I threw hot coffee on him."

"Threw hot coffee on him!" Zagata moved his scar close to the patient. "Listen to me, puke face. We have a police dog named Mike. Mike doesn't go for the throat. He goes right for the balls. Funniest thing I ever saw"--he opened his stance to include Banjo and Dan--"Funniest thing I ever saw was when we had this little nigger kid holed up in some house he was trying to hit. We sent Mike in there. Pretty soon we hear this kid screaming bloody murder. Mike has him right by the cock.

Peeled all the skin right off. So here's this little nigger kid, black as night, with a bright red pecker. Funniest thing I ever saw." His eyes narrowed. "Why did you pee on this man's cornflakes?"

"Because it's shit and shit shouldn't be put into humans."

"I see." Zagata looked at his partner still guarding head of the grocery aisles. "What do you think, Rocky? Should we throw him in the slammer."

Rocky's fingers drummed nervously on his weapon.

"Yeah," Zagata answered for his partner. "We better take him in. The public needs protecting."

Zagata handcuffed him. He grabbed the links between the bracelets and lifted. The prisoner cried out and bent over sharply as his arms levered outward behind him. Zagata asked Banjo, "Will he need to see a doctor?"

"Probably should. We'll take him." He found himself hoping Zagata would approve of the answer.

Outside Zagata's face switched around to friendly. He removed the cuffs and gave the man a shove. "Hot coffee on the prick is punishment enough I'd say. Nice seeing you gents, as always. Come on, Poncho," he called to Rocky who was writing in his incident book. A cigarette hung from his lips and he cocked his head over to keep the stinging smoke from his eyes while he wrote. "Let's saddle up and ride into the sunset." He looked back over his shoulder. "Poncho and I are going under cover for a little while. You won't be seeing us. But," he added, "I'll be seeing you." Zagata laughed, coughed, and slapped the roof of his car so hard it sounded like a gunshot.

*****

Dan asked, "What do you hear from Lauren?" They were parked next to the brown grass in Ruby Hill Park looking out at the city and to the mountains. Winds had cleared out the clouds. The peaks stood sharp and clean.

Banjo had kept track. By listening carefully to passing conversations he knew she and Clayton remained partners. A story floated about that she jammed her flashlight into the throat of a drunk man who threatened Clayton. Banjo wondered if she carried more courage than he gave her credit for. Perhaps he had dismissed Lauren capriciously, looking for a reason to push her away before she did the same to him. Banjo recalled Clayton's straight dive into the man who had without warning dropped him. He wondered what threat Clayton posed to cause Zagata to conspire against him. He regretted that his meddling had got him moved. His mind went back to Eden. He had loved her to the extent he could love any woman; guardedly, conditionally, but needing her nonetheless. He threw her away, too.

Marine Corps friends who died next to him in Vietnam were his true friends. So were Greystone and Dan. They were all gone now, except Dan. What rare, fortuitous feature of this one living friend's personality allowed him to feel safe with him? Sometimes he thought a best friend was someone who could read his mind and know his needs. Banjo wished he knew. If he did he would make that into a pill and give it to every person he knew so he would never feel alone again.

He answered Dan's question with a shrug. "Haven't seen her much."

"Her name comes up in supervisor meetings."

"About time some other name came up besides mine."

"She and Clayton are both turning in to pretty good paramedics."

"Gonna fit the old Denver General mold after all, huh." This interested him. Her skills as a paramedic made her more attractive as a woman.

"I thought you'd be interested since you worked with them."

Banjo stared at the mountains. He and Eden had favorite spots up there. Banjo shifted his thoughts. "I wonder if either of them would have gotten past Greystone's field training."

Dan waited before answering. "We're not using him as a standard anymore. We haven't for years."

Banjo turned sharply. "What's that mean?"

"He and the Chief had a power struggle before Greystone died. The Chief saw stagnation setting into the Division. He wanted to make some changes. One way to make change is to bring in a different sort of paramedic. He wanted to recruit more heavily out of state. He was willing to accept less street experience for people with broader outlooks. Like Clayton and Lauren."

Banjo laughed.

"Clayton has some cultural sensitivities that are important. He's well educated. He can keep this stuff in perspective. He's exceptional on the street. Greystone had a way of letting only certain people through his filter. I think I survived Greystone because the Chief refused to let Greystone fire me."

"So you guys have tossed him out."

"I wouldn't say that, but he served long and well. And long enough."

"If the Chief is getting rid of the old guard why did he want me to be a supervisor?"

"He honestly thinks you have a fresh view of things. And he doesn't want you to self destruct. We both know people who should have gotten out of the business long ago but didn't. I think that's where Greystone ended up."

Banjo stiffened his back. "He cared about this place. He cares about it as much as I do."

"Greystone cared about the paramedic division he wanted to create. He couldn't accommodate the Chief's vision."

"Does the Chief think Greystone picked out the one car in a thousand that would blow the flare line and strolled out in front of it?"

"I've wondered about that."

"That he did that on purpose!"

Dan dismissed his thought with a shrug.

Banjo pushed. "Are you saying he killed himself? I was there. I can tell you he didn't. He stepped out of the ambulance and whop, he was gone."

"I believe you," Dan promised. "But I wonder about Greystone. He was powerful but no match for the Chief. The Chief is always freshening his outlook. He has a genius for finding the change points. You can't keep people and organizations from growing. Anyone who tries will be left behind. I think Greystone saw that happening to himself. The division was moving beyond him. I think that conflict ended his friendship with the Chief."

Banjo remembered the Chief's happy picture of himself with a much younger Greystone. Then Banjo saw Greystone tangled in the brush with blood running from both ears. How alone he looked laying there by himself, dying. How alone. Banjo examined his own isolation and wondered if this was the same road Greystone traveled.

Dan seemed to read his thoughts. "I'm having a get together at my house tomorrow. Kind of a welcoming party for those who just finished their rookie year. Lauren and Clayton will be there. Why don't you come by."

"Mix it up a little with younger minds, huh. Keep Banjo from getting too set in his ways."

"Something like that."

Chapter 11

Ernie Webster laughed at Banjo's admission. "You're the only person I know who is glad he wasn't promoted."

Banjo laughed, too. He was nervous and pushed his words too hard. "Being supervisor would make me crazy. The only place I'm comfortable is the back of an ambulance. Nothing's ambiguous there. I can lay my hands on everything I need. Now all's I need is my night shift and to disappear."

"Isn't that the new supervisor's shift?"

Banjo rolled his eyes. "That's right." He drummed his fingers. "Can't have some kid looking over my shoulder."

"I'm not sure you can have anyone looking over your shoulder."

"That's true. That's true. If I can't be left alone I'd rather be boss. But I'd rather be left alone."

"That's what we all want."

A silence followed. Ernie was patient. "I've been feeling better," Banjo offered, looking away.

"Good." Ernie waited.

"It's a good thing I wasn't promoted. I think dodging that bullet took a lot of pressure off me."

"I think you're right."

Banjo bumped his fist against his mouth. He looked at Ernie's cluttered desk. A spray can sat there. 'Bullshit Repellent' was written on it. Next to that lay a wand filled with glitter suspended in fluid. A sign hung on the wall behind Ernie. It read, 'Pain is inevitable. Suffering is optional.'

Ernie spoke quietly. "I've learned that when you do that something is going on."

"Do what?"

Ernie bumped his chin for Banjo.

"Oh. Well, I'll give you something. Did I ever tell you my dad used to beat me?"

Ernie's face froze. "No. You told me he was alcoholic."

Ernie's frank surprise satisfied Banjo. "My old man'd come home drunk and kick the crap out of me. Once in awhile. Not often. Usually when I did something stupid."

"Stupid or not, beating his child was inexcusable." Ernie took a deep breath. "Well. That helps explain some things."

"Like what?" Banjo asked immediately.

"Like why you need to control situations. Why you have trouble forming relationships. You had no control growing up. The person you trusted most hurt you. Those are strong lessons. That could also explain why you place such impossible demands upon yourself."

Banjo crossed his arms tight against his chest. He shrugged. "I'm pretty fucked up. Huh."

"No."

"No," Banjo repeated, affirming.

"Do you suppose you avoided being supervisor because that authority would make you more like your father?"

His eyes darted. His knuckles drummed against the armchair. "Maybe. I don't know. I've wondered if Dad's the reason I don't trust anybody much. The only people I trust are those who take the same risks I do."

"That's asking quite a bit of someone who wants to be your friend."

"I know. They all became disposable. Except Dan."

"What test did he pass in your mind?"

"I don't know. We were together at the Delphi when he took a round in the arm. Well, more specifically, I was downstairs getting the stretcher. He was up with the patient when the shooting started."

"Do you think you should have been with him?"

Banjo made a face. "He sent me down. That was the right decision. I should've left him the portable radio, though, so he could've called for help. But the cops arrived right away. And I don't know, it was just one of those bad scenes that went to hell. Maybe somewhere I do feel like I owe him something. Anyway... Can I talk about my Dad now?"

"Of course."

"Anyway, when I was a kid I decided the only way I could please my dad was to do incredible things. He never seemed to like me so I guess I never did anything incredible enough. I don't know. There's just a lot of stuff floating around in my head right now. But I do know Dan's about my best friend; even if he is my only one."

"Do you think you have to come close to death to be accepted?"

"Death wish shit again, huh."

"Just a question, Banjo. It's for you to answer in your own time."

"I'll answer the stupid thing now. No. I'm not trying to kill myself. Greystone didn't kill himself. Just because I feel bad when I'm not around when my partners need me doesn't make me crazy." Banjo looked at Ernie. "I don't want to die, Ernie. But sometimes I want to be released."

"From what?"

"From always being responsible."

"From always being in control, perhaps?"

Banjo huffed and recrossed his arms. "Maybe I'm looking for something else to believe in; something else I can trust." His speech slowed. He became thoughtful. "I don't know what I want. But I know I ache for something...more."

"What about yourself? What about God?"

Banjo laughed. "Don't get religious on me. You don't spend a life seeing what I've seen and come easily to God."

Ernie shrugged it off. "It's a thought. As I think about my experiences and listen to yours I have to put my trust in some great who-knows-what. I can let that carry my burdens. I certainly can't." Ernie continued gently. "I think you might be asking the right question, Banjo. Something is keeping you away from wonderful people. Right now my organizing theory is that you can't accept others because you can't accept something about yourself. Your father has a lot to do with that. I don't think you're trying to kill yourself either. I think instead you are trying very hard to live happily. But something deeper may see death as your only alternative."

"Sounds simple enough."

Ernie laughed. "Maybe you can turn this into one of those magnificently impossible situations you so proudly throw yourself into."

Banjo's thoughts stopped. Ernie's casually tossed out comment resonated with challenge.

Ernie's watch alarm beeped. "That's a good place to leave this. I haven't seen you much this summer. Why don't we get together a bit more often for awhile."

Banjo shrugged one shoulder indifferently. "Fine with me."

*****

Banjo dressed for Dan's party. Uniforms, neatly hung and densely packed in his closet, marched down the left side of his clothes rack. Every uniform that ever announced Banjo's professional identity to the world, including his proud Marine Corps dress uniform, waited for duty. Plastic covers protected perfectly creased white shirts. Crisp blue pants hung by their cuffs. Casual off duty clothes hung off to the right. He considered the corduroy pants his best. The blue jeans and polyester shirts were his every day wear. When he wasn't wearing black uniform boots, he wore Hush Puppies, summer and winter.

A welcoming party, Banjo thought, deciding between blue jeans and cords. No such thing took place in his time. Banjo wondered if the Chief cooked up speeches, like at a graduation or something. When new people survived Greystone's field instructor program he told them simply, "You're a partner now. Don't screw up." That was that and it was enough. After that they qualified to meet older paramedics at The Parlour and get drunk.

Banjo picked out the pair of dark green pants, the most formal pair he had.

*****

Wondering, perhaps willing that he should see Lauren at the party, Banjo met her approaching Dan's house. At first recognition, still some distance off, he saw her welcoming smile. He could not control his own and was embarrassed. He looked at the red slab sidewalk, cracked and uneven, until he was more composed. He looked up. She was closer. Dark pants, narrow at her waist and clingy, fired his lingering fantasies.

"Hello, stranger," she called. She carried a wild array of daliahs.

Banjo's face lit up. "Hey."

They met at the foot of Dan's walk and Lauren took his arm. "I haven't seen you in a blue moon." She tantalized him with a look and pulled his arm close. He felt her breast brush his arm.

He said, "I don't work nights."

"Lucky dog. When am I going to see you again?"

"You name it."

"Maybe we can find time for a glass of wine some evening soon."

"I'd like that." He wanted to pin her down but feared a distant date that amounted to no commitment at all. Reaching Dan's wide porch, she rang the door bell without suggesting further arrangements.

Banjo remembered when this house was a run down duplex. Dan and his wife lived above the curious landlady with lavender hair and three dogs named after types of hard liquor. Banjo envied the great spruced up Victorian home with its tall turret and vast cool-in-the-summer porch with a railing wide enough for sitting. When Banjo visited he felt embraced by something old and everlasting, like his grandmother when he was young.

Dan answered the door. Lauren let go of Banjo and hugged Dan in greeting. He felt an old stab of jealousy as he watched the woman of his interest embrace Dan and peck him on the cheek. She handed Dan the flowers. He cradled them like a baby and stood aside to welcome them in.

Dan said, "Nice to see you, partner."

A protective cocoon spun itself around Banjo who reasoned the further he remained from people the less they would hurt him. His answer was noncommittal. "I never turn down free food."

Banjo watched people talk as he would observe them through a window: near but separate; heard but muted. He was present but not engaged. A rookie noticed him standing next to the fireplace and brought the veteran a beer. Banjo curled one corner of his mouth in half smile but did not allow the proud, young paramedic to stay.

From his spot, with his back safely against a wall, Banjo observed the details. He loved Dan's oak floor. He had gotten rid of the orange shag carpeting that smelled of cat urine and polished the oak boards to great, glowing warmth. At the fireplace hearth, Dan had laid dark blue tile.

Dan brought a tall glass vase and set it on the mantel. One by one he slid the Daliahs down the tall, clear neck, arranged them a bit, then centered the bright explosions of color under an old photograph of a small town nestled against a rock outcropping thrusting into the ocean.

Banjo saw Clayton talking to the Chief. Beyond them Snooper stood at the table stabbing carrots into the dip. Like himself, she stood alone and Banjo was thus drawn to her. The new supervisor entered tall and proud from the kitchen carrying a platter of food. He laughed knowingly with Dan who walked beside him.

The door bell chimed. Dan hurried to answer. Roy and his wife waited on the porch. Roy smiled uncomfortably and handed Dan a slender brown bag containing wine. Banjo was touched that Roy came to honor the new people. He turned toward Lauren who moved from person to person touching them, kissing them, saying hello, just like this was her house and her party.

The party bored him. He remembered their old Christmas drunks at the Whiskey Hill Saloon. People drank and smoked and swore and danced hard to deafening music at those parties. Those parties got his insides churned up just like a good shooting or sex did. This party was too polite for that. Banjo finished his beer and made a face, noticing that is was watery, low calorie beer.

Backs were turned toward him. People formed, dissolved, and reformed their intimate groups without him. Even Roy, ordinarily transparent, fitted himself next to the Chief and Clayton. Banjo turned to watch traffic moving on Downing Street beyond the bay window. Lauren sat knee to knee with a woman on a window seat.

Banjo's imagination made one car accelerate sharply, turn hard into the oncoming lane, and propel into a van. The explosive crash shook the floor. Fire glowed beneath the van. Banjo saw no movement within. He dashed past these frivolous people and out the front door. He heard screaming. He saw four people inside the van. The shattered front end pinned two adults. Children cried in the back seat. He pulled at the driver's door. Sheet metal groaned as the damaged door strained opened a few inches then sprang shut. He ran to the other side. Flames and black smoke twirled upward from the tire. Banjo slid open the panel door. The woman pinned by the dashboard cried, "Get my children! For the love of God, get my children!" The dash board lay tight across her chest and her voice sounded squeezed. Color had already drained from her face. Hot smoke stung Banjo's nose. "Tommy! Annie! Can you her me?"

"Mama!"

"Hello, Sunshine."

Banjo jolted. He saw Snooper and felt silly. "Hey Snoop."

"Nice digs here. Did his ex decorate this place for him?"

"No. He's done all this since his divorce."

She grunted, impressed. "The men I've known couldn't decorate a coloring book much less a house. Well, let's have a look around this love nest."

They browsed about. His bedroom, a circular master bedroom, was situated in the base of the turret. The bed was neatly made and covered with a quilt of stitched squares depicting an ocean, a forest, waterfalls and rivers. "Oregon" was embroidered across one square. An over stuffed rocker sat next to the bay window. Books and magazines cluttered the floor around the chair. A telephone sat on a small table nearby. Next to the phone sat a vase of silk flowers and a post card from a place called Cape Lookout.

"Wow. This place is really nice," she said. "He must be gay."

"No," Banjo chuckled. "As a matter of fact he stole a girl friend of mine once."

"Oh?" Then she drove her fists into her blue jean pockets and looked right at him. "Well, I guess it wouldn't be so hard to steal any woman from you."

His jaw dropped. He looked at Snooper. "I beg your pardon."

Her face worked against a smile. "You look like a guy who hangs around with women who always have other places to go. You need a woman who can see past your nonsense; one who doesn't have any nonsense of her own."

"I do, huh?"

"Well, don't you?"

He bumped her shoulder with his. "Well," he laughed. "So..."

They roamed the house together then wandered separate ways. More people accumulated. As Banjo watched he recognized the Chief's hiring pattern. The new paramedics were different. Like Lauren and Clayton, they lacked something that he and Greystone and the Chief came with. They others were so young and bright and untouched. Perhaps that was it. None of these yet had hard faces and cold eyes. No one here looked like soldiers.

Nor was there a common dedication to the division. The present day paramedics were not tightly joined. No war stories occupied conversations at this party. No one asked, 'Been getting any lately', by which they would mean exciting calls, not sex; though both amounted to the same thing to Banjo. Instead he over heard the Chief and Clayton comparing back packing trails. Lauren breezed through the party asking about one person's children, another's graduate school, and yet another's upcoming trip to Taos; catching up on the little bits of chit chat with all the people she hugged and kissed.

The new people were so different. They were not the kind who came to the division to lay it all on the line. These people drew a line. Banjo felt an arrogant satisfaction after making that distinction. Who among these had stepped to the edge;

offered himself up? And after the first time, would they again? Banjo's pride slipped. He hadn't offered himself up either. But his friends were those who would.

Banjo reached the dining room table. A blue runner decorated the broad plank table. He ate Italian olives. He remained glassed in, separated, and safe. Half Deck entered. He wore a black leisure suit accented with white shoes and a narrow, white belt. His hair shined. Banjo smiled. At this party he had more in common with that supervisor than with most of the others. He went to Half Deck. "Hey, guy."

Half Deck's quiet toothpick moved warily. "Banjo."

"Not too many old timers here."

Half Deck looked around in a shifty, calculating way. He nodded. "I'm always fascinized by the way new people seem so dang sure of themselves. I'd like to get them on the street myself."

"Not like the old days."

"No sir."

Banjo nodded toward Eric now chatting with the Chief. "What do you think of your new supervisor?"

Half Deck studied him and the toothpick was still. "Well, like I say. New people seem so dang sure of themselves. He could do with a little less mouth and a little more ears." He looked knowingly at Banjo. "You should have took the job."

"I didn't score high enough."

"You didn't try. Next time it comes around you try harder." Half Deck stabbed Banjo's chest once with his finger and moved off.

So Eric was having trouble. This pleased Banjo.

He went back to the detail of Dan's house. Every place he looked was a view. People sat in wooden sky blue chairs which the oak floor reflected. A northwest Indian mask hung below a beveled mirror in the entry way. He reminded himself to ask Clayton about it. Behind him hung a print of loggers standing next to an enormous fir tree. Pictures of Dan with his parents sat on the fire place mantel. A graceful wooden sea gull in flight sat on an end table.

Dan had so much. Banjo ached for such money and good fortune. The others seemed to have so much, too. Clayton and the Chief still talked about trips into the mountains. He remembered Lauren's house. Though it looked like a cyclone of colors had hit it, she nevertheless had a home. It contained warmth and place. The Debbie J was nothing more than an address.

Then he understood the real difference between these people and himself, and a frightening fire of jealously ignited in him. He had only his job and his stories and his memories. These people had lives. They had friends. They created permanence for themselves. They were anchored. Banjo floated freely.

Clayton approached. He wore cowboy boots, a little muddy at the heels, and his black hair was growing out. Banjo, feeling his emptiness more when near those whose souls were full, did not want to talk to him just now.

Clayton gestured at Dan's living room. "Quite a place."

Banjo was remote. "I'm not sure I could put my feet up here, but it's nice."

"How have you been?"

"Okay."

"Have you been getting anything good?"

"No, same bullshit ambulance calls."

There was a moment of sharp discomfort between them. Clayton said, "Is there something wrong?"

"No. I'm fine." But Banjo was irritable and nervous being in range of Clayton's perceptive sensibilities.

"If you want me to leave you alone I will."

Banjo shook his head. "I've got some things on my mind, is all."

"I can tell."

He threw his hands up. "Now look. I admit you can tell things but don't be poking around inside me. I don't want it."

Clayton watched him.

"I mean it," Banjo told him. "Don't be inspecting me."

"I just came over to say hello."

Banjo remembered the comfort he had begun to feel with Clayton just when Half Deck took him away. Clayton's philosophies traveled frequently through Banjo's thoughts. Banjo said, "It's been awhile."

"Thought anymore about coming hiking?"

Banjo laughed. "I'll hike with you down to The Parlour."

"I don't think so. I don't drink."

Banjo laughed again. "How'd you ever get on down here? Used to be a new guy couldn't wait to join the rest of us for a beer after he got out of his rookie year. Used to be that was sort of a graduation. But not anymore, I guess. You new guys must have a little stronger moral fiber than me. Suppose?"

Clayton's face grew stern. He looked Banjo over then left his gaze drift elsewhere. Clayton turned back and his temper ignited. "I don't give a damn about any tradition of yours that requires alcohol. Alcohol killed my father and grandfather. I drank like a fish until I was twenty. I've been sober for eight years and I'm not about to give all that up just to be accepted by you."

Banjo acted as he would on the streets when confronted with someone who threatened him. He said calmly, "It's all right, partner. You don't have to worry. I'm not going to force anything on you. I was just kidding."

Clayton took a deep breath. "Don't kid about that."

Banjo's guard fell away. "Your old man was an alcoholic?"

He nodded.

And you're an alcoholic?"

He shrugged with his eyebrows.

"How did you stop drinking?"

"My dad started telling me stories of my family. He taught me about my culture, my ancestors, my great grandfather, Shot In The Heel, who was a very powerful medicine man. Over and over he told me these stories. Pretty soon I began to feel like I belonged somewhere and had roots. Then it no longer made sense to use a white man's drink to destroy myself. So I started going to AA meetings and quit. That's where I began to think about the spirituality of my people and the power my great grandfather had."

Something seized Banjo's fascination. "Like what power?"

"His visions, his power to heal. He always knew where to find buffalo, when trouble was near. He was an important leader."

"And you have some of that: visions and such?"

"I think so."

"Visions?"

"On rare occasion."

"Visions of what?"

Clayton narrowed his eyes. "Are you going to take this seriously? I'm not a side show."

"No, no. I really want to hear this."

"A few times when I was a kid old men appeared and told me to prepare myself. They told me if I did not listen to them I would continue my sickness forever. None of this made sense until Dad started telling me about Shot-In-The-Heel's visions. Dad made me realize I had more to do in life than hang sheet rock and drink beer, which is what I was doing."

"So what do you think you have to do?"

Clayton thought. "Well, if this were 1871 when my great grandfather lived, I would be a medicine man. But that was then and this is now. I think I can combine my experience as a paramedic, my visions, and," he chuckled, "my experience as a drunk to help bring emergency care to Sioux reservations."

Banjo smiled weakly at Clayton's reference to drunkenness. A thought struck him. "Do you tell others around here about your visions?"

"No. If I tell people about my visions, I give them away and I lose my power. I tell you because you want to believe them."

Banjo nodded. "I do. There's something about this stuff. But if I were you I wouldn't be talking like this to just anyone."

Clayton's chest bounced with a quiet laugh. "I can be a wooden Indian when I have to be."

"What can you tell about people?" Banjo asked, wondering what Clayton had divined about him.

"The nature of their power. What their spirit is like. What anybody could tell, really, if they paid attention." Clayton looked outward toward the paramedics. "There is great power among paramedics. Much power. But also much searching. They remind me of myself before I found my traditions. Paramedics yearn for traditions but don't understand that people in the business today are here to create traditions for those who will come later. I see that. I see paramedics trying to make the uniform say who they are without looking at their own hearts."

Banjo felt a twinge of recognition in that observation.

"I see paramedics who feel they have to sacrifice their spirit in order to feel worthy of their uniform. Sioux warriors also took great risks in order to be honored by their culture so I understand that."

Banjo said, "I do, too." He added, "Is this ability of yours what made you so sure Zagata killed that prisoner?"

Clayton drew a breath and stiffened. "Zagata killed him. I didn't need the gift of second sight to recognize the fact in his eyes. I'll tell you something else, my friend. It will fall to you to stop him."

Banjo's mouth fell open. "I beg your pardon. What makes you think that? I stay out of his way; like I told you to do. He's a cop. They'll have to take care of him. No, no, no, my boy. Your gift has failed you there." Banjo feigned a yawn. "Well, it's past my bedtime."

Clayton remained serious. "If we were partners once, we're always partners. I'll stick with you."

"Fine. Fine," Banjo answered absently. "I'm going to find myself another beer." He extended his right hand to Clayton. "Congratulations, by the way. It's not easy to break in down here. You're a fine paramedic."

Clayton smiled and took Banjo's hand. "I need to hear that from someone like you. I respect the old guard."

In silence, Banjo answered Clayton's strong gaze. Pride brightened within him. "Thank you, Clayton. I'll work with you anytime." And that was the highest honor he could bestow.

*****

Banjo stayed until the end and found that he did not drink as much as he thought he might. When everyone had left Dan opened two beers. He gave one to Banjo then dropped to the sofa and rested one knee over the arm rest. He looked at Banjo with wide eyes, feigning exhaustion. "How ya doin' partner."

"Quite a party, Dan. You'll make someone a fine wife."

Dan smiled and took a long drink. "First beer of the evening. Can't get mouthy at my own party."

Banjo laughed hard and freely. "This was a nice party. I like these kids."

Dan smiled back. "I'm glad you came. It made a difference to them. Made a difference to me, too."

Banjo ignored Dan's compliment. "I talked to Clayton."

"Did he tell you I give them all Banjo lessons?"

"Do you tell them what happens to Banjo after a few years?"

"Some things they have to learn for themselves." Dan raised his beer. "To old friends and survivors. May we forever be."

"Here, here," Banjo whispered, hoping. He touched his beer can gently to Dan's.

Chapter 12

Banjo walked ahead of Dan through brown grass that was stiff with frost and high and spindly from neglect. He wondered if fleas would jump onto him from the grass and he began to itch under his socks. A car axle with bald tires lay hidden in the dense grass and he banged his shin against it. Ahead, the collapsed gray boards of a shed sparkled with nets of sun jeweled cobwebs. A refrigerator stood next to the shed. The door hung open and orange rust nibbled through its white enamel. Banjo's memory of ancient calls placed a dead boy inside the box.

Only minutes ago Banjo had driven by this place to work. A great snarling guard dog prowled this lot and barked at passing cars as it had done this morning to Banjo. But the police had put a bullet in its brain when they tried to enter after a garbage man had noticed legs protruding from under the fallen down shed.

Banjo rubbed his stinging shin and sniffed the air for the distinctive odor of death. Only the cold air touched his sensitive nose. He looked for the dog and felt a little jolt when he spotted the carcass through crisscrossed grass. For a moment he feared it would leap from the dead and charge. Ahead he saw the pile of old lumber. He saw the shoes, toes pointed toward the dirt. Banjo wondered if the dog had torn out that man's intestines and left the rest to rot. He would be the first to see. He hated being the first.

The legs extended out from under what was once the floor. Dry grass arched over them as though reclaiming them to the earth. Banjo sniffed once more, still unable to catch the smell he expected. "Hey," he called, kicking one shoe. "You hear me?" He shrugged at the police. "You never know. He could be sleeping." Banjo, Dan, and the police pulled on the floor boards. The punky wood peeled away easily.

Banjo heard someone ask, "How long do you suppose he's been here?" He puzzled. There should be a smell.

They revealed his thin, gray face. Pine needles gathered in the hollow of his cheek and rested just inside his dry mouth. Red ulcers over his high cheek bone had eaten through his skin where it pressed against the cold earth. One arm was drawn rigidly to his face. He probed the cold stubble of his neck for a pulse. The stiff, protective arm stirred. Bony fingers gripped Banjo's wrist and pulled it away.

Banjo jerked his arm free and dropped to his haunches. "Who the hell are you?" He rubbed his wrist where the cold hand had gripped him.

The dry mouth closed. It swallowed. Then a hissing voice asked, "Who are you?"

A policeman said, "Damn. One touch and he comes to life."

The man's long arms drew slowly to his sides and he pushed himself up to his knees. He made a high arch on hands and knees and his head and long neck dangled well down between his shoulders. Needles and grass fell from his clothing. He slowly angled one leg under himself and pushed himself upright. Banjo took a step back to watch the man, narrow and gray as the lumber piled at his feet, rising over him.

Banjo said, "What happened to you?"

"I got beat up and I come here to rest."

"How'd you get past the dog?"

"I get along with dogs."

"Well," Banjo told him, "you're coming along with us now."

They placed him on their stretcher. He had to bend his knees and draw in his feet so they could close the ambulance door. Banjo and Dan delivered him to Denver General.

*****

Banjo was writing his patient care record when Dan stepped into the emergency department and said, "Let's go. We have another call." Banjo checked a wall clock as he hurried to the ambulance. Their shift had begun just twenty minutes earlier.

Banjo drove. Dan asked the dispatcher for the nature of the call.

"There's a man believed to be trapped in a garbage truck."

Dan made a face. "Yuk."

Banjo slowed the ambulance at an intersection.

Dan looked out his passenger window. "Clear right."

Banjo punched power to the engine and was pushed into his seat. "Great party last night," he called to Dan over the electronic siren wailing just above their heads.

"Went pretty well," Dan agreed. "I like how the place feels after the people leave. It's like their friendly spirits are all still in the air keeping me company." The ambulance slowed sharply, pitching Dan forward. He looked right again. "Clear."

Banjo said, "I keep thinking I'll have a bunch of people over."

"You should."

"Hell of a mess to clean up afterward."

"It's worth it. Clear. I noticed you and Lauren arrived together. Anything going on there?"

Banjo raised his eyebrows thoughtfully and spun the steering wheel left with the palm of one hand. He accelerated between elm trees lining a neighborhood street. "Might be." He braked hard and picked up the microphone to report their arrival. He motioned with his head. "Check the back of the garbage truck."

Blood pooled below the rear of the truck. "Oh, great," Dan said toward the window.

A policeman waited near the blood and gestured helplessly at the compacting controls. "You know how to operate this thing?"

Dan and Banjo looked at each other. Dan asked, "Where's the driver?"

"No one's been able to find him. I called the fire department. I think we have to cut the hydraulic lines."

Banjo went to the truck and wiggled levers. Nothing happened. He shrugged at Dan and leaned cross legged against the garbage truck. Blood dribbled. It accumulated into a long pool.

Soon he heard the characteristic mechanical growl of fire engine sirens. He liked that powerful machine driven growling-screaming sound much better than the ambulance's whinny electric shriek.

Fire fighters cut hydraulic lines and the rear compacting section popped ajar. A gush of garbage and blood hit the pavement. Banjo told Dan, "Nothin' were gonna do here, partner. Whoever's in there is as dead as he can be."

"Hey!" A man ran from a donut shop. "What are you doing to my truck?"

"This your truck?" asked the fire officer.

"Yes, it's my truck." He pointed "And that's my hydraulic fluid on the ground there."

The fireman also pointed. "Well, that's blood right there."

"Of course it's blood. I just emptied a laboratory. They use cow's blood. That's just a busted jar. Gol darn. Do you know what it'll take me to fix and bleed those hydraulic lines? I'm down for the rest of the day."

Banjo leaned close to the policeman. "Adios."

The policeman smiled. "Adios."

Banjo idled the ambulance around the garbage truck. Feeling happy and chatty, he said, "Well, we've been at it about an hour now. Let's head over to Colfax and grab a cup."

"Think that clerk will let us back in the store?"

*****

After driving a bit Dan said, "You know, I like Snooper."

"She's okay," Banjo answered, wondering why his partner brought her up. "Kind of a goofy broad." Snooper had been entering his thoughts with peculiar frequency. It would trouble him if Dan were interested in her, too.

"I guess that's why I like her. I like people a little off center. Like you. Keeps me from getting too stuffy and boring."

"Oh," Banjo answered with false surprise to draw Dan's thoughts away from Snooper. "So, you've heard the talk."

"What talk?"

Banjo raised his eyebrows at his partner. "People say you're old before your time. Stuck in the mud. Predictable. Boring. Supervisor material."

He stared open faced at Banjo. "Really?"

"You haven't heard? Oh," Banjo concluded lightly. "Must be what they're saying about me."

Dan blinked. Then his face regathered its starch. "Creep. Thanks a lot."

"My, my. Aren't we a little sensitive?"

"I am sensitive about that. I've gotten far too serious. I'm not even thirty-five, but sometimes I feel like I'm the father confessor for the entire division. People tell me what mischief they're about to get into as though they want me to bless it. They never invite me to mess around, though. Why don't people invite me to play?" He sighed deeply. "All I am is a reference point."

"I know all about thinking things aren't what they used to be. Believe me; I know all about that." They exchanged looks and Banjo told him, "You inherited that from Greystone. You and your field instructors are the gold standard. You teach new guys to be just like you. What do you expect?"

"Did Greystone ever complain about this?"

Banjo laughed. "Greystone never complained about making anybody into his image and likeness. He only complained when the Chief stood in the way of that."

"But I don't produce clones."

"No? You had the same agreement with your last new paramedic that Greystone had with you. You do it like I say, kid, and I won't fire you. Right? Isn't that still how it works?" Banjo bobbed his eyebrows knowingly. "You talk about throwing out the old Greystone ways but all you've done is paint an old chair a new color. You're a real nice guy and all, but you're still a hard ass with new people. And after a few months with you and a year or so on the street, those fresh outlooks will turn just as shitty as yours and mine."

Dan sighed again. "So this is how the rest of my career is going to go."

Banjo leaned across and slapped his shoulder. "Tell you what. Next time I'm about to screw up I'll drag you into it."

"Just don't get me into anything stupid. I don't want another dinner at Half Deck's."

Chuckling to himself, Banjo lumbered the ambulance into the 7-11 parking lot.

Banjo left the store with two cups of coffee. Steam from them vaporized in the cold air. They sat in the warm ambulance, sipped their coffee, and talked some more.

"Think you'll ever get married and have kids, Dan?"

Dan blew across the surface of his coffee. "I'd like to have kids. That was a big issue with Karen and me. She wanted her dress shop and I wanted kids. Guess who won that one?"

"You ever sorry you broke up?"

Dan thought. "Sometimes. Sometimes I get lonely and wonder if my divorce was really necessary. But as I run it back through my head, I always come up with the same answer."

"So was Eden worth it?"

"Eden was the consequence, not the cause."

Banjo grinned. "Uh-huh."

Dan did not get defensive. "I've thought about Eden. Getting involved with her wasn't the right thing but she didn't ruin the marriage."

"Think you'll get married again?"

Dan shrugged. "Seems as though I'd have to travel a million miles to find the woman I want. Even if I did find her I'm not sure I could let her into where I need her."

Banjo joked, "I think I've decided I'm just too damn ugly to attract a good woman."

Dan laughed and Banjo joined him.

Then Banjo asked, "What do you think of Lauren?"

"She's a little squirrely."

Banjo nodded agreement. "Good looking, though."

"If I get involved with a woman I want to be sure she'll stick around. I'll be a hard one to get to know. I have to be confident she'll put some effort into a relationship. Someone like Lauren wouldn't give me that confidence."

Banjo nodded again. "But you think Snooper is okay?"

"Well, I'm not thinking about dating her but she's a good and decent woman."

This relieved Banjo whose musings now revolved around two women. "Well, personally, I want a flaming knock-out. Preferably a rich one."

"Number five," the dispatcher called.

"Time to go to work," Banjo said happily.

"On a man having hot flashes," the dispatcher told them.

Dan shook his head.

Banjo said, "I had a guy once who overdosed on Estrogen. He was kind of cute."

"It's getting cold," Dan said looking out the window at the gray sky. The cold window turned his breath to a cloudy film. "We'll be getting people with cooked up problems so they can ride to Denver General."

Banjo looked at his watch. It was just past noon, two and a half hours into their ten hour shift. Banjo's stomach began to growl for lunch. "It's a little early for them to start holing up for the night."

They found a man hunched over an empty coffee cup in a cafe not far from where they were drinking their own coffee. Cigarette butts had spilled from the mounding ash tray. His hair carried the oil of many unwashed days and his face shined. Looking at him made Banjo want to wash his own face and hands. The proprietor called 911 to get rid of him. The man was vague about not feeling well and asked to go the hospital. They gave him a ride to Denver General where he was given a hall pass to spend the afternoon in the waiting room.

*****

"Well, partner," Banjo said happily when he hoped back into the ambulance. "Lunch time, don't ya think?"

But on their way to eat the dispatcher called again, "Number Five, cover a dog bite. You'll be second car in. Fourteenth and Corona. Police are there already."

"Two cars on a dog bite?" Banjo asked his partner. "On the way," he told the dispatcher. Nearing the address another ambulance raced past them, toward the hospital. The paramedic driving was alone in front. "Must be the other half of the dog bite," Banjo thought out loud.

They found police officers pinning a man face down in the intersection. Their knees jammed his neck and back and flattened his face against the asphalt. From the ambulance Banjo saw blood soaking his shirt. He flung the shift lever into park and the ambulance clanked and lurched to a stop. He and Dan jumped out and grabbed their equipment. "He's not injured," called a police officer. "He's just real shook."

Dan and Banjo put their bags down. Sobs broke from deep within the man's chest. An officer leaned close to his face and told him. "I want the paramedics to take a look at you. Can we let you up?"

"You can let me up."

"Okay. I'm real sorry about your little girl but you threatened people and you sounded real serious. We can't let you break the law. Understand me?"

The officers stood, carefully removing their containing pressure. One officer spoke quietly to Banjo and Dan. "A neighbor's pit bull just killed his daughter. He went crazy and threatened to kill the owner."

"Where's the girl?" Dan asked.

"One of your unit's took her in."

"Where's the dog?"

"The owner has it until Animal Control arrives."

Dan nodded. "What do you want us to do here?"

"Well ... I mean, he watched his little girl get torn up. You guys can tell better than me if maybe he needs to talk to someone."

"Is he manageable?"

"I think he'll be all right."

When the girl's father stood Banjo saw blood clots and bits of fatty tissue clinging to his shirt where he had clutched his daughter. "Let me go change my clothes," he said. "I have to get out of these clothes."

"Sure, partner," said the officer.

They visited about the killing and Banjo sickened. A storm rose in his head. Smoke and pig tails and pink, wrinkled up little bodies swirled about. He took deep breaths to settle his grinding stomach.

A door slammed. An officer jerked his revolver free and aimed it past Banjo's head. "Put that down!" Banjo turned to see. A shotgun exploded very near. He felt its thunder. He wondered why the police officer behind him did not return fire. Banjo thought the policeman was hit and spun to him. The officer remained firm, sighting down his barrel. "Put that down or I'll fire!"

Banjo turned back the other way. On the porch, still wearing his bloody shirt, the father held an upward pointed shotgun. A jagged hole in the porch roof above him rained dust and shards of wood. He roared, "I'll kill him!" He pumped another blast that tore more material out of the ceiling. "I'll kill that son-of-a-bitch! Then I'll kill his worthless dog!"

"No, you're not!"

Banjo saw tendons straining in the crouching police officer's neck.

"Get out of here," the officer told Banjo without moving his eyes.

Banjo looked for a place to dive. He checked on Dan and saw him disappearing behind the hood of the ambulance.

"Mister," the policeman called, "we're gonna kill you if you don't put that down. You have a right to be upset but you can't be shooting people."

Banjo hurried toward the trunk end of a police cruiser. His eye caught the shotgun barrel on the porch dropping quickly into firing position. A voice cried, "NO!"

Banjo dove for the pavement. Shots banged like a string of fire crackers. Pain flared in his knee when he struck the concrete. He scrambled behind the police car and he was still scrambling when, in the ringing silence that followed, someone yelled, "Ambulance! Ambulance!"

Banjo peeked from under the police car. The father lay on the porch and blood spread from his chest. Police rushed in, their weapons trained on him. One officer nudged the face with his boot. He looked for Dan and Banjo. "Get in here now, you guys!"

Banjo climbed to his feet and his knee failed. He grabbed it looking for a bullet hole and found instead a scraped and bloody knee. Dan carried two bags to the porch.

"Banjo," Dan called. "Get the car set up. I'll have the cops help me load him."

Banjo threw a switch in his head. The exchange of gunfire had not happened. The mangled girl, for the moment, ceased to be. What he had grieved over an instant ago became dry circumstances he was trained to deal with. Banjo set himself to do certain things he had done countless times and could do without thinking. Automatically, he hung IV bags from the ceiling and prepared oxygen and other equipment he would use to breathe for the man. An officer appeared in the back door. "Your partner says forget it."

"Okey doke." Banjo put things back in order and got out. He went to Dan standing on the porch and took a long stride from the top step to clear the thickening pool of blood. A shotgun blast had caught the man in the nose and his skull was now a crater. Small black holes dotted his shirt. Neither Dan nor Banjo spoke. Silent sadness gathered. Stunned faces peeked from windows in surrounding houses. Blue tinged gun smoke lingered in the air. Banjo smelled the rusty smell of blood that was almost a taste, and as he humanized again, the great, inevitable weight of the moment settled heavily into his shoulders.

"God damn him," cursed one officer.

"Well," said another, "A guy can't be trying to shoot someone and expect to get away with it."

Banjo wanted to cry. Instead he decided it was all over and nobody felt pain anymore. The father and daughter were together in a better place. He wondered if they might soon be eagles soaring together on the mountain winds.

Dan and Banjo did not speak until they had driven many blocks toward their next cover station.

After a time Dan said flatly, "I heard some buckshot hit the ambulance."

"Can you see where it hit?"

"I didn't look." Then as though finally thinking to ask, "You all right, Banjo?"

"Sure. I banged up my knee a little when I hit the ground but I'm fine. You?"

Dan stared out the window. "I saw him get blown away. I saw his face disappear. Now I'm looking around in me for something to feel but I can't find it."

"How are you supposed to feel?"

"I'm suppose to feel something, aren't I? You know when everyone is sad about something but you're not? You feel out of place and inappropriate; like there's something wrong with you. This is Greystone. This is when I hate him." Dan turned his searching face to Banjo. "You know?"

Banjo whispered, "I know." He drew in a deep breath and it trembled when he exhaled. A tear rolled off his cheek. He wiped his fingers across his eyes and tears blurred the road ahead.

Dan said, "At least you can do that, Banjo."

A headache seized Banjo behind his eyes. Thinking it was a hunger headache he turned down Broadway to see if any of the restaurants appeared tolerable.

Chapter 13

Banjo's gathering headache pushed him toward food. "So how's Pie in the Sky Pizza sound?"

"Oh, just out of this world," Dan said bitterly to the window.

"Yep, that's where I'd rather be, too." Banjo parked next to a fire hydrant. "Want anything?"

Dan said, "Not really."

Inside the restaurant Banjo's nose filled with the warm smells of garlic and spices. He hungrily put pizza combinations together in his head. A single siren yelp pierced his headache and caused it to pulse. Another customer heard also and smiled at him. "No rest for the rescuers."

"No friggin' lunch either." The restaurant door closed behind him and snapped the warm smells off clean. Hunger overcame his patience. "Goddamn well better be a good call," he said, settling himself behind the steering wheel.

Dan said, "Police have someone not breathing over in the Lincoln Park Projects."

Banjo liked that kind of information. In his state it gave him permission to drive aggressively and curse drivers who would not pull over. He punched the accelerator. He swung into traffic and forced cars to swerve and screech to stops. Kids on the sidewalk waved at the passing ambulance and Banjo ignored them arrogantly.

Three story brick apartment buildings surrounded a bare, dirt courtyard that was littered with abandoned children's toys. Stiff brown grass pushed through bulges in the asphalt parking lot. A white fire engine grumbled noisily next to an old car propped up on jacks. Banjo stopped next to it. People hurried from their apartments toward a knot of angry residents surrounding police officers and fire fighters. They shouted at them and accused them of murder. Others yelled insults from open windows. Within the outraged circle Banjo saw the plain features of an unmarked police car. He and Dan elbowed roughly through the surrounding crowd. An inner ring of police officers protected firemen who performed CPR on a man. The ring opened to let Dan and Banjo in then quickly closed.

Banjo leaned close to Dan in order to be heard over the shouting. "I'll intubate. You defibrillate."

A fireman compressed the chest of a black man whose jowly face jiggled with each downward thrust. Dan kneeled next to him and tore open his silk shirt. Buttons sprang into the air. He scissored through the tee-shirt.

When his soft chest was exposed, another angry voice demanded, "Show that man some respect!"

A red ellipse of raw skin created by the friction of chest compressions had already developed between the man's nipples. Dan stuck his hand down the man's pants. "Chest compressions are circulating blood," he announced to those near. "They're generating a pulse down here."

Banjo leaned closer to Dan. "What?" His skinned knee hurt when he shifted along the asphalt.

"Shit!" cried the voice. "I said show some respect. Don't be shoving your hands down the man's pants."

Banjo turned toward the voice. "Back off! We're paramedics and we're trying to save his life."

"You don't care about no black man's life. You're just finishing off what these fuckin' policeman started."

The patient's hands were beneath his back. Banjo pulled on one arm to gain arm access for an IV but it remained under him. Banjo tugged again then looked. "Why's he handcuffed?" he called to the inner circle of police uniforms.

"This upstanding figure tried to jump my compadre, Rocky, who was in trouble."

Banjo turned quickly toward the sound of Zagata's voice.

"So I choked him down. Rocky's pretty skinny and not so good at droppin' a goof."

"Take the cuffs off, Zagata."

"Why? He's a dealer and he's been poisoning these kids here." Zagata gestured broadly to the young, belt high faces in the crowd. "I don't understand why you always want to save little men; especially one who wanted to hurt a police officer."

"Jesus, Zagata. These people are going nuts. I know he's a prisoner but let us do our job so we can all get out of here."

Zagata was suddenly defensive. "Prisoner! He's no prisoner. What are you talking, prisoner? I cuffed him to make sure he wasn't going anywhere until you showed up. You saying I hurt prisoners? You saying I did something to that prisoner at the jail? Your partner's been talking out of school about that, you know."

Dan snapped at Zagata. "Will one of you just take off the goddamn cuffs. Argue about it later."

Zagata turned his scar to Banjo and it moved in a menacing snake-like way. "I'm hearing your old partner saying things about me that are highly inflammatory."

"Fine," agreed Banjo impatiently. "Now let us go to work."

Rocky hurried after his handcuff key. "Good Lord, Larry. It ain't that big a deal. He only pushed me around a little. Let these guys do their job. I want to get out of here, too."

Zagata, ignoring the taunting crowd, patiently explained to his partner, "But Poncho, I don't like being falsely accused. His partner was falsely accusing me and Banjo is agreeing that he did."

Banjo felt the crowd surge against the blue circle of safety and yelled, "Goddamnit, Zagata!"

Rocky uncuffed the man then patted Zagata's chest. He said, "I know, Larry. A guy doesn't like being accused of something wrongly. I know that. Now let these people do what they have to and you and I will go talk about it."

Banjo prepared the necessary equipment to slip a tube into the man's trachea. He watched a fireman's efforts to ventilate the patient and judged them good, though he detected a distant gurgling, the sound of air reaching the stomach and threatening to displace its contents. Then he allowed himself a moment to sense the emotional charge around the patient. The predictable urgency was present but the resuscitation was quiet and smooth. The pace did not tumble carelessly over itself. Banjo lost sight of Zagata and fell into the rhythm of their efforts to save this man. He passed the tube into his throat.

"Okay," Dan said. "He's in fib. Clear the patient." Everyone removed their hands. Dan pressed paddles to the man's chest. His heavy chest muscles jerked as a unit. "Let me look first before you resume CPR," Dan told the fireman.

All eyes but Banjo's watched the heart monitor. Banjo fingered the large external jugular vein in the patient's neck. He swabbed it with alcohol and bent the IV needle slightly to accommodate the angle of approach to the vein. He slipped it beneath the skin.

Dan paused. "All right. Let me see."

Banjo stretched across the patient to see the monitor. "What do you have there, partner?"

Dan pointed. "What is that? Do you think those are organized enough to support a blood pressure?"

Banjo put his fingers to the unconscious man's neck and watched wildly changing complexes march across the screen. Dan pressed two fingers against his cheek in thought.

Another accusation rifled in from the outer crowd. "So is he alive, or did this cop kill him?"

Zagata yelled, "Hey! Hey! You just keep your mouth shut or I'll run you out of here."

"Well," Banjo offered, "let's get the epinephrine in him and run some fluid. That's my vote."

"Sounds good to me."

Banjo injected the medicine and opened up the IV flow control. He watched the IV bag shrink as fluid drained from it. He placed his stethoscope on the man's chest and his eyes traveled up and down the patient, watching, watching as he listened. Dan fingered for a pulse at the patient's groin.

Dan said, "His rate's kicking up. Let's see if he has a pulse. Stop CPR, please." The fireman sat back on his knees and blew hard out of his mouth. "Banjo, get a blood pressure. He's perfusing down here."

Banjo wrapped the cuff around the man's arm. He watched the gauge as he pumped it up and he noticed the man's neck muscles contracting with respiratory effort. "Pressure's one sixteen. We've got some respiratory drive, too."

"Okay." Dan looked the patient over and pursed his lips thoughtfully. "Give him some lidocaine and I think we're ready to go."

*****

At the hospital Banjo sat in the back of the ambulance and let his legs extend across the vinyl floor hopelessly stained with old blood and dirt. A tingling weariness settled into him. He shivered and wished he had worn long underwear. Steam rose from his breath and the cold air dried out his face and hands. He looked outside for snow clouds. Half his shift had passed.

He listened to his quiet breathing and tried to ignore the blood surging painfully in his head. Another ambulance idled to the dock and clanked its loose bumper against it. He heard the dayroom door squeak open and bump shut.

Banjo's head fell against the ambulance wall. How many times had he sat here exhausted? How many faces had he looked into from this seat? How many more would he see? His back hurt, having twisted wrong lifting the man in cardiac arrest.

The man would live. In fact, he woke up enough to pat Banjo on the knee in thanks. His knee still felt a little warm on that spot. Banjo's other knee stung and a bloody head appeared in his fresh memory. He tried to shake that clear. A red and shriveled baby floated behind his eyes. He drew a sharp breath and threw his head forward into his hands. "She's dead," he told himself. "She's dead and in a better place than I am."

Why? A small part of Banjo still asked such questions. But he had asked so many similar unanswerable questions that they now bored him.

Someone grabbed his arm. Banjo startled and turned. Zagata's scar trembled with rage inches from his face. "I thought," he hissed, standing in the side door, "that you had

157

more loyalty than that. You should have sat on your partner back at the jail. Now I have to keep an eye on you, too. I'm trying to protect those kids out there; trying to keep my partner from getting killed. Now I have to keep an eye out for a couple of pushy paramedics. That's a lot, Mr. Paramedic Man. That's an awful lot. I can't be doing all that but now I have to." `

Dan interrupted, "Saddle up, Banjo. We're headed to a seizure. Later, Zagata."

*****

After the call they were brought back to Denver General to cover the city from there before getting lunch. Banjo thought more about Clayton's suspicions and said, "Zagata's crazy."

Dan said, "Stay out of his way."

"Clayton thinks he saw Zagata kill a prisoner."

"I've heard him saying that. I told him to stop. Zagata has ears in this division and he's been dropping in on Clayton's calls."

"He's been dropping in on me." Banjo let that fact settle in. He remembered Zagata's sudden insecurity when he referred to hurting prisoners. Fear clutched his stomach and twisted it. "What if Clayton is right?"

"Wouldn't surprise me."

"You're pretty clipped in your answers, partner, and I'm feeling all alone in this ambulance. What are you thinking that you aren't saying?"

"Zagata's name has been coming up in supervisor meetings more and more. He's been buddying up to paramedics. He buys them things, loans them money. He's gotten a few into gambling and who knows what. Pretty soon he's leaning hard on them until they pay back his favors."

"Leans on them how?"

Dan looked at Banjo. "Follows them around first. Maybe calls them up at odd hours. Gives them speeding tickets. I've never heard it getting beyond that."

"What's he having paramedics do?"

"He's got four or five doing little favors. Not much that we can figure out; the names of nurses; gossip around the division. Once he wanted to know how much the division spent on overtime. Personally, I think he's probing. I think he's trying to find paramedics who will steal drugs for him or give him physician DEA numbers so he can forge prescriptions. That's my guess." Dan gestured vaguely. "I don't know. Maybe all he wants is a little Zagata army that will stand and salute him. We're keeping an eye on him."

"Then why is he knocking off prisoners?"

Dan laughed. "If he is he'll probably just get a little administrative leave. Nothing ever happens to Zagata. We're worried that he's trying to build the same structure of intimidation here that he built in the police department."

Dan shifted in his seat to face his partner. "Remember the Delphi shooting you and I were on? Did you ever wonder why the cops were right on top of that? That was right around when Zagata was accused of stealing cocaine from the evidence room and selling it. I've wondered if that wasn't a drug deal Zagata and his buddies put together that went bad. But I don't remember ever seeing Zagata around there."

"Do you really think he'd let us get into that much trouble?"

"Oh, no. I doubt he set us up. I think it was just a screwed up deal."

"But what if he did kill that prisoner like Clayton thinks?" Banjo asked, remembering Clayton's prophecy and wondering if circumstances would twist in that cruel way to require him to stand between Zagata and his black intentions.

"What did you tell Clayton about it?"

"I told him that if he wasn't absolutely sure, to forget it."

"I'd say that's a pretty good answer. Zagata may be probing for soft spots. We're very worried he'll try to turn things rotten around here. The word is to stay the hell away from him."

Banjo itched under his second chance vest and he squirmed to scratch it. "So I feel like a fine, upstanding citizen now." His hunger headache swelled behind his eyes and he squeezed his fingers into them. "Goddamn! If I don't get something to eat my head will explode."

*****

Back at the hospital Banjo marched straight into dispatch. Two dispatchers slouched in their chairs. "Listen to me, gents," Banjo told them. "I understand you promised to take us out of service for lunch after this last call." A status board near one dispatcher showed the location and availability of all ambulances. The single available car was Banjo's. Both dispatchers turned and smiled cunningly.

On their way to cover a district instead of getting lunch, Banjo told Dan, "Goddamn dispatchers all need to be taken out and shot."

"Number five."

"Go screw yourself!" Then Banjo lifted the microphone and answered with his location. "Five's at thirty-second and Irving."

"At the District One Police Station on a cutting."

"All right," he answered with a nasty nasal twang. Then he asked, "This an officer?"

"Didn't say," answered the electronic voice.

Banjo spun around the block, one hand steering, the other pushing angrily against the intrusive microphone. He raced through the streets then hit the brakes hard at red lights. They hit their door panels when Banjo turned corners. At the police station Banjo threw the transmission into park before the ambulance stopped. The gears locked and clanked and the ambulance lurched.

A sergeant met them inside the precinct station.

"What happened?" Banjo asked.

The sergeant looked puzzled. "Nothing happened. Why?"

"Dispatcher sent us here on a cutting?"

The officer jerked his head in surprise. "Well, just a minute. I'll check." He stepped down the hall to the front desk. "Anybody here call an ambulance for a cutting?"

Banjo over heard the negative answers.

"Sorry, gents," the sergeant told them. "Must have been a mistake."

*****

Back at Denver General Banjo again asked, "Now can we get some lousy lunch?"

"You can try."

Banjo repeated nastily, "You can try."

At the 7-11 on Colfax everything looked good to him. He bought barbecued chicken that had been warming since lunch time hours earlier, a pint of chocolate milk, Fritos, and, as a snack later, malted milk balls. He gave the clerk a five dollar bill and got back a few coins. He tried to calculate how many thousands of dollars he had dropped over the years in 7-11 stores, but the mathematics proved too complex for his starved brain.

The afternoon was dusky and colder as Banjo carried his heavy bag of food to the ambulance. The leading edge of rush hour lengthened the lines of headlights at traffic signals and briefly Banjo wished his job so normal he could leave work right now like these people and worry only about what was on TV tonight. He dropped his sack between the seats and reached in for a chicken thigh. After his first greasy bite the dispatcher called and directed them to a freeway accident. Banjo threw the mangled piece back and realized he had forgotten napkins. He wiped his face with the back of his hands and his hands on his pants, which now shined with chicken grease.

Banjo maneuvered onto the freeway and asked Dan, "Am I smarter than the average dispatcher?"

Dan laughed. "Yeah, I'd say."

Banjo swung into the fast lane and shut down the siren. He shot past freeway drivers before they realized an emergency vehicle approached. "Then why am I out here in the cold, starving, and running bullshit calls? Those guys sit in there smug as you please, warm and well fed, telling me where to go. Now, why is that?"

He slowed and yelped the siren at a driver not checking his rear view mirror. The driver look up and the car jerked right. Banjo continued. "I'm tired of jumping when some idiot says jump. Maybe I should be a supervisor. Then I could be one of the idiots saying jump. I'm getting old, Dan."

Traffic slowed. Rows of red tail lights glowed ahead. Plumes of white exhaust billowed in the cold air above the cars. Banjo saw police emergency lights ahead where cars angled across two lanes of freeway. He brought the siren to life to pick his way through the thickening cars.

"I'm old, Dan," Banjo repeated again, coming back to his thoughts. "I can't be doing this forever. Let the young kids get the daylights scared out of them. I don't want to come to work and never go home again. That could've happened to either of us today."

"I've been thinking about that, too."

"You don't have to do this anymore. You're rich. I'm stuck. Nothing else I could do. Nothing else I'd want to do, despite what they do to you." Banjo pointed at a car just ahead. "Give that guy the spot light."

Dan directed the light beam into the car's rear view mirror and wiggled it back and forth. The driver looked up and Banjo shrugged hugely at him. The car merged into the right lane and let the ambulance pass.

Banjo said, "I don't know what else I would do. I know I don't want to be bored. I know I want to do important things. Sometimes I think I'd like to stay right here forever. But God," Banjo added. "I don't know where else I can go in this place."

"Well, stand-by. Half Deck's been saying there may be an opening in the supervisorial ranks."

"Eric?"

Dan nodded.

"If I became a supervisor would you stick around? I mean, I'd need someone close I could trust."

"I'm not going anywhere," Dan answered.

Banjo pulled around the damaged cars and parked so they protected the ambulance from traffic. From the ambulance Banjo saw that the involved cars were empty. A group of people huddled around a policeman. "Looks like none of these people are going anywhere, either." Banjo plunged a hand into his sack of food. "I'll just stay right here and finish up lunch while you check them."

Dan shivered into the cold and made his way from person to person asking questions. Soon he hopped back in the ambulance and slammed the door. "It's cold out there! I think it's going to snow."

Banjo idled the ambulance away from the accident scene. A tow driver jumped into the stream of cars with an outstretched hand. Banjo waved his thanks, reached for his third piece of chicken, and powered into the opening traffic.

They exited the freeway and left the dense rush hour traffic. They heard the dispatcher call another ambulance, "Number six, cover a shooting at the Logan Street Diner, Logan and Louisiana. Sounds good. Use caution. Be awhile before a cover car arrives. The police are having roll call."

Banjo stopped crunching his Frito. "Now that sounds interesting."

The other ambulance answered, "Six copy."

After a few minutes Banjo heard, "Six calling. We've arrived without cover."

"Okay. Use extreme caution."

A few more quiet minutes passed. The ambulance six crew called again. "Six calling. Is this supposed to be in the diner here?"

"That's affirmative. In the Logan Street Diner."

"Okay. We're looking."

Banjo loved sneaking around buildings in tricky circumstances. Even listening to this on the radio thrilled him.

"Six! Six! Get cover in here quick. A waiter and some crazy guy are having a gun fight. Get them here quick. Please!"

"Six," called the dispatcher, "get out of there."

"Six back. They've got hostages and we're being fired on. Bullets are everywhere."

"Number six." Banjo recognized Half Deck's voice. "From the supervisor. Leave now."

"If I leave now they'll have another hostage. My partner's in there."

Dan and Banjo looked at each other, their eyes wide, jaws slack. "What do you think?" Dan asked.

"I'd think we'd better." And Banjo wheeled sharply around the corner and headed toward the diner. He wondered if this call might present him with his crucial moment. He feared it might and felt himself begin to tremble.

"Six calling. Police cover is here but get us a second ambulance. We've got two down here."

"Six. Get out."

"We're pinned here."

Only blocks away now, Dan picked up the microphone. "Number five, we'll cover that. We're two minutes out."

"Copy five. Stay back until police secure the scene."

"Copy," Dan answered.

Banjo took a deep breath to settle himself. Sweat lined his palms. "Hell of a shift today, partner. I'll need a beer when this one's over."

Dan did not answer. He set up an IV bag.

A police cruiser barricaded Logan Street a block from the diner. The officer at the car waved them in. "Keep your heads down," he called. Banjo saw the first ambulance parked near the diner's windows. Stupid, he thought. He idled in and noticed police officers with drawn weapons trotting along side his ambulance to in get close. Banjo stopped. The diner, quiet and empty looking, was only steps away.

Banjo pointed, "Let's get behind that fence there and we'll plan this thing." Both left the ambulance through the door opposite the diner. Banjo clutched the portable radio. Dan carried trauma kits. They crouched behind a low wooden fence. From their spot ten yards behind ambulance Six they saw no sign of the paramedics. Police with shotguns and heavy vests took up firing positions around the diner. "We're not doing any good here," Banjo said. "Let's get over to their ambulance."

Dan hunched near the end of the protective fence. He turned to Banjo. "I want you right on my ass."

"I'll be there."

Hunched over, Dan bolted toward the orange and white ambulance sitting eerily quiet. Banjo plunged after him as he would into icy water, all at once, defying the chilling consequences, hoping he would emerge. He anticipated a ringing shot and a murderous crush into his left side before he crossed the distance. He listened for it. He shot a glance at the diner, but heard only the rush of wind against his ears and the distant shriek of more sirens. A dog barked somewhere. There was even a rustling of garbage cans. But he heard no shot.

He had five more yards to cross. Dan reached the rear of the ambulance. He looked inside. Banjo thought it odd that Dan would look there and not back at his exposed partner. Banjo would have felt safer. He anticipated the shot tragically at his last step and shrugged his left shoulder protectively. He reached the ambulance.

Dan told him, "Everyone's inside." They went to the side door. The crew performed CPR on a woman with a small, black hole in her chest. A man sat on the squad bench watching. Blood darkened the right side of his shirt. The paramedic at the lifeless woman's head ordered, "Get him out of here. He's been hit in the abdomen. He's doing okay so far, though. Aren't you, partner."

Dan said to him, "Can you walk?"

"I think so."

"You understand what's happening? We may have bad guys inside wanting to shoot. But we need to get you out of here now."

"I know what's going on. I shot one of the bad guys."

"All right," Dan said. "We'll worry about that later. Right now you're going to have to run to that other ambulance. My partner and I will protect you as best we can. Let's go." Dan helped him out. The three stepped to the back of the ambulance. It seemed like a football field away. More police gathered behind positions of cover and drew their weapons.

Some crouched behind the ambulance. "We're taking off," Banjo yelled at them, pointing to their patient. He heard Dan tell the patient, "Keep your eyes on that ambulance and keep running. My partner and I will stay between you and the diner. Ready?" He turned to Banjo. "Ready?"

"Quit talking and let's do it."

"Go." The three sprinted. The patient grunted hard.

Panting, Banjo told his partner, "I'm putting this sucker in warp drive as soon as I get behind the wheel. I'm a sitting duck in this thing until we're out of here."

"That's fine. We'll manage."

Banjo opened the side door. Dan and the patient climbed in.

Banjo crawled to the driver's seat through the passenger door.

"Hang on," Dan said. "Give us a second to get secured.

Banjo rolled his eyes and remained sprawled down and out of sight. When he heard, "Okay," he popped into the driver's seat, pulled the shift lever into drive, and hit the gas in single quick motion.

The ambulance shot forward. "Bump!" Banjo called back. He hit the curb and bounced across a lawn to keep a row of trees between the ambulance and diner. He stayed on the sidewalk until he reached the intersection. Then he turned right and picked up speed toward Denver General. "You okay back there?"

"We're fine."

"Was Six coming before we turned the corner?"

"Didn't see."

Safe now, Banjo relaxed a little. He took his right hand off the steering wheel and drove as he usually did with his left index finger and thumb. He sent ambulance Six his best thoughts.

Half Deck and two crews of paramedics met the ambulance and helped wheel the stretcher in. Half Deck, his tooth pick erect, asked, "Did they blow that dirt ball away?"

"Don't know," Banjo answered. The strength even to hold himself straight was gone. "Don't know. This guy we brought in said he got somebody."

"How's Six doing? I tried to get them out of there. But hell, I would have stayed myself. You can't have some damn supervisor back at headquarters running the scene."

"Don't know. Don't know. What time is it?"

"Nineteen hundred hours."

"Good. Just thirty more minutes." Banjo turned away from Half Deck. He walked up to Eighth Avenue and looked eastward to catch the first glint of emergency lights growing more distinct. He trained his ears for a siren. Banjo reviewed the scene, searching for reasons that could have compelled him to stay, for he had to root out any evidence at all that he had run when he should have stayed. He found none. He relaxed further. Now he could safely relive this call and not be found guilty.

A distant yelp caught his ear. Red, white, and blue lights winked at him far up Eighth Avenue. They gained focus and definition as the ambulance sped toward him. By now television crews had gathered.

Banjo remained quiet and within himself as he watched ambulance Six bump safely against the dock. The crew hurried their patient to the waiting surgeons. He walked to the ambulance still hot from its hard drive and considered how moments earlier it had stood witness to gunfire, hostages, and death, and now waited here like a faithful horse for another call. Banjo looked for bullet holes. He found none. Then he remembered with delighted surprise.

Searching the rear of his ambulance, Banjo found several shiny ellipses where shotgun pellets had struck at an angle and gouged the paint. His heart raced again as shotgun blasts thundered in his head. His stinging knee grabbed his attention. That had happened so long ago, he thought, just today.

A member of the Six crew left the emergency department pushing a bloody stretcher. Banjo crowded to him past the Chief, Half Deck, and the reporters. "You okay?"

He shook his head. "I saw my partner go inside then bullets went everywhere. I just knew I had lost a partner and I was damned if I was leaving until I got him back. Then he and your patient drug the woman out. I don't know how they did

167

it." He waved at his ambulance. "I have to clean this shit up." A sheet of blood congealed on the floor. IV needles jabbed in the squad bench after failed IV attempts stood erect like tiny, limbless trees. Oxygen and IV tubing coiled on the floor. Their packaging soaked up blood. Banjo rubbed the paramedic across his shoulders. "You need some help?"

"No, I'll do it."

"You doing okay?"

"No, I'm not doing worth a damn. I just want to be left alone." He climbed into the ambulance. "Close the door, would you."

Banjo slammed the door and stood there with his arms crossed. The Chief saw and directed the press and others into the dayroom. Dan walked from the emergency department. He also sagged. Banjo said, "I used to feel this way after combat. All scared and shook and jazzed. I know I need to rest but I'm going too fast to go home."

"Well, I'm going home. The oncoming crew can clean up."

"How about a beer?" Banjo's joints hurt and his energy had bled out but the shift left him full of electricity. Images spun in his head. His knee stung. A car backfired and he jolted toward his ambulance before remembering where he was. He needed a beer, two beers, three beers; he needed numbness. "Come on, Dan. Lauren's still working. Just one beer. I'll go nuts if I go home now."

Dan motioned slowly with his head. "There's Snoop. Ask her."

Desperate for company, Banjo looked at her.

"Hey, Snooper,"

She turned. "Hey, you," she answered.

"How about a beer?"

"Why?"

Banjo stopped. He thought. He did not know how to answer. Then, without insinuation, he told her. "I had a bad shift and I need some company before I go home."

She shrugged. "Sounds all right."

Chapter 14

Banjo saw steamy car exhaust and gathering clouds in The Parlour's white window etchings. His memory added red tail lights and a whiff of gasoline. He liked the little recollection. It meant his needed sweet journey to numbness awaited inside like a mistress. The door handle was cold and stung his hand. When the familiar warm darkness inside enclosed him, Banjo pointed to the bartender. "Jackson! Two big ones with the usual jolter." His favorite booth sat empty and inviting though many people occupied the bar. Crossing to it, he looked for Snooper but did not find her. A little of his pleasing anticipation slipped away.

Soon Jackson followed with a tray heavy with full glasses. The bartender asked, "Having company tonight, Banjo?"

"If she ever shows up."

"She driving?"

"Don't go being a mother." Banjo put the amber filled shot glass to his lips and inhaled its seducing aroma. Then his head and hand jerked back in a single, well practiced movement. Whiskey burned a trail down his throat. He drank deeply from his cold beer and sighed a great releasing sigh which sounded like water quenching fire. He waved his hand at the remaining drinks. "One more round," he ordered, "to back up these here."

The electricity popping within him quieted and he smiled and the world became a less treacherous place in which to live. Banjo settled himself comfortably and wondered what kept Snooper. He checked his watch. He played with his fractured image in the beveled mirror and was quickly bored.

"Well, hell, Greystone," he sighed to himself. Just you and me again, I guess." Feeling justly deserving, Banjo gulped the other tumbler empty and finished off his beer. Jackson brought more. Banjo took the journal from his backpack and turned to the pages that sandwiched the Denver General shoulder patch. Banjo wrote.

'Hell of a shift tonight, guy. I about got picked off. Twice, in fact. A little girl got eaten up by a dog. Cops blew her father away when he went nuts with a shotgun. Zagata's on my back. Twisted, huh.'

He sipped the foam off a fresh beer.

'I feel like cats are prowling around inside me. You know what Dan said after the dog attack? He couldn't feel much afterwards and he said, This is when I'm most like Greystone. This is when I hate Greystone. You kept all that stuff in. I can't be that way anymore. It's like my closet is full and stuff is spilling out all over the place.'

Banjo drank savagely from his beer. Some dribbled down his chin and onto his uniform shirt. He held the empty glass aloft. "Nurse!" He looked around at the knots of people gathered at tables. "Goddamnit, where is she?" He turned back to the wall. Gloomy loneliness pulled him further into himself. He ran his hand over the page to wipe up a dribble of beer. The ink smeared. Banjo continued.

'How come kids die, John? I try to find explanations. Even after all these years I try. Clayton believes people who die horribly are rewarded in another life. I don't know. Maybe. Where are you right now, old partner?'

Banjo waited as though listening, then continued.

'I want to understand. I want to forgive. But I don't know how. I don't know how to figure this out.'

"Who you writing to, Sunshine?"

Banjo jumped. He placed an open hand over the page he had written on. "I keep a personal journal sometimes. Writing about tonight's shift." He slipped the shoulder patch between the pages and closed the journal back up as Snooper slid into the bench seat opposite him. She took one of his beers and sipped. "One of these *is* mine, right?"

"I thought you were coming right over?"

"I did. What did you expect? I'd drop everything and come running?"

Banjo grunted and looked at her. Snooper's face, framed by squared off bangs and straight hair, was plain and her features resembled a young boy's. She leaned over her skinny arms crossed on the table and looked straight at him. He sipped from his tumbler of whiskey and smiled and huffed a quiet laugh. He liked her sass.

She asked, "What's so funny?"

"You."

"So, what's so funny about me?" she repeated.

"You."

Her back straightened. "What's so funny?"

"You, I said."

The edges of her eyes crinkled up in calculation. "Same can be said for you."

"What's that, Cupcake?"

Her face softened and she laughed. "Cupcake. Is that what you call women?"

"Never called a woman Cupcake before in my life. Where'd you get Sunshine?"

"I call all men Sunshine."

"Uh-huh."

"Men I think amount to something."

Snooper caught him off guard. He squinted one eye, thinking about the comment. Her smile retreated to a hard line across her face. He asked, "So you think I amount to something?" He wanted her smile back.

Snooper took a drink. "Don't you?"

"This is kind of weird, don't you think? You always answer a question with a question?"

"It's like when you're on the streets," she told him. "You're real careful who you trust."

Banjo quickly felt excluded from her world and grew bored.

Snooper's eyes opened fully for a moment. "Sorry. Not too many men invite me out for a beer. I don't know what to think of this." Her mouth remained opened as though to speak words that were suddenly no longer there. "I mean, I don't know you very well. You were my field instructor and I admired you. But we've never been friends. I don't know what you're after here." She gestured at him. "You said you wanted to talk about your shift."

The beer began its anesthetizing magic. Numbness crept into his fingers and exhaustion settled in where electricity had sizzled. In his haze Banjo felt safe enough to start. "Did you hear about the shooting Dallas and Ray had?"

"No."

"Some guy shot up the Logan Street Diner. Dallas was inside when they were still shooting at each other. The cook took a round in the gut. Some woman got it in the chest. Dallas and the cook drug her out."

"Dallas okay?"

"Pretty shook, but he's okay." Banjo remembered running and running and running toward an ambulance that grew no closer. His fist went to his mouth and bumped. He wished she would take his hand as Lauren would and lightly entwine her fingers in his. He wished she could see inside him and touch just the right spot. She folded her hands and shifted so that she looked less angular.

Banjo added, "Dan and I were second in. We heard on the radio that one of them was held hostage. When we got there we had to shuttle a patient from one car to another with the bad guy still in the building."

"Police ever get him?"

Banjo shook his head no. "We left when the Special Services Unit was about to go in. I haven't heard."

"Were you in the open?"

Banjo nodded. "Like I was back in the jungle waiting for the shot I wouldn't hear." Banjo ordered another beer and abruptly added, "Then we had that gunfight. Police killed a guy."

Snooper frowned. "I thought you said the shooting was all over when you got there."

Banjo said impatiently, "This is a different call."

"You mean the shooting that's been all over the news? The one where police killed a man whose daughter ..."

"That's the one," he quickly finished for her.

"You were on that, too?"

"Right in the middle."

Snooper whispered, "Wow."

"The cops fired shots right past my head. I tell you, Snoop, I could almost feel the muzzle blast. And when I dove for cover and my knee hit the pavement it hurt like hell and I thought I'd been shot. Christ, I thought I'd been hit. Twice in a shift I thought I'd gotten it. That's asking a little much." He took a deep breath and gulped more beer. He pressed a hand to his stomach. "The guy's head disappeared. Dan saw that. He said it just disappeared. Can you imagine? There's a shot and his head is gone. Just like that. It's all so twisted. One minute I'm feeling sorry for him. The next minute he's pumping buck shot into the air. Then he's dead." He shrugged abruptly. "All in a day's work." Banjo held his face tightly against what lay beneath.

"That's tough."

Her response disappointed. He made a that's-the-way-it-goes face and swallowed more beer.

She looked at her fingers. "You and I had a call on an infant death when you were my field instructor. Over in the Sun Valley projects."

Banjo nodded, but did not recall.

Snooper continued. "My sister's baby died just as unexpectedly. When I looked into the crib and saw that mottled little body, all I could think of was my niece. I thought I would lose my mind. I didn't think I reacted enough for you to notice but I must have. On the way out you told me something that has gotten me through things like this. You said there was no explanation for such things. The only thing we can do is choose how we respond. That was exactly what I needed to hear. That gave me control over something I thought was uncontrollable. I think I would have resigned otherwise."

Banjo searched his mind. "I said that?"

"Sure did, Sunshine."

"I didn't think I had such thoughts in me."

"I use that baby to appreciate the other children in my life."

Banjo studied her simple face. It was fresh and clear, like morning in the mountains. Banjo let go a quiet chuckle.

She asked again, "What's so funny?"

An expanding smile crossed his face. "You."

She smiled also. "So, what's so funny?"

"You."

"I said, what's so funny?"

"You, I said."

She let it go. "You make me nervous."

"Why?"

"I always get nervous when people laugh at me. Don't you?"

Banjo laughed more. "I like being with you."

"You're a strange guy." Then she hurried to add, "You're strange in a nice sort of way. I mean, I don't even know you but you seem to be always sideways with the rest of the world. I like that. That's the kind of strange I mean."

Banjo warmed. "I always feel like I have to explain myself to people."

"Screw 'em," she said.

"All the way," Banjo agreed.

"Out of our lives."

"Back to their offices."

"Where their small minds can play."

Banjo flattened his hand over his face. He laughed from his belly which no longer felt pierced by a knife. He looked at her. "This is strange."

"What?"

"Don't start."

She smiled. "Don't start what?"

"Don't you think this is really strange?"

"What?"

"Snoop!"

"No. What's so strange about talking?"

"Talking's fine. But this? We cause each other to talk in circles and poems."

She looked back, puzzled. "What do you make of it, Inspector?"

"It's hard to tell, Sergeant."

"Do you suspect foul play?" she asked.

"I haven't had any foul play since I can't remember when."

"Yes," she said. "I recall similar circumstances."

Banjo asked, "Have you been searching out foul play?"

"I've been on guard against it."

"Why is that?"

She squinted knowingly at him. "Leads to no good."

He gave her conclusion thought. He tapped the table with a finger as though puzzling. "We should give this greater consideration later."

Snooper broke character. "Look. Little games are fine but something else is going on here. Men never show interest in me. What do you want?"

Banjo's sweet fun flew away. "Nothing. Company."

"Is that all?"

"What do you want? I should write this in blood?" He gulped a shot glass empty and drank his beer half down. Snooper blurred and he lost sensation in his legs. "I had a lousy shift. I wanted some lousy company. I invite you and what do I get? Suspicion!"

"Listen up, Sunshine, you're feeling sorry for yourself. The way I figure, you like feeling sorry for yourself because you can get other people feeling the same way for you. Not me, Bub. I don't want any part of that. And I am sure I'm not going to watch somebody get roaring drunk because they can't make better decisions about how to handle their job."

Banjo slapped the table with both hands. "Party's over. I don't need some woman trying to impress me with how tough she is." He raised his voice. "I don't need some woman thinking men owe her something. I don't need some woman always after fifty-one percent of everything."

"What the hell does that mean, fifty-one percent? You're crying in your beer and you want me to pat you on the back and say there, there. Well, I'm not going to do it. If you need someone, go see your shrink."

Banjo's fist thundered down onto the table. The glasses jumped. "I am not seeing a shrink!"

She waved a hand in the air as though striking on the obvious. "Everybody knows it."

"You're a goddamn paramedic. We do the same thing. I would have thought you'd support the people you work with."

"Support the people I work with. That's perfect. Just perfect. I don't even know you. We get into these weird little word games and suddenly you're asking me about the last time I had sex and if I'm looking for it now. And you want me to support you?"

"You're the one who started this. You are not going to pin your hang-ups on me. I got enough of my own. No wonder you act so tough. You got nothing underneath."

"What?"

"You got nothing underneath!"

"What!"

Banjo said it deliberately. "You got nothing underneath." He laughed.

"What's so funny?"

"You."

"You son-of-a-bitch." She grabbed up her beer and threw it in his face.

Banjo shot upward and banged his sore knee on the table. "Bitch!" He splashed the remains of his beer across her chest. She wore no bra and her sweatshirt clung to her small breasts. Excitement flamed in him. "You got no tits, either."

She stood and shoved her red face at him. Banjo met her face midway across the table. His jaw stung and his head snapped back. Snooper's tiny fist swung past. He pushed her into her seat. Bar patrons halted their conversations. Forks were held in mid-air, mouths hung open.

Jackson came running. "Both of you! Out of here. Right now. Banjo, you stay gone for awhile. You understand?"

"Me! She hit me first!"

"Her, too. I don't want to see your faces around here for a long time. Now beat it before I call the cops."

Snooper snatched her backpack and broke past the tables. Banjo followed. Outside she faced him, her fists jammed against her bony hips. "Well?" she demanded.

The alcohol and cold air quickly killed his energy. "Well, what?"

She stared hatred at him. "Oh, why don't you just keep walking."

His head jerked with sudden confusion. "This is a sidewalk. Why don't you use it?" He waited. She stood firm. His teeth chattered. "So what's going on here? Are we seeing who gets cold first and walks away?"

She crossed her arms tightly and shivered. She looked like a child refusing to come in from the cold.

"You're freezing," Banjo told her. "Tell you what. I'll do us both a favor and walk away first."

"You're not doing me any favors."

"Fine. Good night." He waved her off and started toward the hospital where his truck was parked.

"Sunshine."

He stopped. "What?"

"I don't like being pushed."

Weary and impatient, Banjo turned. "Listen. We have to work together. Let's pretend this didn't happen. Tomorrow we'll come to work; you'll be sassy and I'll be grumpy, just like usual. Okay?"

Her shoulders bobbed once. "Okay."

Across the yards of cold sidewalk, their eyes still touched. She nodded. So did Banjo.

Snooper said, "That's the foul play I told you about, Inspector."

"You're in a dangerous line of work, Sergeant."

She smiled and her chest moved with a silent laugh.

"What's so funny?" Banjo asked.

"You."

He chuckled. "You're a goofy broad."

"Yeah, once you get to know me."

"Get together again sometime maybe?"

Her face changed. Calculation came into her eyes. "Fat chance, Sunshine. You shoved me once. You'll never get close enough again."

Banjo's mouth hung loose. Snooper slung her backpack across her shoulders. She looked at him and her mouth worked to hold back another amused smile. "A goofy broad," she repeated. "That's perfect. Good night, Sunshine."

Banjo started for Denver General shaking his head. Some trick of the eye, some sleight of hand, some magical curse swept over him a moment ago. Their eyes had caught and rested easily upon each other. Banjo felt her, welcomed her into his closely held regions. He thought he glimpsed past her steel curtain and through her window. Then in that supremely tender instant, sometimes requiring weeks to work up to, for he lived in terror of cold rejection, he had asked to see her again and she slammed her window on his fingers. He did not see that coming. Snooper was dangerous. He would stay away from that one.

Chapter 15

Tenacious yellow leaves quivered horizontally in the elm trees, straining against the cold wind. They reminded Banjo, as he drove to work, of Nebraska winds. Those winds had burned his face, when, as a boy, he was kicked out of the house following a beating to wander alone through neglected fields wondering where, if not at home, he could feel safe. When hard winds blew grass over and tore leaves from their trees he knew the holidays bore down. The holidays, led by Thanksgiving only days away now, raised fears and aches as old and deep as the bones in his body.

At Denver General Banjo's fingers-stepped through his tightly clotted mailbox. He found nothing new and was disappointed. He caught a whiff of pipe smoke.

"Banjo. We need to speak." The Chief did not create a fantasy of mint juleps on the verandah or dips in the lake. He sounded impatient. Heat gathered under Banjo's second chance vest and sweat made his palms slick.

Banjo stiffened his guard. "Whatever you say, Chief."

A spirit thin wash of pipe smoke lay in the air of the Chief's office. He motioned Banjo to a seat with a nod in that direction. The Chief sat. He leaned over his crossed arms and extended his long neck toward Banjo. "Were you in The Parlour last night in uniform?" One eye squinted as though taking aim.

"Well ... yes."

"You were drunk, weren't you."

"Maybe. So what if I was. I was off duty and not the first to have a beer in uniform."

"You didn't just have a beer. You got drunk, again, and, even more incredible, you were in an altercation with another paramedic!" He shifted upright and slapped the arms of his chair. "This is not acceptable. Drunkenness, in or out of uniform, is inexcusable. It is the pinnacle of irresponsibility. Yet, you do it. Your drinking has impaired your work and --by heaven above, how could you do this? It has led you to brawling."

"I wasn't brawling. She hit me first."

The Chief nodded. "She hit you first. I see. Do you have any idea how juvenile that sounds? Do you have any idea how childish that reply is?" The Chief struck a blow to his desk. "Do you have even the slightest notion how such an awful display reflects on this division?"

Banjo's old shame rolled in like a cold fog. He had failed, again. He had disappointed, again. "But I wasn't really drunk."

"Just so. You're more concerned with what I may think of you than what you did to our reputation. Did you notice that Ms. Roberts was not in uniform? To the public one of my paramedics got into a shouting match with a woman, insulted her, then hit her."

Banjo pleaded, "That wasn't what happened!" Ancient pictures swirled through his brain. His father hit him. He threw his arms protectively over his head. His mother ran. Cold winds hit his face when his father opened the door and ordered him out.

The Chief slapped a hand on his desk top. "I had an enraged bartender call me this morning. A nurse from this hospital who saw you last night called in a high snot. Don't tell me what did and did not happen. You struck a woman!"

Banjo dropped his head into both hands. "We both said things. Then she hit me. So I shoved her back. That isn't an excuse but it's what happened."

"Are you still in counseling?"

The question surprised him. He looked up. "Why?"

"You are not asking the questions here. Are you still in counseling?"

Banjo mumbled, "Yes, sir."

The Chief examined him closely. "You are the best street paramedic we have but you are destroying yourself and your career. I decided some time ago I would do whatever was necessary to prevent that. I am no longer sure I maintain that conviction. Banjo, you betrayed this division."

"Oh, come on."

"You made us all look like brutes last night because you were drunk and could not control yourself. I will not allow that." The Chief drummed his fingers absently on his desk. "Effective today you are suspended for four days."

"What!"

"You are suspended. If you act out like this again I will terminate you." The Chief pointed a finger at Banjo. "Mind you, I will go to great lengths to keep you here but, by God above, I will not let you hurt this place. If you choose to let your life drain away in alcohol, so be it. But you will not hurt this paramedic division again. So help me, you will not." The Chief rocked back in his chair. "From this point onward, if you are drunk in uniform you will be terminated. If there is any evidence at all of inebriation at work, you will be terminated. You're next shift is a week from today. That is all I have to say."

"Wait a minute. Who said I was coming to work drunk?"

The Chief held up a hand. "Don't be coy. More than once you have had to either drink or use marijuana before coming to work. I can't prove it, but I know it."

Banjo sat in disbelief. He wondered how it would feel to wear his uniform back to the Debbie J without having soiled it with sweat and city dirt. "I'm calling the union."

The Chief ignored him as his father did after a strapping. Banjo had been beaten, now he was being thrown out of the house. Banjo's fist went to his mouth. He straightened his back against old remembered stings. He dreaded the cold winds outside. He wondered what Snooper would think. "What did you do to Snooper. She was yelling, too."

"Nothing. She was out of uniform and defended herself rather well."

"I suppose she's been in your office crying just like Jackson and that nurse."

"She has not. I sought her out."

Heat rose sharply into Banjo's face. He shoved his chair away and stood. Before bolting he noticed the Chief casually tamping new tobacco into his pipe. His father, just as indifferently, would pick up his own pipe and newspaper. A full aching groan broke from Banjo. He left the Chief's office and walked to his truck. The cold wind cut him.

*****

Dried maple leaves hung from the walls of Ernie Webster's office as though frozen in descent from a tree whose limbs extended well above the ceiling. They were gold, yellow, and brown and had been pressed flat. A child drawn picture of a pilgrim family was thumb tacked to his wall calendar. They wore black hats that looked like squared off tepees and their smiles were crescent moons laid on their sides. Father held a musket. Mother wore an apron. A turkey strutted on stick figure legs.

Banjo remembered his grade school Thanksgivings. He had searched the fields behind his house in Omaha for these same hand dwarfing maple leaves to press flat under books and tape to his bedroom window. He recalled scissoring out huge turkey bodies. He thought of Sonja, a grade school classmate. Her box of crayons contained sixty-four sharp pointed colors all standing straight. His held eight and were blunted and broken like bad teeth. He would offer her his as they colored knowing she would decline and instead push her box toward his desk.

His awful Thanksgiving uncertainties returned. He never knew how drunk his father would get or whether he, Banjo, would reach bed safely without new welts raised by his father's heavy belt.

"So, what's new, Banjo?" Ernie held his hands quietly in his lap.

Banjo looked him over. "Not much."

Ernie remained quiet. His hands were small and slender and his nails looked like he gave them more attention than a man should. He liked Ernie's sweater, though. A stand of green fir trees, accented with brilliant patches of yellow, swept across his chest.

His shift with the dog mauled girl and Logan Street Diner shooting pulled his attention from the sweater. That day had taken on space occupying shape and weight in his mind, like a tumor. His fist bumped at his mouth.

Ernie uncrossed then recrossed his legs. "Something's going on."

"I had an interesting experience with Dan. We had a shift with some real bad calls awhile back. Afterwards he said he envied me because I could cry and he couldn't. I thought that was strange. I figured him for being all put together right and able to get to his feelings and that. I looked at him as sort of a model to work toward. But he envied me."

"Sounds like you've moved past him."

"Yeah," Banjo answered vaguely. "He said he hated Greystone because he was like him. Years back we all envied Greystone for how strong he seemed. He never showed anything. People were circumstances, he used to say. Any paramedic got shook, they were crazy."

"Greystone's inability to show emotions was his disease. Just as it seems to be Dan's." Ernie's voice was flat. He sounded unconvinced that he had reached the heart of Banjo's present concern. "Crying as you did after a bad call is normal. I'm glad to hear about that."

Banjo shrugged.

After another long moment of silence Ernie changed the subject. "You want to try something different?"

Banjo's back tightened and his street instincts flew into place. "Like what?"

"I've been doing this with some of my other clients. It's a relaxation technique. Want to try it?"

"What's it do?"

"It's a way of relaxing by visualizing certain pleasant things. All you do is sit with your eyes closed and listen to me."

Banjo grunted. "You're the gooney bird."

Ernie smiled and his eyes crinkled at their edges. "Find a comfortable position with both feet flat on the floor. Try folding your hands loosely in your lap like this." Ernie lay the back of one hand in the palm of the other.

Banjo squinted an eye in distaste at the womanly pose Ernie struck. He squirmed stiffly in his chair. The muscles in his shoulders bunched when he cupped his hands together. Settled at last, Banjo cocked his head and watched Ernie as he would watch someone suspiciously hanging around a call he was on.

"Now close your eyes."

Banjo shut them. After a moment Ernie spoke, but more quietly than before. Banjo opened one eye a slit and saw that Ernie's eyes remained closed.

Ernie said, "First, let's take a few deep breaths. Take a breath in and hold it for a five count."

Banjo breathed in and held.

"Now exhale quickly."

Banjo let the air gasp from him. As his chest collapsed, some of the tightness left him.

"Again," Ernie said.

Banjo drew in a column of air, held it, then let it fly from him. It took more of his stiffness away.

"And again."

Banjo did so. His jaw began to sag. His shoulders loosened.

"Now," said Ernie Webster just above a whisper, "we are going to imagine the warm and safe home place we would go to during a storm which is now gathering fast. The sky is heavy and black and lowering. Cold winds rise ominously. Soon the first large drops of rain will pelt our shoulders."

A memory returned to Banjo. He sat in his ambulance watching bruise colored clouds lower. Air raid sirens growled to life. At that moment the dispatcher broadcast a tornado alert. They were advised to take cover. Banjo recalled the ironic question that came to mind. Where were they going to hide? Then, just to the west and close, Banjo saw two funnels squirming like snakes out of the clouds. The air turned green.

Ernie said, "But you are not concerned because you have a safe place to go where you will be welcomed, warmed, and loved. I want you to go to that place now."

Banjo's frightened partner had asked, 'Where do we go?'

Banjo considered the question. 'We don't, kiddo,' he said. 'Pretty soon they're going to send us after it to pick up the pieces.' He was glad to follow the storm and be first to the destruction and take charge.

Ernie said, "Now you are there. Imagine who is in the house: close friends, dear grandparents perhaps, people who will hold you and protect you and keep you warm. And those special people are in a wonderful room with a glowing fire. You are with them as the storm rages outside. The sky is black. Rain is slashing sideways across the windows and you can distantly hear it on the roof. But here in this place there is light and warmth, a kind of golden glow, and these people are delighted you are with them."

Banjo left his tornado memory to imagine such a house. He could see it. The house was a great log house with warmly lit windows and smoke twisting from the chimney. But he did not go in for he did not know anyone in the house. He belonged in the storm. In the storm he was strong and clever and could prevail and the challenge was to go as far into it as he could.

The air around the ambulance quieted and Banjo's partner asked again, 'Don't you think we should find a place to go?'

'No sweat,' Banjo answered happily. 'We'll keep an eye on that thing and stay right behind it.' Banjo watched the lengthening tails entwine into a single, thick funnel. He took a deep breath to control his fluttering stomach. He remembered the fearful thrill of bone rattling helicopter rides into the jungle. He awaited the dispatcher's order to a destroyed school or a flattened shopping center. He waited, eager, hoping with the slightest twinge of guilt, that the funnel would touch down within the city limits, his jurisdiction, and not in another's.

"Now Banjo," Ernie murmured, "I want you to fill this house with detail. Make this place home. Give it lace curtains and warm colors. Make it be like Thanksgiving day with those good smells and sounds. Put pictures on all the walls. Give it overstuffed chairs with books and magazines strewn around them. Give it tall floor lamps and wooden bookshelves and put quilts on the beds and line the clean, folded back sheets with stuffed animals. Fill your home with music. Make it the home you want to go to when you are cold and tired and frightened."

Winds now shook the ambulance and Banjo fought to control his building fear. The twister dropped its tail to the earth but Banjo could not see where. He watched debris climb into the whirling column. He put the ambulance in gear.

'Where you going?' his nervous partner asked.

Banjo pointed toward the storm. He hurried the ambulance north. The funnel chewed into buildings somewhere ahead of him and to his left. His anticipation grew. He drove faster trying to catch the storm. They reached the city limits of Denver. He saw no damage. The tornado bounced across the ground to the northwest well outside of Denver and far beyond his reach. He watched the tornado grow smaller and more distant and was a little sad.

Ernie Webster broke into his thoughts. "Now. Take a look around your home and put every piece of it into your memory. Look at it carefully. Lock it away and it will be there for you when you need a safe place to go when you find yourself in a storm."

Banjo opened his eyes. His hands were slick with sweat and his bunched up shoulders ached as they had when he chased the tornado. Ernie's eyes remained closed for a few more moments. Presently Ernie looked up and smiled. "So, what did you think?"

Banjo smiled back. "Interesting."

"Tell me one thing you like most about your house?"

The question startled him. "Ummm. The music," he lied, not wanting to ruin Ernie's efforts.

"What kind of music was it?"

"Oh, I don't know. All kinds. Classical, mostly. Mozart. Berlioz. Chopin." He pleaded with the therapist in his thoughts not to make him extend the lie.

"Really. I guess I didn't know you liked great music."

Banjo diverted Ernie toward truthfulness. "My mother used to teach piano. I would listen to her play."

"Did you learn?"

Banjo nodded. "Actually I had classical training and I was quite good."

"No kidding. Do you still play?"

Banjo frowned and shook his head no.

"Why not?"

"I don't know. I guess Vietnam took the spunk out of me for that."

Ernie raised his eyebrows with understanding. "But music is a wonderful gift."

Banjo looked away. "My old man used to gripe at me when I played."

"What would he say about piano playing?"

"He'd say piano playing's for girls."

"Did you enjoy the piano?"

Banjo recalled that distant time before the war. "When I played the piano there would be nothing else. Sometimes I would hear my mother humming along, but mostly I was carried away. I ached to be a concert pianist." He looked at his hands. "I have the hands for it. They're big. Chopin had huge hands. He wrote music for pianists with big hands. I could play some of his pieces pretty well."

"But your father shamed you away."

"Away from the piano and into the military. Back then I would have done anything just so he wouldn't hit me."

"Was your father in the service?"

"Marines. South Pacific. Iwo Jima. Then he became a cop in Omaha."

"When did he die?"

"When I was in the Marines. He drank himself to death basically. He got drunk one night, passed out, puked, and choked on it. A fitting end."

"Is your mother still at home?"

"Oh, sure. She still lives in the house I grew up in."

"Do you see her?"

"Not really."

"Do you ever think about going back for some more piano lessons?"

Banjo chuckled quietly. "No."

"Why not?"

"I guess I'm mad at her for not defending me. She would always take care of me afterwards but I learned real quick that the only one I could rely on was me."

"What could she have done?"

"Hell, I don't know. The woman could have at least said no before running upstairs with her hand over her mouth."

Ernie's watched beeped.

"She could've at least said no, for Christ sake. Her kid was getting the crap beat out of him and she ran away. You never run away like that. You just don't do it. Even if you're going to die, you don't run away. Isn't that what you learned in Vietnam, Ernie? You never run when you got people in trouble. You never run. She ran. Goddamn her. She ran." Banjo set his jaw and shook his head. Tears stung his eyes. He swallowed hard. "My own mother."

*****

Banjo drove to Dan's house. The heater in his truck no longer worked and he was cold. He was nervous, going there unannounced for Thanksgiving dinner, fearing he would have to explain why he had this unexpected day off.

The holiday's uncertainty quickened his breathing. He thought of Dan. With his steady partner Banjo could spend the day safely. Maybe Clayton would be there, too.

Dan's windows glowed warmly. Tawny, brown corn stalks bound in the middle by twine stood against the pillars of his porch. Orange and yellow gourds were arranged carefully around the spindly stalks.

Banjo took a deep breath, held it, then let it steam from him. He rang the doorbell and braced himself for the warm cooked meat smell. Soon Dan opened the door. "Banjo! What a surprise. I thought you had to work."

"I was lucky. I got it off. How about dinner?"

Chapter 16

Now Christmas carols scratched from Banjo's pickup radio as he headed for work. This music of home and happiness, like so much else these days, was a trial. He needed a beer. Memories crouched near the edge of his consciousness and required numbness to dissolve them. He knew the microwave baby lurked there somewhere. Polka dot pig tails rustled gently in his emotional winds. So did the dog mauled little girl. So did her father and his blood smell mingling with gun smoke. So did his own father.

He had taken a beer from the refrigerator this morning and fondled it. Its heft and color were pleasing. His insides itched for the cold, bitter drink. His fingers clutched the bottle and he raised it to the light and he peered into it. But the Chief's threats still rung in his ears so Banjo only looked at his beer through its impenetrable brown window. Clayton had made a decision about alcohol and Banjo wondered if he had it in him to make the same one.

Now, on his way to work, he clung to the biting cold steering wheel in his rattling Toyota pick-up. His fingers fidgeted. His skin crawled. Memories encroached. He wanted a cigarette and that thought surprised him for he had never smoked tobacco. Then an odd urge struck him. From a remote time Banjo recalled another way to quiet his squirming spirit.

He drove on past Denver General.

*****

Banjo stared through the expansive picture windows of Broadway Piano. Before him, beautiful and majestic as queens, sat the instruments of his boyhood joy. Woods of high polish and rich color curved and gleamed in the light. Black and white keys, sharply bright, waited to be touched. Taut sound boards lay ready. The sweeping shape of one piano led his eye to the adjoining bend of the next and then to the glowing shine of still another beyond. Brass footed legs stood in a crowd. Keyboards extended at wild angles from each other.

Then a baby grand piano, reminiscent of his mother's, arrested his attention. He stared at the clean keys and soon his hands took up the graceful movements of an old memorized piece. He heard himself long ago playing the music he only listened to now, alone in the Debbie J. And distantly audible from within this old transcendent memory, he heard his sweetly humming mother.

Presently, he found himself settled onto a button tufted black leather bench. He scooted forward until the balls of his feet rested exactly on the foot petals. He touched the keys gently. He spread his left hand above the keys. It was stiff and unaccustomed to this stretch and a small ache remained when he relaxed his hand. Banjo reached left again and instinctively settled his fingers on four keys. A soft chord floated from the sound board. Banjo's right hand played a short chord progression. Sour notes made him wince. The key action was very soft. His lightest touch produced sound.

The nervousness of a recital over took him as he searched his memory for sheet music. Banjo took a breath, held it, and let it escape quickly. He closed his eyes and played the opening bars of *Voices of Spring*. His hands had lost their quickness and control. These fingers could not strike the correct keys unless he directed them with his eyes. But there were moments when his music discipline, even after so many years, made the intervals between notes consistent and sharp.

More of the waltz lay in his mind and hands than Banjo would have guessed. Ancient memories found their way to his fingers, though he knew they must soon run out. Music resonated in him. He moved as the music moved him. He felt again in his chest the exquisite lifting pleasure of beauty and was profoundly grateful that he could release a little of it with this piano. He saw his mother, sitting, ankles crossed, facing him; resting one elbow on the piano as she did. Her eyes were closed and her hand moved gracefully to the music her son played. A smile crossed her face.

Banjo jerked his fingers away and drew a frightened breath. Someone towering over him told him to stop. He stiffened protectively and turned to see who had ridiculed his playing. He saw no one and the store remained quiet. His hands fell into his lap and he sighed his discouragement. "Screw you, old man," he said to his father.

Banjo's fingers traced the curves of the piano's body. He opened his palm to stroke the smooth wall of the beautiful sound chamber. He reached inside to touch the tight strings. His fingers played with a few. Then Banjo withdrew his hand and stood. For a long time he considered his reflection within the piano's high polish.

He searched out the store clock. His shift had started nearly an hour ago. Banjo turned away from the grand instrument and he zipped his coat against the cold waiting outside. A deep sigh rushed from him again. "Sure as hell," he said aloud, "I'd need supervisor money to afford one of these."

*****

Half Deck looked at his watch and pushed one of its many buttons when Banjo walked into the dayroom. "Stop watch says fifty-seven minutes. Clock doesn't lie." He showed it to Banjo. "That's what it says. Isn't that right? That'll cost you an hour's wages."

Banjo grunted and turned away.

"You were late. I almost had to run a call with your partner." The toothpick twitched nervously.

"Ron, I'm not in the mood for this." His stomach soured and burned and he craved a beer.

"You ...!" Half Deck jammed his fists into his hips, spun to leave, then turned back. "Into my office!"

Banjo looked at him, surprised by the supervisor's fury. "You have something to say to me, say it here."

He clamped down on his toothpick. "No. You've been horsing me for a long time and you are going to hear me out. In my office!" He went to his office without waiting for Banjo's answer.

Banjo entered, sat on the corner of a desk, and crossed his arms. "So?"

Half Deck's head trembled. His mouth struggled to form words. "Why am I so much gall and wormwood to you?"

Banjo shifted his eyes away in confusion then back. "What?"

"You embarrassed my family."

"What!"

Half Deck straightened himself. "You embarrassed my family at dinner."

Banjo thought. "You mean last summer? What did I do that took you six months to tell me about?"

"Your manners and attitude. You were laughing at us. We were nothing but a spectatulation to you. I was trying to do you a true honor. I was trying to encourage you. But you laughed at us. At me. I would like you to tell me why."

Banjo looked at the desk photo of Elvis and at Half Deck's own long sideburns cutting blackly down his soft cheeks. His chest bulged falsely with the second chance vest. Happy talk disc jockeys chattered from Half Deck's clock radio. Banjo laughed in disbelief. "You really want to know?"

Half Deck's tooth pick twitched. "Most indeed."

Banjo opened his mouth to start. Words would not formulate and an audible sigh escaped. He looked at the overbearing and arbitrary supervisor. "Why?"

"I deserve to know. I suspect your thoughts are similar to the others in the division, as you are the informal leader of the street staff."

Banjo stared at him and said, "You're a mouse."

The tooth pick twitched again as Half Deck braced himself.

"You think because you're a supervisor you can beat up on the crews every three months with your damn schedule. You wear that body armor like you're still a real paramedic, but you sit in this office playing radio games and scratching lottery tickets. How do you expect the street paramedics to look at you? They all laugh at you. They all call you Half Deck. That isn't my doing."

"No."

"I've been here sixteen, seventeen years. You never say shit unless you're going to dump some on one of us. You write memos when you should just talk to a person face to face. You can't just have a conversation, you have to make us understand you're the boss. People think you serve no purpose except to post schedules. You have an image problem, Mr. Supervisor. Nobody around here remembers the last time you ran a call. You're not a real paramedic. There. Is that what you wanted to hear?"

"No. Well, yes. I suppose that is what I thought I might hear."

"Well, it's the truth."

Half Deck's jaw muscles bulged. His tooth pick jutted straight and still. Then, slowly, it drooped from his lips. The office was quiet. Half Deck shifted his eyes from Banjo.

Banjo said, "Now I suppose you're going to leave me on days forever."

Half Deck did not answer.

"So what do you want me to do now?"

"Leave me." Half Deck cleared his throat. "If you've had your say, please leave."

Banjo dropped his eyes. Suddenly he could find no comfortable position in which to stand nor a prideful way to exit. He found himself admiring Half Deck's courage to bear up against personal criticism. This was Dan's courage and Greystone's and what he hoped lived within himself.

Half Deck repeated, "Please leave."

"All right," Banjo consented. Then he asked, "Why did you want to hear this?"

Half Deck crossed his arms protectively and looked at the floor. "I wanted to know the sum truth about what people think of me. Dinner last summer suspected me that you carried the division's regard, such as it is. Took me this long to ask." Then he looked straight at Banjo. "We all need to hear the truth some time or other." He nodded once with certainty. "Isn't that right?"

*****

"Know what I did before work today, Danny boy?" Banjo asked. Dan drove them into northeast Denver.

"Quite a bit, judging by when you got here."

"I played the piano for the first time in years, then I chewed Half Deck's ass. I don't know which felt better."

"Played the piano?" Dan sounded skeptical.

"I finally decided why that guy pushes my buttons. My old man hated my piano playing. He would stand over me as I played and look at his watch. He'd time how long it would take me to get nervous and quit. Then he'd laugh and laugh when I did. Just once I wanted to tell him to go to hell. Half Deck's always playing little games to let you know whose in charge. Just like my old man. Today he came up to me looking at his watch telling me I was fifty-seven minutes late and how he almost had to run a call with you."

"I didn't know you played the piano."

"Actually he sort of invited me into his office and asked me to tell him what the division thought of him."

"Thought of who?"

"Half Deck. I got into his world this morning."

"I thought you said you were late because you were playing a piano."

Banjo thought of Half Deck standing with his arms at his sides, braced against Banjo's brutal honesty. "Actually, I was awfully hard on him." He thought again. "And he took it like a man. Made me feel guilty, the way he was big about it. I tell you, he just stood there. When I finished, he said if I was through, would I please leave. He wasn't afraid of me, Dan. He knew what was coming and he wasn't afraid. Or if he was, he didn't show it. I admire the little rat for that. He stood his ground."

They were at a red light and Dan faced Banjo. "Tell me again why were you so upset at Half Deck?"

"Mr. Humphries, our scheduling supervisor, showed me something today."

Puzzled, Dan looked out the front window. "Half Deck?"

"But I was late in the first place because I stopped in at Broadway Piano to audition an instrument. I played a lot as a kid. Even won a few competitions in high school." Banjo itched again to feel the keys responding under his long fingers. He asked off handedly, "Did I ever tell you I won a scholarship to study piano at the Chicago Conservatory of Music?"

"He didn't say anything back to you?"

"I might have been a Van Cliburn, or something. I loved to play Chopin. He wrote such vigorous piano pieces. I'd feel like I'd just finished a wrestling match -- all sweaty and spent -- after playing one. What a wonderful feeling that was, pouring everything I had into a work. It was like giving myself completely over for something enormous."

Dan said, "You're not listening to me. I asked you about Half Deck."

Banjo shrugged. "Sure." He turned to his partner. "Tell you what. I'll buy one and you can come to my place for lessons."

"Buy what?"

Out the window Banjo added, "I'll need the cash."

*****

The dispatcher brought them into Denver General just before their shift ended. Banjo and Dan entered the dayroom drawing in cold air. The Chief sat in a broken down over stuffed chair, his long legs drawn up close as he rested. Roy sat quietly on the sofa. The Chief said in the direction of Dan and

Banjo, "Oh, wind, if winter comes, can spring be far behind?" He looked at Roy and told him, "Shelley."

"Whose she?"

The Chief chuckled. "Gentlemen," he called. "We're in a story telling mood tonight. The tales are of a spooky genre, befitting the low and gloomy skies."

Banjo still hurt from his last meeting with the Chief. But the Chief's bright eyes sparkled with sympathy and met gently with Banjo's. The urge to bolt left him and Banjo relaxed and grinned like a boy. "How about the night I tracked a patient through a cemetery," he said pulling off his jacket and sitting in a chair across from the Chief.

"Nicely. That will do nicely." The Chief leaned back to listen and crossed his legs. His hitched up pant leg revealed a triangle of tanned and sun toughened skin above the wool socks that piled at his shoe tops.

"We had this car wreck one night. The car's all beat to crap, the hood's horse shoed around a telephone pole, the driver's door is flung open, blood's all over the place. But no driver, no passenger, no nobody. This is the dead of winter, now. It's the middle of the night. The fog's so thick the other side of the road is fuzzy. There's maybe six inches of snow on the ground. So it's all real quiet and hushed and creepy. And here we are with a car wreck nobody should have survived, splattered with blood, and no patient. Then my partner, I think it was Robert, finds bloody footprints leading off through the snow. This was too weird because they headed right toward a cemetery." Banjo shivered. The rest sat fixed in silence.

"Robert says ... I'll never forget this bit of raw courage. He says, 'This is your patient. You go first.' I *hate* being first to see. Anyway, off we go lugging our equipment, me leading and Robert so close I think he wants to hold onto my coat.

"What's really strange is how far apart these foot prints are. The guy must be a giant. But he had tiny feet. We go a few steps and come to an open iron gate and I see tombstones and I'm thinking this can't be happening. This is the Twilight Zone. This is Transylvania. This is anything but regular. But off into the fog and tombstones goes this bloody trail. Robert's telling me to wait for the cops but that's stupid, I tell him.

They don't carry stakes or silver bullets. He hits me on the back. Then, the idiot, he yells over my shoulder into this cemetery, 'Hey! Anybody in there!' Christ. I damn near climbed a tree. So I whack him and tell him to shut up. And in we go.

"We're walking really quiet and talking in whispers like we might wake somebody up. And we're all hunched over like we're sneaking around. Pretty soon we see the foot prints hook around behind this big old monument of a tombstone but don't see foot prints come out the other side. The guy's right behind it." Banjo paused for effect. "I told Robert to go around the other side so we'll both see at the same time, but I have a surprise for him. He goes to the left and I start right and just when he makes the corner I stop and let him go in first. Cheap shot, I know, but he shouldn't've yelled. Next thing I know is he grunts like he's been hit in the gut so I step around.

"I look. And I look again. Then I look at Robert. I had figured we were tracking a man seven feet tall. But laying there snow white, stiff, and dead as a mackerel in her own blood is an old woman. She had a hell of a gash that ripped the inside of one leg, ankle to thigh, and how she got herself into that cemetery or why she took such long steps, I haven't a clue. It's almost like she wanted to milk all the blood out of herself and die right there. Damndest thing."

Silence followed the story and Banjo was pleased with himself. The Chief smiled at him. "You do have a time of it out there, don't you?" Then the Chief told a story. "I had a shooting in a gravel pit one night many years ago. One drilled another in the chest, as they often do. Greystone and I found the poor devil down in the bottom, laying in cold water, still bleeding out of the hole. It was a terrible wound; done with a shotgun, I suppose. Steam rose up from his seeping blood." He exhaled a cloud of pipe smoke as if to illustrate. "I thought of life itself escaping the body. I can still see it. Steam rose in a column from his chest as steam would rise after dousing a camp fire."

"My spookiest," Roy began after a suitable pause, "was the plane crash at Stapleton Airport. I was in the first string of ambulances there. When we got onto the field -- it was during that blizzard so we were barely getting around even with chains -- all we saw at first was one fire engine just visible through the snow. And nothing else. I expected fire and mangled bodies and people all over the place but ..." Roy shook his head. "Just us, and that lonely fire truck. We got closer and saw the fuselage, but it didn't look quite real because it was in pieces and I was seeing it like though a sheer curtain or something. Then even less distinct about two hundred yards off was the tail section. And that just looked like a broken model airplane. That's all I could think of-- this isn't real. It's as if I was outside myself seeing everything from way off. I jumped out first, slammed my door and, I'll never forget this until the day I die, I heard behind me seven more snow muffled door slams. Then there was absolute silence."

Roy looked off and changed his story to the present tense. "I'm not hearing screams. I'm not hearing engines running. I'm not hearing radios. I'm not hearing anything. All I see is this vague shape of an airplane on the ground and it's not making sense to me. Then someone yells from where the tail section broke away, 'Hey, he's still breathing!' Then I know. 'Oh, shit,' I said. "'This is the real thing."' He looked at Banjo and the rest. "But I'll never forget those eight doors slamming and that huge wall of silence that hit me."

Roy shook his head again. "There's no way to train for that much human tragedy. Everyone was frantic; looking for a child, a husband, a wife. No one could be consoled. But my most haunting memory will always be those doors." Roy focused off once more and made a sound for every muffled slam. "Bump, bump, bump, bump, bump, bump, bump, bump." Then he sat back quietly as though within his enormous white silence.

Everyone in the room had been there that afternoon and all were drawn to their own memories of it. Banjo recalled a fireman carrying a baby missing the top of its head. He took it to one paramedic and held it out to him on extended arms. The paramedic looked and pointed the fireman toward a large tarp demarcating the morgue area where bodies had already been placed. The fire fighter then carried the small body to another paramedic who looked and also directed him to the area of bodies. He carried the child to a third paramedic and again hopefully extended his arms. Banjo left what he was doing, he had forgotten now what that was, and went to the fireman. His drawn face and sad eyes pleaded with Banjo. 'I'll take care of the little one,' Banjo had promised. He lifted the light bundle from the bulky arms and carried it to where bodies were already losing their definition to the accumulating snow.

The Chief said quietly to Roy, "Allow me another literary indulgence." He looked into his cloud of smoke and quoted, "There is not life of a man, faithfully recorded, but is a heroic poem of its sort, rhymed or unrhymed." He thought. "Was that Carlyle? No matter." The Chief looked at them. Banjo, who puzzled at the quote, thought the Chief cast a significant glance his way.

*****

Banjo's shift ended a short time later. He shouldered on his coat for his cold drive back to the Debbie J. The Chief stood, his long arms reaching well down his thighs, and crossed the room with two long legged strides. He extended a bony hand. "Merry Christmas, my friend." Banjo took it and felt the strong, warm grip. "Have you a place to spend the day? If not, Mildred and I always have extra slippers and cider mugs."

Banjo had not thought where he would go Christmas just three days off. "No, I expect I'll stay around; maybe go over to Dan's." He grinned over his shoulder at his partner.

The Chief said, "Are you planning anything nice for yourself? You've been through much this year, some of it from my hands, and you deserve a gift."

Banjo shrugged and smiled.

A stern look formed amongst the lines in the Chief's face. "Do not spend the day alone. You drive out. Or go to Mr. Craven's. But your state will not abide Christmas alone in your apartment."

Banjo nodded, thinking instead of the Christmas present he might well give himself.

*****

Again, as he had before work, Banjo wanted a beer. The Parlour with its favored corner tempted him. Greystone could easily be conjured up to offer an audience for his thoughts. But neither the bar nor his dead partner satisfied a new itch now causing his fingers to move delicately across an unseen keyboard, playing music Banjo thought had died long ago with so much else in Vietnam.

Chapter 17

Banjo made a special trip to work for the spring schedule posting. He had given Half Deck no requests and dreaded the supervisor's vengeance for his blunt criticism. Snooper sat in the dayroom, legs crossed -- one ankle resting on the other knee -- and thumbed through a magazine. She glanced his way with vast indifference then quietly turned a page. The door to the communications center was open and a paramedic leaned against it visiting with the dispatchers who also spoke to the electronic voices in their ears. Roy sat alone on the sofa. Clayton, Lauren, and Dan formed a small, waiting group.

Banjo watched Half Deck and the rookie supervisor, Eric, through the office window. Half Deck's heels rested on his desk and the tooth pick stuck from his mouth at a jaunty angle. Eric sat on the corner of another desk laughing, the top two buttons of uniform shirt were vainly undone. The appointed hour was two that afternoon. Half Deck would not make his entrance until exactly then.

Banjo went to Dan's group and stood off his friend's shoulder, listening to conversation. Lauren, Banjo could tell, had just said something which left her sad and resigned and the others shook their heads. Dan told her, "That's too bad," but his offering was mumbled and not comforting.

She smiled weakly and shrugged. "Yeah, it sure hosed up my day." Her shoulders drooped a little, tilting her sad face downward.

The supervisor's door opened. People milled toward the bulletin board but Banjo, in his show of disinterest, let the others edge in front of him. Half Deck shouldered through the gathering paramedics without acknowledging them. He lay the single sheet of computer print out up against the bulletin board and carefully smoothed it off as he would a freshly hung panel of wall paper. He placed thumb tacks at each corner and neatly pushed them to the hubs.

Grumbling arose even before he finished. Ignoring these, Half Deck stepped back for a broader view of the perfect squares and cleverly placed names, then returned to his office.

Once the door closed Banjo elbowed sideways into the tight knot of people. He looked first at the shifts beginning late in the afternoon and running into the early morning hours. These promised the most action. His name was not listed. He searched the night shift hoping to find himself situated there with a good partner. His name was not there, either. He cursed Half Deck and his eyes traveled suspiciously along the day shifts. Banjo looked first at the eleven a.m. shift, then at the ten-thirty shift. He went to his current nine-thirty schedule without finding his name, and, with alarm, to eight a.m.. He did not find his name. "That son of a bitch." Banjo dropped to the shift beginning at six in the morning and there, under Snooper's name, he found his own. "That little son of a bitch."

Banjo spun to leave and found himself chest to chest with Snooper. She stood, fists jammed into her hips, as stubbornly as she had outside the Parlour. She said, "I don't want any of your seniority crap, Sunshine. We're partners. Got it? Equals."

"Cold day in hell before your my match on the streets." He shoved past her protruding elbows. Her arms went flying before she regained balance.

He returned to the periphery where Dan stood. "He put me on mornings. I mean *early*. Like six a.m. in the goddamn morning. I can't get up then. Is he trying to get me fired, or what? And he's got me with Snooper."

Dan laughed. "Guess who I'm with? I'm spending the next three months with Lauren. Every cop and fireman in town is going to be following us around just to talk to her."

Banjo's thoughts flew to her instead. "Why is she with you? She needs more field instructor work?"

"No. Just partners."

Banjo cocked his head toward him. "You got the hots for her? I thought she was still dating some doctor."

"I never get involved with people I work with ..."

Banjo laughed rudely, remembering Dan's intrusion into his romance with Eden. "I'll catch you later."

Banjo went to visit with a group still discussing the scheduling fall out. Roy was red faced and a vein in his forehead bulged. "I told him I couldn't get my request to him until I had the wife's work schedule. Three days late and this is what he does to me. Gol darn." He shifted one foot outward and, like Snooper, jammed his fists to his hips. Clayton stood next to Roy. Clayton's bear claw necklace rested against his chest outside his tee shirt. His sleek black hair brushed his shoulders. "No offense to you, Clayton," Roy said. "I don't have any heartburn working with you. But when am I going to see my kids working the middle of the night? Three days late. Now look at him in there. Sitting like he's the king of us all." Roy turned a full circle and raked a hand through his thinning hair. He extended a trembling hand at Clayton. "One of these days I'm really going to lose my temper with him. And when I do I'll give him down the road good. I'll do that. You wait and see. I'll do that one of these days." He drew a breath and his jaw tightened. He sucked in another long breath. "Well, I have to go tell the wife and kids."

Clayton said. "Three months isn't a life time, Roy."

"Yeah, yeah," he answered going away.

Banjo, irritable and scrappy, observed to Clayton, "Screwed Roy, too, huh? What did he do to you."

"Nights again. I like working nights. It's peaceful." Clayton gave Banjo a look of certain knowledge. "I told Half Deck awhile back that Indians could see further into the night than white people." He chuckled. "He must have believed me because he put me with Roy and Roy's as blind as a bat at night."

Banjo planted his hands on his hips. "Just what allows you to take Half Deck's jerking around so calmly? Is it some Indian way of yours? Don't you ever get sick of the bullshit around here?"

"Things are fine with me."

"Jesus! You're being walked on, man. Don't you ever go on the war path?"

"We're used to it."

"Well, you need to get un-used to it to survive around here."

"I can take care of myself."

"Not in the talking mood today, huh."

"Not when you're talking nonsense." Clayton's eyes flashed. He crossed his arms as though barring Banjo from moving closer. "And what's this war path business? Sometimes you can be a real red neck cowboy. I am a Sioux Indian. I am not heathen red man. I don't scalp white men. I don't steal their women and children."

"Oh, don't be so touchy," Banjo told him. "I'm just being pissy. I get this way when people mess with me."

"Get pissy with someone else then." Then, a moment later. "Who are you working with now?"

"Snooper."

"A good partner. You can trust her."

"How do you know. You worked with her? I've had a little experience with her and she can be kind of changy."

Clayton shrugged.

"Oh. One of your insights, huh. You *are* a spooky cuss, aren't you."

Clayton smiled. Quiet self confidence lighted his face. "Spooky, huh." He glanced over his horizon again then back. "That's good. I like that."

He looked past Clayton to Lauren. Her back was to him. Her hair was full of red highlights and lay so prettily across her shoulders. "Well, I have to go say hello to Lauren."

"Now's a good time."

Banjo narrowed his eyes. "Why?"

"She's available."

"Another flash from the blue?"

"I over-heard her talking."

"So," Banjo declared, "you do stoop to the lower forms of communications."

Her availability piqued his old interest. Her sweet drawly voice and stupendous legs moved him swiftly beyond his conceited conception of her flawed beauty. "So," he repeated, thoughtfully. "She doesn't dig Doug anymore." He looked toward the bulletin board where she visited. She had told him awhile ago she wanted to get together. He looked back to Clayton, squinted one eye, and nodded his good-bye.

Banjo decided to be confident, as though ignorant of her other relationship. He took a deep breath, held it, then expelled it forcefully. Approaching from behind he slid an arm around her shoulder in a friendly sort of way and said, "I see we're in the same time hemisphere now."

Lauren turned toward him. Her hair swished softly across the back of Banjo's hand. "Well, hello stranger. What rock have you been hiding under since I can't remember when?"

"Oh, I've been around. How've you been?"

She sighed greatly. "Sometimes God rather deliberately causes things to happen to teach people lessons. I think that's what happened to me."

"Really. How about that glass of wine we've been trying to have since winter? We can talk about it."

"I suppose that would be all right. Let me look in my little book." Lauren removed a date book from her uniform shirt pocket. She opened it to a page of filled up squares of time. She held her other hand at a right angle to her wrist and delicately wiggled her fingers as she studied.

Banjo took the great leap. "How about this evening?" His heart pounded.

Lauren's eyes darted from her book to Banjo and back as though looking for a means of escape within her calendar. "Sure," she said at last, sighing. "I have nothing important going on. Do you have a place in mind?"

He shrugged. "The Parlour?" Banjo reconsidered, recalling Larry's demand. "No, that place is always so smoky. Let's go listen to some music. The Parchment Farm usually has some nice jazz. You up for a little jazz?"

"Oh," she drawled, "I suppose jazz would be nice enough."

And Banjo had his date.

A sharp siren wail caught his attention. An ambulance bolted into the lot, turned fast and backed hard to the dock. Banjo went to the window. Before it stopped the back doors flew open. Paramedics and two police officers sprang out. One officer carried a police belt which still held a service revolver.

The stretcher rolled out. A paramedic thrust his fists downward on the chest. Another siren cut the air then fell silent. A police cruiser, and another, then another shot into the parking lot sending gravel flying. They stopped carelessly at sharp angles. From one, its emergency lights still flashing, ran Zagata. Banjo looked for Rocky. Banjo searched among the now half dozen officers pushing into the emergency department. He whispered, "Oh, my God." and jerked the dayroom door open.

When he reached the resuscitation room Banjo could not see past blue uniforms crowded at the open curtain. Banjo grabbed one uniformed arm. "Who is it?"

"Rocky Osborn."

"Rocky? Like Rocky and Zagata? What happened?" Banjo strained to see. He caught little flashes of surgical gowns and instruments between the halves of green drapes pulled not quite closed.

"He and Zagata made a drug bust. Rocky went into a bedroom and some guy poked a magnum out the closet door and opened up. He took one just above the vest and another in the face."

"You get the guy?"

"Not yet."

Banjo looked for Zagata knowing he was staying close to his jumpy partner. The policeman now asked Banjo, "What do you think? Does a guy with one hole in his chest and the other in his face make it?" The question was asked softly, as a bewildered child might ask if his run over pet would wake up and be all right.

Banjo shook his head. "It isn't likely."

The officer turned back. Soon activity in the trauma room ceased. The murmur floating among those standing vigil stopped. Banjo heard the slap of latex gloves pulled from hands. He recognized the soft whumps of bloodied surgical clothes thrown into hampers. A doctor exited through the curtains. He faced the uniforms and said, "I'm sorry. He was probably dead when he hit the ground."

A great tower of silence rose up from the officers who faced the green drapes drawn around Rocky's body.

Communication among them was done with their faces. An open, wide-eyed face looked about to cry but did not. Another was set hard as stone and spoke of revenge. Some with pained, searching stares avoided other faces that also revealed their own haunting fears.

One by one they left. Soon Banjo alone remained and he slipped in behind the curtain. Zagata, unaware of Banjo, stood next to his partner. Rocky, skinny and naked, looked frail without his uniform. A black hole punctured his right cheek swelling that eye into a purple bulge. Banjo found a similar hole just under his collar bone. Surgeons had sliced him open below the wound to reach in and control bleeding. Lung, soiled brown from cigarette smoke, filled the bloody surgical opening. Black-red clots on the floor made a slick pool of thick blood underneath Rocky's stretcher and dark red foot prints led about the room. A surgical tray held a bloody disarray of instruments. Banjo sniffed the quiet air and caught that characteristic rusty smell.

Zagata stroked Rocky's hair. He patted Rocky's cheek. Zagata's scar was livid, like a lightening bolt crashing down his cheek, and his head trembled. With the rasp of sand paper over wood he said to Rocky, "You'll see." Zagata nodded. "You'll see." Then he nodded with great certainty. "No sweat, partner. Don't you worry. You'll see. And your family will know." Zagata drew a great breath and his eyes grew wide. He fixed them on something only he could see and squinted his right eye, his aiming eye. His chest filled with deeply drawn breaths and he worked his mouth as though loosening up a sore muscle. He made fists with his free hand.

He spun to face Banjo and Banjo wished now he had not interrupted. He backed away and said, "Sorry, Zagata. Just paying my respects."

Zagata did not answer. His feverishly glazed eyes bore through Banjo. Zagata exploded past Banjo before he detected Zagata's gathering movement. He left behind him a trailing sensation of sweat and blood and hatred.

Chapter 18

When they met at the Parchment Farm, Lauren did not take Banjo's arm and draw it to her side as she had other times. Nor did she engage his eyes with her teasing glances. Though Banjo noticed these differences, he set them aside and enjoyed the music. He thought about this curious change, recalling his keen fantasies of falling in love. Such quickening anticipation had filled him even today thinking of the evening. But her distance, immediately sensed, caused Banjo only fleeting disappointment. Some long injured deep spot was healing. The salve of femininity seemed less needed. He was comfortable. She, however, fidgeted.

Banjo propped his fist on his chin and was transfixed by the quick fingers dancing on the keyboard and after watching them for a long stretch he brought her into his thoughts. "I love pianos. They are infinitely complex and beautiful and there is no limit to the music they can make."

"Mmmm," Lauren answered in a polite, dreamy fashion. "They are pretty, aren't they."

Banjo's fingers moved with the pianist's. "I'd love to play like that. What a gift it is to reach someone deeply with your music."

"I'm afraid my fingers are just plain old stumps when it comes to that. I couldn't play chop sticks." She turned full face to him. "Say, do you like Roy Orbison?"

Banjo shrugged a shoulder and she went back to her wine.

The piano player stopped. In the new silence Banjo tried another line of conversation. "So, what's happening that's got you down?"

"Oh ..." She picked at the napkin under her wine glass. "Boyfriend trouble, I guess you could say." She twirled her wine, thinking. "He said he needed space. Space. Well. I took that to mean he wanted me to quit hanging around so much. He said that wasn't it, exactly." She squared off and looked at him. "Honestly Banjo, I didn't just fall off the turnip truck. I know dumped when I hit the dirt." Lauren struck a pose. Her mouth went ajar and she jabbed the outside angle of her bent wrists to her waist. "Well, what is it then, I asked." After a moment Lauren broke character and sipped her wine.

Banjo sipped his, too, then asked a question to nudge her. "Did he ever say what was bothering him?"

"Well, he wanted me to be a sweet little ole doctor's wife. And he wants a family and all that when he finishes his residency. Now tell me. Do you take me for someone who can sit home all day? He figured that out, too, I guess. What he wanted space from was me. That's alright, though. If we was married, why, before a week was out I'd be twiddling my lips. He's such a sweet boy, though.

"When we started dating he told me he was interested in a family. I told him I was, too, but in my own way of sayin' so that says maybe, could be, someday in the sweet bye and bye. You know how I do. Well, he finally told me to fish or cut bait. I hate being done up that way."

Banjo's mind wandered gently over his wants. "I can see what he's saying. A family sometimes sounds nice to me, too. I've been divorced for ..." he looked at the ceiling. "... a long time. I've had some girl friends." He shrugged. "Nothing real serious. Nothing stuck. Lately, though I've been thinking maybe there's more to life than running calls and seeing the occasional woman. I guess I'd like to meet somebody."

"Well, when you do, sooner or later you'll also meet up with their quirky needs. That can really hose up your day; getting up when they do, watching their kind of movies, listening to their radio station. Pretty soon all you're doing is their stuff. That's the way they're gonna do ya. That ain't right but I never figured out any other way."

Banjo traveled deeper into his thoughts. "When I think of meeting someone I think of losing her. I never just enjoy the moment. My mind goes to when it will all fall to pieces. I think I've spent my whole life assuming that whatever I have I'll lose. So I piss everything away before it's taken.

"Lately," he went on, "I've had this fantasy of moving to the mountains and writing music. One day I was looking at the Rockies and it suddenly occurred to me they might not be there by the time I can afford a house there." He stared into his wine. "It's hard to trust someone when you take it for granted they won't stick around."

Lauren said, "I worry about the opposite. I don't want to be stuck with someone who makes me lose track of myself. A year's about all it takes to feel crowded. That's how long Dougy and I saw each other." Lauren slid a hand across the table and slipped it under his. He squeezed and felt warming pressure in return. "We're a fine pair," she said.

Banjo thought about this. For so long he wanted Lauren. Now, this evening, at the moment of her availability, something was letting go. Lauren drew the hair away from her face and swept it behind one shoulder. She leaned back and shook her head. Red highlights flashed. Banjo watched tight little wrinkles in her neck crinkle and smooth out. Something surged beneath his stomach. He dallied again with his pleasing fantasies. How nice the house he had created for them would have been. Better, he decided now, to forget it. Better he go no further, now that ending the fantasy seemed no longer to tear the flesh of his soul. Though he feared loneliness, better he remain alone. He knew that desert. At the moment of her skittish availability he turned away. He asked, "What sort of relationship are you looking for?"

She searched off somewhere. "I don't know. Maybe I want a man who'll feed me, love me, and let me come and go like a hound dog." She rocked her head again letting her hair brush softly against her shoulders. "Think I'll ever find one of those, dear boy?"

Banjo smiled at her.

"Tell me," she said. "What are you hoping to find? What impossible conditions are you looking to impose on some unsuspecting woman?"

Banjo took a long time to answer, discovering much as he traveled inward. He had returned to his music. He had allowed Dan into a secret region where he let no person. And

Clayton's mystical spirituality had struck some harmonious chord. Still, he was lonely.

"Hello?" Lauren drawled at him. She tickled his hand with a finger. "Are you still in there?"

Banjo jerked his hand away, laughing. Her hand, fingers wiggling, searched his out once more. "Talk to me, dear boy," she said in her sing-song way.

"I want to get married."

She took two gulps of wine and fluttered a hand at him. "Banjo, I need a break from relationships. I'm not sure I trust my own judgement. Lord, don't I think that you're a good looking man and why wasn't this world different."

Banjo opened his mouth to speak but she interrupted.

"I'm a wounded woman. Don't you see? I want you in my life, but not as a lover. Not right now, anyways."

Banjo smiled at her sudden flight from his wish to marry, a wish that came as a surprise to him, too, but seemed true nonetheless. "I was speaking only in general terms."

She pursed her lips and took a moment to regain herself. "Oh." She sipped more wine. "I run my mouth sometimes."

And there, Banjo knew, his fantasy of Lauren ended. But no bolt of loneliness struck him. Presently he felt a lessening of pressure, as though a constant head wind ceased blowing in his face. With this ending he knew something else could begin. Across the table, redness was still settling out of her neck. She glanced at him and smiled curtly only with her mouth.

*****

Snooper pushed herself into the corner made by the seat back and cab of the ambulance. Her legs and arms crossed angularly forming a barrier of limbs between herself and Banjo. She dozed, though sounds startled her awake from time to time. After stern looks toward Banjo, she drifted back into her noisy sleep breathing.

Banjo read the paper, the ads specifically, looking for pianos. But he too, glancing frequently at the black morning horizon, fought to hold his eyes open. Coffee steamed from a styrofoam cup propped on the dashboard and it caused a circle of fog on the cold windshield. Banjo snapped the paper to make it lay flat on the steering wheel and it rustled loudly in the silence. He squeezed his eyelids with his thumb and index finger and stared vacantly at traffic thickening on the freeway below him. He could not remember the last time he watched rush-hour build from this end of the day.

A pick-up, its cab lighted, grumbled slowly through the parking lot where they sat waiting for a call. The driver wore a plaid flannel shirt and his rolled up sleeves revealed white shafts of long underwear. He extended his head to a sniffing position and sipped from his steaming coffee mug which he then returned to the dash board before him. Then he reached to his breast pocket and took out his pack of cigarettes. Several popped up to a well practiced flick of his wrist. His lips took the one furthest extended. He turned his head toward the ambulance and Banjo's eyes caught his. Banjo nodded his respects. The sleepy, immobile face nodded back. Then the pick-up cab lights went out and through the dark rear window as the truck moved past the ambulance, Banjo saw a small hot circle of orange move to the man's face.

How many years, Banjo wondered, had this man risen to get out before the sun. He recalled the kitchen noises his mother use to make getting his father out this early. After the kitchen noises he would hear the screen door squeak and slam shut and, after a predictable interval, his old man's muffler shot pick-up would roar to life. All the while Banjo, cozy in bed, would be glad he did not yet have to leave his soft warmth and shock himself against the cold morning. Covers tight to his chin, he listened to the loud truck noises decrescendo toward his father's police station.

Banjo's mind went to his pick-up. It too roared and smoked and left a long trail of noise. This morning any child in any bedroom along his route to work could have followed him. Banjo had a flash of odd familiarity. As his father had done so many times, so had Banjo this morning. And so had that working man in his pick-up. For a moment Banjo's long dead, still hated father came alive in that ordinary looking man heading to work. And he flickered to life in Banjo who also awoke much sooner than he wanted. His father became a working man, an ordinary man with friends and secrets and haunting memories doing, like Banjo, the best he knew how. Banjo turned this over in his head, moving from his father to the everyday man then back to himself. All looked very much the same. None were perfect. They all could have done better. Banjo looked at his father's memory a little longer. Old anger reared up. He shifted his attention.

A pinkish gray line raised off the horizon and the quality of light changed. Freshness spread across Denver which awaited the gathering day clean and quiet and ready. Banjo felt similarly clean waiting there peacefully without the usual noisy urges surging just within. Wind kicked up, swaying the dry grass just down the hill from him. Darkened buildings now sparkled with recently lighted windows.

Traffic noise on the freeway just beyond grew audible above the ambulance engine generating heat against the morning cold. Banjo sipped from his cup and felt the coffee tension rising in his nervous system. The dispatcher, quiet for some time now, sent out two ambulances. One hurried to a man awakening with chest pain, another to someone found dead. The early morning DOA, Banjo recalled. It had been years since he responded to one of those predictable calls. Remembering this feature of early morning shifts, it seemed those days rarely opened without pronouncing someone dead first thing.

Another ambulance hurried to a passenger short of breath at Stapleton airport, another to a seizure. Banjo knew they would soon be shifted to an area of Denver emptied of ambulances. "Hey, Snoop. They're going to be messing with us soon."

She remained still.

"Come on. Rise and shine. No more time for beauty sleep."

"Do we have a call?"

"No. Not yet."

"Then leave me alone."

"Might as well stir those lazy bones now. The dispatcher's going to find us sooner or later."

Snooper did not answer but Banjo saw that her breathing had quickened. He swallowed more coffee then etched designs in the cup with his thumbnail. The tiny intersecting grooves resembled the provoking designs on The Parlour door. He thought he caught a whiff of gun smoke. A slick, thickening pool of blood hung in the air. The blood congealed on the floor under Rocky's stretcher. He heard Zagata's murmured threats and recalled the hot smell of his sweat. Banjo swallowed hard and focused on the passing traffic but his seeing would not penetrate beyond the visions. He opened the door, hoping the cold air would jar the memories loose.

"Number One," the dispatcher called.

Banjo heard this from far away. He stared into the morning light and forced his mind empty. The memories dissolved, letting go as quickly as they had seized him.

Banjo picked up the microphone. Snooper had not stirred from behind her bony fence of arms and legs. He said to her, "Time to go to work."

Banjo answered the radio and the dispatcher told them, "Number One, you're going to 2301 Clay on an unconscious party. Caller states this person in not breathing." The address was near Zagata's precinct station. Banjo looked toward the station to see if a cruiser might be slipping quietly into the early morning light toward this call to surprise him.

Snooper fumbled with her seat belt. He did not use his siren on the way to the nearby address, wishing to preserve the peacefulness of the morning. Speeding through the deserted neighborhood streets at dawn he saw women in kitchen windows fixing breakfast. An early morning paper boy threw the heavy **Rocky Mountain News** at porches. A backing pick-up stopped in its driveway to let the ambulance pass. Banjo watched the droopy tail of a garbage truck disappear down an alley and remembered blood streaming from just such a mechanism.

Banjo stopped in the street. He told the dispatcher they had arrived. The eastern sky now glowed beautifully, as if an artist had cast bold stokes of blue and orange and pink along the horizon then blended them with his thumb.

Snooper's eyes were still puffy as she straightened from her slouch to leave the ambulance. She got the equipment and started up the walk without Banjo. Her stride was loose and powerful like a man's. Banjo had to hurry to catch her.

A woman held her bathrobe closed at the top with one hand and the front door open with the other. Her face worked against tears. "He's in the bedroom," she said, standing aside, gesturing fearfully down a tunnel dark hall. "Please don't look around too much. The room's such a mess." Snooper whispered something to the woman and touched her shoulder as she passed.

Banjo reached to the back of his pants and realized, in his sleepiness, he had left his flashlight in the ambulance. He searched for a light switch. He found one and flipped it on. Nothing happened. When his eyes adjusted he saw an empty socket in the ceiling. The bedroom also was dark and it smelled of stale air. "Smells dead," he heard Snooper say, though this was not said to him. She reached behind for the long flashlight slipped inside her pants. Banjo looked for another light switch and sniffed the air himself.

His sensitive nose detected no odor of death. To diminish her intuition he cautioned, "Don't assume until you've checked."

She continued about her business. "Uh-huh. Right." Snooper's flashlight beam traveled to the windows. "Open the drapes," she told him.

The draw cord was jammed. He forced the curtains open, standing on tiptoe and pushing the folds apart by hand, to let the early light fall into the room. He saw dirty clothes on the floor where they had been dropped. He stepped through them carefully so they would not tangle his feet.

Long legged TV trays stood crookedly on either side of the bed amid the clothes. Each held a mixing bowl. Banjo found a few unpopped popcorn seeds lying in the greasy bottom of one. Empty beer bottles were stashed upended in the other. A television guide opened to last night lay next to that bowl. Sniffing again Banjo recognized stale beer.

Snooper pulled the covers back. The man lay face up. His mouth was slack, lips tinted blue, and stubble bristled from jowls that settled loosely at the angle of his jaw. Snooper placed two fingers behind the angle and tugged. His mouth remained stiffly open. She lifted his fingers curled in a half fist. The length of his arm moved then popped back to its resting position when she let go. Banjo sniffed again and caught a whiff of feces. Snooper slid one hand inside his pajama top and felt his chest. She peeled open an eye lid. Then she returned the covers across his chest and smoothed them a little so they fit neatly under his chin. "Find out where the cops are. I'll go talk to her." She did all this and spoke these words without laying her eyes on Banjo.

Banjo stood still in the quiet, his back to the man dead in his bed. He listened to the distant indistinguishable voices from the living room. He heard bird songs outside. And way off he felt more than he heard a rhythmic mechanical sound like a dishwasher or clothes dryer and Banjo wondered if the woman, in her need for distraction, found some chore to tend to. The quiet deepened and soon he sensed that curious yet eerily familiar presence of the newly dead. He turned to the man. Still, after seeing so many hundreds, the utter silence of death struck him. The inert body lay stiffly as though frozen. But something lived, invisible and nearly palpable, in the air about him. Something remained just beyond the immediately detectable. Banjo always felt this. After a death this sensation climbed his spine and caused a shiver, then left a tiny residue of peace finally come.

He radioed the dispatcher from the bedroom. His voice and the electronic answer boomed disrespectfully in the silence. Then he picked up the arm load of medical kits Snooper left behind and sidled clumsily down the hall.

Snooper sat close to the woman on the sofa. Their knees touched and Snooper rubbed her shoulders and back. A single lit candle sat exactly centered on the coffee table before them. The tiny flame burned cleanly and caused little wrinkles in the air above it. The woman cried into one hand.

*****

Back in the ambulance, the dispatcher assigned them back to their earlier position. Banjo sighed with great dismay as he settled behind the steering wheel and looked out across downtown now busy with cars and people. With this single, first call Snooper had reduced him from a senior partner to a servant opening drapes and carrying her bags. Black fantasies jumped to mind. He saw her committing a great error that he, just in time, would correct. He saw her pick a fight in which he sustained injury while rescuing her. He wanted the Chief to fire her for something.

*****

Banjo went to Broadway Piano after his shift. The ambulance calls that left grass stain on his knees and tiny flakes of dried skin on his jacket existed elsewhere now that the black, curving, luminescent body responded beneath his fingers.

Though many years had passed since he played, the musician's discipline remained. Giving himself over to the music, he reached a distant memory source. From there he could perform what, until now, he could not remember. The sharply black and white keys flashed under his fingers. The keys answered lightly. He did not feel their action. He did not have to look at his hands.

Chapter 19

Banjo raked brittle elm leaves from the narrow flower bed squeezed between his patio and the fence. His rake was too wide to fit the bed and it clawed the cement. When the wind circled there last winter he heard these leaves scratching along the cement sounding much as his rake did now. Preparing to plant as spring advanced, he cleaned away the low banks of wind-rowed leaves.

He bored a finger into the freshly revealed well mulched dirt. He raked twisting lines in it, reminiscent of the tortuous etchings on The Parlour door and a vague, familiar foreboding overtook him. Something troubling disturbed the fresh light of spring and the green haze growing in the trees overhead seemed sinister and made him uneasy.

Banjo finished his beer, got another, then put some music on, turning it up loudly so he could hear it outside. Returning to the rake, he gouged the swirling dirt etchings into straight furrows.

The raking was soothing and Banjo enjoyed this gentle interaction with his tiny rectangle of earth. Fresh smells reached his sensitive nose. These were boyhood smells, well remembered from when he had lain on the ground to closely examine grass blades and watch insects. The sweet smells were a companion, as close to him as his music and his mother, and gave him peaceful spots of time that allowed him to sit still amid quietness. He reasoned this was why he found such joy in the details of dirt and grass and music.

Banjo considered what to plant in his skinny flower bed. Last year the clematis climbed his fence. Perhaps columbine would be fitting this summer. For a moment he considered planting a juniper tree. He loved the smell of juniper berries. An elm tree would be nice, too; this being his optimistic challenge to the elm disease taking the older trees in Denver. He had thought of planting trees other years, too, but annually decided he would not remain in the Debbie J long enough to witness their small increments of growth that represented continuity and permanence. He thought of Greystone. He would plant something for Greystone.

He felt the ominous disturbance rumbling within him again like an approaching thunderstorm. He recalled that Greystone had died in the spring and thought perhaps the coming anniversary caused this troublesome feeling. But naming the strange sensation did not calm it. Something frightening approached. His thoughts turned to impermanence.

He moved to the Debbie J promising himself to settle somewhere nicer soon. He put off gathering the symbols of home, occupying this dark space only superficially, waiting for something else. But some incompleteness these past ten years kept him from sinking his roots. From time to time a woman seemed necessary for that dimension. Eden brought a layer of contentment. He was sure he could have remained still with her long enough to feel settled. Then, briefly, there was Lauren.

He floated on the wind like a dandelion seed. He ached to touch down, take hold, and stubbornly root.

He leaned for a moment against his rake and listened. *Beethoven's Fifth Piano Concerto* played on his CD. This was the last piece he learned before joining the service. Banjo closed his eyes and imagined playing it before an audience in a great concert hall. He had expected to do so with the Lincoln Symphony, having been invited to perform with them as a young artist. The newspaper had written about this. Smiling music teachers told him to expect a stunning soloist's career. He had his scholarship to the Chicago Conservatory. He had this gift; this extraordinary gift within his heart and within the grasp of his nimble fingers. He stood on that threshold his final year of high school. It should have worked. He should be Arthur Joshua Stanley, performing artist, not Banjo, a nickname acquired in Vietnam when someone thought he should play that twangy instrument rather than a grand piano.

That was fitting. For war robbed him of the spirit that otherwise flowed into his music. There in the jungle his sense of beauty, thus his spirit, withered. Since then he had found nothing into which he could pour himself. He felt wetness in his eyes. He reached for his fresh beer and finished it.

Small shoots of grass poked greenly from the black flower bed. They pulled up easily and he smoothed off the dirt with his hand. He imagined a bigger flower bed, a brighter place to live with room for a piano. Through the sliding kitchen doors, his dark apartment looked like a cave. He wanted to come out and live his life in the light.

This was not a new thought. Banjo wondered how he had reached his forty-third birthday today, still hoping but somehow not attaining. Dan had much. Clayton's life was so spiritual, Lauren's so colorful. And the Chief, vastly wiser that he, had a home, a family, and the division to give himself to.

Banjo had balked at his opportunities. He was married for a time but had refused children. Women since had shown interest, but he had discarded them. He made decent money but had little to show for it. The Chief had worked hard but in vain to bring him into the administrative fold. Often Banjo imagined himself growing a comfortable little belly and a beard, and wearing bedroom slippers around the division as a supervisor. He threw that image back as well.

Somewhere along the line he had not taken a step; somehow he had missed his initiation as a man capable of settling and committing and growing. Over and over he tried to prove himself but nothing seemed to do. Somehow he had missed an extended hand.

Banjo heard rustling near the front door. A thick manila envelope slipped through the mail slot and dropped to the floor. Stopping first at the refrigerator for another beer, Banjo picked up the envelope and saw his mother's handwriting, recently grown unsteady, another marker of time gone by. The bulky envelope had a curiously light heft and he turned it over and fingered the rectangular shape inside, puzzling over why she sent him a birthday present now after so many years of cards alone. Many carefully placed strips of tape sealed the flap. Her need for thoroughness and certainty remained as strong as it

had been when she insisted on those from him at the keyboard.
He picked at the layers of tape briefly then tore the top off the
envelope. A thin box and a letter slid out. He read:

Son,

*I thought you would like your father's old war
medals. Though I searched high and low I could
not find the letter explaining his commendations.
He told me the stories only once just after he got
home from the war and said he never wanted to talk
about them again. I suppose he wanted to forget
all that. I wrote down all that I could remembered
of them. He told them in such a chilling way. They
weren't hard to recall.*

*I don't know if you're aware, but he died when he
was 43. Why did I decide it's fitting that I give these
to you when you turned 43? I know you never cared
for him much. I guess I hoped that someday you
would at least feel some ties to him. He was a good
man but so troubled. The war changed him.
Afterwards he drank too much and smoked. But he
was a good man. The war changed you, too. You
never told me your stories and I often wondered. It
was so odd. You went off to Vietnam, your father
died, and when you returned you were more like him
than my young virtuoso.*

Well, here's what he told me about the medals.

Banjo uncurled his arm and let the hand holding the
letter hang at his side. He calculated in his head. His father
had died in 1969 at forty-three. He must have been in high
school when he joined the Marines. He would have lied about
his age. Banjo added this to what little he knew about his
parent's early life. They must have been high school
sweethearts to have known each other before the war. He
chuckled cynically and wondered what the war had stolen from
his old man and hoped that it, too, had cost him deeply.

He looked at the closed box in his other hand. His father's war years had always remained hidden, understood but never discussed. That his father may have won medals never occurred to him. Medals, Banjo thought. He went to Vietnam to get home alive and earned no medals.

He opened the box. Resting in a bed of now fading royal blue felt lay a Purple Heart; next to it, a Bronze Star. He lifted the Purple Heart carefully. A dark, decades old impression remained perfectly outlined in the felt. The ribbon was faded. Banjo gently placed it back and brushed his finger over the old star. A sense of enormity overcame him. He recalled his own war terrors that merited no medals and wondered what his father had to fight through to win his. He read again from his mother's letter.

> *Your father, after only a short time in combat, became a sergeant, being promoted from corporal on the battlefield, and in this capacity had men under him. He cared very much for these boys. He was scarcely older than they were but he had more fighting experience.*
>
> *On patrol one afternoon (he was stationed in Borneo) they were walking through tall grass out in the open when machine gunners opened fire on them from a hill side. They dropped into the grass which covered them but each time one of them moved the grass moved also. The Japs were able to spot them and they killed two of your father's men this way. As long as they lay still the Japs could not see where to shoot but as soon as the grass rustled, they fired. They lay there a long time waiting for something to happen. The sun was right in their eyes and it was hard to see where the firing came from. One of his men was badly wounded and needed medical care. At last your father called out for everyone to fire at the next machine gun burst. Then he rolled over fast as he could to draw fire. The machine gun opened up, followed by such a volley of fire from his men as to sound like a tearing sheet, and the machine gun*

*fell silent. When the noise died away and your father
turned to see about his troops, his leg would not work
work. A machine gun bullet had struck his thigh
and for this he learned the Purple Heart and was
shipped back to Australia for R and R and to heal.*

*The next year (he spent three and a half years in
the South Pacific) he again was leading men on
patrol when a Jap tank burst through the jungle at
them. His men panicked and ran off. Your father
was so disgusted he picked up the large Browning
Automatic Rifle one of his men had dropped and
stood there firing at the little slit the tank driver
looks through. The way your father tells it he stood
there more angry than anything. He said he was
damned if he'd let a Jap tank scare him. (He wanted
to show his men something, too.) The tank bore
down upon him and he kept firing. Suddenly the
tank swerved off out of control and crashed back into
the jungle. He said he just turned and looked at his
men. For this he was awarded the Bronze Star for
bravery. He laughed at that saying he wasn't being
brave, just hopping mad.*

*This is what happened and these are his medals
for it. I was always proud of him. He was a good
man.*

*I hope you enjoy these. Take care of yourself.
Happy Birthday.*

*Love,
Mother*

Banjo backed up to his chair. When his calves bumped he
sat hard, letter dangling from one hand, medals held firmly in
the other. His chest filled with fluttering and he gasped to
catch his breath. Something huge had happened to him. A
great guiding myth cracked and was proved a lie. His father,
previously a brooding, violent presence became tangible,
reduced, and familiar. He was too much like that man in his

pickup: easily seen and almost touchable. His father was too much like himself: a combat veteran, a drinker, a good man.

Banjo grabbed his beer. He finished it on his way to the refrigerator for another. He saw a different kitchen where a shiny film of grease covered the appliances. A microwave containing a hideous form sat there. Somewhere he caught a whiff of cooked meat and he had to bend over and concentrate so he would not vomit. He heard maniacal laughing and saw Zagata's scarred face. Zagata spoke. 'You and me, little man. You and me.' Then smoldering pigtails rustled quietly in a breeze. A little girl with a hole torn in her belly floated there. Next to her drifted a man with no face. Screams filled his head. Banjo threw his head back and guzzled his beer.

He found himself in his bedroom rooting through clothes. He rolled a fat marijuana cigarette and pulled on it hard after lighting it. He carried the cigarette and beer into the living room and restarted his music, turning it up until the room shook. The images circled. Banjo made fists and beat his head to kill the faceless screams. He drank the beer and sucked in the marijuana smoke. The floating images obliterated his room and blackness caved in on him. Banjo squeezed his eyes tighter but the visions grew sharper. Screams pierced though he clapped his hands over his ears. He listened for his music but could discern only heavy vibrations beneath his feet. Banjo cried out and beat the beer bottle against his head and he sucked the cigarette down until it burned his fingers.

Then he grew lighter and the images dulled. Screams grew quieter in the distance. His room appeared as though through holes in clouds. He found the medals on the floor and kicked them away as he would the source of a noxious smell. He stumbled to the bedroom and rolled another joint. Clumsy now, he upset his beer and it soaked into the brown shag carpet. He lit the cigarette and fell onto his bed. He prayed the joint would outlast the memories. He inhaled hard and held his breath against the stinging smoke and the visions softened. His breathing eased. The muscles of his shoulders loosened. He could close his eyes now without seeing vividly. The hand holding the burning joint dropped to the bedspread and soon he was jolted awake by a hot smell. Banjo raised up and dropped the burning ember into a shell casing next to his bed. His weight rolled him onto his back. He raised a hand and let it slap against his forehead. "Why couldn't she just leave him dead and buried?" he groaned. "Goddamn her. Why couldn't she just leave him where he belongs?"

Chapter 20

Banjo slouched in the cab with his arms crossed and stared out the windshield. He cast a quick glance rightward toward the intersection. He mumbled, "Clear."

Swiveling her head left and right, Snooper idled the ambulance under the red light. She picked up speed so gently Banjo could scarcely feel it. Cars passed the ambulance by. Banjo called to her over the siren, "I'd like to get there while I'm still a young man."

She drove carefully with both hands placed properly on the steering wheel and ignored him. Cars filled the next intersection. None moved for the approaching ambulance. She turned off the siren and slowed, waiting for jammed cars to loosen.

Banjo bolted upright. "Blow them off the road! They'll get out of the way. Just light it up and blow them off the road."

"Hey. Hey. Hey. Settle down, Sunshine." Her eyes remained straight ahead. "They'll clear out."

"You drive like an old woman. Makes me nuts." He slumped again. "Wake me when we get there."

Zagata met them. A quite-pleased-with-himself grin filled his plump face. He held a man by the scruff of his coat, as though he had just caught a bad cat. The scar was quiet, though he met Banjo's eyes with a hard stare.

"Damn," Banjo wondered aloud. "What is he doing here?"

When the ambulance stopped Zagata opened the side door and flung the man in. The patient struck the diamond steel plated step and fell onto the stretcher. Outside now, Banjo watched the man settle himself on the bench seat. He rested his alligator boots on the stretcher rail and rubbed his scraped shin beginning to ooze blood. He wore cut-off jeans and his tanned legs were shaved clean.

Banjo watched Zagata from a ways off. He remembered Zagata's hot fury as he spoke his last words to Rocky and worried something lay beneath Zagata's cheerful grin. He would be careful around the erratic policeman. He asked, "What do you have?"

"This nut can't control himself."

The man spun on the bench. A tiny earring glittered from one lobe. "That's not fair!"

Zagata told Banjo and Snooper, "He's got a doctor's appointment this afternoon. Okay? He wasn't supposed eat or drink since midnight last night. Right? So what's he do? This morning the dumb son-of-a-bitch gets loaded. Now he's craving food."

"Well ..." he called from the ambulance. "You going to arrest me for that. Come on big guy." He held his wrists together as though they were handcuffed and puckered his lips. "Let's do it. Lock me up." He spread his arms. "So come on now, is this such a big deal? I get the starving munchies when I smoke. I don't trust myself not to eat. Somebody needs to watch me. Is that such a crime?"

Zagata's scar flashed. "Fag." He hopped into the ambulance. A single swing, so quick Banjo scarcely saw it, sent the man to the floor. Zagata said to Banjo, "You want him? I can throw his tight ass in jail for something."

Watching Zagata, Banjo asked the patient, "What's you doctor's appointment for?"

"I'm HIV positive." He made a sassy grin at Zagata. "So you better glove up before you touch me. And I have this abdominal condition. That's what my appointment is for. Can we go now?"

"In a minute." He inquired about Rocky. "Find the guy who shot him?"

Zagata took a deep breath. The scar undulated like a snake. "He's still in town. We know that." He looked off and his eyes flashed hotly. "He'll do something stupid pretty soon."

Snooper, watching from near the back bumper, caught Zagata's eye. He looked at her then turned back to Banjo. "You working with cutie pie here?"

"Cutie pie," she chuckled. "That's perfect. Just perfect." She stepped to the policeman and patted his scar.

Zagata jerked away as though burned. His eyes narrowed hatefully and he pointed. "Don't you ever touch me, woman."

Snooper crossed her arms and appeared merely curious about the cop.

Slowly Zagata relaxed and he said to Banjo, "She's a pisser, that one. I think I might like to fuck her."

She huffed. "In a pig's eye." She got in the ambulance.

The patient leaned out the side door. "Excuse me? But I believe I'm paying for this little ride and I would like to get along now."

Zagata offered, "I can still arrest him for something. Maybe get him for being an asshole in public. Take him out to the landfill for a little target practice."

"No," Banjo answered. He felt gritty and unclean. His dry throat croaked. "We'll take care of him."

"Suit yourself." Zagata dropped into the driver's seat of his police car. "See ya." The car door shut. He jerked the shift lever down. Tires barked.

Banjo felt the ambulance slipping under his shoulder. He stood to catch his balance. "Hey, Snoop! I'm not in yet."

"I know. Let's go. The city's getting busy."

Banjo got in back with the patient but leaned through the door into the cab and said to Snooper, "Never get cross with Zagata. You understand me? Keep your sassy mouth shut around him."

*****

At Denver General Snooper backed the ambulance to the dock and touched it softly with the bumper. Lauren stood on the dock looking in at Banjo through the ambulance's back window. She pointed to her ambulance and motioned for Banjo to help lift. She held her arms away from her sides and bulged her cheeks. Banjo poked his head into the cab. "Take this guy

228

in. I'm going to help Dan and Lauren lift a heavy patient." He enjoyed giving her the order.

"We got her in the ambulance with some firemen," Lauren told him standing at the back of her ambulance. "But I'm done in now. I need some help." Dan nodded from behind the patient's head and made wide eyes at the weight on his stretcher.

The heavy woman told them, "It usually takes four of five of you to pick me up." She lay beyond the stretcher width and the side rails could not be raised. The straps squeezed deep furrows into her jiggling flesh. Her stubby sausage fingers relaxed then regripped the stretcher rail. "You sure only three of you can manage?"

"We'll manage." Dan answered through his grunt. He lifted his end across the gap between the ambulance floor and dock. "This is just a straight up lift." Lauren stood and arched to stretch her back muscles. "Ready?" Dan asked her. "You ready, Banjo?"

All three squatted. Banjo took a breath. He exhaled forcefully at the first resistance to the lift. The stretcher legs slid downward as the patient rose. Near the top, just before the legs locked, Dan's face filled with disbelief.

"You okay down there, partner?" Banjo asked.

"Put her down," Dan told them urgently. "Put her down." His legs buckled and he struggled to control the stretcher's descent. He sat on the ambulance floor and the stretcher dropped the last few inches onto his knees.

The woman cried, "Oh! Oh!" and her doughy hands whitened around the stretcher rail. "Don't lose control of me. Don't let me tip over."

Banjo hurried to Dan. He lifted the pressure off Dan's legs. The stretcher slid onto the dock and Dan stared dumb-faced out to nowhere. Banjo told Lauren, "Go get Snooper. Have her help you wheel her in. I'll hold the stretcher." Lauren disappeared into the emergency department.

The patient dropped a hand over her heart and she gulped in air. "I told you boys it took more than you had to lift me." She turned her head toward Dan. "Is he all right? Oh. Oh. I'm sorry if you're hurt. Oh, dear. This has never happened.

This is so terrible." She reached a hand toward Dan who remained unaware. "Are you all right? Are you hurt?"

At last Dan focused on her. He seemed to think about the question. After a moment he nodded his head and whispered, "I believe so."

Lauren and Snooper brought orderlies. They leaned into the stretcher as though pushing a stalled car. Banjo sat next to Dan. He repeated the woman's question. "You hurt, partner?"

His eyes searched about. Dan shifted his right leg and cried out. One hand shot to his groin and the pain left his mouth drawn back in a tight line. "I tore something. I felt it rip when I lifted her." He looked at Banjo. "I think it's really bad."

"You'll be okay. Give you a couple days to sit around and you'll be back at it."

Lauren returned with a wheelchair. "Let's get you inside so's they can look you over."

Dan shook his head. "I can't get up."

She locked the wheels. "Oh, hush now. Banjo you grab him by that arm there and I'll take this one here."

Banjo stood and pulled under Dan's arm. Dan cried out again and he shrugged away from their hands. He planted both palms on the ambulance floor. "I said, I can't get up."

Now, curious on-looking people enclosed Dan and Banjo. The Chief in his slippers looked down at them. Half Deck, feet spread, arms akimbo, stood next to the Chief. His toothpick stuck straight out, clamped in his teeth as he thought. Nurses and physicians wearing green scrubs gathered and looked over the shoulders of others to see. Concern wrinkled a few brows. Lauren stepped back and put a hand to her mouth. Snooper crossed her arms and looked clinical.

"Well ...," Banjo hinted indignantly.

The circle shrank. The Chief kneeled down and slid an arm across Dan's shoulders. "Is it your hip?"

Dan nodded. "Somewhere in there."

Half Deck took charge. His toothpick jumped impatiently. "All right. All right. Let's get a stretcher out here." He looked at the Chief. "He going to need a dose of pain medicine before we lift, boss? He looks about half agonized there."

"Perhaps. Perhaps," the Chief replied absently.

"Get the stretcher right along side," Half Deck ordered. When it was positioned he ordered, "Banjo, you go around behind and take him up under the arms." He motioned to others on the dock. "You people here take his legs and be danged careful about it." Banjo kneeled behind Dan, slipped his arms under Dan's and took his wrists. He said quietly, "This is going to hurt, but we'll do it quick and be done with it."

"It already hurts," Dan answered, stiffening as hands slid under him.

"You people have him now? Careful not to drop him. Watch you don't hurt yourselves, too."

Banjo complained, "Goddamnit, Half Deck. This is Dan. Not a sack of potatoes."

"I know it's Dan. I can see him sitting there. All right, people. On three. One, two ..."

"This will be real quick, Dan," Banjo whispered.

"Three."

Many hands lifted carefully and Dan was elevated. The stretcher rolled beneath him. He was just touching down on the sheet when the next cry broke from him. Banjo patted his shoulder and noticed Dan's face was near the color of the white sheet under him.

******

Banjo drummed his fingers on an armchair in Ernie Webster's waiting room. He crossed his legs and bobbed the suspended foot. Hating to reveal very much, he supposed he could tell Ernie about Dan's injury last week and how no one was sure he'd be back on the streets. The therapist had come to know many things about his friends. Deep down, guiltily, Banjo wanted Dan's field instructor position. Then he'd always have new paramedics to send in first. He could probably talk about the medals. God, the medals. Why on earth did his mother send those things? The alarming sensation he felt just before they arrived must have been the universe's way of warning him. They were buried under clothes in his dresser but he could almost feel a cold spot through the closed drawer when he passed near. At least he'd have something to talk about. He hated the waiting game Ernie played so well.

The string of bells hanging from the front door knob jangled. Banjo hoped the person entering was not a client for one of the other therapists in the office. He hated sitting here with someone else. He sized them up for what was making them crazy and he believed they did the same. Ernie's door opened. He escorted a woman from his office, waved and told her to take care of herself, and, seeing Banjo, extended a hand inward toward a wing back chair. The hot seat, Banjo thought immediately. He didn't like taking turns with other people for that chair. It was always weirdly warm. And with its back too straight to slouch and cross his legs, it wasn't comfortable either.

He entered and sat down. Ernie Webster sat, smiled, and folded his hands. And they waited. "So," Ernie began after a moment, "What's new? I haven't talked to you in awhile."

Banjo shrugged. "Not much. Same stuff." He crossed his arms and looked out the window to the fire station across the street. The white fire engine sat on the ramp and fire fighters washed it. He talked out the window. "I got a letter from my mom."

"Your mother. I didn't realize you corresponded."

"I don't. She sends a card at Christmas and for my birthday."

"Did you just have a birthday?"

"Uh-huh. Forty-three big ones." Banjo found a green thread unraveling in one arm of the chair and he dallied with it.

"I just turned forty-two myself. Somehow this one was worse than forty or forty-one. I'm certifiably in my forties now, not at the edge anymore. I remember when my parents were this age. They seemed so old."

Banjo laughed. "My old man died when he was forty-three. So what's my mother do for my forty-third birthday? My mother sends me his war medals."

"He was decorated. That's more than I can say for my war experience."

"Me, too. I had a platoon leader that kept us out of those spots. He'd tell the chaplain he was going to kill the Colonel whenever he thought the Colonel was sending us on a stupid mission. Chaplain would go talk to the Colonel. We got pulled off patrol in time for Thanksgiving dinner that way. 'Chaplain', Leon would say, 'Colonel's trying to kill me. I'll kill anyone trying to kill me. I don't care what uniform he's wearing.'"

Ernie smiled. Banjo noticed a tiny, sparkling blue earring in his ear lobe. He stiffened and regarded him suspiciously. Ernie said, "I got my chest stomped during an ambush one morning. I'm not sure who did it but several ribs were separated from my sternum. I figured that was good for a Purple Heart, but it never happened."

"Dad got a Purple Heart and a Bronze Star."

"A Bronze Star. He did stand up and face the music, didn't he."

Banjo laughed. "He drove off an enemy tank with a BAR. Stood there firing at it until it rumbled back into the jungle."

"Do you feel one-upped by him again because he came home with medals and you didn't?"

He thought about this, searching for tell-tale stomach churning that told him Ernie was on to something. Banjo remained comfortable. "No. I never ducked anything. I wonder what I would have done, but situations never came my way. He deserved his glory."

"Sounds like you might not be as angry at him."

Banjo's hand bumped his mouth. Ernie waited quietly. Banjo drew a breath. "When I got those medals ..." He nodded his head. "When I got those and read mom's letter it was like something collapsed all around me. Mom talked a little bit about him and it was like I was reading about myself. I'm my father's age. We both went off to war right out of high school. Mom said he drank too much but that he was a good man, like she was asking me to forgive him."

"Your father sounds a lot like you."

He folded his arms tightly across his chest and stared at the triangle of chair between his legs. "At least I never beat up kids or stole their dreams."

"Don't you do that to yourself sometimes?"

Banjo avoided the question and looked back at the fire truck. "I always hated him. But all of a sudden he and I are just the same. So how could I hate him and not hate myself? I mean I've done some snakey things but nothing to make me hate myself. I don't know what to think of him now. But I don't want to spit on his grave anymore. What do I do with all of that?" He laughed. "This was a guiding principle all these years: my old man was worthless, he died a puking drunk and he screwed me up. Now, what do you know. Zip, squat, plunk. He's me.

"I got loaded, really loaded after that. I got so loaded I passed out before I could toss the joint. I woke up smelling smoke and there's a hole burned in one of my blankets. People could just as easily be saying the same thing about me that I say about Dad. He got looped, passed out, but, in my case, I burned the damn apartment house down."

Ernie waited. Banjo watched the firemen backing their truck into the station. He removed his fist from his mouth. "I know what plagued him. I know what he saw. He was still a son of a bitch but I know what followed him around."

"You both heard the same screams," Ernie told him. "You saw the same shot up bodies. You smelled the same blood and puke and shit. The memories are the same. Sooner or later, Banjo, we all have to see our parents for who they are. And they're very much like we are and the sooner we get used to that idea the sooner we can get on with things."

As they talked, Banjo felt something settle inside. New pieces fitted themselves into his emotional puzzle. He whispered an understatement. "This is quite a shock."

Ernie laughed. "Isn't this fun. I love my job." He watched out the window and Banjo turned there also. Leaves thickened in a walnut tree. Blue and yellow crocus shoots poked from the flower beds. Ernie turned back to Banjo. "Say, didn't Greystone die about this time of year?"

Banjo nodded. "Eleven years ago this month."

"How have you been doing with that. People often revisit their grief on the anniversary of a death. After Robby was killed I thought about him every January for years."

Banjo knew his drinking was heavier now that the iron touch of cold had lifted and the colors uncurled for spring. The Chief appeared to know this, seeming always to have a supervisor present when he showed up late for work. He lifted one shoulder. He curled one corner of his mouth. "I don't know. Maybe a little."

"It's something to be aware of."

"Sure." Within his reflections Banjo heard the polite beep of Ernie's watch alarm. The front door bells jangled.

"I think we should stop there, Banjo."

"I agree. A guy can only take so much in the way of revelation.""

*****

Banjo looked at his paycheck and figured. He added up his bills then looked off thinking harder. Money evaporated from his checking account. This he could not understand, though during his honest moments he knew he spent money loosely without any regard for later needs. He folded the check into his wallet and wiggled the torn open pay envelope back into the thickness of paper plugging his division mailbox.

"Banjo!" Half Deck's call was hard and sharp and Banjo's shoulders bunched instinctively. "How's about lunch? Tuesdays they have turkey and dressing in the cafeteria."

Banjo said, "Pass."

The supervisor tempted. "I have some thoughts on the directionality of your career around here, given that Dan is probably off the streets for good." Half Deck grinned. His toothpick pointed toward the ceiling.

"What?"

Half Deck continued past Banjo toward the door. "Let's go eat."

Banjo followed, feeling hooked but too curious to heed tiny warnings.

Fat women wearing white aprons and hair nets served up food in ladles. "How's the paramedic business?" they joked with Half Deck. "Picking up?" They chuckled and clucked, their faces bowed toward the plates they filled.

"As per usual." Half Deck answered. "And sometimes doesn't it stink, too."

"Oh Ronald," one said. "You're bad. Too, too bad."

Another threw her head back and barked one loud laugh at the ceiling. "You are bad," she agreed. "Uh-huh. They should make you go back to where you began and start all over again."

Half Deck wiggled an index finger at his plate. "Maybe a little more dressing on mine there, dearie."

"I don't know how you can work up such a appetite hauling all those sick people around. I don't see how you do it. No, I don't. No, sir." She dropped another spoonful on his plate and it dipped in her hand under the added weight. "Little bit extra gravy, hon?"

"A little bit."

She ladled on mud colored gravy until it dripped thickly off the plate. "Take some of that blueberry pie. They did a good job on it this morning. Not like it usually is."

Half Deck gave her a fish eye. "Just how many pieces did you have this morning?"

"Why, only one. On-ly one. That's my usual. Besides, how else can I recommend it to our customers?" All the women murmured jesting accusations back and forth and they chuckled knowingly.

"Just one piece," he repeated. "One piece of each pie is more like it. I never come through here when I don't see a piece missing from every pie in there."

They all laughed hard and waved him off. The cook dishing up Half Deck's plate passed it to him. "Now don't you be telling stories out of turn. Our new customer here," she nodded toward Banjo, "might get the wrong idea." She said to Banjo, "You new here, sugar. I've never seen you."

"No."

Searching for a table Half Deck said, "I love those old gals. Sometimes they'll tell you a joke that'd like to turn the air blue."

Seated, Half Deck sliced his turkey. He thumbed a mound of cranberries and dressing onto his fork then stabbed a piece of meat. It dangled and dripped gravy on its way to his mouth opened so wide the skin of his cheeks stretched.

Banjo picked at his thin white slices. His mound of dressing broke apart in hard chunks. He forked a solid square of dressing and raised it to eye level. "I see why you asked for extra gravy."

In time Half Deck sopped up the gravy with his bread leaving a brown swirl on his plate. He returned for that with his last bite of bread. "I swear," he sighed, sitting back and letting his belt out a notch. "I've been off the streets for ages but I never broke that habit of gorging my food down like I might get a call any second."

Banjo raised the subject. "What's going on with Dan?"

Half Deck bobbed his eyebrows as though he alone knew. "He's bunged up good. Tore some muscles, a ligament or two. It's a real bad injury. Almost had to operate to patch him together but they decided to wait on that. Anyway, he's off the street for good and we're looking for a new senior F.I."

Banjo bolted forward in his chair. "What's he going to do? The division isn't going to toss him away, is it."

"The Looner always takes care of the faithful. Isn't that right." Half Deck squirmed a little in his chair to get comfortable. "No, Dan will join our supervisorial ranks and Eric will leave them."

"Dan didn't take the supervisor's test. How can the Chief do that?"

"He can put anyone he wants into an acting spot. When the list expires Dan will take the new test and you can bet he'll be hired on for real."

A hard, physical sensation hit Banjo. "What about those still on the list?"

"There's only two. You and a burned out ex-supervisor." Half Deck lifted the lid off his coffee cup and sipped, satisfied to leave Banjo's question there. He removed a lottery ticket from his pocket. "I always like to scratch these after dinner with my coffee." He wiggled a fingernail along a row of covered numbers, mouthing each as they were revealed. "I swear if I ever win this thing I'm out of here. Did you hear I won a couple passes to the antique car show at Currigan Hall? The radio station had you call in and you had to name eleven kinds of cars in fifteen seconds while you're actually on the air. I nailed it in thirteen."

Banjo felt his strings being pulled. He stood and picked up his tray. "I'll go congratulate Dan."

"Now wait a minute. Hold on a minute," Half Deck chuckled and slipped the lottery ticket back into his shirt pocket. "We haven't talked yet."

Banjo sat and leaned over his tray. "We agreed some time ago we didn't like each other. Don't jerk me around. Now what do you want?"

"I said we're looking for a new senior F.I. I'm here to tell you to think about it because the Looner plans to ask."

"Ask... me? Last time I was field instructor it took exactly two months before the Chief busted me back down. Said I didn't set a good enough example for the rookies. I haven't changed much since then."

Half Deck shrugged and held that pose. "Like I say, the Looner takes care of those who keep the faith. Isn't that right. Didn't I say that? You have been keeping the faith, haven't you?" His left eye squinted so slightly Banjo nearly missed it and he knew Half Deck was working out a strategy. "Truth is, it's not a lot of extra money, maybe a hundred seventy-five a month. But you get your pick of the shifts and any partner when you don't have a new guy."

"When's he planning this?"

"Don't know for sure. Maybe toward the end of the month. We have some new hire-ees starting in May." Half Deck ran his tongue around the inside of his cheek to clean out food. "You and I have our own uniqueialities and we get at each other wrong. But we both want what's good for the best paramedic division in the USA."

"Chief ask you to talk to me."

"No, sir."

Banjo looked at him hard. "I'll think about it."

"I hope you do."

Banjo prepared to stand but a thought struck him and held him at the table. He leaned across to Half Deck. "Tell me what you know about Zagata."

"Bad cop. Stay away from him."

"You were a supervisor during all the police department drug business. What happened?"

"You mean when Mr. Zagata was conscripting cocaine and heroin and selling it? Don't know. Nobody never told me anything officially. But I heard. They say he blackmailed his captain someway to take the fall. Then that captain just happened to go off and kill himself. That's the action-summary of what I know. Except when I went to cover that shooting you and Daniel got mixed up in at the Delphi."

Banjo waited. "And?"

"And while you two were dodging rounds he was sitting as warmly as you please in his police car. My guess he was counting money from the drug deal that went to smithereens up there. That'd be my guess. I never had much use for him since. So you stay away from him. I keep telling you that. Don't I tell you that?" Half Deck picked at his teeth with his toothpick.

"Anybody else that might know something about Zagata?"

"Aren't you listening? I said avoid him like the plaque. Why are you obsessiating on him anyway?"

"He started showing up on my calls and I can't get him out of my mind. Gives me the creeps. It's like he's my curse."

"Go read your newspapers. They had lots about that business. Even did a piece about Zagata himself, as I remember, when the cops investigated him."

"When did all that happen?"

The supervisor frowned in thought. He belched and his cheeks bulged. "That would have been about ... Well, when were you and Daniel ducking lead at the Delphi?"

Now Banjo thought. "I don't know. About 1980."

"Well, that's about it then. I'd start looking about the spring of '79. Uh-huh, I believe that'd be about right. Captain Bancroft shot himself January of 1981. I remember that because I drove my new 1981 Oldsmobile to his funeral and it was the slickest car there, excepting the hearse."

The proximity of factual information quickened his pulse. Zagata's increasing appearances seemed to correspond to Banjo's growing worry. He wondered if Zagata had some extrasensory means of knowing of secret and unusual interest in him. He wondered what Zagata would do to someone he found meddling. His rage flashed when Snooper simply touched him. His rage would probably explode if the vulnerable areas of his past were probed. But if Banjo was being preyed upon, he should learn of his predator.

Chapter 21

The library at the **Denver Post** was less than he expected. A few microfiche machines were lined up against one wall in a small room. Scores of dated microfiche files were stored in gray file drawers against the opposite wall. Thus, decades piled upon decades of Denver history were organized in a small, uninspired room. A sign admonished library users to keep the blue celluloid slides in proper order when returning them to their files.

Banjo browsed along the files. Nineteen sixty-nine arrested his attention for that was the year his father died and the year he returned from Vietnam. An eerie sensation crawled up his spine. It was as if he returned from his war exactly when his father died in order to continue his father's disordered and unsettled life. Now he was forty-three, as his father was when he choked to death on his vomit, and Banjo sensed he was at some vital moment that would decide if he, too, would die his own disordered death or live on. His thoughts went to Zagata and he wondered how dangerous that cop might be.

He found the files for the year he started at Denver General and knew, if he looked, he could find accounts calls he responded to that year. He remembered his very first: a ten year old boy who had drowned. A priest was giving the child last rites when Banjo snatched him up and rushed him away. He learned later that the family had understood he was dead and did not want him transported at all. The boy's mouth was full of water that sloshed out when Banjo picked him up. Banjo never forgot pressing his mouth against the boy's wet face to breathe for him and hearing gurgling deep within his small chest. That was seventeen years ago.

In fact, every memory that tore through his head lay quietly within these flat sheets of blue film. In 1978 he and

241

Greystone pulled two burned up children from a garbage dumpster. Banjo touched 1980 and heard shots in the Delphi Hotel which he feared might kill his partner.

The Golden View Apartment fire that the Chief had recently painted from memory was contained there in 1981. And, of course, that was the awful year, the year John Greystone was killed. A grave silence tugged at Banjo as he looked at that year. Therein lay the details of that night. But he did not tear the vault-file open to revisit them as he might have other years when the anniversary was imminent. He found himself instead wanting to pass it by.

Nineteen eighty-two was the year a Christmas Eve blizzard paralyzed Denver. Banjo worked sixteen hours a day seven straight days until other paramedics could dig themselves out and come to work. He remembered responding to a man whose throat had been cut and stalling his ambulance in a snow bank. Banjo never made it to the call. He still wondered about that man.

During one shift in 1986, his first three calls were for people in cardiac arrest. He resuscitated all three and each woke up and thanked him before they reached the hospital. Somewhere in there was an article about him. For a day, he was the paramedic who could raise the dead. He was very proud of that day and believed then he could do this work forever.

The winter of 1989 was the winter of the jet crash. He saw again the snow covered bodies on the runway and the pitiful fireman trying to find a paramedic who would save the baby whose head was nearly torn from its body.

Banjo came to 1991 and stopped. A warm, cooked meat smell washed over him and he turned sharply away. That was just a year ago and his memory of the baby killed in the microwave was too fresh to let it into his consciousness. He returned to 1979.

Banjo removed several weeks of slides. He drew a deep breath as he slid the first into the slide tray and scrolled the machine toward fall. The police department drug scandal was headline news back then and would not be hard to find. He hoped Zagata would not detect some disturbance.

Banjo worked his way through the front pages of the daily papers from that fall. He started out scanning each methodically, but as he looked deeper he grew anxious and hurried, as though he had only so much time before his search was discovered. He passed through September. His breathing quickened when he positioned the slide bearing October's papers for he was sure that month would bear news. He found that his hand trembled and he could not steadily control the scrolling knob. He approached the end of October and thought it would be to ironic if the first account of this was on Halloween. It was not.

He removed October's slide, tossed it aside, and replaced it with November's. He moved the page finder to November first to begin his search. And there was Zagata's face. Banjo startled as though found out. Zagata. He was in his uniform picture and he sat stoically before the American flag staring intently at nothing. But his cold eyes took Banjo in nonetheless, just as they had last shift.

This was Zagata. Showing up not on the day when witches and warlocks rose to their wickedness, but surviving that night to infect the holy day that followed. Banjo shivered. His stomach began to grind.

He read. The headline stated that Zagata was suspected of stealing drugs from the police department drug locker and was placed on administrative leave. An informant claimed this to be true, stating he had purchased cocaine from Zagata. Banjo wondered what had happened to him. The Chief of Police pledged to investigate this thoroughly in order to regain the public's trust.

There was nothing more in the following addition or the day after. Within three days there were more headlines. The police were not giving the press satisfactory answers when asked how many officers were being investigated or how high the investigation was extending. Banjo sensed an immediate suspicion and impatience in the articles.

A later addition focused on Zagata. He leaned close to the screen as he would to study a viper enclosed in glass.

Zagata was emerging as a central figure in the police investigation, though he denied any illegal activities. But the newspaper reporters also found other higher ranking officers in the police department of greater interest. Banjo found Captain Bancroft's name first mentioned here.

The Denver Post cast Zagata favorably; sympathetically, Banjo thought. He was a decorated veteran officer, having rescued two women from a house fire, and was noted for his unorthodox methods of police work. Banjo had to chuckle at this. The account told the story of Zagata hiding for seven hours in a trash box, waiting for a contractor to throw away building materials containing drugs which he would later claim after the garbage truck he hired hefted the box and carried it away. Zagata went with the box of trash and arrested the contractor and truck driver when the two re-opened it. Out of radio range, he had to handcuff the two to the trash box and use a pay phone to call the local police department, which happened to be the Weld County Sheriff's Office, many miles north of Denver.

Zagata admitted to being in and out of the drug locker during the time under investigation but knew nothing about the illegal activities. He alluded to difficulties with superior officers who criticized some of his methods.

Then Banjo read something of great interest. The article mentioned that Zagata had been shot in the face and his partner killed in a drug deal three years before. The murderer had gotten away. This, Banjo decided, was the reason for the article's soft touch and Zagata's lightening strike scar.

The reader at the time would be left believing Zagata was set up to take the fall for the Denver Police Department. Banjo wondered. He looked through more editions without finding anything new until reaching the end of November. This reflected a news conference at which the Chief of Police announced the early retirement of Captain Harry Bancroft who was the commander responsible for facilities and internal security and ultimately responsible for the loss of items seized by the police. The investigation, the article promised, would continue. Banjo searched into December and January but found nothing more.

His eyes were tired and his bunched up shoulders were sore. He wasn't sure what he had learned but he was impressed by how quickly Zagata had disappeared from the investigation after Bancroft was sacrificed. He vaguely remembered the old Captain. He was a useless old alcoholic whom Zagata still talked about, but he seemed inoffensive enough. The intensity of his search receded as the harmless nature of the information grew apparent.

Then Banjo remembered that Bancroft had killed himself. He took the slides from early 1981 and searched through the obituaries. He found the account then scanned the rest of that issue for a related story. He found it in the *Metro Denver* section.

Bancroft was found dead in his van in City Park east of downtown according to the article. He died of a single gunshot wound to his head, evidently self inflicted. His service revolver was still gripped in his hand. An empty gin bottle lay on the floor of his van. Blood alcohol tests revealed he had been drinking heavily at the time. His wife, Harriet, told the reporter that they were planning to move to Arizona nearer their children. Banjo took a wad of paper from his jacket pocket and wrote her name.

Banjo switched off the microfiche machine and forced his tired eyes to focus on items in the present. He noted the late afternoon time. He looked outside. Tired of old memories, drugs, dead partners, and suicide, he got up and returned the slides to their proper place in time.

Outside, the spring sunshine warmed him nicely and he smelled a flowering plum tree nearby. But the heaviness of Greystone's death returned with the freshening breeze of spring and this year Banjo found himself resenting the old intrusion for it always ruined the sweetness of the season. It was time to pay his respects to his old partner and perhaps to say good-bye.

*****

Banjo stood before the twisting designs etched in The Parlour's frosted windows and hefted his backpack higher on his shoulder. The same old recollections came to mind. On earlier anniversaries of Greystone's death he had welcomed these remembrances for their familiarity. Now their painful intrusions were not desired. The urge to honor Greystone's death this way had not been strong this year and he wondered why he had come.

The darkness inside closed in heavily. The yellow-orange lighting he once longed to recreate in his home left him feeling melancholy.

Banjo looked for Jackson. A flat faced woman with stubby hair jerked open taps instead. She looked at him in a business-like way and arched her eyebrows high in question. He answered, "Coors, I guess."

His booth remained as empty as his wish to occupy it. But this was the eleventh anniversary and tradition and duty were important. He settled himself and soon the amber glass of rising bubbles was placed on a napkin before him. He took the corduroy journal from his backpack while keeping one eye on the bar to catch movement elsewhere. He opened it to the shoulder patch which he fingered respectfully. He took a pen from his pocket, clicked it open, and held it just above a clean page, waiting for inspiration. When words did not come, Banjo grew frustrated as he would when sleep would not come. He let his eyes travel around the bar. He was bored.

This place did not please him anymore. Too many memories lived among these booths and tables and the agony they carried was no longer a payment he wished to make. He wondered if by simply choosing he could control the blazing memory flashes. He remembered a story in which a demon disappeared when the little girl he vexed told him at last that he had no power over her. Banjo wished Zagata would disappear that easily. These thoughts concerned Banjo for he had never been without fear or pain and in their absence he worried he would have nothing left to feel at all. He sipped his beer. Its cold bite was not enticing.

He wrote in his journal. *'Sometimes I wonder if you did step in front of that car.'* The sentence shocked him. He whispered, "Aw, Christ. I'm sorry." Suddenly breathless, he gulped his beer and he held the empty glass over his head.

Jackson's familiar tug did not come. Banjo shifted to see the bar. The short haired woman talked with another woman at the bar. He called, "Excuse me. I'll have another." She took her time. When she brought it he wanted to reach up and rub her hair that was cut to an erect one inch all around.

Banjo hunched over the journal. *'But how was it for you around the division? Were you feeling like all your options had run out? Did you wake up one day and suddenly realize you blew it somewhere along the line? Did stuff inside get to churning so hard you thought you would explode? What happened? Did your heart finally break? Did you deliberately step in front of that car?*

'I am where you were. The young guys look up to me but I'm only a stake in the ground; something to aim for then move beyond.' He toyed with the napkin that soaked up dribbles of beer. He worked thoughts around but they would not take on words. *'How could you not have seen that car? I realized awhile ago that it didn't hit your door. The car went wide. If you had just stood next to the ambulance it would've gone right past. But it got you. How could you miss seeing something that close, coming so fast?'* Banjo clenched his fist and he saw an image he had denied before. Several steps beyond the ambulance sitting properly next to one another on the asphalt were Greystone's shoes, left behind when he was torn out of them and flung rag doll fashion into the bushes. Banjo drew one hand hard down his face and whispered, "You should've looked." Fearing someone might hear, he secretly wrote to his old partner, *'But maybe, you son-of-a-bitch, maybe you did.'* His eyes traveled wildly about the bar searching out those who could have heard this. He swallowed to quiet himself.

'Did you do that on purpose, John Greystone? Did I live all these years thinking I'd gotten you killed?' Banjo looked up from the page. *'I don't know, either. But that ain't my problem anymore, old partner. I got enough going on. I got some crazy cop following me around. Goddamn Zagata. You remember him. I swear he's killed a couple prisoners and I'll bet he had something to do with old Bancroft's suicide.'*

Banjo finished his beer and slid the empty glass to table center. *'I was at the newspaper library today and walking past all their files was like walking through a grave yard of old memories that won't go away. Standing there I realized how old they were. You died eleven years ago, old partner. I'm sorry you're dead. You don't know how sorry I am. You don't know how much I miss you. But this is my last entry. I'm not driving my stake in the ground next to yours. I have to keep moving. Things are changing too fast. There was a time I would've thought this was running out on you. But you're not the one in trouble, partner. I am. And I'm thinking I'm not the one who ran. Maybe you were.'* He shifted so that his back leaned against the wall. He lifted one foot onto the bench seat so he could see throughout the little place.

Banjo recalled Dan's awkward entrance years ago into the Greystone centered clique that had gathered here frequently. During that visit Banjo watched Eden's fascination with the handsome young rookie. Two years later they all celebrated here when his old friend Robert at last was accepted to medical school. He mourned here when Eden returned home to Pennsylvania. Annually he sat here to conjure up Greystone. And he remembered fretting that, as a supervisor, he would be welcome here no longer.

Few living friends came here anymore. He alone was left to tell the paramedic division stories that lived within the Parlour. These were numerous but old. Something dragged him forward now. Banjo closed his journal and put the shoulder patch in his pocket. Remembering something he turned back to the booth and whispered, "I planted a rose bush for you, old friend. It's over in Cheesman Park where you and I liked to hang out." Banjo recollected a call he and Greystone had run on there but let it go. "Oh, by the way," he added. "I sold my pickup and bought myself a piano. I'll think about you when I play."

Banjo turned sideways to maneuver between the close tables. He passed the bar, nodded to the stranger drying glasses, and opened the door to a bright, clean blast of spring sunlight.

*****

Morning sun warmed his face as he sat cross legged in the grass of Ruby Hill. Stabs of light ricocheted off downtown buildings. Details were sharp and clear and so close Banjo felt he could tap his finger on the tops of buildings or run his hand along their smooth sides. He reached for the styrofoam cup steaming within the circle of his legs. Little waves wrinkled across the coffee surface when he blew on it. Snooper, sitting next to Banjo, reached for her cup also. Banjo liked this silent morning clarity for its restoring powers. As the sun warmed his skin something else penetrated deeper to warm him.

Snooper cleared her throat. "Talk to Dan lately?"

"I saw him the other day," Banjo answered through a yawn. "Surgery's definitely out." Then Banjo wondered when the Chief would ask him about the field instructor's job. He asked Snooper, "Who do you hear is filling Dan's old job?"

"I hear talk about filling it with one of the other F.I.'s, then adding a new instructor. Clayton probably."

"Clayton! Clayton's a rookie."

She shrugged off the observation. "He's been here a couple years. You look at the instructors. They're all in the two to five year range now, except for Dan. Besides, Clayton has a gift. He sees things coming. It's almost like he can read minds. He'll keep himself out of trouble." She looked at him squarely. "Besides, you're not really interested, are you?"

"Maybe. I thought about it. Half Deck told me they were thinking about me to replace Dan so I was giving it some consideration."

"Half Deck? He has nothing to do with it. I catch the talk but, I have to tell you, your name never comes up."

The hand holding his cup slashed away flinging the coffee into a luminescent sheen. It held an undulating surface for an instant then splattered steaming to the grass. "They need experience in there. New guys need to know our traditions; our ways. They need discipline. They need to be taught respect. I see kids been here a year think they're the best paramedics God

249

ever put on this earth. Whose that new guy working with Roy? Big fat kid, wears a belt buckle that says "Paramedic" on it. Saw him write in the dirt on the ambulance under where it says Paramedic Division, 'The best in the country'. Anybody has to tell people they're the best, isn't." He needed to prowl about. He rolled to his side and pushed himself up. "Half of the guys down here are so new they never even heard of Greystone. And the Chief is turning the whole division over to those dweebs."

Snooper watched him pace about on the grass. "I thought you just wanted to run calls and be left alone. Why do you care who becomes the next field instructor?"

"Look at me! I'm forty-three. Do you know how old Greystone was when he got it? Thirty-nine. How old is Dan? Thirty-five, thirty-six? One lift got him. One car got Greystone. That's all it takes down here. One of anything. More and more I get to thinking maybe there's one of something out there waiting for me." His fist went to his mouth and he turned to face another direction. "But when I think about gettin' off the streets... You're not a real paramedic when you leave the streets." He pointed downtown. "That's my world. When I see all the pretty lights of Denver spread out I think there's a half million people down there who depend on me. There's a half million people I'll lay it on the line for. And I'm proud. I am genuinely proud. I'll go anywhere those people ask. No questions. That's who I am. That's all I want.

"But I see these kids zooming right on by becoming supervisors and field instructors thinking they know what's best for a place. They don't plan to stick around but for a few years, yet they tell us older guys what has to change when they don't even know our soul. Then the Chief threatens to fire me and Zagata is prowling around out there like he's keeping an eye on me." Banjo crossed his arms tight across his chest and felt the pressure of his second chance vest. "I don't know what I'm going to do. I do not know what I'm going to do. Dan's job looked like a way out. A little advancement, I could pick a shift away from Zagata's. I'd have someone to send in first on calls."

Snooper picked at the bristling grass next to her. "What do you have left to prove, Sunshine?"

"What?"

"What do you have to prove to the rest of us."

"I don't have to prove a damn thing to you guys."

"I know." She dallied with the grass more and looked puzzled. "I told Half Deck I wanted to work with you."

Banjo stopped. He looked at her. "You did this? You're the reason I get out of my warm bed and freeze my ass in the morning?"

Her shoulders bobbed with a quick, little shrug.

He scrunched his eyebrows. "You got your way with Half Deck's schedule?"

"He was more than eager to stick you on early mornings with me."

"No doubt. What'd you want me for?"

"I admire you."

Banjo looked at her from narrowed slits. "You admire me?"

She didn't answer but pulled blades of grass from the dirt.

"You admire me for what?"

"I hear talk." Snooper pooched out her lower lip and raised an eyebrow as though to say the talk had merit. Banjo tightened his arms more protectively still against what she intended to say. "People know you're going through a hard time and they talk and they see. Some folks down here get a look about them when their time is running out. You've got that look, Sunshine. Some say you'll be gone in a year. Some hope a miracle will happen and the Chief will forget the past and make you a supervisor. Actually most the people I talk to like that idea."

"Only most?"

"So I took the opportunity to work with you."

"Why?"

"Why not?"

He laughed to himself.

"What's so funny?" she asked.

"You."

Her back straightened. "What's so funny?"

"You."

"I said, what's so funny?"

251

Banjo asked again, "Why me?"

Now Snooper laughed. "Once you're gone there's never going to be another Banjo, except for maybe me. Suppose I just wanted a closer look at the original before you vanished?"

Banjo grew stubborn. "No way anybody is forcing me off the street. Not the Chief, not these hotshots, not-no-way-never nobody!" Banjo thought again. He smiled a little. A bit mystified, he said, "You got Half Deck to change the schedule so you could work with me?"

They fell quiet and Banjo warmed to her. He felt fully seen and Snooper, having taken in the good and the bad, nevertheless chose to stay near him. Banjo trusted her.

She spoke again. "I don't give many people my respect. Sooner or later everyone compromises a value or hides behind a lie. You never do. You're right out there for everyone to see and people can be damned if they don't like you. That's standing full face to the wind. That, I can admire. You're also the best paramedic down here so how could I resist."

Banjo sat once more and the stiff grass pricked him. His mind quieted and his focus opened once more to the clean morning. He laughed again within his chest. "You are one goofy broad."

*****

He touched the piano keys as he might absently touch a pet curled in his lap. In a state sweetly absent of thought he played nice chords and easy stretches of music he knew well.

The blonde piano fit against the wall only after he had shoved his vinyl recliner into the middle of the room. Banjo admired the piano's soft light reflecting glow. His apartment was less a cave for it, though his narrow living-dining room space was far too small for such a piece. Crowded now, he could extend his arms from his rocker and nearly touch both his stereo equipment and his new piano.

Old sheet music piled up next to the brass tipped legs near Banjo's left foot, this sent after a telephone call to his mother. Banjo had placed a TV tray next to the piano for his coffee cups. He used paramedic division patches as coasters. Geranium blossoms floated in a bowl of water sitting on top of the piano, next to a photograph of Marine Corps friends. He loved his well tuned instrument and daily enjoyed running a dust rag over its smooth surfaces.

Banjo dabbled with the various music scores sent by his mother, trying out his memory of them. He could still read through a few and the strength of his old music training pleased him. Banjo paused and took his coffee cup. As he sipped, his eyes settled on the scrap of paper he had set near the keyboard after returning from The Parlour. Harriot Bancroft, it read. He thought.

Banjo went to the dining room table where the telephone book was. He cradled it in his right hand and thumbed through it backwards. At a certain page he drew his index finger down the list of names. There were many Bancrofts. But he found an H. Bancroft, and he recognized the address as a residence for the elderly not far from him on Ellsworth Avenue. He closed the book and set it aside. He paced the short length of his dark apartment. Suddenly anxious, he went out for a walk, knowing if he did not he would sit in his cave and drink. Headlights and grills faced him in the parking lot when he opened the door. He edged sideways between the cars. If he knew where Snooper lived he would go by to talk. Instead he wandered obsessively along Ellsworth Avenue.

Chapter 22

At the 7-11 on Colfax Snooper told Banjo, "Get me some, too. The usual cream and sugar."

Banjo went inside and poured two cups. It smelled pretty fresh. He filled his to the top and left Snooper's an inch below. He poured cream into hers and stirred. He added another dab and stirred again until a certain smooth, muddy color swirled up. Then he poured in two packets of sugar and twirled her coffee still more. Banjo enjoyed fussing with Snooper's coffee. She took pleasure in having it just so.

At the counter Banjo heard the siren pop. "Time to go to work," he told the clerk. "Catch you later." Settling himself into the ambulance he asked, "Did I ever tell you about the call Dan and I got out of here? The manager threw coffee on some guy's pecker who was peeing on the corn flakes. By the way, where are we going?"

"We have a stabbing out on Colorado." Snooper took a couple sips. "Oh, Banjo," she sighed. "You are very good with my coffee." She steered with one hand and held her coffee with the other. At corners they tilted their cups to compensate for the ambulance sway.

They had to park nearly a block away from the address at the end of a line of police cars. No police officers smoked their cigarettes and visited outside as they did when the event no longer held their interest.

"There's something mighty different about this one, Sunshine."

"Maybe they're still looking for the guy who did it." They loaded their equipment on the stretcher and bounced it along the cracked and uneven red rock sidewalk.

Neighbors gathered in the front yard trying to see beyond the hedges that arched over the porch steps which formed a cave-like entrance to the front door. Women stood with their arms crossed telling each other that they knew trouble lived in that house. Men smoked their cigarettes and yelled at the kids to let the ambulance people by. A frowning policeman guarded the door. Banjo said, "Hey." There was a discomforting give to the front porch floor.

"You remember Rocky?" the policeman asked. "The jerk in there with the knife sticking in his chest did it."

Banjo asked, "Get the suspect?"

"Whoever stabbed him was long gone before we got here."

"How's he doing?"

"I said, he killed Rocky."

The ammonia smell of cat urine made Banjo's eyes water. Yellowing newspapers covered some of the windows and cast the room in dim and old looking light.

"Where we going?" Snooper asked generally.

"Medical! In the bedroom! Here!" It was Zagata. Banjo nearly dropped the trauma kit out of astonishment. It was always Zagata. Everywhere he went, it was Zagata. Cynically, Banjo wondered why the cop was in such a hurry to help his partner's murderer.

In the bedroom Banjo saw the knife first, twitching with each heartbeat, glinting rhythmically like a weak light flashing. Zagata knelt next to him. "I think he's stuck right in the heart, Banjo. What do you think?" Zagata held the hard side of his face toward Banjo and his livid scar shifted.

Banjo whispered, "Holy shit." To Zagata he said, "Don't move him. If the knife is dislodged at all he'll bleed out."

The man turned his face and fastened his eyes on Banjo. "Don't let me die, man. Don't let me die." Then he said, "They set me up."

Zagata interrupted. "Let's get him going. We wasted enough time looking for the suspect."

Banjo said to Snooper, "We have to be real careful with him. Get one of the cops to bring in the stretcher. I'll try to stabilize the knife."

Zagata bolted upright and leaped over the patient. "I'll help her. You can do more good here where I am, Banjo."

The light was dim and Zagata's quickness startled Banjo. But Banjo caught his mean smile and Zagata's fierce eyes engaged his for a moment. He heard a little grunt which could have risen from the patient, or from Zagata in his sudden movement. And perhaps there was a change in the way the knife glinted in the available light. This flashed by in an instant. Banjo looked down. He gasped. The man's eyes focused nowhere and the erect knife stood still.

*****

At Denver General Snooper hosed the man's blood from the back of the ambulance. Red water rushed along the curb and dropped through a grated drain. Banjo scrubbed at clotted blood stuck to the stretcher frame.

Snooper screwed the nozzle shut to listen. She laid a hand on the top of her head and twisted up her face. "What exactly did you see again?"

He wished he had said nothing to his partner. Had he really seen Zagata touch the knife? It angled differently after Zagata sprang over the patient. He was sure of that. And he *was* sure of Zagata's pleased and cunning look that seemed to dare Banjo to say anything at all of this. Banjo closed his eyes. There again was the man, watching a knife bob in his chest, pleading with him to save his life. Zagata said something about looking for a suspect but another officer said the suspect had run off before they arrived. He pondered what the patient was trying to say.

What did Banjo see during that dimly lit second? He had seen nothing. No one could be so precise, so quick, so subtle, and so sure of himself to look Banjo squarely in the eye and execute a man. No one. Not even Zagata. But something had happened. He knew that as surely as Clayton had known something had happened in the jail cell a year ago.

Banjo looked at Snooper. "Forget it. I didn't see anything." He scraped at the blood with a piece of gravel that lay on the floor. "I just got a feeling."

"You going to tell anyone?"

"Tell them what? That Zagata maybe willed some guy to die?"

"If you raised it through the Chief and the Chief made a formal report, my guess is it would get looked into."

Banjo snapped the latex gloves off his hands and brushed the residual power against his pants. Dusty hand prints remained on his thighs. Banjo remembered the livid, flashing scar. Zagata had directed it at him, exactly, and only at him, not his partner's killer. "I don't know what I saw."

"Listen Sunshine, if you think something happened you need to tell the Chief."

"And what do you think would happen then? I can hear those Internal Affairs guys now. 'Tell us, Mr. Stanley, exactly what you saw.'"

"'Well sir,' I would say, 'I saw a guy die of a stab wound to the heart.'"

"'And what did you see Officer Zagata do?'"

"'Well sir,' I would say, 'I saw Officer Zagata hop over the patient to help my partner get the stretcher.'"

"'I see. Then what did you see?'"

"'Well, sir. Then I saw the guy dead.' Not too compelling, I'd say. Wouldn't you, Snoop?"

She said quietly, looking straight at him, "You never pulled up short before. Why are you doing it now?"

"Listen. You don't turn in a cop just because you got a feeling. I don't read minds. I don't see into the souls of men. Leave me alone. I don't need another conscience riding in the seat next to me."

Snooper turned her head but a side-long look of disgust trailed along behind. Pressure grew in his chest. Heat rose behind his second chance vest. He stepped from the ambulance but found no relief outside from his prison within.

*****

Before leaving Denver General Banjo found a new memo folded precisely and tented neatly over the wild outcroppings of paper protruding from his mailbox. It read, *'Until further notice or until you professionalize your mailbox your mail can be picked up in dispatch between the hours of ...'* Banjo wadded Half Deck's memo and flung it straight at Half Deck's office. He said, "Like I need this shit." It plunked quietly off the window and skidded under the sofa.

He heard the Chief's door open and a little change in his stomach told him that the Chief must be prowling for him again. He feared the Chief knew of the stabbing and would question him. Instead Dan came from the office leaning heavily over his cane. He carried a thick file folder under his arm. He smiled. Banjo saw the curling file and the faded pencil notes on its jacket. Some of the notes were smudged under old gray coffee stains. Banjo asked, "What's the Chief have you doing there?"

"It's an old proposal Greystone put together to train new field instructors."

"They need it. I understand Clayton is the newest among your rare breed."

Dan watched Banjo for a moment. He nodded. "I think Clayton will do well."

"Not many whiskers on his shiny chin."

"I know. But we see advantages in using younger paramedics."

Banjo raised a hand. "Spare me. I don't need to hear this."

"The Chief wants me to dust this off and see if I can't put a program together."

"You want to do some good, you'd make a field instructor's program for all those supervisor's. I even know what I'd call it. I'd call it the Phoenix car for all those desk bound supervisor's rising from the ashes. I'd love to get Half Deck on the street and watch him squirm. But then I probably wouldn't qualify for your elite program, would I?" Banjo again noticed Dan watching. "What in the hell are you looking at me like that for? I hate it when people look at me that way. Makes me think they know something I don't want them to know."

Dan motioned with his head. He turned using small steps and walked to the Chief's office, tilting heavily over his cane. Banjo followed. Dan sat in the straight back chair in front of the Chief's desk. Unsure for a moment where to sit, Banjo thudded into the Chief's high back swivel chair and kicked his heels onto the scattering papers. He entwined his fingers behind his head and waited.

"I'm sorry things haven't worked out for you," Dan said.

Banjo laughed bitterly. "You have no idea how things haven't worked out for me, partner. I've got a crummy shift with a bitchy little partner and nowhere left to go. That's pretty much the state of things."

"Don't do this. We've been through too much together."

"*WE'VE* been through too much together." Banjo kicked his feet down and planted his palms on the desk top. "Your landlady gave you a whole damn house. You became the Chief's golden boy field instructor. Now you're his fine new supervisor. You even got my girl friend. I, on the other hand, am still busting my ass on the streets wondering when something's going to take me out. You can bet if it does the Looner won't find me a comfortable little job in here. He's still got people watching that I don't come to work drunk."

Now Dan stiffened and grew stubborn as he did on the streets. His voice fell quiet. "People make their own beds."

"What does that mean? Did I make the Chief hire a spooky rookie to be a field instructor? Did I get you hurt so you could jump right into a spot I might've wanted?"

"No. But every time the Chief approached, you proved yourself too unstable, insubordinate, and drunk to do this division any good."

"Oh. So you mean I'm not a kiss-ass like Half Deck or Eric." Banjo stared right into Dan's eyes. "I've been down here a long time. I'm the best paramedic in this whole division. Nobody tells me what to do. Not the Chief, not you, certainly not that eunuch Half Deck."

"How long do you think you can work the streets?"

"Looks like I'll have to work them indefinitely, doesn't it Danny-boy. I mean, I don't see many openings in upper management."

"What do you want to do?"

"Well, right at the moment I'd rather be out getting my car ready than listening to my best friend tell me I'm too damn drunk to do this place any good. That's kind of the way it's gotten around here. The new guys telling the old guys what's best and where they should go. That's what's happening to me! Damn new people trying to tell me what's right and what's wrong."

Dan struggled to his feet and jammed his cane across the desk into Banjo's chest. "What do YOU want? Don't tell me what you think others are doing to you because they aren't doing anything. What happens to you is your own doing." Dan jabbed his cane at Banjo's chest with each word of the question. "What do you want?"

"I want to be left alone."

"No! None of us is ever left alone." Dan used the desk for a crutch and circled the desk for Banjo. Raising his cane like a club he proclaimed, "You cannot be left alone," and struck Banjo feebly across his shoulder. "You are a part of this place yet you push everyone away." Banjo scrambled to his feet and shouldered against the Chief's wall of pictures. One of them fell to the floor and shattered. Dan struck again and a photograph of the Chief standing with Greystone fell. "I try to help. The Chief tries to help. But you tell us all to go to hell. Well, I'm telling you to go to hell. Go rot on the streets. Go bitch about those who work hard and make something of themselves. Turn into a ghost like Roy. You're a damn coward anyway and you don't deserve any more than you have."

Banjo bolted straight up. "Coward?"

"**Coward**!" Dan thundered, arching more weak blows upon Banjo. "You're afraid to let anyone close, you're afraid to take chances, you're afraid to make commitments. You're afraid to do anything that isn't easy. Well, I'm not. The Chief isn't. And I'm damn tired of hearing you tell me that because I'm ahead of you something must be wrong with me. You want it all on your terms. Well, nothing ever is." Dan rested, panting, leaning heavily on the Chief's desk. Watercolors and photographs lay wrinkled and torn amid glass shards at Banjo's feet. Slowly Banjo lowered his arms. He heard Dan's hard breathing in the sudden silence. Pain twisted Dan's face and he pushed a hand into his groin. His legs began to give and he dropped into the Chief's swivel chair.

Banjo looked for red welts on the backside of his forearms. An old horror rose in him. He fought back tears. "Why did you do this?" His voice cracked. "Why did you beat me? You know my old man used to beat me like that. You know how I hated it. Why did you beat me? Christ, Dan, look at me. I'm crying. I want to crawl right into the floor."

Distant and weak, Dan answered, "You're as messed up in the head as I am in the hip. The only difference is, I know I have to move on."

"Only difference is," Banjo wiped an eye with the back of his wrist, "you have options and I don't."

"Make your options. What do you want?"

Banjo sniffed and wondered. "I don't know. I do not know."

Dan pushed himself upright and cried out softly. "It isn't easy being your friend. I'm afraid if I can't figure out what you need you'll go off the deep end again like you did when Greystone died. I'm tired of doing that but I don't want to lose you, either." He reached out and patted Banjo's shoulder then grabbed a handful of shirtsleeve to help pull himself up. "Help me clean up this mess. The Chief's going to be pissed."

*****

Banjo walked along Cherry Creek but the weight on his mind kept him from giving it much attention. He knew it ran diagonally southeast out to somewhere or another and Banjo wished he could follow it to its disappearance. He recognized the message of necessary change Dan had delivered in his hail of flimsy blows. He also knew that not changing was to remain alone in his cave at the Debbie J fretting over what others might have in store for him.

Perhaps he would not be alone. He had had some luck over the years finding friends with the gift of insight who could make their way near to that deep and secret place where he needed human touch. Eden had. Especially Eden. Clayton had a magic way about him that Banjo still missed as a child would miss being picked up.

But Dan had called him a coward. Banjo's chest swelled each time the word rolled painfully through his thoughts. Dan was no longer willing to put the effort into the friendship. Dan had beat him and pushed him away. Now he wandered by himself, wishing to disappear. Nothing had changed since he was a boy. He had only grown older.

A police car approached from an intersecting street. Banjo noticed it slowing for no reason he could see. Reflecting sunglasses shot a ray of sunlight at him. The face wearing them turned and Banjo saw the scar. Zagata stopped the cruiser and rolled down the window as if to speak. Banjo's throat caught with dryness. He waved feebly. Even from several dozen feet Banjo could see that the scar moved restlessly. Zagata extended an arm from his window and pointed his finger at Banjo. His thumb cocked back as a hammer on a revolver. It snapped downward and his hand jerked. He held his arm extended this way for a moment then drew it back inside. He shifted his shiny sunglasses elsewhere and eased the police car away.

*****

Banjo hurried back to the Debbie J. He took a six pack of beer from the refrigerator and rolled a couple marijuana cigarettes. Memories were kicking up and he needed to kill them. He fantasized a call that proved his bravery but left him dead. The dispatcher would send them on a sick case ...

But Banjo, seeing the old apartment building, had a feeling. Inside with Dan behind him, Banjo had to wait until his eyes adjusted to the dark. Banjo sniffed and looked down the long hallway of doors. The carpet smelled musty. Someone had been smoking a cigarette nearby, or was that gun smoke?

Dan said, "What are you waiting for? Let's go get this guy then find some lunch."

"No, something isn't right." Banjo pulled the long black flashlight from his belt and held it club like above his shoulder. The beam searched down the hall for the room number. "It must be upstairs." And Banjo started up. Dan followed, stepping noisily, and Banjo knew that he did not feel it. "Would you be quiet. I don't want the whole building knowing we're here. We may have to rabbit out real quick."

Dan said, "You worry like an old woman."

Approaching the landing Banjo twisted to see up the next flight. Shadows hid those steps. He directed his beam of light there and dust swirled in the white shaft as though just disturbed.

And Dan said, "Don't be such a coward. Let's go."

Dan shoved Banjo forward. He stumbled and fell. When he lifted his face from the worn carpet, smooth side by side shotgun barrels looked at him. The twin black holes were cold like snake eyes. He heard Dan stumble backwards and vomit. Banjo rose slowly. He said, "How you doing, partner," as though to say, 'Nice day if it don't rain.' No answer. He wondered where Dan was and feared to look. "We're paramedics. I understand someone is sick here. Do you happen to know who called?" The barrels followed Banjo's nose as he stood. Then a face materialized behind the blue-black barrels and it was badly scarred. "Hey Zagata. How ya doin', Zagata. We're not here to hassle anyone. We'll leave if you like. It's all right."

From behind him Dan yelled, "I'm getting the hell out of here and calling the cops!"

Banjo cried, "Dan, no! Wait!" Then he was lifted from the landing. Banjo gained altitude through the gun smoke cloud but could not smell it and he watched himself tumble down the stairs rag doll fashion without a head and bowl Dan over. That struck him so funny and he laughed but made no sound. He watched his legs tangle around Dan's as Dan pushed and shoved to free himself. So this was the great Field Instructor, Dan Cravens running like a rabbit and getting his partner killed to boot. Then he saw Zagata's livid scar settle and his face return to its beer drinking friendliness.

*****

Banjo took a last hard pull off his marijuana cigarette and dropped the tiny butt into a shallow bowl of milk. It spit a sizzle then floated cold amongst the few remaining corn flakes of his supper. He drank beer and it dribbled from the corner of his mouth. A little of it sprayed when he raised his head and cried into the silence, "You're some fuckin' hero, Danny-boy. Some fuckin' hero. Leavin' your partner like that. Shee-it." Banjo's head fell against the vinyl rocker. He set his beer on the piano bench. Brown flower petals floated in a vase on top of the piano. The cornflakes rested nearby on the CD speaker, next to the shoulder patch that had marked his place in the journal. In his lap lay his father's medals and a picture of his old platoon. He stroked these gently.

He said again into the apartment's darkness. "I never thought you were a coward, Dan. Just shows that you can't trust anybody but yourself. And here you were calling me a coward. Me! I make sure the old values are maintained; make sure the old guys are respected. That's courage. I stand up for what this division stands for. That's courage. I lay it on the line every day out there. Every day. One car, one bad lift, one knife; one of anything and I'm done. That's courage." He sat forward to grab his beer. "Even if I knew going in that I wouldn't be coming out, I'd go anyway. That's real courage. And you're telling me I'm a coward!" He drained his beer and threw it, bouncing the bottle off the brown shag carpet. He lifted another from the six pack set next to his rocker. He lit another marijuana cigarette.

"And what do I get? I get shit. Sometimes I wish I'd've taken it in the chest instead of Rocky." He barked out a laugh. "Maybe I will! At least that way I'd get a nice funeral and maybe a plaque on the wall next to Greystone's. A fine tribute to dying dinosaurs. At least we weren't cowards!" A sob caught in his chest. "I truly do wish I'd've taken it instead of Rocky."

Banjo lifted his father's medals. He held them close to his eyes and tilted them to catch the yellow light refracting dimly from the street lamps outside. He imagined them decorating his father's proud chest and touched each carefully to find some remnant of his warmth. He touched lightly upon his own terrible memories of combat which had earned him no honors and fell awestruck at his father's acts. Banjo drew on the cigarette. "That Dan's some fuckin' hero, huh, Dad. He'd've been one of those guys who ran when that Jap tank came at you. He'd've never made it in combat with either of us. Not that one." Banjo lifted the Bronze Star and placed it gently over himself so much younger in his platoon photograph. "I just thought of something. We were both sergeants. I about shit bricks when I got my third stripe. Took just six months after I got in country. I was lucky though. I had a charmed life over there. Only led my patrol into a bushwack once. 'Course that was probably because I was lost most of the time--always where the enemy wasn't. Had one guy killed. Roland Yantes was his name. But I never ducked anything, though. I was available if anything was to come my way. Honest, Dad. I never ducked anything.

"From Mom's letter it sounds like you had a hell of a time. Sounds like you always did the right thing, too." Banjo puffed thoughtfully on the cigarette and he began to disconnect from his chair. "I'll bet you were a good cop, Dad. I'd've like to have worked with you. I'll bet you never ran. I'll bet you never gave up on the department or sold yourself out or turned on your partner."

Banjo snatched the medals into his fist and flung them. "But why the hell did you beat me? What did I ever do to you? All I ever wanted was to play piano. But no. You wanted a soldier. So that's what I did. I did that for you. Why did you beat me?" Banjo threw his second empty bottle after the medals and grabbed another. "What did I ever do to you! Well, you got what you wanted. I'm a drunk just like you who brings nothing but trouble to everyone around him. Look at me. Look at who I am! Shame on me!

"It's true." Banjo squeaked as his mouth twisted to cry. "Look at me. Here I am. I live in this shitty apartment. I got no family close. No kids. My best friend just kicked me out of his life. I see this fuckin' cop kill a guy and I don't have the guts to do what's right. My life's black and it's going to stay black." Banjo hugged his Marine Corps photograph to his chest and believed that in these still faces lived his only true friends. "You're dead. You don't have to worry about this stuff anymore. But I gotta get through it and I don't know how."

He spilled beer into his mouth and down his shirt. He lost his lighted cigarette and lit another. "I have to fix this. You know what I'm saying? I have to fix this or I know I'll die because I want to, but then I know I don't want to. Do you understand what I'm saying, you son of a bitch? You know what I'm saying? What do I have to do to fix me? My God, Dad, you broke me. You're the only one who can understand. What do I have to do to fix me? I'm waiting." Banjo listened to the echoing silence. *"Dad! Talk to me. What do I have to do to fix me? For God's sake tell me what do!"* Hard sobs broke from his chest. "Dad?" He rested an elbow on the speaker and leaned his head against his fist. He grasped the shoulder patch that lay there and pressed it to his face. Tears damped it. Tears fell amongst the cereal bits and rippled the milk. "Dad, please. Talk to me." He waited. "Dad. Daddy?"

Within his marijuana cloud he felt himself floating in a continuous backward somersault. Clouds banked around him. Lightening bolts slashed. A shotgun fired and he bunched his left shoulder. He remembered a cooked meat smell and swallowed hard to hold against vomiting. A brittle skinned baby with squinty eyes and tight fists hung there and no matter how painfully Banjo pushed his fingers into his own eyes, the red image remained. He beat a beer bottle against his head. He buried his face in the crook of one arm. But the dispassionate storm raged on. He saw a young girl, her belly torn open and bleeding. Then pigtails shifted gently in the breeze. He heard screams and he was not sure if they existed only within his head or if they sprang from his throat.

Banjo flung his fist outward and beat against what he could reach. A discordant sound rose sharply from his piano.

His fist crashed hard against the keys each time a new memory flashed behind his shut eyelids. Bangs, loud, dissonant bangs exploded as methodically as a march.

Banjo stopped. He lifted his heavy head. Sniffing his runny nose dry, he shifted himself to the piano bench and toyed with some keys. He set his beer aside and used his shirt sleeve to wipe his runny nose. He sniffed again and swallowed a time or two as he gathered himself. The notes of music on a page in front of him blurred. He played an imprecise short chord progression that clanked with wrong notes. He tried a little of the *Moon Light Sonata* from memory but, drunk as he was, his fingers were awkward and dumb.

He turned on the bench. He could identify the power switch on his CD and he believed he could drop a disc into his player. He did so not knowing what he chose and pushed the play button. He closed his eyes as he fell back into the wide rocker. Then quietly, gently, a Mozart sonata flowed from the sound system and softened the darkness in his apartment. Soon the storm in his head abated and his memories began to fragment and fall away. He floated on the music flowing around him and filling up his tired heart.

He spoke again to the darkness. "I'm sorry I got so drunk. I'm trying not to." And before he lost consciousness he promised himself never to drink so much that he could not play his new piano.

Chapter 23

Banjo woke and willed one heavy eyelid to rise off his cornea. He raised himself up a bit and worked to bring the clock into focus. It was five. He had to hurry but he craved sleep as other times he craved beer. Banjo fell back to his pillow and roused his reasoning capacity.

If all movements were precise he could sleep fifteen more minutes before showering, giving him a thirty minute walk to get to work by six. He closed his eyes.

When he checked the clock once more to be sure he had calculated correctly, his fifteen precious minutes had passed. Banjo rose and stumbled from many days of incomplete rest. His worry filled sleep and achy weariness reminded him of the killing he could not bring himself to report.

He shaved without much thought to his movements. From within his lingering near-sleep he wondered if he dreamed his awakening and hot shower. He did this again before he was finally sure that the journey from ragged sleep to blurry wakefulness had ended.

*****

His shift passed slowly under the anticipation of his afternoon appointment. He feared he had used bad judgement, though he knew it was hardly the first time. He worried he was dredging up things that should be left alone.

He had wandered past the Ellsworth Towers the other day when walking. Impulsively, he went in and asked the woman at the desk if a Harriet Bancroft lived there. Banjo's heart thumped when she said yes. 'Was her husband a police officer?' Banjo had asked. 'Indeed he was,' answered the receptionist who also asked, 'Are you acquainted with Mrs. Bancroft? Would you like to leave a message?'

He could have said no and left. But that, he reasoned, would have raised suspicions and, God, what if the receptionist had called the police. For sure Zagata would hear about that. So Banjo found himself again trapped by his own heedless act. He left her a note saying he was a paramedic who knew her husband and wished to chat. She called that evening and Banjo found himself traveling down a new road before he realized he had even gotten into the car.

Banjo wondered how he would venture into this conversation. The direct route was to ask if she thought Zagata had anything to do with her husband's suicide. He reconsidered. Perhaps the better question was if she thought her husband killed himself at all. But that might tear too deeply and he did not want her to cry in front of him.

He bussed home after work, changed, and walked to Ellsworth Towers. Within a block, the closeness of the tall retirement center turned the illusion of his little investigation into a probing, even painful, conversation that was about to take place. He said out loud, *"Christ, what am I doing?"* What if she remembered nothing of Zagata and grew suspicious of his questions? How many angry mouths would drop when it was learned he was associating Zagata with Bancroft's death? The Chief, assuming more drunken behavior, would fire him on the spot.

What if she was insulted by the intrusion and threw him out? Then called the Paramedic Division? What if she said it was all nonsense? What if Zagata had charmed her somehow years ago and she was actually fond of him? Then -- what irony this would be -- Banjo would become the aggressor in her eyes and Zagata the victim.

He stopped on the sidewalk in front of the building and shook his head. *"This is crazy. This is absolutely nuts."* Within one of its small rooms she waited, probably wondering about him this instant, anticipating his ring of her room buzzer. Banjo walked on past.

He walked around the block. What if she laughed in his face and demanded an apology for his insolence? What if she had company? For God's sake he couldn't talk to her in front of the bridge club. Maybe she was senile and had forgotten who he was. He could imagine her puzzled voice squawking through the intercom. "Who are you? What do you want?"

He came back around to the front of the building. The fluttering in his stomach strengthened. What if? he wondered. What if? What if he told her his story about the prisoners who died peculiarly in Zagata's presence and she fastened her clear eyes onto his and said, it doesn't surprise me one bit.

Banjo pressed the button corresponding with her room number.

"Yes? Is this Mr. Stanley?"

"Ah, yes it is, Mrs. Bancroft."

"Well, good afternoon to you, then. Won't you come on up. Six-thirty six. Last door on your right at the end of the hall. You'll recognize it by the brass door knocker." Her voice was strong, not age weakened and Banjo liked the friendliness it carried.

The elevator took him six floors and opened. He stepped into the hall and sniffed the air out of habit. He noted the room numbers running either direction along the hall. He noticed her door knocker shining from the hallway's end. Approaching it, Banjo soon saw that it was a brass rendering of a basset hound. Banjo smiled and pulled on the nose to raise its upper jaw then let it bang noisily down upon its lower teeth.

He heard barking and claws clicking madly on the linoleum just inside. When the door opened Mrs. Bancroft was bent over holding back an eager, panting beagle. She gestured inward with a hand, her face smiling up at his. "Come in. Come in. Princeton isn't known to bite strangers, though he's apt to slobber. Princey," she said, cupping the dog's jaw in her hand. "You be good. You hear me? No jumping." She let him go and straightened herself up. Even erect she scarcely came to Banjo's shoulder and Banjo was not tall. The dog danced at Banjo's feet then shook his head. His floor dragging ears paddled Banjo's pant leg. "The darn dog," she said, "has a way of greeting people, doesn't he."

Banjo smiled and still felt nervous and awkward. He could see down the entry hall to her living room. Wide windows let in the long afternoon light. A sofa and comfy looking chairs were situated around a glass coffee table. Cookies and a steaming tea pot sat there. He said, "This is a pretty small place for a dog with that much energy."

"Oh, yes. He can be a little windmill when he gets excited." She made a high voiced chuckle, which she self-consciously cut off, that would irritate Banjo no matter what mood he was in.

Banjo liked her immediately. She was quick and bright and her hair was white and cut short like Peter Pan's. Expressions flashed across her agile face, changing it like a sudden breeze would rustle leaves on a tree. She was disarming and a bit flustered by her rude dog, but Banjo sensed she could take a man's chin as she had Princeton's and scold him just as easily.

Banjo said, "Thanks for having me over. I imagine you find this strange."

"Not so far," she said. "Come sit down." She led him to the living room and offered him a chair. She poured him tea. "I spent a year in England awhile back and found afternoon tea wonderful. It adds a bit of grace to the day. I'm glad for company at tea time." She handed him the cookie plate without comment as though taking one or two was an expectation. He took two. The dog nuzzled his knee until he scratched his ear. Mrs. Bancroft settled herself with cup, saucer, and cookie and smiled at him. "Well, Mr. Stanley. Harry always had a particular warm spot for you paramedics. Indeed, so have I. This is the first time in many years, though, that I have met one face to face. What can I do for you?"

He drew a deep breath. "Well. Actually." Banjo cleared his throat. "I wanted to ask you about one of the officers in your husband's command. His name is Larry Zagata."

"A long time ago, Mr. Stanley." Her observation was stern. She looked off, thinking, squinting, pursing her lips. "Big man. Roundish face. Scar?"

Banjo nodded.

Her voice flattened and her mood cooled. "Yes, I remember. Interesting man." She sipped her tea. "Anyway."

Banjo squirmed. "Anyway. He's been bothering some of the paramedics."

"Perhaps you should report him."

"Well, I'm thinking about that. But it isn't easy reporting a police officer. I guess I wanted a little informal background information, I guess you could say."

"Is he bothering you?"

"And one of my partners."

She pursed her lips to a bird's beak and held her cup and saucer absently as though she had forgotten she held them. "You should report him. But you don't need my advice for that."

"No."

"Young man." She found the saucer and cup she held and set them down with a clatter. "What is it you want?"

"To be honest, I'm afraid of Zagata. I've heard him talk about your husband like he had something over him." She abruptly crossed her arms and looked away. Banjo knew of no other direction then straight ahead, clumsily. "He liked to say how he could do anything and Captain Bancroft couldn't touch him. And I was noticing when I went through old newspaper clippings written during the drug scandal years ago that Zagata was the one everyone was looking at when all of a sudden the attention was on your husband. Then he retired."

"What on earth does all that have to do with you?"

"Well, I don't know, but it's all part of the reason he scares me."

"You and many others."

"The truth is ..." He closed his eyes. "Please don't tell anyone this. But ..." He stumbled over the thought. "Mrs. Bancroft, I've been a paramedic in this city for close to twenty years. The police have gotten me out of more scrapes than I can count. I have nothing but respect for them. But Zagata ..."

"Is a bad cop," she finished for him. She came back to her warmth.

"I believe that. A couple times my partner and I witnessed events that troubled us and I wanted to ask you if you thought they sounded plausible. For example, we can't really prove it, but we're both sure he, I don't know how to say it, sort of killed prisoners."

"Sort of! My good man. Sort of? How do you mean?"

This was rapidly becoming a huge mistake, Banjo saw. This was stupid, irrational, poorly thought out, and would probably get him into more trouble. He wished he could roll back time by half an hour so he could continue his walk around the block and go home. Then he would not be here stammering over his words in front of a stranger once married to a police captain. But here he was, so onward he went. "My partner thinks he choked one to death in a fight at the jail and I think he deliberately moved a knife sticking in a man's chest causing him to die. And he choked another guy down who jumped his partner."

"Now he's tracking you."

Her terminology was more chilling than he liked but it was accurate enough. "Pretty much."

"Yes, well." She wadded her napkin and dropped it on her untouched cookies. "I can't speak to what you saw or didn't see. But I can tell you he was a man who accumulated power by intimidating officers. Harry watched that many times. Zagata would probe and probe at an officer, particularly females, looking for soft spots." She shivered. "Social intercourse for him was prospecting for souls. He would befriend someone perhaps a little weaker than the rest of us. And oh, how he could spot those.

"Mrs. Osborn, the young wife of his last partner, and I met recently over lunch. She told me stories of how he would burrow into her husband's teetering confidence. He lent Officer Osborn money, gave him watches and all to make him feel grand because big Zagata was his friend and partner. He continually bragged about his guns and how many men he had killed in Vietnam. I remember one time Zagata bragged to me about how easy it was to hire someone to kill a man." She shuddered. "For the life of me, I haven't any idea why he said such a thing to me. Veiled threats, I suppose. He certainly made me think.

"But some of these young officers ate this up, especially poor Mr. Osborn. Great and powerful Officer Zagata was his friend." She moved in her seat as she gathered energy for this story.

"Harry observed him worming into some female officers' confidence so he did a little investigating. Pretty soon he learned Zagata was offering them money if they would meet friends of his, other officers. Once he told these women that he could sell their pictures to **Playboy** magazine if he let them take pictures of them without their clothing. One woman actually did it. The ones who didn't told my husband. Pretty soon she was getting phone calls in the middle of the night. Or he would show up on her calls or follow her home. One night she was raped. Everyone suspected Zagata but she refused to identify him. She's since left the department.

"He's not a nice man, Mr. Stanley. But you asked me about that old drug business. Harry was not sure what happened. But he believed Zagata had other officers steal for him." She diverted her eyes and stopped. A sad look of shame crossed her face. "Of course Captain Bancroft had a drinking problem. And it is true that on more than one occasion Zagata caught him drinking on duty and once or twice driving drunk. Everyone knew it but poor Harry would have been mortified if the public found out. The news was so active on this back then. Harry had nearly thirty years on the department so he decided it was easier to take responsibility as the commanding officer for losing drugs from the evidence locker than to bear what Zagata would tell everyone if Harry did not." Tears brimmed in her eyes. She dabbed at them with her crumpled napkin.

"Harry was deeply shamed that he let such an evil man bargain him into retirement. I can just hear that awful policeman using his twisted logic on Harry. My husband was very proud of his years of police service. He was a fine, fine officer. His men loved and respected him and he felt he let them down by bowing to this man. It is really no mystery to me why Harry killed himself." Her lips tightened again to a little beak and she spat, "He is a filthy man, Mr. Stanley. A filthy and evil man.

"I don't know if Zagata did the things you are talking about. But he is capable of poisoning your department like he did my husband's police district. He's a predator and he will devour your paramedics. My husband, God rest his soul, could not find the bravery to stand up to him."

Banjo listened with growing dread. He remembered Clayton's prediction that he alone would have to stop Zagata, but he doubted he had the necessary strength either.

*****

Wind up toys stood at odd angles on Ernie Webster's desk and Banjo wanted to twist one up and watch it clatter about. A new wooden toucan with a great red banana beak balanced on a brass ring. Daffodils arched from a thin vase next to him. A year ago great lavender peonies sprang from this vase and he felt so low and raddled then that he believed he could crawl inside the complex petal pattern and disappear. He wished for the same today now that Zagata seemed to be everywhere and more dangerous than he imagined. The box of tissue sat discreetly close by, next to the flowers. As discreetly placed on the carpet near the chair was the waste basket. A wadded tissue lay at the bottom, tossed there from an earlier session.

Banjo sat in the wing back chair where he always sat. Still, after three years he felt splintered in many pieces. He was drinking less but his life kept getting more complicated. He sighed.

Ernie looked up from the notes he was making. He said, "I'll be right with you, Banjo."

Banjo found this so unpleasant, telling of thoughts deeply held, terrifying, and not well understood. Sometimes he felt patronizing of Ernie, telling him instead of odd things of no importance; old, unwanted items laying around on the floor of his brain. The therapist's unsettling patience drove him to this. He would give Ernie some of this discarded junk today, being too frightened to speak aloud of Zagata.

He noticed the familiar sign on the office wall: 'Pain is necessary, suffering is optional.' He seemed to have plenty of both. Dan beat him with his cane. Snooper was not sympathetic of someone who would not let his own wounds heal. And the Chief gave Banjo the choice of this chair in Ernie Webster's office or unemployment. Now Zagata.

Banjo had no greater understanding into which these painful perplexities could fit. Clayton seemed to have such broad spiritual shoulders. Even the unsolved murder of the baby in the microwave wasn't the arrow through the heart for Clayton as it had been for him. Abstractly, Banjo recognized he could choose to respond differently. Wallowing in his pain was not mandatory. But to choose he needed options and he knew no other way.

Suffering thus was how he believed he was meeting his obligations. His mind drifted over to Snooper. Though she was not agreeable to listen to any of his sufferings, his mind rested easily on her. He liked her certainty. She looked at him squarely as he wished women who interested him would. Women who did not look at him directly built trap doors they could disappear into at any moment, like Lauren and Eden. Every bit of Snooper occupied the space she stood in. Banjo had confidence in her. She was not attractive but neither was he exactly a movie star. He experienced pleasant stirrings when he thought of her.

Ernie Webster looked up from the notes he jotted. "I apologize Banjo," he said. "I've hardly had any time between clients." He sat up and folded his hands in his effeminate little way and Banjo stiffened at the gesture. "What would you like to talk about today."

He shrugged.

Ernie sat quietly, waiting.

Banjo felt a little stiffness climb his spine. "I had this weird dream I guess I could tell you about. I dreamed Dan and I were on this set of stairs when this shotgun was leveled down on us. Dan panicked and ran and I took it in the head. I remembered watching myself tumble down the stairs from some point above. And the guy who shot me was this cop I run calls with sometimes." Banjo thought it too suspect to admit

276

that this was a conscious fantasy. He added quickly, "I do not, repeat, do not have a death wish."

"Would you like to talk about the dream?"

The 'Oh-so-like-a-shrink' question irritated him. "Not much to say about it really."

"Do you think something like that will happen to you?"

He answered quickly, "Doubt it."

"I remember last winter you were telling me about an awful shift with Dan."

He picked nervously at a fingernail. "But I never came right up against it, you know? Besides peeing my pants, I don't know how I would act if I thought I was about to lose my life ..." Banjo let that thought trail away.

"If I did what you do I would consider myself plenty tested."

"I mean I've been scared before but I never had my life flash before me or think this is it, I'm not getting out. I don't know how I would react. Before I leave this business I need to know I would do the right thing."

"What's the right thing?"

"The right thing is to do your job and never leave your partner."

"Just because you haven't experienced exactly that doesn't mean you're not heroic. My goodness, Banjo, you do very dangerous work."

Banjo dismissed the observation. "Not really." He cast about for something to say. "My biggest fear is finding someone in mortal danger. I'm not sure I'd go after him. I might. I hope I would. I tell rookies that I would and that they would have to go, too. But I've never really been there like Greystone and Dan. I'm a little ashamed of that, in fact. But that's the truth."

"You aren't obligated to lose you life for others, Banjo."

"Would I do the right thing?" The question arrested all of Banjo's attention and he did not acknowledge Ernie's comment.

"You said yourself many times that you never dodged anything." Ernie shrugged. "You've done your duty, Banjo. You've done more than enough. You can rest. Let someone else do this."

Banjo stared at the flowers. "But would I do the right thing?"

"You're not responsible for everybody. No one is."

Banjo tired of this conversation. He wished he could crawl into the daffodil blossom. He wished he could go back to ten minutes before that stabbing and take himself out of service for lunch. He wished Zagata had not scared him that way. He wished he had not gone snooping in Mrs. Bancroft's life.

Ernie leaned forward and rested his elbows on his knees. He spoke with quiet certainty. "Let me tell you something, Banjo. You belong to a great family. You are a single member but you carry the memories of everyone who has given much for others. Every honorable soul who has sacrificed in this way also carries your memories. This is the blood of your family and it is in the veins of all of you who have served. You have lived a spiritually true life." He pointed at Banjo. "Many people remember you as the one who saved their life. They think of you on the anniversary of their crisis or when they hear a siren or when they see their children and bless you for giving them more time with them." Tears rolled down Banjo's cheeks and he was dreadfully tired of all the crying he had done in this office. "If these thoughts were sparks to be seen in the sky, they would flash all across Denver.

"Over time, slowly, you will have to let go of your pain and your self imposed obligations and your belief that to be loved you must sacrifice yourself. As that happens you will find there is plenty left of you. And you will find that at the center is your wonderful and accepting and understanding heart. If this weren't true, you could not have done all that you have. You did your duty, Banjo. You've done enough. You've given all that you can. It is not necessary to give up your life in order to live. You can quit, my friend. You can rest."

Banjo cried into his tissue but not for the letting go he knew he must do nor for the loneliness he knew he would face. He cried instead out of fear of the one remaining scar faced obligation that he knew stood squarely before him, legs apart, fists jammed to his hips near his pearl handled weapon.

Chapter 24

Banjo and Snooper waited in Ruby Hill Park. Eastward the sun shimmered exactly on the horizon. Noting the time of this, Banjo knew that spring had progressed past the indifference of a late frost. He would plant his annuals soon. He wondered if Snooper liked flowers or if any man had ever given them to her. His eyes crept over to catch her unguarded face. Her blond hair, cropped chin length, shined with light and formed a straight curtain, and the profile of her eyes and nose and lips and chin peeked from behind it. The curtain of hair rocked gently with her movements as she read the newspaper, alternately obscuring then revealing the line of her face. This line was fine and smooth when not wrinkled in suspicion and her skin was clear. He wondered if any man had ever touched this skin and made her shiver. He followed the smooth line of her neck down to her T-shirt and wondered about the shapes that lay within. Banjo traced this line again with his secret stare, now noticing how gracefully her slim neck moved. Muscles shifted delicately each time she swallowed coffee. Snooper raised her head and Banjo's eyes darted back to his coffee.

Every morning they came to this place. Here before the day's nervousness began to rise, he found clear moments of peace. He wondered if he might feel this way if he could ever shake the ugly dog Zagata out of his life. It was possible, for these daybreak moments next to Snooper seemed to come more often.

His fingers ached. Banjo touched finger tip to finger tip and pushed. Then he balled his fists and stretched his fingers again. Playing the piano into exhaustion became his means of reaching sleep. He would push himself relentlessly to perfect a certain passage. That he might do so, he would practice until the hours vanished and he awoke with his cheek against the keys and he had to shower for work.

Lost within the tiny details of music he discovered new subtleties and deeper understandings, as though squinting through the eye of a sewing needle he found shiny new worlds. He passed into these lands during his deeper moments of artistic passion. Only after stopping and showering did he know his hands hurt and Zagata waited.

His arms still carried the symbolic ache of Dan's blows. His heart carried the same pain, so perpetual, so familiar, which followed an important loss. He would miss Dan's mothering most. He came closer than anyone to knowing his needs. Mind reading was such an important criteria for a best friend. That Dan could do so made his rejection such a damnable act.

Snooper said less to him since the stabbing though his affection for her grew. He returned again to study her face. He watched her fingers hold the paper and carefully turn pages so that each fell straight and even in her hands. These movements charmed Banjo. Each was patient and quiet. In his hands the newspaper would rustle and snap as he hurried from page to page, not respecting the paper's natural fold and lie. Hers was the calm he longed for and he was drawn to Snooper. He asked, "Have you heard the talk about Dan and me?"

She said as she read, "You mean about your little tiff?"

"I guess that about does it for him and me."

"Why so?"

Banjo wished for more than clipped Greystone-like responses.

She folded the paper to her knees. "Listen, Sunshine. A fight is a fight. It isn't the end of the world. People are supposed to fight. It unclogs the arteries, gets stuff flowing again."

Banjo grunted, glad that she spoke to his fears.

"I fought with my sister all the time. We'd even throw stuff around a little bit."

"You still mad at me?"

"For what?"

"You seemed to think I should report Zagata."

"Shouldn't you?"

"I don't know."

She pressed him as she had after the stabbing. "What did you see?"

"I don't know."

"You saw something. Otherwise you wouldn't have said anything to me."

"So are you mad?"

Abruptly, "No."

"Now you're holding back."

"I guess I expected more."

Banjo spun in his seat to face her. "Do you know what he did? That day, that very day I was walking home and he drove up? He stuck a hand out the window and pretended to shoot me. Do you suppose it's a coincidence we bumped into each other? He followed me! He knew where I was. Zagata's telling me, 'Don't you dare.' He's done that in the police department for years. He even forced a captain to retire. Now, given that I'm really not sure what he did and given that he as much as threatened me directly, don't you think it's prudent to stay out of it. That bad guy killed Rocky, after all. I'd've wanted him dead, too."

"If Zagata didn't do anything why is he threatening you?"

"Maybe it wasn't a threat. Maybe it was just his weird way of saying hello."

"Uh-huh."

"Go be somebody else's conscience. I have enough trouble with my own."

"I'll bet you do."

"Shut-up. Just shut-up."

Snooper changed the subject. "Listen, if it helps, Dan's upset, too. I heard him talking on the phone." Banjo turned his head just a little as if to say he was interested but not terribly. "He said he thinks he laid it on a little too thick. He thinks you're never going to speak to him. If you ask me, this whole deal's cooked up to try to get you squared away. It seems that there are some real important people down here trying to help you. This is a family trying to help out one of its own. But then you ought to know; you being the keeper of the great Denver General Paramedic Division traditions." She narrowed one eye. "So don't piss it away. And think of this, Sunshine. If you report Zagata, this whole division will be with you. He's a bad cop and we all know it."

"Who's trying to do that?"

"The Chief is always tinkering with something. Why don't you go ask him. I just wish someone would pay half as much attention to me."

Loneliness lingered on Snooper's face a moment longer than her comment. In this shutter speed instant Banjo saw her world which looked so much like his own. His heart began to hurry and this frightened Banjo for he suspected that in the midst of his tightly twisted life he was falling in love with her.

"What's the matter now, Sunshine?"

Banjo wondered what change she had detected in his face. "Nothing."

"Well, you're the one in trouble so I guess you deserve all the energy."

"Do you care about what I do?"

She answered too quickly again. "No."

"Oh." He sneaked another look at Snooper who had returned to reading the paper. He met her sidelong eyes glancing back at him. This time each held their glance; Banjo wanting to pull away but not and Snooper looking with her head cocked a little and her eyes full open as though having just asked the sweetly difficult question, 'Are you worthy of me?'

*****

On the last day of June the spring schedule expired and Half Deck exercised his arbitrary changes. Banjo had submitted no requests, relying on Half Deck's enduring grudge to keep him where he wanted to stay; with Snooper at sunrise drinking coffee. He was afraid to ask what shift she requested.

She may have wanted to remain with him. On the other hand, she may have had her fill. Both thoughts frightened him. Banjo calculated he could keep himself happy and avoid admitting anything to himself by consenting to let Half Deck continue his punishment. Tricking Half Deck in this subtle way seemed fitting and just.

Banjo went idly to the bulletin board before going home. The morning shift with Snooper was the first place he looked. The schedule told him Snooper was to work with Lauren now and he felt like something had been taken from him. He looked through the supervisor's window. Half Deck sat in there scratching a lottery ticket. The two made eye contact. Half Deck stopped and came into the room. "I gave you Clayton and an evening shift. Figured it was time to bury the satchel. Know what I mean?" He turned back through the door and closed it before Banjo could answer. He did not know if Half Deck really meant to favor him or, noticing his growing closeness to Snooper, exerted his calculating influence.

*****

Banjo rubbed a hand against his sweat slick chest exposed by two undone buttons and flapped his sticky uniform shirt. Clayton took a long drink from a canteen of ice water. They watched heat waves wiggle off the asphalt in parking lot next to the old Safeway store, and across from the dark apartments that left Banjo feeling gloomy. A smog curtain obscured the Rockies and the sun glowed orange through it. Heat had increased for a week and the news reported the extraordinary spring temperatures. Zagata fell from sight but Banjo knew he was attentive. Banjo remained a prisoner.

Clayton said, "You're brooding, aren't you?"

Banjo liked him. His meditations, far off looks, and trips into the back country were no longer spooky now that Banjo had taken his own journeys into the depths of music and his soul. They had something in common. Even though Banjo did not feel necessarily illuminated by his wanderings, he felt stronger knowing where to find quiet moments.

Clayton said little and waited patiently and this balanced Banjo who now felt like cats prowled inside him. He drummed his fingers restlessly on the arm rest and said to Clayton, "You ever notice anything about Zagata after that druggie we had last year died?"

Clayton turned abruptly. "Why?"

The response alarmed him. "What did he do?"

Clayton took on his far away look and turned to his open window, toward the Rockies, ghostly through the hot pollution. He returned after a moment. "He followed me around for awhile. He gave me a button with Mickey Mouse superimposed on a yellow star. The word 'Superstar' was written across the bottom. Zagata said, 'Here, this is for you. Don't do anything to disgrace it.' I took it for his strange way of being friendly."

"What exactly did you see on the bottom of that pile of people?"

"I don't know."

"Why did you suspect something happened?"

Clayton thought. "I saw a quick movement and I saw that man's face startle then relax and I saw Zagata. He looked satisfied."

"Like a predator?"

"Exactly." Clayton sounded relieved as though someone finally understood.

"Why didn't you report that?"

"I didn't want to take such a terrible step on a feeling alone. Besides," he added, "you told me not to."

"Never should've listened."

"You saw something." This was not a question.

Banjo fidgeted. "I get so sick of sitting in these damn ambulances. Stupid dispatchers telling me where to go. Go here, go there, wait here, wait there. New people trying to tell us older guys what's right and what's wrong. I've been sitting in these ambulances so long my knees creak from being bent up. I'm sick of eating greasy 7-11 chicken in ambulance cabs, sick of being on someone else's string, and I hate this spot. I hate looking at that damn apartment house over there. I hate smelling those goddamn garbage dumpsters on hot days. I hate smelling like this!" Banjo raised one arm. "Smells like goddamn chicken soup.

"You ever think about what else you could do, Clayton? What you could do with all the time you waste sitting on corners staring at drunks? Now I see why guys go to school. They can study their brains out down here waiting like this. I never figured that out until just now."

"You used to say there was no place as much fun as the street."

Banjo huffed. "You believe everything I say?"

Clayton's inward vision left again for some other horizon.

"I feel like my life is wasting away. What's going to happen today that I haven't seen a zillion times? And what are my chances of getting hurt? Pretty ever-lovin' good, I'd say." Banjo remembered Zagata's out stretched gun barrel finger. He jerked his head toward the side window and his heart pounded. "Zagata's scum. How many guys has he intimidated?" Banjo puffed out his chest. He imitated Zagata's voice. "Once you're a supervisor you're nothing, little man. You're nothing if you're nowhere on the streets, little man." Banjo slammed his door. "That scum! He deserves to be shot right in the spine so all he can do is move his eyes and need a machine to breathe for him. He probably shot Rocky."

Clayton said, "You're letting someone else's behavior dictate yours."

"Lay off the metaphysical shit. Jesus Christ, every time I say something you say something weird and deep. Makes me crazy. Don't you ever say anything stupid? Huh? Don't you ever say something a regular guy would say like, 'Boy, that really sucks' or 'That's the shits'. I mean, get a life."

Clayton looked at Banjo.

"And sometimes, Clayton, you just turn away and disappear. I've never seen anyone who can check out so completely. You're just gone. I could fall right out of this ambulance and you would drive away without noticing. I really think you would."

Clayton's gaze remained steady and peaceful but Banjo noticed a little droop at the corners of his eyes that looked like sadness. Then Clayton blinked and dropped his eyes.

After a moment Banjo reached across and squeezed his arm. He confessed, "I saw the son of a bitch do the same thing. I saw him kick a knife in a guy's chest. He died because of that. I know it. I know it because I saw the knife pointing a different direction after Zagata jumped over him. I know it because I saw the victory flash in his eyes. I know it because Zagata threatened me. And I know it because I know it. I'm going write it up for the Chief."

*****

They were sent to a man thrown against a garage wall when a car battery exploded in his face. This gave Banjo a little jolt. He hated to see destroyed faces. After that they saw another man whose car battery also exploded into his face. Banjo flushed these eyes with saline and poured water over the reddening skin. And after that a chain saw bucked into a third man's face. With interest he noted the torn sinuses that the saw had chewed open and wondered what this injury must feel like. Banjo had only ever had hunger headaches. Clayton was right there like a good partner, anticipating moves, quieting family and bystanders, watching his back, reading his mind.

Banjo recalled his terrible fantasy with Dan. He saw Zagata's finger extending like a gun barrel. He shivered and wondered if these injuries today were strange forebodings of how his own face soon would look.

Toward the end of their shift, Banjo sat stiffly quiet with his eye closed nursing a headache. He sat this way for along time and Clayton did not disturb him and Banjo was grateful for his partner's understanding. With their great secrets held in common, Clayton's importance grew. Clayton, having seen his secret first, validated Banjo's. Banjo did not have to be the first to see. His partner had borne this brunt for him. This further compelled Banjo toward Clayton's trusting friendship because partners joined in this way did not leave each other. He asked Clayton, "Will you stick with me? Will you remind me I wasn't crazy?"

Clayton roused from his meditation. His voice rumbled from within his chest. "Zagata has no power over you. We both saw. I won't leave you."

Chapter 25

The act seemed so simple. He knocked on the Chief's door. The Chief listened, his brow furrowing tighter as Banjo spoke. When he finished the Chief lifted his heels off the desk and leaned forward over his arms. He said quietly, reverently, "Banjo, I cannot advance this."

And Banjo said, "No?"

"No. This is circumspect. You waited, what ..." He looked at a wall calendar. "More than a month." The Chief cocked his head. "What did you see, exactly?"

Banjo propped his forehead on his fingertips.

"If you saw something, then clearly we advance this. If there was deliberate action. Most certainly the police would already be undertaking their own investigation. Surely you understand how this could antagonize the police department. You can see the risk to the division." The Chief frowned and looked intently at Banjo. "Did you actually see him strike that knife? Did Officer Zagata threaten the suspect in any way?"

Banjo shook his head no.

The Chief nervously took his pipe from the child made ash tray, tamped in fresh tobacco, and lit it with a trembling hand. "This is very serious," he said to the sweet smoke. "Very serious. How differently was the knife angled after he leapt over?"

Banjo slid his face into his hand. The Chief picked up the telephone. "Uh, Mr. Humphries, is Daniel there with you? Could you send him in, please. No, I'm fine. Everything's fine. Just send Dan in here."

Dan entered, still listing over his cane but looking sturdier. Half Deck followed. He said as he entered, "Chief, the last time you sounded like that Greystone got himself killed." His tooth pick pointed straight at him.

With a distracted wave the Chief motioned them to chairs. "Mr. Stanley has something to tell us. I would like your opinions." The Chief searched the ceiling through his billowing pipe smoke.

"You leaving us, Banjo?" Half Deck asked.

Banjo answered, "Not just yet."

With a deep breath Banjo, again, told his story which, having lost the intensity of the first telling, sounded like a school yard tale. He avoided eye contact until finished. The room rang with silence. Banjo felt Dan's hand on his shoulder and Banjo took it.

"He's a bad cop," Half Deck answered immediately. "Didn't I tell you that once, Chief? Isn't that right. He's the same SOB I saw sitting right outside the Delphi during that shoot out that almost got these two here. You remember that night, don't you, Daniel. You should. You got the scar to prove it. I swear that SOB is mixed up in hooch, dope, drugs; probably selling L.D.O. or S.D.S. or whatever that shit is on the side. Why else would he just sit there while these two were dodging bullets? Couple police were busted down the river for that. A captain up and kills himself. Dang, you know Zagata was mixed up in that." Half Deck's voice rose with his certainty. "I'll bet he fixed to have that Mexican killed that these two worked on that night. I have no doubt that he himself did this thing here." The tooth pick was still aimed at the Chief who let his eyes linger on Half Deck for a moment before shifting toward Dan.

Dan ignored the agitated supervisor. "What exactly did you see, Banjo?"

Banjo exploded to his feet. "Nothing! Not a goddamn thing. I'm making this all up." He stared furiously at his old partner. "I don't know exactly what I saw but I saw enough be willing to stick my neck out and report it. You'd think this damn division would have the balls to follow up."

Half Deck thrust out his chest. "Who said the division won't support you?"

Banjo looked at the Chief who answered as he had to Banjo. "I cannot advance this." He exhaled another cloud and searched it.

The tooth pick shot from Half Deck's mouth. "What! Can't advance this. What kind of looner crap is that?"

The Chief slammed his pipe to the ashtray. The force of this blow shot ash into the air. "No! I will not advance this! It is circumstantial. I will not jeopardize the police response to our calls. That would endanger our paramedics. I will not send this."

Half Deck stabbed a finger into his chest. "Well, damn sure I can. And damn sure I will. I'm the senior super around here and if I put something to the police it'll get a response."

"Ronald!" The Chief said, "You will not go around me."

Half Deck eyed him. "We need a little come back-to-Jesus talk here, Chief. We all walked around here tippy-toed after the Delphi shooting. We all knew Zagata was up to something. The police department knew there was something fish-bait about that situation but they wanted us to be all hush hush so they could investigate. Bull shit! So they could ignore it. Our people are under fire and the cops want us to sweep it under the grass. We did it the first time and nothing happened. We aren't letting the police obliterate this again. As far as I'm concerned this division has a little fessing up to do. And by God, Chief, if you won't, I will."

The Chief rocked back in his chair and crossed his arms protectively. Banjo was frightened for he had never seen the Chief in such a fearful posture. The Chief denied Half Deck's accusations. "We did not avoid any issue surrounding the Delphi shooting. The police department specifically requested me to furnish certain information, which I did."

Half Deck reached a finger into a breast pocket for another toothpick. He clamped it between his teeth and bit through it. "You didn't send my personal eye-view of the Delphi thing, did you? You told me not to tell anyone what I saw, didn't you"

The Chief said, "I was specifically requested by the police department ..."

"To keep your mouth shut! They were getting shot at and you let Zagata muscle you."

"I did no such thing!"

"You did. It was Zagata's commander, Captain Bancroft, who stood right here and begged you to keep this quiet because if you didn't Zagata would turn up the heat on him. Isn't that right?"

"You have no such information."

"My old man was a cop. He worked with Bancroft. Jesus Jones. I can't calculate how often Harry Bancroft set in our front room drinking and crying in his beer over all this to Calvin."

The Chief did not answer and Banjo knew that his boss, sitting mute, hands trembling, had bowed as Half Deck declared. A terrible truth stuck Banjo. An old certainty crumbled to dust before his eyes. You never leave your partner. Banjo lived by that rule. Now the Chief was leaving him undefended and was proposing to do so again. Heat built up under his second chance vest. Storms gathered in his head. Banjo began a fantasy. The Chief would do something stupid on the streets and get Banjo killed. In that wakeful nightmare Banjo felt the hot stab of justified rage at just the precise moment his life ended and Chief's eternal guilt began.

Then Banjo remembered that he also had shied away from what was true to avoid Zagata's danger. His anger softened. The building storm tattered. The fantasy dissolved. Banjo looked closely at the Chief. The older man looked more worn out than haggardly wise. But he was no longer the same in Banjo's eyes.

The Chief thought. He let his pipe burnout in the ashtray. "Daniel? Your counsel, please."

Without hesitating Dan said, "Send the report."

*****

Word exploded onto the streets. Banjo retold his vague story so many times. With each telling it sounded less credible. The Internal Affairs interview went as badly he expected. Banjo watched the skeptical glances between the two officers who were dressed in sports coats and cheap ties, and asking the same tired questions:

'Tell me again exactly what you saw?'

'Did you actually see Officer Zagata touch the knife?'

'Were you distracted at any time during these events?'

The interview ended with unfriendly thank-you's and uncertain references to remain in touch. He feared the episode had ended there.

Then the television reporters learned of this report. The Chief released an unusually clear statement but the news people were disappointed with a story based more on intuition than fact. They put Banjo's allegations on television anyway. The next afternoon Banjo heard that Zagata had come to the division looking for him. The Chief took him into his office. People outside could hear Zagata without trying. He accused Banjo and the Chief of lies and betrayal and promised to take it up with them personally. A day later Banjo saw an unmarked police car sitting across from the Debbie J. Zagata caught Banjo's eye. Then, as if nothing in the world was wrong, he started the car and drove away smiling wide, looking like he had just won a million bucks.

When he went to bed that night, two days after reporting the incident, he closed his eyes but the nervousness rushing around inside him would not let him go. He wished his great test of courage had been like Greystone's or Dan's. Physical courage was ever so much easier to get to sleep with.

The phone rang. He checked his watch. Only supervisors needing overtime coverage called after midnight. He ignored it. Well past ten rings Banjo threw the covers off. "Like I need this shit." He jerked the receiver to his ear and told the caller, "It's two in the morning!" There was silence. Then the line clicked dead.

*****

Great relief settled Banjo's nerves when he opened the dayroom door the following day. A crew of paramedics watched a soap opera. The Chief's door was open and Dan leaned against the frame speaking to him. Dispatchers spoke to voices in their ears. Roy had not gotten his schedule request in on time and complained to Lauren about his shift. She sat on the edge of the sofa holding a plastic garbage can in her lap and eating a powdered sugar donut above it. Between bites she chatted her drawly, comforting words at Roy. Clayton came from the equipment room with his arms full of supplies for his ambulance. Snooper looked at the new schedule, standing like a man with one hip shifted outward, fists jammed into her back pockets.

Banjo sighed aloud. He was normal now. This was home. These were his friends and he felt safe. Clayton noticed him first. He emptied his arms into a chair and extended his hand. "He's a bad cop." Banjo nodded and smiled his thanks. "I believe you, Banjo. I know what you saw."

"I'm not sure what my eyes saw."

"But you saw other ways and those are the more important ways."

Someone lay a firm hand on his shoulder. He jumped and electricity fired painfully through him. Roy squeezed his shoulder. "Hang in there."

"Yeah, thanks, Roy." Banjo laughed nervously. "I'll try."

But when others saw him, little looks of disgust darted across their faces. Eric looked at him darkly then left the dayroom with two other paramedics. Lauren put the garbage can down. "Oh, Banjo," she said still chewing. "Isn't that how they do you when you try to do what's right? I hear that jerk is following you. Is that what he's doing?"

"I've seen him outside my apartment a couple times."

"Well, why don't you just find yourself somewheres else to stay. You know, an extra precautionary thing, to cover all your bases, until this thing works itself out. Lord knows that man's the sort to settle up." She stabbed the angle of her wrist to her hips and jutted her jaw. "The insufferable gall. Why, if that man does this, what will he do?"

"I've been thinking that myself."

"Well, don't you pay any attention to what he does. I don't care. Maybe I'm just the phone company, but I just don't care.

He's just trying to scare you, that's all. He's got no right to go around hosing up your day like he's doing. Call the Chief of Police. Tell him to call off his dog."

"Lauren!"

She startled.

Banjo closed his eyes and took a moment to catch his breath. "I don't need this."

"Well, I am sorry," she said with a little upward lilt to the last syllable, making it a jaw thrust, not an apology.

Banjo's fear returned. She saw this and touched his sleeve. "I am sorry," she said again. "I run my mouth sometimes. You know that."

"Thank you."

Wood smoke touched his sensitive nose. "Banjo, why don't you come talk to Daniel and me."

Two chairs sat before the desk. The Chief gestured graciously toward his office. Banjo entered and sat. Dan had settled into the chair next to him. The Chief put his pipe in his mouth and sat also. One hand fidgeted with the fingers of the other. He asked, "How are you, Banjo. Do you need anything? Is there anything I can do?"

Banjo said, "No."

The Chief shifted his eyes away and seemed puzzled. He removed the pipe and poked distractedly into the sooty bowl with his long index finger. He and Dan exchanged knowing glances. Banjo waited until the silence roared in his head.

"Something you guys wanted to say to me?" Banjo asked.

"There's talk around the police department," the Chief replied. He lit the tobacco. "Loose talk, careless talk, the sort," he told the cloud roiling from his nose and mouth, "that one must place in its proper context."

Banjo sat forward and his stomach began to ache. "Like what?"

"Well, they're angry. We have to understand that. If one of them made allegations about you, we would be very upset and vindictive."

"Vindictive. What have you been hearing?"

The Chief gestured uncertainly. "Has Officer Zagata confronted you or made any threats?"

"Not really. He parked in front of my apartment a couple times." Banjo remembered something else. "The phone rang in the middle of the night last night but nobody was there. Why?"

"I think it would be good, very good, if you found someplace else to stay for a few days."

Banjo drew quick breath.

"As a measure of prudence," he added quickly. "I don't expect anything to come of this."

Dan broke in. "Chief, tell Banjo what's going on."

Banjo looked from Dan to the Chief then back to his friend. The Chief deferred to Dan and Banjo was glad of that because he could no longer trust the Chief.

"Listen, Banjo. We have some contacts inside the police department. There's talk that this is going to reopen something they don't want reopened. Zagata's been drinking real heavy and getting a little crazy. He threatened to kill another officer a few days ago. We're not sure why. They suspended Zagata for that but somehow he's still on the job. Zagata knows there are people in the police department who resent the drug scandal and want to believe you. They hope this will go to the Grand Jury. If it does, it could blow up big and nasty. That might be what Zagata is reacting to. He's been bragging that he's blown away people before and gotten away with it." Banjo closed his eyes, folded his arms across his stomach, and bowed his head. "But this time someone from inside, you, has made a formal complaint which sounds entirely plausible to many cops. There may be a case here if other officers at the scene have similar stories. The talk is that Zagata might try to intimidate you. That's the bad news. The good news is there is support within the police department." He shrugged. "Of course Zagata has his soldiers and minions, too. And some of them," Dan added, "work right here."

"What's Zagata say he's going to do to me?"

"We don't know that, Banjo," answered the Chief. "But we want to make sure you are protected and watched over."

Dan said, "Banjo, my renter moved out awhile ago. The apartment upstairs is fixed up. I know you've thought about moving. Why don't you bring some things over and stay there.

If you like it, call it home and move in. I'm a reasonable landlord."

Banjo felt Dan's hand rubbing his shoulders. He jostled about under the massaging. Zagata's scar danced in front of his eyes. He saw Zagata's grandly satisfied smile. It made Zagata look like he had something perfectly worked out and now waited like a cat for the opportunity. "Are you advising this or are the police?"

Silence again was the first answer. "Both," Dan said.

Banjo threw up his hands. "Oh great. The police department is warning me about one of theirs. Why the hell don't they lock him up?"

Dan's voice was dull and flat. "Because he has done nothing against the law. If he threatens you in any direct way or tries to ..." Dan let that trail off and tried again. "It's a police matter after ..."

"After they have a fuckin' body!"

Dan struck the Chief's desk with his cane. "There's no way in this city, no way in this day and age of reason that a cop is going to kill a paramedic."

"I agree," the Chief added vigorously. But the menacing thought hung there cold and steely. All were struck dumb. At last the Chief gathered his thoughts. "Let's develop a plan."

Banjo interrupted. "I already got a plan. I'm getting a gun."

The Chief's head fell back. "For the love of God."

Dan told him, "Banjo, you're not getting a gun. You'll shoot yourself in the foot."

"I'll tell you what, Danny-boy. I shot a lot of things in Vietnam but my foot wasn't among them." Banjo's voice grew pressured and abrupt. "When it comes to Zagata it looks like there isn't a lot of backbone around here. I'm getting a fuckin' gun. And I'm going to carry it all the time."

"Not on duty, Mr. Stanley. I will fire you on the spot."

"Fine. Dump me. But I'm not going to be a target for some nut. Not me. He's crazy. I'm protecting myself."

The Chief planted his hands on the desk and rose. "Not in a division ambulance nor within these walls!"

"You're not the target!"

"Absolutely not!"

Banjo jumped to his feet. He felt something tapping his chest. Dan's cane wiggled back and forth between Banjo and the Chief. Banjo swatted it down. A blow stung his neck and he spun toward Dan.

"Settle down." Dan pointed the cane like a long nosed pistol at Banjo then at the Chief and back. He nudged the Chief. "Sit." Dan tapped Banjo's chest again. "You, too."

Banjo said, "I'll break that thing over your head."

"This is our plan," Dan told them. "Banjo, you stay at my place. Half Deck already has you on a shift away from Zagata. Get rid of your telephone. You can use mine and I'll always keep the answering machine on. You and the Chief will write a report of Zagata's activities and send it to his commander. I don't know what that will do, but at least it means we're not rolling over." The Chief nodded.

"What about when I'm on the street?"

The Chief said, "We will prepare a temporary position within administration."

"No way. That jerk is not driving me off the streets. Don't even think about it."

Dan and the Chief looked at each other. Banjo's eyes darted from one to the next. Dan said, "Will you move in with me? It may not make you more comfortable but I'll feel better."

Banjo huffed. "I ain't going through this alone. I'll sleep in your bed if you want me to." A thought struck him. "Can I bring my piano?"

"Bring anything you want."

*****

Snooper waited in the dayroom. She sat angularly reading a magazine and tossed it aside when Banjo came from the Chief's office. He sat next to her and wanted to lay his head down on her shoulder.

"Scared, Sunshine?"

Banjo whispered, "Yeah."

She patted his leg. "I know." Her hand remained. Banjo felt her warmth against him. "Let's get out of here and talk."

They walked along Cherry Creek where the trees were leafed out and fully green. A few daffodils blossomed down next to the fast, muddy spring run off. Banjo thought of his own flowers just blooming that he would have to leave.

"What did you guys talk about?"

"They think I may be in some danger and that I should move in with Dan. Zagata beat up another cop and he's been acting weird toward me." He looked at her. "I got the distinct impression that they think he may try to do something really crazy."

"Like what?"

"Like the craziest thing."

She wrinkled her face in thought. She stopped and Banjo walked a few paces on before noticing. He turned. Her mouth hung ajar. She asked, "They think he might want some kind of revenge?"

"The goddamn police department thinks he may want to."

"Oh, Banjo. Why don't they lock him up?"

He laughed. "Because he hasn't done it yet. That's why." He turned down a street toward the Debbie J. "Let's go this way."

They walked and said nothing more to each other. At the Debbie J Banjo unlocked his door and stepped aside for Snooper who entered without hesitation. Banjo asked, "Can I get you something?"

"Just water."

He gave her a full glass and opened the sliding door to his patio. Banjo kneeled next to great maroon peony blossoms. Their weight bent the stems onto a small wire fence he had sunk into the loose dirt to hold them upright. He ran his hand gently across the petals feeling their softness. Banjo found the most perfect blossom; the one with the greatest complexity and depth of color and with shears, cut the stem near to the loose dirt. He took this to Snooper. She saw him coming with the flower and drew her legs together in a feminine way and sat up. "I have something for you," he said. He felt awkward and flushed. He handed it to her and sat on the arm of his wide vinyl chair where she sat. With her delicate fingers she reached for it and drew the bloom to her nose. Her head remained bowed in this way for several moments. Banjo lifted his hand to her head and faltering and fearful, lay it lightly against her hair. It's softness frightened him.

She whispered into the flower, "What are you doing, Sunshine?"

"This is a dangerous line of work, Inspector."

"Yes, it is." Snooper leaned against his hip.

Banjo asked, "What's your name?" She did not answer. "Before I really knew you I gave you that nickname. But I never knew your real name."

"I like Snooper better." Still she had not looked up from the flower. She turned the stem between her thumb and first finger to see all around it. "Alice," she told him finally.

"I like Alice better." He ran his hand through her soft hair.

Snooper drew a quick breath.

"I'm not sure what I'm doing, Snoop."

Now she looked up and her face was open and searching his.

"I'm going to move in with Dan. I mean I'm dumping this place and I'm going to rent Dan's upstairs. I can't get through this by myself. I can't come home by myself and find that cop laughing in his car across the street."

She nodded her understanding. Banjo took a deep breath, held it, then exhaled hard. "I don't know what I'm doing right now, with you. But I know how disappointed I was not to be partners anymore."

She nodded again and Banjo knew she agreed.

"I guess I'm saying I'd like to be ..." He worked his hand around in the air. "I came to like our mornings up at Ruby Hill. And I came to like how I feel around you. And I know that especially now I'd like to keep on feeling that way."

Snooper hooked her arms around his waist and lay her head against his hip. She squeezed. "I like that feeling, too."

He circled her bony shoulders with an arm and hugged her. He held himself against her and tensed when a frightening need to express himself arose. He felt her body tense, too.

She asked, "What's the matter?"

Into her silky hair he told her. "I love you."

"What?"

He looked down into her face. "I love you. Is that okay?"

She looked steadily into his eyes and Banjo felt her relax. She rested her head against him again and held on tightly. "That sounds good to me, Sunshine." She patted his back. "This will all work out. You'll be fine. You'll be all right."

Banjo listened but remained unconvinced. Soon his back tightened, sitting twisted as he was on the chair's padded arm. Banjo stood and took her hand. She rose gently and hugged him first then kissed him. Then she allowed Banjo to lead her into the bedroom.

Chapter 26

Eric slapped the wall of the ambulance as Banjo cleaned out the back before shift change. He stood sternly, his chest bulging under his tightly tailored uniform shirt. He wore shiny black loafers, not dusty boots. A thin beauty chain circled his neck and a ring sparkled uselessly from one little finger. He smelled of after shave. Banjo greeted the fancy looking paramedic with the minimal nod and hoped he would leave.

"You mind if we talk?"

"No." Banjo continued with his cleaning chores.

"You judge and jury now, are you?"

Banjo raised his head. "Excuse me."

"I understand you decided Officer Zagata killed a man, though you didn't see how. Is that a fair assessment of the circumstances?"

"I guess the circumstances are none of your business."

"I guess they are, now that you just cut off police cover for every paramedic down here."

"I doubt that."

"Zagata's a good cop. He's fished me out of many tight spots."

"You shouldn't've gotten into them in the first place."

"Listen Banjo, he taught me more about the streets than anyone down here. Field instructors don't hold a candle to him. He knows people all over this city. Something happens out there and he knows somebody who knows about it. You get him fired and a lot of crooks are going to shake your hand." He shook a finger at Banjo and a pinky ring glinted in the light. "I'll tell you something else. There are more than just one or two paramedics down there he treats like family. He's given me money when I needed it. He saw that Joe Boyd had money to fly back to Pittsburgh for his dad's funeral. He'd give you the shirt off his back. Sure, he's a little coarse, a little rough around the edges, but he's a good man. Leave him alone."

Banjo turned back to his cleaning. "You have no idea."

Eric placed a foot on the side step of the ambulance and leaned in. "You're not listening to that bunch in administration, are you?" He tapped his muscular chest. "You listen to me and this is from the street paramedics. We like Zagata. He shows up when we need help. Half the time you call the cops they're either in roll call or drinking coffee. But not Zagata. You know that. He's there every time."

Banjo tapped his own chest. "I'll tell you something about Zagata. When Dan and I were dodging bullets up in the Delphi Hotel, goddamn Zagata was outside in his car counting a big roll of money. What was he doing that night, Eric? But then you don't remember that, do you, because you were still diddling girls in the back seat of your daddy's car." Now he fired his finger at Eric. "Don't tell me about Zagata. Zagata doesn't have friends. He has tools. And he doesn't give money away, he buys people."

Eric crossed his arms and straightened up. "You're right. I don't remember the Delphi, but I hear stories about higher ups in the police department who want to get rid of Zagata. He doesn't follow rules, just goes out and does his job. So it makes sense people would make up stories like that about him. They even tried to set him up to take the fall for stealing heroin from the evidence room. Banjo," he declared. "There are things in the police department you don't understand. This is one."

"You watch too many movies."

"No, I'm telling you." Eric's voice was whiny now. "I'm not here because this is my idea alone. There are a lot of nervous street paramedics out there. Some of the people you work with wanted me to talk to you."

And Banjo knew power was over to him. He said, "Let them say it themselves."

"Zagata's a good man. He doesn't like certain people. That's true. But he's like a father to me. I've been to his house. I've met his wife."

"He threatened me."

Eric hesitated, momentarily at a loss. "How?"

Banjo was vague. "Telephone calls. Following me."

"Oh, that's just Zagata. When he does that to cops they just tell him to go to hell and he stops."

Banjo fixed his eyes on Eric. "Do you know he was suspended for threatening an officer?"

"He's not suspended. I just saw him on a call yesterday."

"Do you know," Banjo continued, staring hard at him, "that the police are telling the Chief that Zagata's dangerous, that I should be protected?"

"I don't know what the Chief is thinking." He forced a laugh and rolled his eyes. "In fact I never understand what he's thinking. Those supervisors have no idea what it's like for us on the streets. Those guys aren't real paramedics. They're little men." Eric uncrossed his arms to wipe his hands then recrossed them. He removed his foot from the side step and placed his other foot there.

Banjo watched his growing restlessness. "Is that what you amounted to when you were a supervisor?"

"I didn't like being off the streets. What they said they wanted from me changed dramatically after I got in there. Suddenly, big news, they didn't want an advocate for us. That's happening here, Banjo. Things aren't what they seem. You really have no idea what you saw, do you? At least the way I heard it you didn't actually see anything. Zagata was only going out to help your partner. If he had room he would have walked around that patient. He likes people. He's knows how rude it is to step over some one like they're a log on the ground. For some reason those little men in administration don't like cops and you gave them a reason to go after one. Paramedics aren't mad at you. You thought you saw something and you had to report it. We understand that. We can't understand why the Chief is running with such a flimsy story and why you are being so stubborn. But I'll tell you, Banjo, if one of us gets hurt because the cops don't show up, folks down here are going to be looking at you."

"You're pretty tight with him, aren't you?"

Eric shrugged. "We get along."

"Uh-huh. Well, tell your friend to quit calling me on the phone then hanging up. Tell him to stop parking outside my apartment. Tell him if he didn't do anything he shouldn't have to intimidate me. And tell Officer Zagata of the Denver Police Department that if he has something to say to me he should come say it himself, not send one of his boys. Now you run along and tell him those things for me." Banjo pushed Eric aside and left the ambulance.

*****

Snooper spent each night of the following week with Banjo. On Sunday morning he made them coffee and they read the paper in bed. He gave her the Living section, which she showed little interest in, while he read the front page. He played symphony recordings on his CD. She recognized none of them and told him they sounded like church music. She prepared a few meals for him during the week, but she went about them in a perfunctory get-it-over-and-done-with kind of way. Her clattering about sounds were not homey and her indifference toward his chosen routines created fearful moments when Banjo found her presence tedious.

But their moments of deep connection remained sweet. They cuddled in bed one night and Banjo said into her soft hair, "What do you hear from the other paramedics?"

She pulled away to look at him. "What do you mean, kiddo?"

"Eric caught me at shift change awhile ago and told me that some of the paramedics don't believe me. They think the Chief and Dan and the rest are just looking for a reason to go after a cop. He thinks people will hold me responsible if anybody gets hurt."

She lowered her eyes from his and Banjo knew she carried news. "I don't hear."

Banjo relaxed. "I thought Eric was full of crap."

"No. I didn't mean that. I mean I always hear the gossip. Now I don't. I think Eric's right. There are paramedics down there who resent what you did."

"So what talk do you hear?"

"The supervisors. They wonder if this will ever get to the Grand Jury. Half Deck is sure it will, Dan doubts it, and the Chief, the good old Chief, doesn't have any idea."

"Dan doesn't think the Grand Jury will get this? He told the Chief to make the report." Banjo flopped to his back. "I'm beginning to feel set up. The Chief didn't want to send it. Half Deck threatened he would. Dan was the swing vote."

Snooper snuggled again. "Must be Dan's clever way to get you out of this apartment and latch onto a good renter."

"Son-of-a-bitch," Banjo complained. "Do you hear anything from the street paramedics? Anything at all?"

"Just from those who believe you."

"How many is that?"

"Lauren, Clayton, Roy, and others, the older ones who remember the Delphi shooting and the drug dealing inside the police department."

"So what you're telling me is the whole damn division is split over this." He rolled his face into a pillow. "Great." He bolted upright and flung his pillow from him. "I need a beer. Want one?"

"No, and you don't want one either," she called after him.

He returned with three. He drank one straight to the bottom. "Zagata's threatening me. He calls on the phone. He's probably sitting out there right now. Eric tried to tell me I didn't see what I saw. He actually tried to tell me what a great guy Zagata is. To hear Eric, the guy's a damn scout leader. And you're telling me half the division is shutting me out."

Snooper made a little sound of protest.

"Don't tell me that isn't happening. The reason you're not hearing anything is because you're in the other camp" He drank part of the next and set it aside, preferring to stay sober. "I've poured my life into that place. There aren't half a dozen street paramedics who've been around longer than I have."

"They support you."

"He killed somebody. And you know something else. Clayton saw him do the same thing about a year ago. Only I sat on him and told him not to say a word."

"Why?"

"Why? For the same reasons Eric gave me; for the same reasons the Chief used. Don't antagonize the cops. You don't know what you saw. This could put us at risk."

Now Snooper sat up. "So what's the difference between that event and this one?"

"Because I saw this one!"

"You mean you didn't trust Clayton."

"He was a rookie."

"Rookies have eyes."

"You're not giving me a lecture. Not now. Not tonight."

"You don't trust anybody, do you? To tell you the truth, I'm not sure you trust me. Sometimes I wonder if I'm nothing more than a security blanket you'll put away when you're not afraid anymore."

This question frightened Banjo for he had asked it himself and found no answer. "Well, I've wondered if I wasn't just some port in the storm for you. The first guy in forever to be interested so what the hell, beats sleeping alone. When are you going to decide that this is too crazy for you? When I move into Dan's, are you going to think poor Banjo is taken care of now and run off?"

"I don't run, Sunshine."

"I don't either." But a little tug in his stomach made him recognize that love frightened him.

She looked at him. "I expect a lot of you because you seem to have so little fear."

"You have no idea."

She said, "I act brave because I'm afraid of so much," and she pulled him back down so she could tuck her head into his chest.

Banjo sighed very deeply. "I remember being afraid that I would fall in love with you."

She nodded.

"I remember being afraid you would laugh at me if I told you."

She murmured an acknowledgment.

"And to be honest, I don't know if I'm clinging like this because I love you or because I'm so afraid of what's going to happen."

She looked at him. "But you had some feelings for me before all this happened, right?"

That was the truth. "Yes."

"And it wasn't like I was some bombshell every guy wants to hop in bed with."

He admitted to himself that this also was true.

"That's the way I put it together. Something started happening months ago. This stuff just moved it along. Is that how you see it?"

Banjo deferred to his touchy stomach. It remained comfortable. "Yes." And confidence in his feelings for this woman of boyish features and demanding expectations grew.

"To tell the truth," she said, "I'm not always sure myself that you weren't just the first man in a long time like you said. But I can't imagine that. I set very high standards for men."

Banjo told her, "Don't be demanding. I always did my best before you came along. Nobody's going to make me do any better."

She shook her head quickly in agreement and snuggled closer. "I love you, Banjo. You set something free in me. You make me feel in a way I never thought I could. I want to make you happy. I want to love you in so many ways."

Banjo felt himself arouse. He nuzzled his nose into the softness of her hair.

"I won't run off when you move," she said, brushing a hand across his belly. "I don't want someone else taking care of you. We'll be fine. This will all work out. Pretty soon everyone will forget this and we can all go back to the way things were."

Banjo rolled her onto her back.

She whispered, "That's right, baby. That's right." She stroked his hair. "You're such a good man. You give so much. You try so hard."

Banjo kissed her tiny breasts and his breathing quickened. He rubbed his belly against her smooth skin now beginning to glisten in the late evening heat and soon they were both slippery and frantic.

Breathlessly, finding that her words urged Banjo on, she told him more. "You don't always have to try so hard. You can rest. Let me help you." Banjo slipped inside her and she yelped, "Oh, Banjo." He felt the hard grip of her fingers. "You can relax now," she said. "You can let yourself feel good."

Banjo nuzzled against her neck and allowed himself to remember his mother's great comfort. He heard the words of his mother and felt Snooper's passion. Snooper spoke more quickly. She punctuated her words with cries. Banjo drove hard against her and felt himself separate from his body and float with her as though in a vast, warm pool. He Stiffened. Then he disappeared into her. A cry burst from him. Presently, as he relaxed, he became aware of her continuing pleasing movements beneath him.

"That's what you needed, my lover," she said. "That's what you wanted. I want to give that to you so much." She gave his face little kisses.

*****

Banjo lay nearly asleep next to her. A car door outside slammed and alarm shot to the ends of his fingers. He heard the car start and back from its close by parking place. Banjo searched Snooper's slack face for a sign of wakefulness. His headache returned and his mouth tasted foul.

Chapter 27

Banjo lay hot and awake in bed. Unable to sleep, Banjo watched Snooper sleep. He had been to the window already. Zagata sat out there: a heavy figure waiting in his police car, patiently moving a burning ember toward his face until the ember brightened suddenly. He threw the covers off to release heat. The glowing red clock numbers had advanced little. He stood and pulled on his shorts.

Light fell across him in the kitchen when he opened the refrigerator. Three cold bottles of beer side by side on the top shelf tempted Banjo. He thought about it but changed his mind. He pulled open the sliding screen to his patio and stood in the cool gusts that swirled between the building and close fence. He drew a sharp breath and shivered. Clematis greened the fence behind his peony blossoms. He could smell their freshness. He burrowed out some weed shoots with his big toe. They had grown in the loose earth during his weeks of distraction and neglect.

Within this still night Greystone came to mind. What would he have done? Would Greystone leave the streets as Dan and the Chief urged him to do? Absolutely not. Would he move in with Dan as Banjo was planning to do? Banjo doubted that. What would Greystone do about the brooding figure waiting out front? Greystone, Banjo resolved, would look Zagata in the eye and tell him to get lost. That's what Greystone would do. Banjo's courageous father would, too. Banjo took comfort knowing his father's brave blood coursed in his veins.

He dressed, slipping his long black flashlight down the back of his pants and put on hard toed work boots. He pressed a hand against his stomach, took a deep breath, held it, and exhaled forcefully. He opened the door and went outside. The dark head lights of parked cars stared blankly at him. Silvery street lights cast hard shadows. A few birds chirped but those were distant and lonely sounds against the heavy night silence. A breeze puffed and moved his hair a little and his eyes were scratchy from poor sleep.

The police car sat across the street, idling, waiting like a wolf. The figure in it looked straight ahead, ignoring the new activity at Banjo's front door. The ember moved again. Banjo walked sideways along the length of the parked cars. He stopped at the sidewalk and looked for cover to dive behind just in case. He swallowed hard. The breeze cooled his sweaty skin and was cold and he regretted not wearing his second chance vest.

"What'n the hell are you doing over there, Zagata?"

The figure made no move. Cigarette smoke twisted quickly from the wing vent and disappeared.

Banjo crossed the street. "Zagata! What do you think you're doing here?"

Zagata picked at his tongue as though pulling off a strand of hair. He rubbed his fingers together and spit toward the upright shotgun next to him.

Banjo reached the rear of the police cruiser and stopped out of range of the car door if it were to spring open. "You're not scaring me off, Zagata. I'm not backing down. I don't know how you whacked that guy but you did it."

Zagata remained still.

"You going to talk to me? Hey! You can hear me. Open the damn window." Banjo moved forward a step. He watched Zagata's head dip slightly as he puffed on his cigarette. Banjo shined his light at the rear view mirror. The reflecting flash illuminated the inside clearly and Banjo saw many empty coffee cups in the back seat and on the floor. Zagata reached up and turned the mirror away. Banjo slammed the car roof hard with his flashlight. The noise rang out like a gunshot. "You going to just sit there? You afraid to open a window and talk? You afraid a Grand Jury is going to say you murdered that guy? Looks like there's nothing you're not afraid of, huh?"

Zagata drew a finger along his scar and held it there as though thinking some intriguing thought. Banjo heard a distant laugh within the police car and watched Zagata's right arm move ominously to his side. He raised his hand and it held his service revolver. Zagata twisted in his seat.

Banjo said, "Oh, shit," and looked where he could run. His closest protection was across the street among the cars, but if he ran there and Zagata fired, the bullet might penetrate his apartment and strike Snooper. The car window slid down. Banjo couched at the car trunk and coughed in the exhaust smoke rising into his face. He pivoted, preparing to bolt along the side of a nearby house.

Banjo heard, "Move away from the car, little man. I have a call."

Banjo raised up and peaked through the rear window. Zagata used his weapon to gesture Banjo away as he might try to brush away a pesky fly. Then the car roared away from the curb enclosing Banjo in a choking cloud of fumes.

Banjo trembled and coughed. He stood to breath. Electricity popped in his chest. He remembered his first patrol in Vietnam. He nearly cried after returning from it safely and he wanted to cry now.

He returned, trembling, across the dark street, past the cars in the parking lot, and to his front door. An envelope was taped to the door knob. He snapped it up and tore off one end. Photographs slid into his hand. At first, in the dark, he could not make out the figures caught in a bed, but their surroundings were familiar. He held it up to the silvery street light. He cried out in horror and fell against a car. The photograph was of Snooper and him. A note was typed on the back. It said:

'I have the audio, too. Who knows where these will show up?'

There also was a sickening, breezy post script:

'By the way, just so you know, I'll have to fuck her for you. You don't last long enough.'

Fear seized him. He thought he would collapse. There was no safety here. Zagata could reach him where ever he was.

Zagata could reach him even in bed. Banjo's skin crawled and he felt exposed and weakened as he did when his father beat him and turned him out into the cold Nebraska winds.

He burst through the front door. It crashed against the inside wall.

Snooper cried, "Banjo!"

Banjo rushed to the bedroom. Snooper sat up clasping the sheet to her neck. He turned on the light. "Get dressed and help me look." Banjo tore the shade from his lamp and examined the light bulb.

Snooper curled herself protectively in the bed. Her sassy self assurance was nowhere near her worry filled face. "What is going on?"

He threw the photograph at her. "That! He's got this damn place bugged, too."

She looked at the picture then turned it over. He heard her gasp. He ran to the tool drawer in the kitchen and returned with a screw driver. He removed electrical outlet covers. He probed one with his screwdriver and received a shock. Banjo threw the screwdriver down and ran his fingers along the upper ledges of the windows and door. He found nothing in the usual places where electronic devices were located in the movies and dropped, panting like a chased animal, to his bed. He looked at Snooper. Tears dripped from her cheeks.

"That scum!" he screamed when he saw her tears. He jerked a drawer from his dresser and emptied his contents. "We're getting the hell out of here. This place is contaminated." He threw clothes into his old Marine Corps duffel bag. "He's been leering into this bedroom. He's been watching us; listening to us. He heard the things we said. Who do you suppose he'll be showing that to? Paramedics! People we work with! That scum. I'd like to shove this flashlight right up his ass."

Snooper said, "Do you think he'll hurt me?"

"No, because you're moving with me into Dan's house. If he touches you I'll kill him. I swear I will." Banjo looked out the bedroom window through which the photograph had been taken. "Jesus, Snooper, he stood right there. Right there! I'm going to see if I can find footprints." But as soon as Banjo flung open the sliding glass door from his kitchen to the patio he realized that concrete extended to the bedroom window and there would be no footprints. He returned and Snooper had dressed. Once more Banjo looked outside. Darkness reflected back an image of different eyes piercing into his. What was the right thing to do? they asked him. What will you do this time?

A memory that had been buried since Vietnam flashed in his mind. It triggered the same painful explosion of terror he felt moments ago when Zagata withdrew his weapon, when he recognized himself and Snooper in the photograph, when, in Vietnam, he had faced his first extraordinary moment of truth. He looked away from the window quickly but the questioning eyes stayed with him. He paced the length of his apartment and looked outside. The curb across the street remained vacant, but the eyes hung in his memory.

Snooper said, "Let's go back to my place."

"I'm not going to run from him," he promised. "I don't know what I'll do, but he will not scare me off."

Snooper placed her toiletry items into her back pack. "That's fine, but just for tonight can we go back to my place. I need to get out of here, now." The declaration was made quietly and the last word, spoken in a whisper, heightened its insistence. Banjo, settling some now, rolled his toothbrush and razor inside clean underwear and placed them in the backpack with her items.

When he locked the front door he thought of Zagata feeding the two of them to his vulgar eyes.

*****

All that Banjo owned was scattered about the upstairs rooms of Dan's house. His piano, which required a moving company to hoist at a fee that would force Banjo to work overtime, was perfectly situated. Snooper sat on the edge of a kitchen chair and bent over a box of books. She looked at an old cookbook. There were stains on a few pages left by an earlier cook. Watching her and remembering this book Banjo supposed his mother had given it to him when he left home. He imagined Snooper looking through cookbooks in a home they had made together. This was a strange thought, he knew. His intellect told him that such things required time and the opportunity to grow naturally. But his emotional composition, especially in times as uncertain as these, required quick and certain answers, so he hurried to realize his happiness. Their moments of uneasiness, however, grew more frequent and he was resigning himself again to failure in this new grasp for happiness.

She lifted his platoon photograph from the box and held it close to her face. "You in here, kiddo?"

Banjo sat on the floor next to her and pointed himself out. "Right there. Brave, proud, and true. That was taken about a month before we were sent overseas."

She looked at him and teased. "Not exactly at your old fighting weight these days are you?"

He smiled faintly at the photograph. Then the smile faded. He said, "You know why I got into this business?"

She rubbed her hand across his shoulders. "Why?"

"To make up for what I did over there." Her hand stopped. He saw the alarmed expression expand across her face. "I was a Marine," he answered. "I was expected to fight."

She closed her mouth and swallowed. "What did you do?"

"I killed people." The words jarred him. Trembling now, because fear grew in him, he said, "I never said that before. For a long time I lied. I told people I was a terrible shot and couldn't hit anything. I was glad in a way my dad died before I got back. I didn't want to swap war stories with him. I had every expectation of being a concert pianist; of bringing beauty into the world. Instead I ..." The word caught in his throat. "killed people. When I came back I had to make up for that. I decided helping injured people was a more direct way than making pretty music."

She was silent. After several silent moments she asked, "What exactly did you do?"

"Nothing heroic," he answered vaguely. "What I was told." His fist went to his mouth. "Is it important?"

"Is there a reason you wouldn't want to tell me?"

He flicked his hand as though discarding something held in it. "That stuff belongs locked up in a closet. I get sick when I think about it."

"It's important."

"Why? There are things I don't know about you."

"You don't know about my old boyfriends because they haven't come up. You don't know how I fell and broke my arm playing soccer when I was twelve. But those aren't secrets and there's nothing horrid about them."

"My things are secret and they are horrid." He stood abruptly and went to his piano. He listened to a few bars of Chopin in his head, then started to play. As abruptly his hands flew from the keyboard and he turned angrily to her. "I tortured a guy." He said. "Did you hear that? I tortured a prisoner, then I threw him in a river to drown." Banjo trembled and he swallowed hard. "Then I puked my guts up. My stomach's never been the same since."

She took a breath and waited.

"We were out looking for some Viet Cong that had been hitting our patrols. Some kid brand new in country tripped and fell over a leg that happened to be hooked to one of the enemy. He was wounded and played dead at first but when the lieutenant jabbed him in the ass with his M-16 he perked up. We figured he knew where the rest of them were. So the lieutenant and I took him for a walk down by the river." Banjo picked up the photograph and pointed to a boy. "This bunch of VC had killed a few of our guys. One of them was him. Nicest kid. He was the only Marine I trusted to tell I was an artist. He always called me Arthur out of respect for my music. Everyone else called me Banjo. When they blew him up it seemed like my last claim to the piano died."

Banjo gulped in more air. "We took the prisoner to the river and the lieutenant would ask a question. 'You with such and such unit?' he asked. The prisoner knew one word. 'Farmer. Farmer.'

'Where are the rest?'

315

'Farmer. Farmer.'

'How many?'

'Farmer!'

The lieutenant got tired of that and gave me his service revolver and he told me to shoot him in the knee.

"I said, 'Lieutenant, I can't do that.' And the Lieutenant said again, like he had not said it the first time, 'Shoot him in the knee. He'll talk.'"

He asked the prisoner questions and, like he was ordering a sandwich, told me to shoot him. I said I couldn't. I just couldn't.

"'Where are the rest?' the Lieutenant asked the prisoner. He didn't even acknowledge my refusal."

"'Farmer. Farmer.' the prisoner answered."

"Then the Lieutenant looked at me like I was the lowest kind of life that ever walked. I was nineteen. I didn't know what he would do to me if I disobeyed his order but I knew I couldn't stand him looking at me like I had let the whole platoon down. He said, 'Shoot the little bastard, Marine!'

"So I shot him. A patch of clothing erupted black and red like a tiny explosion when the bullet hit him. The prisoner hardly winced. I knew I was going to pay for that someday." Banjo stopped to catch his breath. He groaned and turned away from her, "God help me, Snooper."

Banjo began to tremble and he realized he had trembled this way when he aimed the lieutenant's weapon. Then he saw the source of the faceless eyes that had trailed him for more than twenty years. The prisoner had fixed his eyes upon Banjo and -- how the prisoner had mustered such bravery, Banjo could not imagine -- made Banjo look at him directly each time he fired. The eyes may have jerked a bit as each round thudded into his flesh but they remained otherwise immobile.

Sweat slickened Banjo's armpits and dampen his forehead. He drew another heavy breath to steady himself. He clapped a hand over his mouth to hold back vomit he felt churning upward. He gasped again and swallowed. "God help me," he said toward the ceiling. "I'll do anything but I don't want to go to hell."

He turned back to her finally. The shock in her face frightened Banjo. He drew another breath to settle himself. "I'll tell you this once and never again. Bargain?"

She had crossed her arms in an angular fashion and turned her head aside as though having to look at something she would rather not see. "I'm not sure I want to hear it now."

"Then he told me to shoot him in the other knee. Everything in me screamed, don't do it. Don't do it. But I did. I told myself I was only following orders, but I knew it was murder.

It went on like this. Every time he said he was a farmer I had to shoot him somewhere else. Arms, legs, hands. Pretty soon it was clear he wasn't going to be helpful, so we drug him to the river, rolled him in like a log, and used our weapons to shove him into the current. He was too shot up to swim. His head bobbed a few times along the surface like a fishing bobber with eyes then sank."

He stopped and looked far away, into a long time ago, into dark, fiercely held eyes. "I never forgot those eyes, accusing me until he sank. He never cried out. He never betrayed his comrades. He only looked at me like that until he was gone.

"The next morning his unit attacked us. That's when I woke up looking at the wrong end of a rifle. I was about to bravely scream my head off, but there was a shot and the head of that VC exploded. I rolled over and pissed my pants.

"There. Those are my heroic adventures in Vietnam. We caught a prisoner by accident, I killed him, and somebody I never saw saved my life." He tossed his hand and said with feigned casualness, "Oh, I had the usual repertoire of friends dying, bullets zinging past my head; I even remember what my bullets sounded like when they thunked into an enemy chest." He stopped and thought. "I admired that prisoner. I promised to honor him by being brave myself. But I never had the opportunity to be brave enough." He looked at her. "That's the heart of the matter."

Snooper stood and came to him. She wrapped him in her arms and said, "I'll call you Arthur if you like. I will."

"No," he said. "Banjo will do."

He felt as though he had pulled the scab off an old wound and instead of finding healing tissue, found something squirmy and black and festering.

Chapter 28

The summer wore on. Its heat grew as intense as the pressure on Banjo. Once every few days a car trailed him a little longer than coincidental destinations allowed. It was a different car each time, keeping its distance, and Banjo wondered which one Zagata drove, which one might be Eric, and if one was driven by a person whose identity Banjo could not imagine. Upon seeing one car Banjo dashed into a service station rest room and watched out the door. But the car did not pass by.

Zagata waited outside Dan's at night. The telephone still rang at odd hours and Snooper used this for her reason to spend fewer nights with him. They both felt a sad distance growing. Banjo could not stop it and it did not surprise him.

Their eagerness for each other declined. This sad ebbing away was apparent to Banjo in the little, sweet things he no longer said and in the absence of enthusiasm in Snooper's voice. Their long Sunday mornings in bed reading the paper grew tiresome. She fidgeted and flung the covers off and showered. She sullenly put off making meals. Her directness turned to evasiveness and Banjo concluded her energy for him had disappeared.

Banjo found it in him to forgive her, though, and this surprised him because he had never fully forgiven any woman when the relationship ended. Anger still rose when he recalled the afternoon his wife left. He would probably react irritably toward Eden today if he saw her. He remained upset at Lauren for being so beautiful. But even as he examined himself closely, he found it remarkable that he held no resentment toward Snooper. He missed her, though the final discussion concluding their truncated relationship had not yet taken place. The wearisome anticipation of it left him lonely.

How curious, Banjo reflected in his sweaty state there in Dan's breezeless second story. He loved her. He knew this because his love had grown stubbornly through a hard layer of disbelief that such could be happening at all. It had not sprung aggressively from a passionate need to possess a beautiful woman. Even though the protective steel doors to his heart stood ready to snap shut on her, they had not. That was peculiar. Now that she was inside he did not want her to leave. But Banjo assumed that whatever mysterious damage had occurred to the relationship was irreparable. Her distance represented exclusion and that, to Banjo, meant finality. He would have to spring the doors and terminate the loneliness.

He wondered where the misstep had taken place. Perhaps his confessions were too troubling. Maybe the pressures of Zagata were too great. He was bewildered that she would leave him at such a time. Banjo believed partners should not leave partners, ever. It troubled him deeply that this might be the reason.

Banjo removed himself from those thoughts to examine them. They were very unlike the erratic lashing out he was liable to do when he felt unduly wronged. But there they were and his untroubled stomach told him that he was not keeping something hateful somewhere else. He did not know where this strength came from. In his danger and loneliness he felt a quiet place.

He went to a window. From his high perch in Dan's house this morning he saw a dirty column of smoke to the south, probably a brush fire somewhere, owing to the dry heat and winds. He glanced automatically at the street. His thoughts settled on Zagata and he grew agitated. He picked up the newspaper and snapped from one page to the next looking for anything regarding the police department.

The stories had flourished alarmingly when he reported Zagata. Now there were none. Police investigators concluded their discussions with him weeks ago. The inactivity demoralized him. The Grand Jury which Banjo had looked to like a protective big brother now appeared unlikely. The word on the street, carried to him gladly by Eric, was that no other officer in the bedroom recalled seeing anything. Life seemed to go back to normal for everyone except Banjo.

He drank bottled water from the refrigerator and rubbed the cold drink against his chest. He listened at sounds periodically, hoping certain creaking noises were Snooper's foot fall and not Zagata's on the bottom step. Cars slowing and stopping in front of the house startled him alert. The unrelenting heat made sound sleep a memory and drowsiness a routine of life. He sat at the piano but his fingers were clumsy. He fell into a numbed reverie.

It was noon time and hours had to pass before his shift began. Distant jack hammering wormed into his preoccupation. Somewhere someone used a power saw. Deli's and burger joints would be filling. People hanging around the paramedic dayroom now would be watching Perry Mason and digging into their brown lunch bags. Everyone around him had purpose. He sat hot, bored, and too jumpy to go outside. He waited anxiously for Snooper to call, though she had not indicated she necessarily would. He wished that Dan, away on errands, would return soon and make some homey noises downstairs to help him feel safe. Then time would resume.

Banjo went to the kitchen and made a peanut butter and jelly sandwich. He sat back down on the piano bench and tried a few pieces but he was sleepy and his fingers dumb.

*****

Banjo jerked his head off the keyboard and turned to his clock radio. He whispered, "Oh no," and struck his knees painfully against the underside of the piano when he stood. Hopping and running to the bedroom he removed his cutoff jeans and kicked them into a corner. He stripped off his tee-shirt. Aggravated that he had no time to shower first, he forgot his second chance vest. He grabbed his flashlight and jammed it down the back of his pants. When he opened the front door to his landing the heat stopped him. He drew a breath before jogging down the stairs.

He kicked something furry. At first he thought a child had left a black puppet on his landing. He bent close. It was a cat, a dead cat. Blood puddled under its head. A bullet hole, pencil size near the left ear, drained from a ragged hole where the right eye had been. Banjo clapped a hand over his mouth. "Oh, my God." He turned to see if anyone stood near. "Oh, my God." He turned back to inspect the bullet wound then looked for Zagata. "Oh, God." Banjo ran down the stairs and banged on Dan's door. "Dan! Are you there? Did you see anything? Dan? Where in the hell are you? Let me in! Zagata's out here somewhere." Banjo peaked fearfully over his shoulder. A car approached, slowed, and coasted to a stop. He banged harder. "Jesus Christ, man. Are you in there?"

The door opened. Banjo shoved past Dan into his cool living room. "Did you see him? Did you hear the shot?"

*****

Dan stood behind his friend who sat in the chair before the Chief. Banjo held his face in both trembling hands. The Chief looked helplessly over Banjo's head to Dan and his eyes asked Dan what there was to do. They heard a noisy commotion in the hall outside and the Chief's door banged open. Half Deck burst in as though late for something very important. Dan snapped protectively, "Half Deck!"

The Chief distractedly waved the supervisor away but Half Deck did not see that.

He gripped something in his tightly squeezed fist. "Oh, Lordy." There was an excited flutter in his voice. "Oh, holleration. Oh, sweet Jesus, you have come at last." Half Deck thrust a lottery ticket into Banjo's hand. "Read the numbers."

Banjo dropped it. The ticket fluttered to the floor between his boots.

"You idiot!" Half Deck dropped to his knees and snatched it back. He shoved it into Dan's hand. "You read it, I said."

"This is not the time."

The Chief warned, "Half Deck."

"Tell me these numbers!"

Dan sighed. "Then get out."

"For sure," Half Deck answered.

"Fourteen. Seventeen."

Half Deck held another slip of paper close to his nose and nodded with each number Dan read.

"Thirty-two. Forty-two."

Half Deck's studied face brightened.

"Forty-four. Sixty-seven."

He shook his head and laughed wildly. "Eight point two million. Oh, I hope no one else had these numbers. I could buy this place if I wanted." His giggle reached a high pitch. "But I don't."

The silence of the others deepened. "Mr. Humphries," the Chief began carefully. "Let me ask the question. Is that the lottery?"

"Ten-four. Roger-D. Eight point two million." He said again like he was tasting each syllable. "Eight point two million. Eight point two million! Erma called. She always calls with the lottery numbers. I wrote her numbers down here." He held up paramedic division stationary. "And I looked at my ticket here." He snatched the ticket from Dan's fingers. "And they match! Eight point two million smackaroos." He looked at the Chief. "I quit, Chief. I duly, hereby, tenure my resignation effectively ten minutes ago." His giggle hurt Banjo's ears. "I'm done. Maybe Banjo here can mangle the schedule." He bolted from the office. Through the windows they watched him gather his Elvis trinkets. Then he threw up his hands and left. He called to them through the window, "You can have them. I'll go buy Graceland." He pulled the dayroom door open and with a flourish of his hands, was gone. A strange, stunned silence hung in the air behind him.

The twisted irony struck Banjo hard. Fate had put his danger and Half Deck's new fortune in such proximity that it

323

seemed to him he could have just as easily grabbed one circumstance as another.

Dan said, "I don't believe it. Of all the people."

The Chief chuckled in disbelief. "Perhaps he could give us a few hundred thousand dollars to help replace our communications equipment or remodel our quarters."

"I don't imagine," Dan answered, "that Half Deck's likely to help us out that way. He's stingy with his money."

"And he has his vacation to Graceland to consider."

Banjo interrupted them. "Excuse me. Now what was it you guys wanted to say to me? Just how are you going to make me feel better now that the one person I like least in this division has struck it rich and I'm likely to get taken out by a crazy cop?"

The Chief, still not fully returned to the moment, offered casually. "We can have someone take you back and forth to work if you like."

Banjo shrugged.

Dan patted Banjo's shoulder. "We're not done with this, Banjo. Don't try to be a hero."

"I am not getting off the streets if that's what you mean. That guy is not chasing me away."

Banjo watched the Chief's face tighten and turn again to see over his head to Dan and knew this was the same impossible snarl they were in when the conversation started. Then the Chief said, "I must say this, Banjo. The police have warned us. They consider him dangerous. I will say it again. You need to get off the streets until this matter is resolved."

Banjo said it slowly, deliberately, to make himself clear. "I will not leave the streets."

Dan started. "But Banjo ..."

"No! I'll stay where I am."

*****

Banjo did not hear Clayton. Without the encompassing squeeze of his protective vest, Banjo's senses extended further out, inspecting the corners of buildings and slowing cars. His eyes darted and he determined not to let a shadowed recess slip his attention.

"Banjo."

Banjo scouted from the cab. He felt presences everywhere and several times looked into the back of the ambulance. He hoped they would not be called into apartment buildings. There were stairways and so many doors and long hallways and slow elevators. He feared Zagata would be in an elevator when the doors slid open.

"Banjo."

Banjo saw eyes bobbing along a river's surface. A rifle pointed at his chest then the head above it disappeared. He saw Greystone facing down that shotgun. He saw the blue barrel of Zagata's revolver pointing at his nose.

"Banjo?"

Something touched his arm and electricity jolted him. He lurched hard against the door. When he realized this was Clayton's hand he swatted at it as if it were a bee and cried, "Jesus Christ, don't ever just grab me. I liked to had a heart attack."

"You hungry?"

"Hardly."

"When this is over let me take you hiking. I know some places not far from Red Rocks. It's a good place to go when you need to find your way back."

"Sure. Whatever." Banjo's response was clipped and intended to quiet Clayton but he recognized the content of Clayton's offer.

Clayton turned away. After a moment he spoke. "I have come to lose myself in immensity and to know my littleness. To lie in the lap of my mother and be comforted. I am alone, yet not alone. My soul is my companion above all companions."

Banjo turned. "What the hell is that?"

Clayton shrugged, seemed at a loss. "That's by an Oregon poet. I think about that when I'm over my head. It reminds me of greater things, of an order, of attainable peace. It was the only thing I could think of to say."

"Thanks, partner. But what I need from you is to keep your eye on my back, not saying peculiar things." Clayton's poem had been nearly said before Banjo paid much attention to it, but one sentence had found a place in his comprehension. 'I am alone, yet not alone'. That resonated. He understood that. He had been thinking strange thoughts which he attributed to his distracted state of mind. He pondered the significance of receiving his father's medals when he did and whether his father's spirit might be looking out for his son, assuring that Banjo, unlike himself, would survive his forty-third year.

The dispatcher sent them to anther district. Banjo's knees ached. His sticky shirt felt prickly, like biting ants crawling on his skin. Banjo thought perhaps he should go the cool mountains with Clayton. Since rejoining as partners, Banjo experienced different kinds of moments with him. His meditations were no longer bothersome and Banjo found the silences inviting, though Clayton's mystical responses could still be irksome. Clayton's keen sense of moments yet to come fascinated Banjo. He wondered if he could acquire this gift if he learned to sit quietly long enough to read whatever invisible signs Clayton saw. Perhaps Clayton could teach him his medicine man ways if Banjo followed him into the mountains.

But Zagata might follow. He always did. On his way home, Zagata followed. At work Zagata remained close by. Zagata intruded like a storm into his thoughts. Banjo did not want that for his friend. He considered calling Snooper. But that would lead in difficult directions. Banjo rubbed the sting in his arm where he had banged the door handle at Clayton's touch. He opened the door and walked away from the ambulance to a shade tree and sat. A police car passed and slowed. It picked up speed immediately before Banjo could identify the driver. Banjo jumped to his feet and scooped up a hand full of rocks. "Hey jerk, how 'bout this?" He skipped to gather momentum and threw several stones. His follow through nearly tumbled him to the sidewalk.

Sweat ran slickly down his back. Banjo tore his shirt from his pants and worked it around like a towel. He kicked the fender of his ambulance.

Clayton motioned him to get in. He said, "Let's go. An officer stacked it up."

Banjo froze in midstep. "It'll be my luck he got hit covering one of our cars."

Clayton shook his head. "Dispatcher didn't mentioned that. My guess is Zagata's involved. But that's just a guess."

Police cruisers were protectively parked at odd angles around another cruiser crumpled against two parked cars. An officer sat on the driver's seat with his feet on the pavement. He held a towel to his head. The police gave the approaching ambulance no mind until it was very close, then one of them gestured sharply at it to slow down and park at the curb. Banjo felt obvious and embarrassed when he got out. The policemen ignored him. They made no room and he had to edge between them sideways. Banjo said quietly to the injured policeman, "How you doing, partner?"

Zagata pulled the towel from his bleeding forehead. "Oh great. They sent you? I'm better off waiting for a taxi than going in your meat wagon." He waved the bloody towel at Banjo and said to the others, "Know who this is? This is the guy who thinks I kill suspects."

Banjo said flatly, "What happened, Zagata?" If he gave his voice any inflection at all he worried his fear would leak out.

"I dodged a goddamn kid and hit these cars here. That's what happened. And would you like to know what I was doing? I was covering one of your cars running on a stabbing." Methodically and with high drama he looked into the face of each officer surrounding him. "Goddamn. He accuses me and I'm the one who gets it trying to help them out."

Banjo said, "Let me take a look."

Zagata jerked away. "You keep your filthy mitts off me. You're not taking me anywhere. Christ, whose the victim here anyway? I was covering your asses." He stood and cried to the other officers, "And I damn near get myself killed. You can bet I'm slowing it down from now on. You paramedics are on your own. You're not team players. You don't care." He shooed them away with the bloody towel. "Go on. Get out of here. I'll go in with one of these guys."

Banjo asked, "You going to let me examine you?"

"Hell no."

"You going to let my partner here look at you?"

"Just get back in your little truck and make tracks."

"You don't want us. Is that what you're saying?"

Another policeman dropped a hand menacingly on Banjo's shoulder. "That's what he's saying."

Banjo shook out from underneath the hand. "You guys heard him. I don't want him saying later that we refused to take him in."

"Get the fuck out of here, little man."

Clayton asked him, "Where's the stabbing?"

Zagata waved in no direction. "Somewhere over southeast. My head injury makes me forget."

"Over southeast," Clayton repeated. "We'll check on that car; make sure they're all right. That way you won't have to worry."

Zagata huffed at them. "I'm not worrying about you people anymore."

In the ambulance Clayton made a point of calling dispatch while the window was down and the police could hear. He asked if there was an ambulance responding to a stabbing in southeast Denver. "Negative," the dispatcher replied. Clayton looked importantly at Banjo then at the policemen. He waved the microphone at them.

Chapter 29

Banjo heard her footsteps on the stairs outside. Muting his excitement, anxious to know what was on her mind, fearing a bad mood, he hurried to the door. She handed him a clay flower pot. Geranium blossoms drooped against the red terra cotta. "Here. These are for you. Needs water."

"I guess they do."

He stepped away from the heat to let her in. With long, man like steps she went to the refrigerator and bent over in front of the open door. "Any beer in here? Ah, good. Want one?"

"No thanks. I'm watching that."

"Water then? You need to maintain your fluids on hot days." She drank to the bottom one of his bottles of water.

Snooper passed him on her way to the sofa. Taking his hand with a squeeze, she led him along. Sitting, she swung one knee onto the cushions so she could face him. She reached across and played one hand through his hair. She took a hand full and tugged gently in frustration. "Things have gotten so bunched up here, Banjo. I care for you but I want to run away."

Banjo jerked his head away. "If you're going to rabbit, just go. Do it now. I don't need another problem." Doors in him began to slam.

She crossed her arms. "Banjo ..." She dropped her chin against her flat chest. "Banjo, we made love six weeks ago. We've been together almost every day since and I feel like I'm supposed to make some fantasy of yours come true. On Sunday's we have to stay in bed so you can read the paper. You have to have your music on. You talk about how you want to fix this place up and insist on my opinion. I get this real eerie sense that you want to make a place for both of us. Six weeks,

Banjo. Not much more than a month. You don't even know what kind of pizza I like."

He pushed himself protectively into the corner of his sofa and gathered in his dreams. "I like to read the Sunday paper in bed. I like to have company. I love great music. What's wrong with that?"

"You get a dog. I'll go for a run."

"And what's wrong with asking your opinion on things around here?"

"I'll tell you what ..."

"No," Banjo insisted, preferring to throw her out before she said she was leaving. "I'll tell you what. You don't like me, get lost. You don't like how I do things, there's the door."

"Listen to me, Sunshine ..."

"Don't call me Sunshine!" Banjo's heart pounded and tear pressure grew in his eyes. She would leave, that he knew. And he would be alone again. Just like always, his love drifted down this same mean road. This woman threatened his dreams. Her arguments meant anger and he did not know his way through angry words. Anger was his father's beatings and they taught him that he was safest when he severed connections. It was he who required understanding. He needed to fit his life together exactly. He needed to control the course and pace of life. He had to know that at some indiscriminate moment a beating would not occur. So he tried his best to dictate all the moments. And this was so much easier alone. She had to go. He could forgive her for this but she had to go. He looked at Snooper's unhappy face.

She said, "I'm sorry. I'm simply saying I'm afraid of this. I haven't felt this way in a long time. It's hard for me to trust a man. I thought about just calling up and saying play time is over. Something stopped me, though. I decided I don't want out of this."

His great emotional pendulum stopped its wildly outward swing and cautiously suspended itself. She was not running away. Then fear shook his insides. He wasn't sure that he could hold onto something as precious as love. He may drop it and break it to pieces. His ex-wife had loved him and she ran away. He managed to bungle his romance with Eden as well.

Now Snooper sat here already speaking of frustration. Banjo craved the protection of a solitary life even as he ached for love. Pain waited to flood over him regardless of the shore on which he chose to land. Banjo snapped his consciousness alert. Frantic states of gloom such as this were just the murk from which his memories sprang. He waited. He searched about looking for them. They remained distant and indistinct, like lightening from a storm already passed.

He returned to his confusion. But Snooper had proven herself. And she had passed through his locked gate into his remote feeling area and planted a small seed that had blossomed. He loved her.

She said, "I don't even know the language. I don't know how to tell you things. I like you." She corrected herself and whispered, "I mean I love you." She swallowed and gestured vaguely. "But I don't like this."

"What?"

"This! What's going on. I feel like I'm playing a role here. I can't do that."

He saw his angry father, he saw his wife screaming about something or another, the Chief, Dan, Zagata. What he said stunned him. "Are you going to hurt me?"

"Banjo," she said as to a pained boy. "Oh, Banjo." She reached to him and wiggled her fingers for him to settle against her. Into his hair she told him, "I'm not trying to hurt you."

"Are you leaving?"

"No. I want to be with you. But on my terms as much as yours." From the comfort of her warm chest and enveloping arms this sounded less frightening. "But do you understand me?"

He admitted, "I have a certain way of living in mind. There is music and light and calm. And peace. Mostly peace." He felt her nodding above him. "I try to impose that. I know I do." He felt her shrug. He asked, "Do you have fantasies?"

"I don't talk about them."

"I never talked about mine until now."

She was silent and he listened to the warm thumping of her heart. She said, "I want to trust without a doubt. It doesn't matter what the person looks like or where we live or how much money we have. I have to know I can trust the person not to leave." Banjo nodded. Snooper pulled back to see his face. She brushed the hair away from her features. "Do you think I look nice?"

He looked at her finely shaped face and nodded. "You look fresh and young and like you'll always be that way."

Hugging him, she said, "That's nice, Sunshine."

"I don't know where my fantasies come from," he said to her. "I create these fabulous lives for two people who finally come together after many years of trials, like traveling alone in the desert. They fall into each other's arms and I know she knows me all the way through. And, he repeated, "there is music, light, and peace. But mostly peace."

Warming once again to earlier thoughts she said, "But Banjo, I know there won't be any peace unless I can make my own music and my own light. That's all I'm saying." Emphatically she asked, "Do you understand?"

He had never before understood that he would have to understand. He nodded. He shrugged. He shuddered with fear. He wondered and he noticed his stomach, stirring slowly like an awakening cat. He could understand Snooper if he could likewise be understood, he answered to himself. If he knew that when he let his guard down and was himself without his best behavior, if Snooper could see that and accept him, then he could risk the effort to understand her. Banjo relaxed again, for the warmth present in Snooper was deeper and sweeter than that conjured in his one sided love fantasies.

"What?" she asked. "You're shaking your head all ways but the right way."

"I don't know my way here," he said more to himself than to her. "No. No, I don't. What if we start driving each other crazy? What if we loose this feeling?" He pulled away from her. "What if you get tired of me? I'd rather be alone than love someone I have to let go of."

"Like I said, Sunshine. I don't even know the language. If something comes up you talk about it. I don't know. Fighting isn't so bad. It kicks things loose, keeps the friendship interesting, clears the air. I can't guarantee anything and neither can you. But I can promise that I'll tell you what's on my mind" She asked again, "Do you understand my fears?"

Having stated his fears, he destroyed their stature. And having heard them, Snooper remained. She took these in and she confessed her own. Thus, each of them having revealed much that was closely held, Banjo consented to let himself rest against her again. He understood her fears. They were his. His pendulum swung rapidly toward relief. "I understand," he said. "I understand."

She remained throughout the day. That night they made love and afterwards Banjo fell solidly asleep.

*****

Banjo cried out. He saw Zagata in the bedroom leering at Snooper. His lightening strike scar flashed in the street light. He sat up, breathing heavily, and looked through dark, blank window into the quiet darkness. He thought about getting a beer. He thought again about buying a gun. He got out of bed and drank cold water. "The son-of-a-bitch really is that crazy," he said shaking his head widely back and forth. "He is going to track me down. He will track me down." The terrible tragic waste of his own death again lay over him. He sat in his vinyl chair in the darkness for a long time listening to mournful music before he went back to bed. Once more he could not sleep.

Snooper shifted on the coverless bed. She mumbled in her near sleep, "Are you okay, sweetie?"

*****

The early morning was fully bright and heating up before exhaustion let Banjo sleep. The telephone rang. It jarred him painfully and his anger flashed like electricity through him. In his ragged wakefulness he heard Snooper answer. He was

333

unaware of the conversation until she shook his shoulder. "The Chief says he needs to see you now."

*****

The Chief turned back from the window. Absently he reminded himself, "Must fill out Mr. Humphries' termination papers." He glanced seriously at Banjo who waited, spent and bitter from lost sleep, for the Chief to break away from his distant musings. His boss cleared his throat. "The District Attorney called this morning. The case of Officer Zagata is going to the Grand Jury. Perhaps this development prompted the incident on your porch stoop."

Banjo raised his head, too tired for happiness. "But I thought they didn't have a case."

The Chief looked absently into his blue cloud. "Interesting. Interesting," he said, and Banjo thought he was commenting on some odd connection in his mind. "Seems that Officer Rocky Osborn's wife is friends with one Harriet Bancroft who was married to Captain Bancroft; the same captain who took his life during all that drug business. The two of them grew quite close after losing husbands in circumstances involving the same man. Evidently Officer Zagata went so far as to brag to his partner's widow about how he waited before calling you in, then wiggled the knife while you were distracted, or," the Chief added significantly, "thought you were distracted. It is damning testimony and the attorneys have no idea why he revealed such detail to her or why she waited so long to report this. The DA believes Mrs. Bancroft played a role in persuading her to speak out against Zagata. So, Officer Zagata is on administrative leave. The Grand Jury convenes next week and you will be called. But you are no longer the key witness."

For a moment Banjo thought of mentioning his conversation with Mrs. Bancroft. But he let it go. "If he's putting dead cats on my front porch, what is he doing to her?"

The Chief shook his head. "We have no idea. I hope that even his code of ethics prevents him from preying on a widow." He sighed wearily. "But who knows." There was another thoughtful puff on his pipe. "There is much astonishment within the police department," the Chief said. "On the other hand there are others who are not surprised."

Chapter 30

Clayton, erect in his seat, meditated. Banjo slouched in his seat with his knees jammed to the dashboard. He held a quart of cold chocolate milk on his stomach, felt gritty, and hoped sleep would not overcome his vigilance. The newspaper lay at odd angles on the floor between the seats. They waited for a call in the sparse shade thrown by a 7-11.

A car approached the gas pumps in front of the store. Banjo sat up. He strained to see through the glinting windshield. Not until the car blocked their exit did he see the scar. Banjo jolted and spilled chocolate milk. "Clayton, look at that." Zagata stared at Banjo who strained to see hand movement. Zagata wore no jacket and Banjo could see his shoulder holster. He raised his right hand. "Clayton, what's he doing?"

Clayton started the ambulance and shifted the transmission into drive. It lurched forward a little. "Get on the radio. Call in some police cover. If he fires, this ambulance is going to cut his car in half."

Banjo picked up the microphone. His eyes were riveted on Zagata's rising hand. The hand was empty but his arm with one finger pointing extended toward them out the window. Zagata's white scar moved angrily and his hand jerked as if it shot at Banjo. Then the hand withdrew into the car and inserted itself into Zagata's right ear. He snapped his thumb against his index finger and his hand jerked again with fake recoil. Then Zagata's eyes released Banjo's and looked through him and the scar fell quiet. Zagata's car moved away. It turned the corner and disappeared.

"Shit," Banjo said, collapsing back into his seat. "What was that all about?"

Clayton shifted the transmission back to park and rested his face in his open hand.

Sweat made Banjo's armpits slippery. It trickled down his chest. He trembled and his breathing came fast. "That son-of-a-bitch was telling me how he was going to kill me. That was it, wasn't it, Clayton? The son-of-a-bitch is planning to shoot me in the head."

"We better report this. I'll see if we're clear into Denver General."

"Let's just sit here a second. Let me get out of this tin can. I'm burning up."

He got out and a swirly puff of breeze cooled his skin but his insides were wild. He searched his memory for the location of a close by gun shop and wondered if Colorado law would make him wait to buy a gun. He saw the finger in Zagata's ear and wondered how a gun barrel would feel jammed into his ear at the moment it was fired. It would be quick. He saw his prisoner jolt each time he pumped another round into his body. Banjo remembered his moment of high terror in Vietnam when that enemy rifle was trained on him. Banjo figured Zagata must be his payment for his wartime actions. He worried who would protect Snooper if he were killed and Zagata went after her. He hoped Clayton would look after her.

He put his hand in his pocket and folded it around his father's bronze star. Banjo squeezed the old war medal as Clayton sometimes took his bear claw into his hand. "Oh, please," he said under his breath to the spirit of his father. "Give me the strength to do this honorably and give me the opportunity to survive." He squeezed again and the points hurt him. He squeezed until the points of the medal, which his father had held in his fingers and had worn on his breast, opened tiny wounds. In this way and in his desperate state, Banjo believed some of his father's courage would seep through the broken skin and into his blood.

He looked for Zagata's car which may have come lurking back into proximity. He thought of Snooper. Somewhere in the ringing silence a car started and accelerated away.

Banjo heard Clayton open the ambulance door. "Banjo, they want us to cover a sick case. I can tell them we need to be out of service for an incident report."

Banjo returned to the car. "No, let's take it. Zagata's had his fun for the day. Where are we going."

Clayton told him the address and a hard clutch seized Banjo's tender stomach. "That's Snooper's address. What do they say is wrong there?"

"Just some kind of sick case." But Clayton looked off toward the nearby park where the address was. He turned back to Banjo. "Zagata is there."

"Let's go," Banjo ordered. "Get your foot in it. I'll call in police cover." When Banjo did so he was told they were in roll call and help would be delayed.

Hurriedly buckling himself in, Clayton said, "You told me that you struck Zagata's police car with your flashlight. You counted coup on him. That means you have power over him. Don't forget that. Counting coup is a sign of bravery."

Banjo heard, but he wasn't so sure about that Sioux tradition. Even in the heat he shivered and could not stop.

Zagata's car sat empty in front of her house. Banjo slipped his flashlight into the back of his pants, though he did not know what use it would serve against Zagata's pearl handled service revolver. He jumped out and glanced over his shoulder for Clayton. His partner spoke into the radio microphone then hopped out after Banjo.

Banjo stood to one side of Snooper's door and banged with the flashlight handle. Clayton stood to the other side and looked through her window. "Snoop?" Banjo called. "You in there? The dispatcher sent us here on a sick case. You all right?"

Banjo listened. There were no sounds of steps approaching the door. He sniffed out of habit. He looked at Clayton.

Clayton nodded. "Someone is in there."

Banjo snapped, "Can you see them or you just know that?"

"We need to get in there. Something terrible is about to happen."

Banjo ran down the front steps and hurried along side the house looking into windows. Clayton circled the house in the opposite direction. Banjo remembered Zagata's vulgar intentions for her and swore to strangle the cop until his eyes popped out if he touched Snooper. He saw no activity through the side windows.

He met Clayton at the back step. "Did you see anything?"

Clayton shook his head and tried the back door. It was locked. He broke the pane of glass and reached in. They listened. There were no sounds. Banjo stepped inside. "Snooper?"

Her cry split open in the silence. "Banjo!"

Banjo jerked his head to a door just inside the kitchen. "He's got her in the basement." He tried the basement door but it was locked. Fear grabbed his insides and shook him. "Snoop, is Zagata down there?"

There was no answer. Then he heard heavy foot steps climbing the basement steps. The door lock released and the door swung open. Zagata stood in the doorway and his snake scar shifted angrily. Banjo froze. He forced his stare to hold steady on Zagata's broad nose and away from his eyes and scar. He expected Zagata to laugh when he saw Banjo's pant leg trembling. Banjo said, "Get her up here, Zagata."

"She's fine."

"Get her up here."

He ground his teeth and the scar quivered. "I said, she's fine."

Banjo slammed the butt of his flashlight against Zagata's chin. He crashed backwards down the flight of stairs and struck his head on the concrete floor. He moved one leg and Banjo thought he was trying to stand. Banjo and Clayton thudded quickly down the steps. "Snooper! Where are you? We have to hurry."

She did not answer.

They could not find her. "Snooper! Are you down here?"

"Banjo?"

They looked about frantically. Zagata, still on the floor, grew more active. A small puddle of blood gathered on the concrete floor under his head.

"Goddamnit! Where are you? We have to get you out of here while Zagata's still down."

Banjo heard rustling behind the black furnace with vents running all directions like octopus arms. She slipped from a narrow gap behind it. He grabbed her arm to run up the stairs. "Are you all right?"

Cobwebs clung to her tear dampened cheeks. She smelled musty. Banjo looked her face over for wounds. She shook under the grip he had on her arm.

Clayton said, "Banjo." His voice was calm and Banjo was alarmed for it was the quiet voice one would use when confronted by a wild animal.

Banjo turned. Zagata rested the barrel of his revolver in Clayton's ear. Clayton's eyes were closed. Zagata's face was sad and he said as though deeply sorry, "You really shouldn't have pushed me down the stairs like that. I'm a police officer. That's assault." He added a thought which seemed to have just struck him. "No, actually, that's attempted murder of a police officer. At least I thought I was going to die."

Zagata added, "You know why I'm here don't you?" His face began to harden. "I was sent here by my dispatcher."

Snooper shook her head no.

"Yes."

Banjo said, "Turn loose of my partner. He's here because he's with me. You don't have a quarrel with him." Banjo trembled so hard he feared Zagata would hear.

Zagata's expression shifted instantly to curiosity. Banjo feared these spooky mood swings would lead him to say oh-what-the-hell and pull the trigger. "Say," Zagata commented. "Isn't this the rookie that was always getting in your way? I remember you saying what a pain in the ass he was. And I'm almost sure he's the one who tried to tell people I killed that prisoner in the jail. Is this the same guy, Banjo?"

Banjo lied. "Different partner." He took deep breaths to calm himself, for if Zagata sensed calm he would also know he had no power over him.

Zagata removed the gun from Clayton's ear and pointed it over Banjo's head. He fired. The shot exploded in the concrete cellar. Snooper jumped. Banjo ducked. Soot from one of the

340

black furnace arms trickled down on them. Chuckling, Zagata nonchalantly put the gun back into Clayton's ear.

"You're bullshitting me, Banjo. This is actually the guy, isn't it? I mean, you can tell me."

Banjo changed the subject. "What are you doing here, Zagata?" he asked casually as he might ask why he was out of district.

"My dispatcher did send my here," Zagata said. "Really."

Banjo said, "I thought you were on administrative leave."

"Not me. They just told people that. I'm undercover."

"Then what are you doing here?"

He motioned to Snooper. "She called. Said there were prowlers in her house. I came over and found her all shook. So I called you guys. It looked like she needed some help. Banjo, you always seem to think the worst of me. Why is that?" He moved his revolver once more and scratched his temple with the barrel. Then he let the weapon hang to his side. He gave Clayton a shove. "See. You're not afraid of me. You know I'm just kidding."

Clayton hurried to Banjo and Snooper. Banjo could smell his sweat.

"Actually," Zagata continued. "I came to fuck her. I was just curious to see if I can fuck her better than you can. I imagine so. She was going to let me. She had her pants half off and I was getting ready to enjoy some real tight pussy when you yo-yo's came banging on the door."

Snooper spat at him. "You pig! You broke in and tried to rape me!"

Zagata shrugged. "Well, I was more or less telling the truth." A fast storm of anger swept across his face. He gestured at Banjo with his gun. "You shouldn't be spreading lies about me, little man. You really shouldn't." Zagata's voice was tight and cool and his hard brown eyes tried to make Banjo blink. "You and I got along fine up to a point, Banjo. Now that's fouled up. Now why did you foul that up?" The scar moved snake-like. Banjo shivered again then forced himself to hold steady. Zagata smiled like a predator. "You're shaking, little man. You're scared of me." He fired. The report stung Banjo's ears. More soot dribbled onto his hair and some of the gritty black dust got into his mouth. Zagata said, "You shouldn't have raised that stink about me."

Banjo stared back as hard as he could. He blinked many times holding his eyes level at Zagata.

Zagata shifted his mouth and crinkled the corners of his eyes with sinister amusement. He nodded toward Snooper. "I'll bet she's a tough little shit. I'll bet fucking her is like riding a washing machine."

Banjo tried to shift Zagata's thoughts. "Why don't you let these guys go so we can talk?"

"You shouldn't have ratted on me, Mr. Paramedic Man. Any real paramedic knows that. Guess that means you're not a real paramedic. Maybe you should get off the streets. Take that supervisor's job before your Chief decides you're just too fucked up on your booze and grass. I know that about you, Banjo. I do know that. And I know you're old man died a puking drunk ..."

Banjo exploded across the room and jammed the flashlight into Zagata's chest. "You leave him out of this!"

Clayton called out, "Banjo! No!"

Zagata looked at the flashlight with mild surprise and said very quietly, "That looks like a weapon to me, Banjo. That looks a lot like a weapon."

Banjo felt his lower lip tremble and he bit it, wondering what he would do now. He tried to remember tricks of subtle manipulation which he used on the streets. But those were silly and frivolous now that he had lost control, and perhaps his life.

Zagata grinned and stepped into the flashlight and pushed it back into Banjo's chest. "I also know you're about to lose your job if you don't kick the sauce. You're under a lot of pressure; the kind of pressure that makes people do stupid things, like pull a weapon on a police officer."

"Jesus Christ," Banjo gasped as the enormous truth struck him. "You did kill him, didn't you."

"Zagata," said Clayton. "I told the police that we were responding to a shooting with the suspect still in the house. They'll be here real quick."

"Oh, nonsense," he told Clayton. "If you'd really done that, they'd be here by now. Besides, I'll just tell them I was first in and found three dead paramedics." An idea struck him. "Better yet, I'll shoot you guys with my second gun. Then I'll put it in your hands, Banjo, and everyone will think you killed them and then killed yourself. Seems reasonable for someone under your kind of pressure." He glanced toward Snooper and Clayton . What do the rest of your guys think?" He waited for an answer. He focused his attention back to Banjo. "You probably ought to get off the streets while you still can, little man. I think you should do that. You stay with Dan like they told you and you take that nice supervisor's job. Then we won't have this kind of trouble." Zagata pushed his face into Banjo's. The dark eyes merged into one. Banjo held his breath against Zagata's foul breath.

"I'll go ..." Banjo cleared his dry throat. "I'll go talk to whoever it takes to get you hung, Zagata."

Zagata drew himself up straight and expanded his chest with a noisy intake of air. "You do that, jerk-off. You just do that. Then you'll see what kind of police cover you and your candy-ass paramedics get. You just do that." Zagata's breathing quickened. A vein in his forehead pulsed. The scar shifted nervously.

Banjo said again, "You really did kill him, didn't you?"

Zagata's face changed. He raised the gun over his head. His fingers worked at the pearl handle, gripping and regripping. The gun barrel lowered.

Banjo back stepped. "Zagata, what are you doing? Jesus Christ, man, put that back."

But Zagata was in an automatic machine state. Banjo knew iron masks such as this from combat and understood he was no longer a man but a target. Events were now inexorable and the great waste of his own tragic loss filled him. His chest jerked with near sobs. He wanted one last look at Snooper.

Clayton spoke again. "The police department and paramedic division know about you, Zagata. Our dispatcher knows where we are. Someone's going to come. You are the first one people are going to think of if anything happens to us."

In his determined state, Zagata seemed not to hear. The smooth blue barrel lowered slowly, passing Banjo's face, brushing his nose. The barrel was warm and smelled sharply of gunsmoke. Banjo could see lead slugs bulging at him from their chambers and the dark holes of the two empty chambers. He begged in his mind that Zagata would not fire into his face. The barrel continued slowly past his chin, his chest, and stopped at his belly. His chest spasmed and his stomach felt gripped by claws. He wondered if he should run. Would this hurt? Should he spin to protect his chest and stomach sacrificing another part of his body: his back, his legs, his arms? Would he die instantly?

"Please don't shoot him!" Snooper cried. "If you want me, then let's go upstairs to bed and get it over with. My God, don't kill anyone."

Banjo knew Zagata heard nothing of this. God, he had seen so many agonizing abdominal wounds. Maybe he should grab the gun, swat it away. Maybe if he ...

The gun jumped. A sharp report crashed through the still basement. Banjo doubled, recoiled, grabbed his stomach. His arm stung curiously and Banjo wondered if this is how it felt to be shot. The pain was not as severe. Perhaps surgeons at Denver General could save him. Banjo's thoughts paused. He remained on his feet and ... he felt no pain in his abdomen. He looked at his hands, his shirt. He saw no hole nor any blood. A black slash cut across his shirt sleeve and blood leaked from his arm.

Zagata laughed hard. He flashed a victor's smile at Banjo then shouldered his holster. "Probably time to get off the streets, little man. Probably time to do that. Next time I won't tweek my aim at the last second."

Zagata holstered his weapon and clumped heavily back up the stairs. He limped a little from his fall and he checked his temple to see if he still bled.

Banjo's legs gave out and he coiled to the floor. Snooper ran to him. Clayton stepped to the stairs and dropped onto the bottom step. He sat there holding his head in both hands. Snooper rolled up Banjo's shirt sleeve. His arm stung when she pulled the sleeve away from the wound. He saw a blackened narrow ellipse of raw tissue. Blood oozed. She hugged his neck and kissed his hair.

Banjo heard a pop outside and looked up wondering. He recalled a police officer who shot himself in the foot years ago during a quick draw contest. That was in the District 1 police station and Banjo, sitting outside in the ambulance, heard the shot. It sounded like that pop.

Banjo asked, "Did you guys hear something? I thought I heard something outside."

Banjo climbed the stairs on shaky legs. Snooper and his partner followed. From the front porch Banjo watched a police cruiser lurch to stop next to Zagata's car. So did another one followed by a third. Banjo saw a wet splat of hair against the driver's window of Zagata's car. He drew a sharp breath. Lines of red descended from it and thick drops hung darkly at the end of each. The heavy figure slumped against the seat as though tossed against it. One arm was extended casually across the seat back.

Banjo walked to the car, aware of commotion among the police, but was insulated from it by the shock of his own near death. He heard their voices. They asked, "How is he? Is he dead? Did he really do it?" But Banjo walked in a bubble of disbelief and did not answer, fearing if he did some other naked reality would burst noisily through his shimmering, surrounding sheen.

He opened the car door. He smelled the acrid gun smoke and the characteristic rusty odor of blood that was almost a taste. Carefully, fearfully, Banjo felt for a pulse at the neck which was slick with blood. His eyes were drawn to the scar lying slack and drained of color. Banjo lifted his hand from the neck and held it hovering above the quiet disfigurement. He wanted to touch it as he might touch something ugly and horrid and fascinating that had finally died. He wondered if he should. His fingers danced at it as if testing for heat, and finding none, tapped it once, then again, and finally laid them along its length. He found the scar only a shallow recess.

A police officer poked his head in next to Banjo's and asked, "How is he?"

Banjo's hand flew from the scar.

"Is that Zagata? Good God, it is. I'll get a sergeant in here."

Now Banjo noticed a white fragment of brain on the car seat very near his knee. This sent him searching for the bullet trajectory. Banjo tracked from the pearl handled revolver in Zagata's right hand upward along his arm, to his shoulder, to his right ear. There, inside, beneath the bloody mat of hair covering the ear was the black, finger round entrance wound. Banjo pulled Zagata's head away from the seat. A large jelly glob of brain rolled down the seat back and lodged against the door. "How is he?" someone asked.

Surprised, as though not believing it himself, Banjo answered, "He's dead." In a memory's flash, he saw Dorothy and the Scarecrow and the Tin Man and the Cowardly Lion. They are jumping and hugging. 'The witch is dead!' they cried joyfully around a steaming puddle. 'The wicked witch is dead!'

Banjo withdrew from Zagata's car. He saw a policeman drop heavily into his cruiser and say to another, "I was close enough to see it. I knew who it was as soon as I saw the service revolver. I don't remember the shot but I saw the smoke and watched him jump and sag down." He saw Banjo and said to him. "You know what? I watched that paramedic get it years ago, too. I watched him step right in front of that car."

Banjo rushed to the policeman. "What paramedic? Are you talking about John Greystone?" A lightening storm rose in him. He saw the freeway and he saw the red, white, and blue lights shooting at odd angles through the fog. Flares, eerie orange circles of light on the pavement, guided him in.

"Your paramedic. The one killed up on I-25 by Mile High Stadium."

Banjo hissed at him, "That was my partner. I was with him. I was there when he died."

"He picked an awful way to die; stepping in front of car like that."

He grabbed his arm. "He saw the car coming?"

"It looked to me like he watched the car coming and timed exactly when to step in front of it."

"He saw the car coming?"

The officer looked at Banjo then at some point a thousand miles away. "You know how some things never leave you? Zagata will never leave me. I'll always be able to say exactly how he raised his service revolver, pointed it at his temple. Then changed his mind and put it in his ear, then he lurched about, and fell quiet. Just like that I'll always be able to tell you how your partner climbed out and never took his eyes off that car, and how he was lifted onto the hood of it. He went limp against the windshield and seemed to ride there slow motion forever before he slid off into the brush."

Banjo, still in his bubble of astonishment, his arm still stinging, his stomach still twisted, walked toward Clayton and Snooper. His world was fully hushed. This new information about Greystone was frightening. It ended eleven years of burden and he wasn't sure what he would do, as he was never sure how he would cope with any fearful loss. He might lose part of himself with it.

But as he walked, the stinging lessened and a brightness settled on him. He reached in his pocket and held his father's medal for a moment. He had stood before Zagata and the gun barrel and faced his death. And having survived, he knew his strength. He found his honor and survived the year of his father's death. He found his father's spirit and could, at last, release Greystone's. The brightness became warmth that started where his belly had been working. His step lightened and a smile forced its way across his mouth.

A breeze picked up and it made him feel fresh and clean. He stepped sideways between police cars parked at sharp angles from each other and surrounding Zagata's bloody car. Officers busily took photographs, interviewed witnesses, and shooed people away, but Banjo left that inside the jagged circle of cruisers. He walked into the sun, out from under the shade trees where Zagata had parked to blow his brains out. He walked into the light. He walked toward his freedom. He walked to friends who had not left him. He walked to a woman whose love he trusted. He walked to a man whose spirit had helped him find his own.

He reached them and the hush lifted from him. Sound rushed in like water roaring over a waterfall. "He killed himself," he said, shouting.

Snooper and Banjo looked toward Zagata's car and nodded.

"No." He clamped a hand on Clayton's arm. "He killed himself, Clayton. Snooper, John Greystone killed himself. Do you understand? I didn't kill him."

Chapter 31

"The Chief is leaving. Did I tell you that?"

Ernie Webster's eyebrows arched in surprise. This pleased Banjo, burrowing mischievously into Ernie's professional demeanor. It gave him some control.

"No. You didn't say that. Where is he going?"

"I hear he's going back to Georgetown and just stay home. His wife," he added with a knowing tip of his head," is a doctor. Darn sure I'd stay home if I had a doctor for a wife." Banjo waited a moment. A smile irresistibly worked about his mouth. "Guess what else?"

Ernie placed his palms out and shrugged. His large return smile said take it away, I have no idea.

"I'm a supervisor. I took the plunge; the leap of faith; the kiss of death. I have crossed into the void. Dan is the acting Chief. I figure we can handle about whatever they throw at us. I'm putting together a program that rotates supervisors into the street. It's called the Phoenix car." Banjo stopped and fear over came him. "But I don't know jack about being a supervisor. I never even noticed if those guys punch the time clock or not. I don't know how you lead or how you discipline right. I've never planned anything. Why in the hell did they choose me?"

"You can be an inspiration; a role model." Ernie used Banjo's words. "You stood where you needed to stand. That seems like sufficient raw material."

"The Chief likes to tell me how creative I am and how resilient. I think at right angles to the rest of the world. Actually what I think he really wants is another whacko in there after he's gone."

"I don't think the Chief ever made a decision without very careful consideration. He has a reason for promoting you. Why don't you ask?"

Banjo pictured himself proud and sassy, driving the clean, sleek supervisor's car, earning that extra money. "I think I'll save for a down payment on a house. It's been great living above Dan these past couple months but I feel like I need to be on my own." Banjo chuckled at this. "I'm forty-three and still talking about being on my own. What do you make of that, gooney bird."

Ernie chuckled at that. "Gooney bird. Isn't that just perfect?"

Banjo's mind flew to Snooper. Lately he had moved off his dreamy flights of love and home to the practical considerations of a big house; big enough for Snooper and himself and -- Banjo's breath caught -- kids. He and his lover had talked about this in a very abstract way, seeing how far the other would wander into such thoughts. This discussion filled Banjo with great hope. He pondered how to open it again. He squinted an eye suspiciously. "You ever meet Snooper? She says that all the time."

Ernie frowned his negative answer.

Banjo regarded events of the past year. There were moments when circumstances seemed too well put together for chance. People talked about an invisible power the Chief seemed to have. Banjo never believe it. Now he wondered. "You and the Chief ever talk about me?"

Ernie frowned again. "I never discuss my clients. Surely you must know that by now. Why?"

"The Chief is cagey. Sometimes I thought there was a big scheme out there intended just to help me; like the Chief was pulling the reins behind some curtain. I think he was. He could do that." Banjo thought. "Too many things fit together. Difficulties came at the right time. Clayton and his way of seeing bigger things came at the right time. Dan beat me with his cane when I needed it. The Chief pushed when he had to. Snooper kept after me and I fell in love. Zagata was even important. He taught me I could do more than I thought I could. There was a plan. Somebody was watching over me and

I didn't see it. I feel like it took all those people a year and a half just to kick me loose. And now here I am."

"And where is that?"

Banjo thought about this for many deep and comfortable breaths. "I think I'm finally human."

"That's a good place to be."

"And I think there is a God out there; maybe in Clayton's mountains or maybe in the way we all need each other or in the feelings that pass between good people. It makes me feel like I belong to something huge and important that can never be taken away. I've been thinking about that a lot lately. I like believing that."

"I think God is in all those places."

Banjo said, "I like that."

Ernie asked, "What about Greystone?"

"He's dead," Banjo answered. "He died a long time ago. But he also stayed with me a long time. I needed him. He was all I had to talk to. Did I ever tell you I used to write letters to him? I would go to The Parlour where we all used to hang out and I'd write long letters to him in my journal. I would mark the end of each with one of his shoulder patches." Banjo stopped. His eyes grew weepy. "Clayton and I took the journal into the mountains and we burned it in a ceremony. We delivered the letters to him on the wind. If John is up there somewhere, I hope he gets them. I kept his patch."

*****

In the Chief's office Banjo heard the Chief's bedroom slippers slapping quietly at his heels. The Chief proceeded toward them along the short hallway from the dayroom where others still mingled about after his going away cake and coffee. Dan and Banjo participated also until the Chief caught their eye and urgently nodded them back to his office.

The office was naked and echoy and the steel desk was clear of files. A few black heel marks scarred its surface. The

Chief's crudely made ash tray cradled his sooty white pipe. The walls had faded. Those portions once protected by photographs and watercolors now created a ghostly mosaic of rectangles and squares. Banjo's delicate sense of smell detected pipe odor. These things alone in this empty office remained of the Chief.

The door opened in a silent arc and the Chief pushed a shock wave ahead of him. He did not recognize Banjo or Dan but went to his desk as if to sit, then seeing its emptiness, stopped. His rigid body slackened and Banjo feared he would collapse as a puppet without strings. The Chief saw the two sitting in chairs before the desk and pointed at Dan. "May I sit there?" Dan took the desk top to help himself stand. Banjo held Dan down and stood to offer his chair. The Chief pointed Dan to the swivel chair behind the desk. "Take your seat there." Dan shook his head no. Banjo thought this was as much to avoid the pain of movement as his show of respect. The Chief commanded, "You're the Chief, man. Sit there!" Again Dan rose again. When he had carefully resettled into the chair the Chief said, "It suits you."

The Chief snapped up his pipe and lit it with agitated movements and focused into the smoke. He said again, but not to Dan, "Yes, It suits you." He drew strongly on his pipe and held the smoke tightly in his lungs before exhaling. He looked at Dan before him then turned to see Banjo. He said, "I feel as though I died." He sucked again at his pipe and tamped it further with a long finger. The ember died and he had to re-light it. The Chief forgot to blow out the match. It burned his finger tips.

Banjo watched the Chief and was sad. A silence grew around them as the Chief cooled his fingers in his mouth then dried them absently on his pants.

The Chief returned his attention to them. "This is a small death in a way. Don't you think?" He did not seek their answer but continued. "It was my privilege during my years on the street to hold a woman's hand as she died. Her passing left me very sad; so sad and wondering who would attend my passing. I was the last person she saw in this life. I tried to say the right things. I puzzled about what to say, whether I should touch her, or tell her frankly she was dying. She asked me straight out. As she passed on I leaned close to her ear and whispered good-bye. I tried to do well for her. I hope I did well." From beyond the smoky haze the Chief's eyes came to Banjo's. "Did I do well?"

Banjo waited, expecting the Chief to continue his melancholy drifting.

"Did I do well, Banjo? Dan?"

Banjo said, "You did your best, Chief."

"No, no. Did I do well enough? Did I leave that woman with something comforting? I'm one who notices the fall of every sparrow, you know."

And Banjo affirmed, shaking his head yes, and he gripped the Chief's knee. "You comforted her. I know you did because you intended to do that and she knew. I knew when you took care of me. When you did all the right things even though I didn't deserve it. But you did and you helped me."

The Chief said, "I tried to suppress that nasty episode with Officer Zagata. Mr. Humphries rescued you from that."

"You did what was right in the end."

"Aye. Yes, I did." The Chief spoke to his cloud, "That was a shameful thing. Hiding from the truth of that. But it was very hard for me to say no to Captain Bancroft when he came asking me that we let him handle that nasty drug episode. He was such a proud man, but having to bend to his knees for Zagata." He thought a moment then added. "Greystone saved Captain Bancroft's life. Years earlier he was shot in the shoulder and bled terribly and almost to death. Greystone stopped the bleeding and rushed him to Denver General. He supported us at every turn after that and in my own peculiar rationalizations, I decided we should also save him from this awful state of affairs." He stopped once more to examine his blue smoke. "I believe that was the worst thing I did during my tenure as Chief. I did not have your courage, Banjo. I could not bring myself to incur such a risk as I knew Zagata would bring. I wonder if I might shake your hand and offer my sincere apologies."

The Chief's grip trembled and was cold like an old hand. In the Chief's eyes Banjo found veneration, as though he were the elder and the Chief the boy. "This is my passing, you know, and you are my attendants to it. I place this division of stubborn paramedics into your hands. Truly," he said. "I wonder if they are worth the heartache and effort. But they perform worthy work and my job was to allow them to do that well. But Daniel, Banjo, did I do well?"

Dan said, "Chief, you saved me years ago when Greystone wanted to fire me. You saved Banjo."

The Chief smiled distantly. "Yes, I suppose I did." His smile brightened and the Chief drew himself energetically back to the moment. "Yes, I did do that. What genius that was really. The two people I enjoy most are the two I struggled hardest to keep. Now you are among those who take over for me. Fine progeny you are and good reason to have worked so hard."

He changed the subject. "I thank God for Mildred and the children. Sometimes when I agonize over something I am tempted to get down on my knees and pray thanks for my family. They are where I go now. Jonathan. Poor Jonathan. He had nothing but this place. Banjo, you also nearly withered away from having nothing else but this place. Find something more, both of you. Find something that sustains you outside these walls. This is only how you make your living. Do not make it your life. Thank heaven for my family and for my feeble talent as a painter." He looked at his bare walls as though searching for some picture. "They are the reason I am leaving, really. I am so tired of this place. I decided I had given enough, that my family had given enough. I wish to be with them more. And I want my paramedic division given to stronger hands."

The Chief heaved a great sigh and Banjo knew he was ready to go. He tapped charred tobacco from his pipe bowl into the crude ashtray then emptied that into the round metal garbage can. He swept his finger across the ashtray to clean it and dropped it into his sweater pocket. His fingers left a gray smudge on the fabric.

The Chief stood and reached across the desk for Dan who stood to shake it. Banjo stood. He also shook the Chief's hand which was now strong and gripping tightly. The three stood there mute. Dan averted his eyes and Banjo saw Greystone's discomfort with such touching matters. The Chief looked at them both, absently scratching at his beard. Banjo remained still and took in their warmth. This calmness registered with the Chief who let his arm uncurl away from his face. Dan fiddled with a drawer pull for a moment before working himself nearer to the Chief and Banjo. When he reached them he cried out silently at some pain in his hip and leaned heavily on both Banjo and the Chief. Banjo felt Dan's fingers digging into his shoulders. Banjo drew him near. He slid an arm across the Chief's back and pulled him close to complete the circle. "Yes. Very good," said the Chief as though requiring such self permission before embracing. Their interlocking arms tightened. The Chief said through a sigh, "Yes. We do the best we know."

Banjo thought about that. "Easier said than done, boss."

And Dan asked, "Can I call you from time to time, Chief?"

*****

Banjo touched the keys softly and music lifted from his piano. He closed his eyes and opened himself before the music. A Mozart concerto formed under his hands. Banjo touched the keys and music rose from his instrument. It was simple and quiet and he was quieted. He allowed the beauty to fill him.

He stopped and held himself rigid. He heard a distant thump. Someone screamed, 'Oh God. No!' Banjo drew a deep breath and focused on his breathing as Ernie Webster had taught him to do and waited for the old memory to pass. Soon it slipped over the horizon of his consciousness. He resumed playing and the motion of the music touched him inwardly and stirred in him and he murmured little sounds of joy.

He felt something at his side. Snooper settled on the piano bench next to him. She sat quietly and held her hands in her lap, her signal for wanting him to continue as she sat close.

He played. Her felt her close warmth. The music became his gift to her. Banjo turned as he played and nuzzled into her hair and kissed her. She lay an arm across his shoulders.

He played. The music revealed a simple truth to him. This stillness in him was as true as the scar on Zagata's face. The beauty and love filling him now were as real as his memories. The simple joy of this moment was as strong as his fear when facing Zagata's weapon.

Banjo had his road now and a place to go that was great with sweetness and peace and was no longer fragmented as the images he once created of himself in the beveled mirror at The Parlour.

He played. He felt Snooper's hand moving across his shoulders. He played for her. He played for himself. He played for Greystone. Banjo raised his eyes to the top of his piano. His picture of old Marine Corps buddies rested there. Next to it, neatly situated within a frame, was John Greystone's shoulder patch. The patch brought a memory but no storm. Thus, Banjo knew, he could allow his old partner to rest. Thus, Banjo knew, he had found his own place to rest.

The End

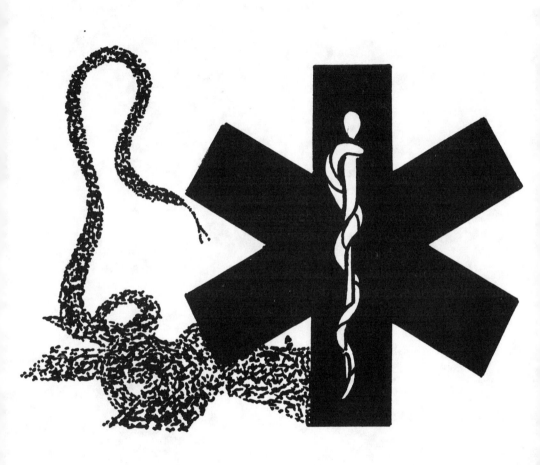